PERFECT STORM

BETH BOLDEN

AUTHOR NOTE

PERFECT STORM AND THE Toronto Thunder series take place in the wider Beth Bolden universe: a universe that is more inclusive and welcoming than our own.

In Beth-world, the first professional athlete to come out of the closet was Colin O'Connor (*The Rainbow Clause*), and after this happened, approximately ten years ago, there have been numerous players, coaches, and even owners who are living their best queer lives freely.

Chapter I

May

"You're sulking."

Aidan Flynn looked up at his brother-in-law's words.

Okay, Levi wasn't his brother-in-law, not technically. Not yet, anyway. Aidan's younger brother, Riley, and Levi's oldest brother, Landry, weren't even engaged, in fact, but the truth was they were the most married couple Aidan knew, ring or no ring.

Also, brother-in-law was easier and shorter to say than younger brother of his best friend. But *yes*, thank you, Levi, he was indeed sulking, and if he had the opportunity to use three less words while in this atrocious mood, he was going to do it.

"No, I'm not."

Levi flopped down on the couch next to him and smacked Aidan on the shoulder. "You sure fucking are, bro."

Funny, Aidan had kind of thought he'd done a decent job of hiding his bad mood.

Not that he was sulking. Men did not admit to sulking. They experienced protracted periods of sadness-induced frustration.

"You're annoying." Levi *was* annoying. Persistent, in that way he apparently believed was charming but was actually just plain annoying. When all four Banks kids were together, they were a lot to handle, but they also absorbed much of their own energy. Landry's twin, Lyla's, deadpan sarcasm negated much of Levi's manic cheerfulness, and Logan's chill energy meshed well with Landry's way-too-responsible-adult, team-leader vibes.

But Lyla was in Atlanta, where she'd moved last year, and Logan and his boyfriend, Dylan, were spending the summer training in Miami, where they both played for the Piranhas.

So Aidan was stuck with only two out of the four, and since Landry was distracted by Riley—as he usually was now—it was up to Aidan to entertain Levi.

Or in this case, be harassed by Levi, who was apparently more observant than Aidan had given him credit for.

"Annoying but right." Levi smacked him again. "What's wrong?"

"I don't want to talk about it," Aidan said stiffly. The last person he wanted to discuss his sulk with was Levi Banks. He'd actually hoped he might talk to Landry about it. Landry had been *his* best friend first, before he'd become Riley's boyfriend, and even though he'd finally come around, happy that his brother and his best friend were so blissful, there was a part of him—a very tiny part, undeniably adding to his sulk—that wished it was still just him and Landry.

He could at least get a minute of his time to say, *dude, I'm kind of going through it right now.*

"We've got nothing but time." Levi spread his arms. "You might as well tell me."

Aidan really did not want to go into it. Thus why he had spent the last twenty-four hours, since Riley, Landry, and Levi had descended onto his Michigan summer house for a week on the lake, pretending like nothing was wrong.

"Why are you like this?"

Levi grinned, not even remotely offended. "Benefit of being the youngest."

"Riley isn't like this."

"Which is shocking, actually, considering how much you tried to spoil him."

And *yes*, at one time, Aidan had been in serious contention for the Overprotective Brother of the Year award. He was being better. He *was* better. Ever since Riley had become the starting QB for the Condors and began dating Landry three years ago, Aidan had taken a step back. Riley was an adult now. He could make his own choices and his own decisions. Even though Aidan's first and last and every instinct in between was to take care of him, to *shield* him, the way he'd shielded him their whole childhood, he wasn't doing that anymore.

Of course, Levi was going to bring that up now, though.

"Anyway"—Levi was clearly not giving up without a fight—"I know you're trying to hide it. Pasting on a very content smile and shit, but it's clear you're not okay."

Great.

Aidan made a face. "If I said again that I don't want to talk about it, would you leave it alone?"

Levi scoffed. "As if. You're my *bro.*" He slung a huge arm around Aidan, like they might actually be brothers, which they were certainly not. Aidan was best friends with Levi's brother and *their* brothers were dating, or married, or exchanging blood soul pacts or whatever it was that they did these days. Not the same thing at all.

Aidan attempted again to change the subject. He shucked Levi's arm off. And that was *not* as easy as it seemed, either. "How are you the biggest of all of you?"

He gave Levi an up-and-down look. He really was *huge*, and all muscle. Landry and Logan were big and broad, but somehow Levi was even bigger. Not many people managed to make Aidan's six foot three feel *small*, but Levi managed it.

"Luck?" Levi laughed, like this was delightful.

Aidan was not delighted.

Vaguely, he considered getting up from the couch and going to look for Riley and Landry, who he'd left in the kitchen to do the dishes after dinner, but then he remembered that if they were taking half an hour to do the dishes, they were probably not just doing the dishes. Aidan clamped his lips together, trying not to think about his younger brother and his best friend currently defiling a public space.

"Bro, you keep changing the subject."

"And you keep calling me *bro*," Aidan retorted.

Levi just shrugged, clearly feeling zero shame about this. "Listen, *dude*, it's always better to have it out than to keep it in."

Aidan disagreed with this assessment. He'd been keeping shit in his whole life, and he'd turned out just fine. Thirty-four and one of the most acclaimed quarterbacks in the NFL? Yeah, he was doing just fucking fine.

"I'm fine, it's totally fine," Aidan said. Maybe if he thought it and said it enough times, it would be true.

He ignored the pulse of pain he felt every time he thought about football. It wasn't fair that Mo could ruin football for him too.

It had been bad enough when he'd lost him on the field. Then he'd finally fucking manned up, told him how he felt, and how had that gone? Pretty much as bad as it could go.

"Bro, you are *not* fine," Levi said softly, his voice losing that smug charisma for the first time all evening, "I can see it. And maybe Landry can't, because he's . . .I don't know . . .dickmatized for the first time in his life, but I can."

"Can someone still be dickmatized after three years of getting dick?" Aidan wondered. Then considered scrubbing his brain with bleach because that was his *brother's* dick he was referring to.

"If the dick's that good," Levi said, waggling his eyebrows.

Aidan regretted a lot of things. He definitely regretted bringing up his brother's dick to Levi. But there was no question what the top of the list was: telling Riley he'd be spending the next month in Michigan. With only a text announcement that he was arriving, Riley had shown up less than two days later with not only Landry in tow, but Levi as well, with only the explanation that Levi needed a distraction from his contract negotiations with Seattle.

Aidan had intended to lick his wounds in peace, but instead he was going to be heckled and harassed by his best friend's younger brother.

"Whose dick is that good?" Landry appeared in the doorway from the kitchen, hair mussed and face flushed, making it painfully obvious whose dick was good.

But before Aidan could let him have it for fucking in public spaces, which Riley knew *perfectly well* was off-limits, Levi squawked loudly. "God, dude, *no*," he announced, tossing a throw pillow in Landry's direction with deadly accuracy. "Keep it in your pants, *God*."

"Can I second that?" Aidan said.

Landry just rolled his eyes. "We were doing the dishes!"

"Fucking liar," Levi muttered. "If Lyla was here—"

"She's *not* here," Landry said self-righteously.

"Yeah, well, if she hears about this—"

"She's not gonna," Riley said, sauntering in, sounding very sure of himself. "You wanna make s'mores? I got the firepit going outside."

Aidan did not want to make s'mores. He wanted to sit here and keep drinking the whiskey he'd started with dinner and pretend that he was 1) alone and 2) that Mo hadn't looked so fucking sorry when he'd let Aidan down as kindly as anyone had in the history of being let down.

He'd be seeing that bluntly sympathetic look in Mo's eyes in his sleep. But not in his dreams, more like his nightmares.

"Moving is overrated," Aidan said. He lifted his glass. "Unless some-one wants to move and get me more whiskey."

Levi shot him a pointed look, but actually stood up and grabbed the bottle and another glass. "If I have to deal with these two," he said, pouring a few fingers for himself and then heading back to the couch, giving Aidan a generous pour of his own, "I gotta be at least a little drunk."

"Unfair," Riley said.

"You two just fucked in the kitchen," Levi said. "Some of us are mourning the lack of available options out in the middle of backwoods nowhere."

Aidan considered telling Levi that if he didn't like the *options* here, he could leave. And he could take Landry and Riley with him.

But he was afraid if he said it, Levi would announce, loudly and with zero subtlety, that Aidan was drowning his sorrows.

As much as Aidan had attempted and thankfully *failed* to fuck up his relationship with his brother, Riley wouldn't take that sitting down. He'd demand to know what was going on, and he wouldn't be easily distracted like Levi had been.

And Aidan *still* didn't want to talk about it.

"You could always fuck Aidan," Riley said to Levi, grinning.

Landry squawked in outrage, like hearing about *his* best friend fucking was somehow different than Aidan having to know what he'd just done in *his* kitchen, with *his* brother.

"Aidan's straight as a fucking arrow," Landry said.

Oh, that was cute. Aidan *wished* that was true. That it was as true today as it had been his whole goddamn life, all the way up until his close friend Morris had signed a blockbuster deal with the Raiders and fucked off to the other side of the country, and Aidan had realized, way too fucking late, that maybe his friendly and brotherly feelings about him were not nearly as platonic as he'd always believed.

"Like you were straight?" Riley waggled his eyebrows at his boyfriend.

Landry flushed. Looking, like Levi had just said, *dickmatized.*

Riley was a good-looking kid, but the eyebrow waggling was not his best look. That didn't seem to matter. Landry always looked like this around him. Like he was constantly dazed by the good fortune that Riley had ever deigned to look in his direction.

It was gross, and maybe a tiny bit cute.

Aidan ruthlessly cut off the thought that, at one time, he'd hoped that he might be able to look at Mo like that. That he might be *allowed* to look at Mo like that.

Levi shared a commiserating glance with Aidan. Of course he didn't know what he was commiserating, but it was still more comforting than Aidan might have imagined five minutes ago. "Wouldn't that be a little . . .I don't know . . .incestuous?"

"And when has that *ever* stopped you?" Riley asked in disbelief. "You and Logan both fucked Carter Maxwell."

"Not at the same time!" Levi yelped, like this was an important detail that everyone hadn't already assumed.

"Ew, gross. I *know* Carter," Landry muttered.

Aidan took a long gulp of whiskey.

"I don't know, I don't think it would be," Riley said slowly. "You're not actually related."

He didn't want to lie to Riley or Landry. Lying to Levi was more fluid, but he was present, too, so Aidan supposed he counted. Thus, he could not stand up and declare that yes, he was way too goddamn straight to fuck Levi.

Just way too caught up in someone else.

"True." Levi looked contemplative, like he was actually thinking about this. And that was not going to happen. Not now, not ever.

There was nothing to do about it, but change the subject, *again*.

God, did he have to do *everything*?

Aidan pulled himself up from the couch, whiskey sloshing in his glass, dripping onto his hand. He licked it off and ignored the face Riley made about it. "Come on," he said, "let's go outside. S'mores, right, Ri?"

Riley looked like he knew what Aidan was trying to do, but the more important thing was that he didn't call him on it.

"Yeah, let's go," Riley said.

Aidan hesitated in front of Levi, still sprawled out on the couch, big thick thighs exposed with his pair of short neon yellow shorts. Aidan couldn't say his fashion sense was the best, but at least he didn't unironically wear neon.

Levi shot him a pouting look. "Not gonna help me up?"

"This isn't a double date," Aidan said flatly.

"And I even got you a refill."

Aidan sighed and extended a hand, and it took more strength than he'd imagined to yank Levi up, but he did it without embarrassing himself too much.

Ignoring, deliberately, how during the whole discussion of Levi hooking up with Aidan that Levi had never said, not once, how he wasn't attracted to Aidan.

He didn't need that brain worm too, on top of all the others currently eating away at him.

Levi's fingers were sticky with burned marshmallow and the remnants of the chocolate bar he'd stolen from the box and eaten without even bothering to sandwich it between graham crackers.

Across from him, Aidan was still morosely staring into the fire, like he might find all his answers in its dancing flames.

Riley and Landry were lost in their own world, sharing one of the big Adirondack chairs, Riley practically on Landry's lap, his head resting on Landry's shoulder. If they were paying any fucking attention at all, they would surely see that Aidan was not himself.

He was always full of dry sarcasm. Always knew better than anyone else what they should be doing. Was never the loudest person in the room, but usually the most self-righteous, an authority he no doubt believed he'd earned by usually *being* right. But from the moment when the three of them had descended onto his vacation house, right on one of the Michigan lakes, it had been obvious to Levi that Aidan was even quieter than normal. Something bleak and unpleasant lingering in the back of his blue eyes.

Physically, he was like the original and Riley the younger copy. Taller and broader, with darker blond hair and darker blue eyes, it was ridiculously easy to tell they were brothers.

But Riley's smiles came so much easier, especially now.

Levi and Aidan had never been particularly good friends. That had always been Landry and Aidan, but Levi had spent enough time in Aidan's orbit to know something was up.

It was kind of shitty that neither Landry nor Riley had noticed, but then, they were still caught up in their own world, giggling under their breath, feeding each other little bits of melted marshmallow, while Aidan gave himself whiskey dick on the other side of the fire.

Aidan was normally kind of a chill, loose drunk, but not tonight. The more booze he drank, he just grew quieter and quieter, until Levi wanted to get up and demand he tell him what was going on. Be annoying enough he couldn't brush Levi off anymore.

He didn't even know why Aidan's steadfast reluctance to tell him the truth bothered him. They weren't really friends. Aidan's shit was his own business.

But Levi felt bad. Unlike Levi with his three nosy, over-involved siblings, Aidan only had Riley, and Riley was kind of the best, but he was a little—or a lot—distracted right now.

"Dude," Levi said, moving his chair closer to Aidan's. Further away from Riley and Landry's.

Aidan's gaze slid over him lazily. "What?"

"You're really not going to talk about it?"

"God, you're persistent," Aidan said, not sounding that perturbed by it. Maybe that was the whiskey talking.

"Youngest sibling's prerogative. We're built this way."

"I meant it. I don't wanna talk about it." He was definitely sulking, no question about it. Aidan's lips practically turned down.

"Doesn't mean you shouldn't," Levi pointed out.

Aidan opened his mouth and then snapped it shut again. His gaze flicked over to where Landry and Riley were giggling together, and it occurred to Levi, that even though they were very clearly not listening, Aidan still didn't want to risk saying anything either of them could overhear.

And suddenly, Levi was more worried. Because if the thing had been a minor issue, Aidan wouldn't have cared. Wouldn't have tried to hide it so hard.

"Dude," Levi said flatly.

"I'm not sure that's better than *bro*," Aidan said.

"You're still going to be playing, right? Like you're not retiring early? I didn't hear you were injured—"

"I'm not injured," Aidan interrupted. "It's not . . . it's not anything to do with football."

"You didn't get a girl pregnant, did you?"

Aidan gave a short, unamused bark of laughter. "No."

"Okay, well, what the fuck is it, then?" Levi hoped he could stop guessing. He was running out of legitimate ideas and he had a feeling bringing up his less legitimate ideas was not a surefire way to get Aidan to open up, only to annoy him.

Aidan clamped his lips shut. Didn't shake his head, but the message was clear enough.

Ugh.

Levi wasn't just worried, he was *curious*.

But then Riley slid off Landry's lap and Landry was up a second later, wrapping an arm around Riley's waist.

"We're going to bed," Riley announced.

"Thank God, *finally*," Aidan said dryly.

Riley shot his brother a look. "You think you're cute, but you're not."

And of course Aidan was. Probably not the way Riley meant, but Levi was trying to be smart about this. Aidan might be hot, but he was straight, and Levi had long given up lusting after straight boys.

"I don't know, I think I'm pretty cute." Aidan fluttered his eyelashes, something Levi was pretty damn sure he wouldn't have done if he hadn't drunk all that whiskey.

"Alright, you keep thinking that," Landry said, detouring over to him to pat him on the shoulder. "Chug some water, okay?"

"Sure, Dad," Aidan retorted.

Landry barked out a laugh. But thirty seconds later, the back door was closing behind them.

Levi didn't *pounce*. He knew if he did, Aidan might not tell him.

But he did glance over and waggle his eyebrows. He'd never have done it if he thought there was a chance in hell of seducing Aidan, but this was Aidan Flynn. There wasn't a chance anyway.

"You're ridiculous," Aidan muttered.

"You know you wanna tell me. You wanna tell *someone*. And you're clearly not gonna be telling Riley or Landry."

Aidan groaned low in his throat, his frustration evident. "I *might* have."

"No way. You wouldn't have tried so hard to hide it."

Aidan just pinned him with a heated look. It shouldn't have made Levi hot, but it did. Levi was bigger, but he had a flash of a vision—Aidan and his broad shoulders and intense blue gaze, pinning him to the bed.

But Levi didn't let himself dwell, because lusting after straight guys lay certain insanity.

Then, before Levi could say anything else—could even shake his mind entirely clear of the fantasy, even—Aidan said in a low, resigned voice, "You know Mo Jeffries?"

"Morris Jeffries?" Levi was surprised and couldn't hide it. Morris had signed a new contract with the Raiders three years ago, despite Aidan working his hardest to try to get the Thunder to keep him.

But that had been *three years* ago. Surely Aidan wasn't still throwing a shit fit because one of his closest friends and certified favorite wide receiver had gotten his payday from a different team?

"Yeah," Aidan said morosely. "I . . .he's one of my best friends, you know? We played together for years on the Thunder. And I thought I knew what he meant to me—"

"Trust me, dude, you made that plenty clear."

Aidan glared at Levi's interruption. "I thought I *knew*. And then he left and I realized it wasn't what I thought it was. I'd . . .I don't know . . .buried the part of it that didn't feel platonic."

Levi felt rocked.

"You had *feelings* for Mo Jeffries?"

Of all things Levi had anticipated, this hadn't even been on the less legitimate list.

"Uh, yeah. *Have*, I guess."

Over the years, plenty of players and friends and even vague acquaintances had come out to Levi. He'd always been pretty open about his sexuality, and thus accessible when someone wanted advice, or an opinion, or even just simply to be heard.

But he just sat there, jaw dropped, as Aidan Flynn came out to him.

"Holy shit," Levi said.

Aidan rolled his eyes. "Somehow I suppose that's on-brand. You didn't give me a *bro* or a *dude*, so I guess I should count that as a win."

"Come on, I'm a little shocked here," Levi complained. He took a moment, tried to recenter himself. Reorient himself in a world where, *holy shit*, Aidan Flynn was not straight. "I appreciate you being honest with me, bro."

"There you are," Aidan said with a ghost of a grin.

"So you're with Mo Jeffries. That's cool." Levi tried not to be jealous and tried not to picture them together. It was hard, 'cause they'd be hot. Aidan with his broad shoulders and insane abs. Mo with his tall slender body and ripped chest. Soulful brown eyes meeting Aidan's deep blue. They'd be gorgeous together.

"Uh, no. Not exactly."

"Not exactly?"

Aidan made a frustrated noise. "Not at all. I . . .I didn't tell him right away. I thought it might go away. That everything might go back to . . .normal."

"What's normal?" Levi asked, because at twelve he'd felt this way, too. Wanting to be normal, hoping for it so fiercely, with such pointed intent, but it had never happened. Eventually he'd been forced to acknowledge that he wasn't going to miraculously become straight. It had taken another ten years for him to realize that even if he was gay, that didn't mean he *wasn't* normal.

Normal was a construct. Anyone could be normal if they decided they wanted to be.

"Yeah, exactly," Aidan said. "What the fuck is normal? I guess it means, would they ever go back to the way things were before? And they didn't. Last week we met up in Vegas, for that charity golf tournament thing? And I . . ." He paused, licking his lips, and Levi saw what was coming, like a car crash, and he couldn't look away, even if he wanted to. And he *wanted* to. "And I told him how I felt."

Aidan didn't have to say it didn't go well. If it had, he wouldn't be trying so fucking hard to mask his heartbreak. Because that was what it was. Aidan Flynn, golden boy of the NFL, didn't get everything he wanted, after all.

"I'm sorry, dude," Levi said, heartfelt. Heart crumbling a little, just at the bleak pain in Aidan's eyes.

Aidan shrugged awkwardly. Like it wasn't a big deal, even though it very clearly was. "I . . .I shouldn't have done it. I knew what he'd say. I knew before I even told him. I just thought—*ugh*, this is so dumb. So fucking dumb."

"No, it's not." Levi moved his chair closer and didn't even think, just reached out and cupped Aidan's knee, squeezing it. It was strong and warm under his fingers, the faint brush of Aidan's wiry hair.

"I thought, even if there was even a tiny chance, it was worth it." Aidan sighed. "But it wasn't."

"Yeah, it was. Now you know everything. Now you can move forward," Levi argued.

Aidan made a scoffing noise. "How the fuck am I supposed to do that?"

"It's not gonna be easy, but the world's your oyster now, bro."

"What the hell is that supposed to mean?" Aidan frowned.

"I mean, you're free to do anything. If you want it, you can do it."

Aidan didn't look particularly happy about that. "I guess so."

"Okay, how about this. You could hook up with *anyone*. You're hot and rich and famous."

Aidan still looked skeptical, which was ridiculous.

"Please tell me you're not disputing any of those," Levi said bluntly.

"No, just none of that fucking matters because it didn't get me . . ." Aidan cleared his throat. "What if all I want is him?" Aidan squeezed his eyes shut, like he regretted saying it. Regretted baring his soul that completely.

"Maybe now," Levi said, reaching over and squeezing Aidan's knee again. "But that won't always be true. You're gonna see someone else someday. Maybe a girl. But maybe it's a guy, and now that you know what this feels like, it's gonna be different. You're going to know what you want, and you're gonna go after him. And because you're Aidan Flynn, you're gonna get him."

"Sure," Aidan said sarcastically. So flippant it was obvious he didn't believe Levi. "And at like . . .thirty-five or whatever, it's going to be cool for me to be like, I've never done this before, so walk me through it."

Levi chuckled. "Of course you'd be neurotic about being a rookie."

"Shouldn't I be?" Aidan demanded. "If it had been . . .well, I wouldn't have minded looking stupid in front of him. But in front of anyone else?"

"I get it." Levi had never felt that way, but he understood that Aidan might. He'd built his entire career on the idea that he was right and excellent and experienced. It was a foundational corner of his whole identity.

"No offense, dude, but have you *ever* cared about that?"

It wasn't hard to forgive Aidan for his mercilessness. He was clearly hurting and lashing out.

"No, but I'm different than you," Levi said gently.

Aidan's mouth clamped shut again.

"How about this," Levi said, and it was very stupid, and he should shut up, because the idea forming in his head was insane and terrible, but he didn't shut up. He kept fucking talking. "How about if your guy doesn't come around—"

"Trust me, he's not going to," Aidan muttered with a fatalism that made Levi's heart ache a little in solidarity.

"If he doesn't come around," Levi continued, like he hadn't heard the interruption, "by this time next year, and you still want to try sex with a guy, we'll do it."

Levi had known what was coming. After all, it was his stupid idea. His impossible-to-resist idea, because apparently the idea of getting Aidan Flynn into bed circumvented any reasonable logic. But Aidan hadn't.

He looked floored.

"What the fuck, dude?"

Levi just shrugged. "I mean it. You want someone to experiment with, I'm happy to volunteer."

"But . . ." Aidan looked him over, top to bottom. And he didn't seem *against* it, just shocked. Which boosted Levi's ego, no question.

"But what?"

"But why the fuck would you want to do that?"

Oh, that was wild. Poor Aidan. Feeling like because Mo didn't want him like that, nobody would ever want him like that. Levi would be more than happy to show him that was not true.

Levi cleared his throat. The fire had almost gone out now. Aidan was at least three glasses of whiskey in. Levi wasn't exactly sober either. Maybe this was an even worse idea than it had been before, but that didn't mean Levi was going to smash the brakes now.

He wasn't sure he *could*.

"Trust me, bro, it wouldn't exactly be a hardship."

Aidan actually had the nerve to grin, all that cocky confidence that always drove defenses insane, the smile that meant he had you, and he was going to show you exactly how much of a crap hand you'd been dealt. Levi felt it too, hitting deep down. Making his cock twitch.

"What? 'Cause I'm . . .what was it? Hot and rich and famous?"

"The first one is plenty reason," Levi said dryly.

Aidan mumbled something under his breath. Levi was pretty sure he heard it, but he wanted to make one hundred and ten percent sure he'd gotten it right. Because the last thing he wanted was to assume incorrectly here.

"Sorry, what was that?"

Aidan made a face, and yes, he was *still* hot when he did that. "I said, *sure, yes, why not?*"

"Score," Levi said and held his hand out to high five. Aidan gave it a skeptical look.

"It's a sex pact, bro," Levi said matter-of-factly. "We gotta high-five to seal the deal."

"Are you fucking joking?"

Levi wondered for a split second if this would be enough to change Aidan's mind. But it didn't. He actually reached out and high-fived him back. Rolling his eyes the whole time, but he did it.

Tomorrow, Levi was going to go out and buy a lottery ticket. In a year, he was going to get to nail Aidan Flynn. He was in the middle of fantasizing about how good it would be—what they'd do—how it would feel, when Aidan spoke up again.

"Why'd you give it a year?" he asked, sounding genuinely curious.

Levi shrugged. Why *had* he given it a year? He could have given it six months. Or six weeks. Or six days.

Except that he wasn't masochistic and he didn't want to fuck Aidan while he was still internally crying over Mo rejecting him. When and if Aidan finally landed in his bed, he was going to be thinking of only one person: Levi.

"Seemed like a nice round number," Levi said, "and I imagine that in a year, we both might find ourselves back in Michigan. And I meant it before, pickings are slim around here."

Aidan looked mildly disgruntled by that reminder. "So it's not because you feel sorry for me?"

"That I gave it a year? Well, I sure as fuck don't want you crying in bed over another man—"

"No, no, *no*," Aidan said. "I meant, why you offered it in the first place. 'Cause you feel sorry for me."

"Dude," Levi said flatly.

Aidan laughed, a bark that made Levi feel reassured, like he *would* get over this. Eventually Aidan would be whole again and ready to move on, and if Levi was lucky, he might end up reaping the benefits of all that.

"I'm serious!" Aidan argued, but he was still smiling.

"I wanna say, we should work on your ego some, but we both know that's not normally a problem. It's just . . . right now . . ." Levi waved around Aidan's body. "You know."

"I'm unusually pathetic right now?" Aidan grimaced. "Thanks for the reminder."

"Hey, you said it, not me."

"So if I . . ." Aidan leaned in a little closer, and then it was *his* hand landing on Levi's knee. But then his fingers stroked upwards, hesitating at the high hem of his shorts. Levi willed him to keep going, to slip his fingers underneath the fabric, even if he knew how bad an idea it was.

He was full of those tonight, apparently.

"If you groped my leg?" Levi questioned.

Aidan groaned. "No, *no*."

"If you came on to me tonight, drunk and pitiful, if I'd turn you down?"

"If anyone should be worried about my ego, it's you," Aidan muttered. But he didn't move his hand. Just stroked the skin of Levi's upper thigh with his rough and distracting calluses.

"I'd say, if you *did* try anything, that I'm very flattered and my bed is gonna feel really fucking lonely later, but yeah, no. Not tonight." Levi made a face. Why was he being so stupid about this? Five years ago he wouldn't have cared if he took a guy to bed and he thought about someone else the whole time. It wasn't like Aidan was drunk enough to hook up with Levi and imagine he was Morris, who was his complete opposite physically.

"Alright." Aidan shrugged and moved his hand away from Levi's thigh. Levi tried not to be disappointed. Repressed the desire to grab it and put it right back where it was.

"You gonna be okay?"

Aidan glanced over at him, blue eyes wide. "You worried about me now, Banks?"

"Obviously," Levi retorted. After all, he'd been the only one to notice Aidan was hurting *and* he'd made Aidan tell him about it.

"It's annoying, but you're probably right. Nothing to do but move forward. Every day's gonna be a little better than the last one." Aidan looked more contemplative and less drunk, then, which was good.

"That's the spirit," Levi said, patting him on the knee.

Didn't let his touch linger, even though he was surprised at how much he wanted it to. And here he thought he'd avoided the same cliché Riley had ended up falling prey to: finding the older brother hot.

"Come on, let's go to bed," Aidan said, hefting himself out of his chair. He paused. "*Not* together."

Levi laughed. "Don't sound so relieved, bro."

Chapter 2

Aidan woke with a pounding head and a nauseating combination of panic and relief swirling through his stomach. He'd told someone. And not even a Riley- or Landry-shaped someone.

Levi had been—Aidan rolled over, putting that thought on hold and gulped Gatorade from the bottle next to the bed, praying that hydration might save his life—well, Levi had been pretty cool about it. Chill, even.

And that was when Aidan remembered what else he'd promised last night. He'd promised to have sex with Levi. *Levi Banks.*

God, he'd even been a few inches away from literally groping Levi's dick in those ridiculous neon yellow shorts.

The Gatorade he'd just drunk lurched unpleasantly in his stomach.

He flopped onto his back. Willed his organs to cooperate. When he was at least seventy-five percent sure they would, Aidan considered his options.

Riley hadn't told him how long the trio of them would be staying in Michigan but there was no way they'd leave this soon. They were around for at least the next few days. Could he hang out with Levi and act like it was all cool between them?

There was the boat and the lake. And Landry had been making noises about going on a long hike one day. Surely there was enough to do around here between goofing around on the water and workouts and meals to distract him from the fact he'd told Levi and Levi's suggestion that they have sex about it. And not even *now*, but in a *year*.

And you, you stupidly agreed, his conscience told him. *Who does that when they're in love with someone else?*

Conclusion: he'd been drunk and stupid and desperate.

Positively, he was at least not *one* of those things this morning, and maybe he could pull Levi aside and acknowledge the other two. Say, *thanks but no thanks.*

That very logical thought got him through getting out of bed and hauling his hungover ass into the shower. By the time he made it downstairs, his stomach had mostly calmed and he felt way less like death. If he never drank that much whiskey again, it would be too soon.

"Hey, it's alive," Riley teased as he walked into the kitchen. He was sitting on the counter, legs dangling off the edge, coffee cradled in one of his hands.

Landry turned from where he was at the stove, flipping pancakes.

There was no Levi in the kitchen yet.

Aidan let out the breath he'd been holding.

"How you feelin' this morning, buddy?" Landry asked, grinning.

"Fine." Aidan did not feel fine, but he was not going to give anyone the chance to give him shit about it.

"Coffee's in the pot." Riley shot him a knowing look. "Bet you need the whole carafe."

It was difficult to pretend around these two who knew him so well. Of course, if that was really true, then why had Levi been the one demanding to know what was wrong with him?

Aidan steadfastly refused to sulk about it, though. He'd done enough of that yesterday. Instead, he moved over to the coffeepot and poured himself a big cup. It was strong and hot and his stomach settled a little more as he sipped it, watching as Landry filled a big platter with more pancakes.

"We were thinking of taking the boat out today," Riley said.

Aidan glanced over at the big picture window. It was sunny and bright, not a cloud in the sky. "Sounds good," he said. *One day down, way too many to go.*

"Levi's in the shower." Riley gestured to the spare cup in front of one of the empty barstools. Aidan hadn't noticed it before. But of course, he was the last one down this morning. "Landry told him to hurry up, 'cause breakfast is almost ready."

"Yeah, he said he was going to drag you out of bed if you weren't out of it already," Landry said. It was clear from his completely normal tone of voice that he hadn't meant it *like that*, but then why would he? As far as Landry knew, Aidan was straight, and there'd be no funny business at all about Levi pulling him out of bed.

"Good thing I made it out first, then," Aidan muttered weakly.

"Yeah, he's not real nice first thing in the morning," Landry said, laughing.

"Spoken like a true older brother." Riley nudged him on the leg with a foot. "Those almost ready, babe? I'm starving."

"Yeah, yeah, I got you." Landry shot Riley a look full of gooey fondness.

Aidan looked away, fingers drumming on the counter. He was beginning to remember why he'd drunk three large glasses of whiskey last night.

Of course, that was the moment Levi decided to show up, wearing another pair of extremely short shorts, neon pink with a bright orange triangle pattern today.

Aidan's eyes flicked down to his exposed thighs, thick and meaty and kind of gorgeous, actually, now that he was thinking about it. Then he remembered, suddenly, like he'd been electrocuted, that he'd *groped* that thigh last night.

He'd absolutely shamelessly put his hands on it and had even considered, in his drunken desperate stupidity, putting his hands on something else.

Aidan choked out an unsteady breath.

"Yo, dude, you're awake."

"God, it's too early for those," Aidan complained, gesturing to the shorts, "and definitely too early for *yo* or *dude*."

"Come on." Levi grinned, slapping Aidan on the shoulder. "You know you love it. All of it." His shameless smile made it clear that he wasn't going to be pretending that last night hadn't happened.

Aidan guessed he should be grateful at least that he wasn't bringing it up in front of their brothers.

"Hey, *dude*," Riley teased, "can you grab the fruit from the fridge? We got the pancakes and the bacon." He hopped off the counter and was about to use the edge of a kitchen towel to pull the pan of bacon out of the oven, but before he could, Landry noticed and made literal *tsking* noises.

"Use a fucking oven mitt," Landry insisted, holding one out.

"God, you're such a mom," Levi complained, as Riley took the oven mitt, rolling his eyes the whole time.

"No, I'm a tight end who wants his quarterback to not burn his fingers off two months before training camp starts," Landry said.

"Sometimes, I'm really not surprised that you and Aidan are friends," Riley said.

Aidan refilled his coffee mug and then moved to the kitchen table, collapsing into one of the chairs. "Shot right through the heart," he proclaimed dryly.

"He means it with love," Landry said, tone brimming with unspoken loyalty.

"Sure, babe," Riley said impudently, the look in his eyes brimming with just as much fondness as Landry's had been earlier, making it clear he didn't mind in the least.

Levi set the big bowl of fruit on the table and took the chair next to Aidan's, even though there were other spots. Aidan told himself it was just coincidence, but then he swore he felt a foot brush his own before he moved it back.

Waggling his eyebrows at Aidan, Levi grabbed the platter of bacon from Riley and took a handful.

It was by no means the first time they'd all sat together like this, eating a meal. Sometimes Logan was there, and after he'd started dating Dylan, he'd come too. Occasionally even Lyla deigned to grace them with her presence, but they'd all been hanging out together for years.

But this felt like the first time.

It's just the hangover, Aidan told himself firmly as his fingers trembled around the fork and he gripped it harder, trying to stop the giveaway shake.

But it was hardly the first time he'd been hungover around Landry and his brothers.

"You're being really quiet," Riley said, after he'd demolished a whole stack of pancakes and was going back for a second round. He pinned Aidan with his intense light blue stare.

"Dude, he's practically dying. Cut him some slack," Levi inserted. His glance over at Aidan was pointed. Like, *get your shit together.*

Aidan wanted to bury his head in his hands and cry. *If I could do it, if I could actually fucking pull that off, I'd have done it already.*

Riley's gaze narrowed. "Maybe." He didn't sound particularly convinced.

"Ri," Aidan said, sighing heavily. "I sorta am." He didn't say why. Was perfectly okay with Riley believing that his hangover was the only reason.

Riley's expression softened. "Want some more coffee?"

"Yeah, that would be great."

Riley got up and poured him another full cup and thankfully didn't say anything else about how weird Aidan probably was this morning. Trust him to notice when he was not just sober, but suffering.

By the time the food was gone and Aidan's cup was empty, he felt marginally more human again.

"You really okay taking the boat out?" Landry asked, stopping Aidan from rising from the table with a hand on his arm. "If you're not feeling it, we can go without you—"

"And leave you two lovebirds alone with Levi? I don't think so." Aidan snapped back a little meaner than he'd intended. A headache was still teasing at his temples, and there were the hundred knowing looks Levi had sent him during breakfast. And then, worst of all, the empty chasm of his heart after Mo had looked at him, so fucking sympathetic, and turned him down.

Considering all that, it wasn't really all that surprising how tightly he was wound.

Landry paused. Staring into his eyes. "Aidan," he said softly. Aidan suddenly worried—abruptly and horribly—maybe he'd recognized Aidan's sulk after all.

"No, no, sorry. I'm fine. We'll take the boat."

Landry let it go, but there was still concern lingering in his eyes as he watched Aidan take the empty plates to the kitchen, piling them up in the sink.

He'd hoped that maybe in the chaos of getting ready to go on the boat he could corner Levi and clarify that he'd been drunk and stupid and desperate last night and it turned out the whole triad was required to agree to insane sex bets with your brother-in-law.

But Riley conscripted Levi to make sandwiches as Riley piled bottles of water and Gatorade and beer into the cooler, and there was no way to get him alone.

Just when Riley finally ducked into the pantry to gather together a few bags of chips—not the best opening in the world, but Aidan was desperate—Landry showed up.

"Hey, let's get the boat ready to go," he said.

Aidan stifled his groan of frustration. Maybe once they were on the lake, Riley and Landry would get absorbed in each other again, like they often did, and he could snatch a moment to tell Levi they'd both been drunk and dumb last night.

"Sure," Aidan said, plastering the same smile on—the one that hadn't fooled Levi—and followed Landry down to the attached boat dock.

He checked the supplies in the boat while Landry blew up a few inner tubes with the air compressor and tossed them in.

They'd just finished up when Levi and Riley appeared, carting what seemed like half a grocery store between them, their arms overflowing with towels, reusable bags, and the gigantic cooler.

"Did I miss the apocalypse?" Landry joked.

Riley glared, but like *fondly*. Aidan grimaced.

"No," Riley said. "We needed *supplies*."

"Apparently," Landry said, but didn't hesitate to take the bags from his boyfriend's arms and help him onto the boat, even though Riley was an NFL quarterback and could figure out how to get from a dock to the boat.

Levi and Aidan exchanged a glance about this whole performance. They'd been doing this for years now, since Landry and Riley had started dating. It felt very normal. Routine, in fact. It had always been easy to give their brothers shit about how pathetically gone they were for each other. But there was a new layer to these looks he shared with Levi now.

A knowing that Aidan couldn't forget.

He wished he'd never touched Levi's thigh.

He wished he'd never told Mo how he felt.

He wished he'd never fallen for Mo in the first place.

Honestly, a lot of wishes that were never going to fucking come true, so he might as well resign himself.

"Come on," Aidan said, pulling the brim of his hat down, trying to shade his eyes more. "Let's go."

It was his house and his boat, so he always drove, even though Landry made lots of noise about wanting to take a turn. Aidan let him *occasionally*, and only when he wanted to take his turn on the wakeboard.

He drove them around the edge. Riley sitting in the back with Landry, Landry's arm over his shoulder, Levi on the opposite side, head tipped back like he was trying to absorb the sun.

"That's the Barnes' house," Aidan pointed out as they passed it.

"Barnes?" Levi asked, frowning.

"Avery and Charlie? Well, I guess now Ethan, too. He just got drafted. They all play in the NHL," Riley told him. Levi made a weird, confused face as Riley laughed. "Hockey, bro."

"They're cool guys. They work hard. Play hard, too. Young, but serious." They'd inevitably crossed paths a handful of times when Aidan had bought this house, at parties and barbeques. Last time they'd run into each other, he and Avery had even exchanged numbers, promising to hang out more. He should've texted Avery that he was coming here, but honestly the thought hadn't even occurred to him. He'd only wanted to be alone and this had seemed like the most logical place to do that, if he wasn't interested in hauling his sad, brokenhearted ass all the way to Antarctica.

"Now I think I remember," Levi said. "Hockey, you said?"

"God, you're an idiot." Landry smacked him on the leg. "It's lucky you're cute."

Aidan steered the boat towards the middle of the lake, taking them across to one of his favorite inlets, with a tucked-away beach that didn't tend to get a lot of traffic, even in the summer. It was almost impossible to reach by foot, and even though it was easy enough by boat, it was off the beaten path enough that most people didn't even know it existed.

They helped Riley empty the boat of the cooler and the food, spreading towels out on the sand, a fringe of trees overhanging on the beach just far enough to give a nice amount of shade.

Riley brandished the sunscreen and everyone submitted dutifully. "I don't know why you're like this when we all tan," Levi griped, tugging off his shirt.

He was built like a tank, wide shoulders—wider even than Landry's—and all rippling muscle. Not underwear-model muscle, but *real* muscle. Like he could probably pick up Aidan and bench him or something. Aidan ignored the prickling of his skin and turned away, staring out at the lapping water on the shore.

"Skin cancer is a thing, dude," Riley reminded him, ignoring his yelp when Riley sprayed the cold liquid all over his skin.

Landry said he wanted the first go, so Aidan took him out first, watching as he carefully balanced himself on the board. He didn't tend to try a lot of fancy tricks, but when it was Riley's turn, his smaller, more compact body made every single one he tried look effortless.

"Hey, you want a turn?" Aidan called over to Levi as he pulled the boat up to the tiny dock. He'd sprawled out on not just one towel, but two, laid out side by side, and he looked blissful.

"Nah," he called back. "I'm good right here. Might take a dip later."

"Come on, bro," Riley said, nudging him with a wet arm. "I'll drive. You take a turn."

Aidan wanted to argue. Say he was still feeling like shit. Which was . . .well, not *technically* true, but true enough. But Riley had that determined look in his eye. The same one he'd worn when he'd insisted to Aidan that he'd end up in the NFL, even though everyone—including Aidan—had thought he was too small.

It was easier to argue with a wall than to circumvent Riley when he wore that look.

"Sure," Aidan said.

They switched places, Riley piloting the boat out with a soft, expert touch.

Turned out that Riley was right about this, like he was right about most things. It was refreshing and good, to use his body in this way, in a way he knew how to. It stretched muscles that had gotten a little too lazy in the last few days of inactivity.

By the time he lifted himself back into the boat, he was feeling good. Loose and warm and with a tiny tendril of an emotion he was pretty sure was happiness winding its way through him.

Of course that was the moment Riley decided to strike.

"What's going on with you?" Riley said, tone of voice deceptively casual but the intentness of his gaze making it clear just how serious he was.

Aidan grabbed a towel and scrubbed it over his wet hair before shoving his hat back on. "What do you mean?"

"*Bro,*" Riley warned.

So much for Riley not having any clue that something was up. And if Riley knew, Landry knew.

Aidan wouldn't have said that was a downside of them dating, necessarily, but it was *something*. A mild annoyance, maybe, on any normal day. But actively frustrating today.

"What do you want me to say?"

"I want you to tell me what's up with you," Riley said.

Aidan still didn't want to lie. Didn't want to tell the truth either.

But maybe . . .maybe it would be better to just spit it out and get it over with.

"You know how last week I was at that charity golf thing in Vegas?" Riley nodded.

Aidan had picked his words carefully with Levi last night. But now he didn't even think; he just talked. "I've been struggling with this Mo thing, for awhile. You know that." Riley knew, but probably thought it was just Aidan's frustration that the friendship was more long-distance than it had been. That he no longer had Mo to throw to on the field. "Anyway, I thought I should say something. I'd been thinking about it for awhile. What exactly I should say. That it was . . .that it was more than just friendship for me. I decided finally, what the hell. And so I told him. We talked."

"You told him you're in love with him, then?" Riley asked archly.

Aidan froze.

"How did—"

"*Bro*," Riley stressed. "You were not very subtle about it."

"Oh."

Riley pushed off from the driver's seat and flopped down next to Aidan. "It's cool, you know? That you love him."

Aidan scrubbed a hand across his face. He probably should've shaved this morning. But he hadn't wanted to accidentally cut his jugular, not as hungover as he'd been.

"It's not very cool," Aidan said.

Riley didn't say anything, just looked sympathetic. Unlike Mo's sympathy, it didn't make Aidan want to fling himself in front of the nearest moving vehicle, so that was something.

"You don't look surprised in the least."

Riley shrugged. "I didn't think he liked you like that. But you liked *him* like that."

Aidan tried not to tense. "It was that obvious?"

"Maybe not to everyone, but to me? Yeah. Football's the most important thing in the world to you, Aidan, and you held out in camp for a new contract, and your only fucking requirement was that *he* get one too. For you, that's kind of crazy."

He'd known it was. Even as he'd done it, even as his agent had repeatedly insisted he was acting insane, he'd felt so desperate and unhinged, he'd stuck to his guns. Until finally, the only person who could've talked him off the ledge had done it. Mo had sat him down and gently told him he was going to Vegas. That it was over.

Aidan hadn't understood then why that had felt like the end of the universe.

Now he knew, but that didn't make it any easier to swallow today than it had then.

"Didn't work," Aidan said, and suddenly he was dangerously close to crying. He hadn't cried before, three years ago, when he'd wanted to. And not since he'd gotten back from Vegas, because part of him had worried that if he started, he just wouldn't stop. And he wasn't that guy. He'd never been that guy.

"No, but you tried. You were brave, putting yourself out there like that. There's something actually kind of beautiful about that, to be honest. Balls-to-the-wall crazy Flynn behavior."

Aidan choked out a laugh. "How can it be beautiful if he doesn't feel like—like I do?"

"Love is always a gift," Riley said softly, "even if it's not returned. I think you'll see that eventually."

Aidan made a scoffing noise. This feeling, a *gift*? He wanted to return it, receipt be damned. Dropkick it back into the maw of the universe.

"And," Riley added even more gently, and this time it was him, wrapping an arm around Aidan's bare shoulders, "I do think he loves you, just not like that. Someday, you'll feel differently, and you'll love him again the way he loves you. It'll be good again."

Aidan almost said that was similar to what Levi had said.

But he didn't want Riley to know about Levi. That he knew, or what else had happened with Levi last night.

Because again, whatever Riley knew, *Landry* knew.

Landry didn't operate on the same unhinged overprotective-older-brother frequency that Aidan did, but he would *not* be happy about Aidan being in love with someone else and agreeing to fuck his younger brother. Even if the younger brother had been the one to suggest it.

"I hope so," Aidan said instead. And he did. He wanted to not feel like this, not anymore.

"You're gonna get past this, I promise," Riley said, squeezing him tighter into his side. "I'm gonna be there for you."

"Thanks, Ri." It was a little jarring for Riley to be acting this way. But, Aidan supposed, this was all he'd really wanted for his younger brother. To be so happy and secure and mature that he could comfort others, when they needed it. Even if the person who needed it the most was Aidan.

"Landry, too," Riley added.

Aidan groaned.

"What? Of course he knows. He might've put it all together before I did," Riley said. "But I think he might like it if you *told* him. He's your best friend, was your best friend long before you met Morris. You were friends when things were shit, back then, with our parents. And he's still your friend, even when things are shit, now."

Aidan knew Riley was right. "Yeah. Alright. I'll talk to him."

Riley smiled. "Good."

It was impossible to hold his long resigned sigh in. "How did you get like this?"

"Like . . .emotionally mature and shit?" Riley grinned. "You, bro. All you. And not the way you think."

"How do I think?" Aidan asked dryly.

"I mean, you think it was because you babied the shit out of me and protected my ass and somehow kicked it at the same time, never letting me settle. But here's the thing, that was brave as shit, being all those things when you were too young considering Mom and Dad were . . .well, like they are." Riley didn't say what their parents were like, but Aidan knew all too well. Too caught up in their own petty hatreds and rivalries after their divorce to remember they had two sons. "But the bravest thing you ever did was to take a step back and let me sink or swim."

"You'd have killed me if I didn't," Aidan said, swallowing hard. It had been tough. One of the toughest things he'd ever done. Every molecule of his body had been screaming at him to do anything else. But he'd known if he did, Riley would never forgive him.

He'd had to give Riley the space to figure his own shit out. Even if he failed in the process.

And he hadn't.

"Yeah, and it was scary as shit, no lie. I was afraid I'd fuck it all up, but I didn't, because you raised me right, bro."

Aidan didn't say anything, staring out at the gentle waves, listening to them lapping at the side of the boat. Thinking about everything Riley had said. About that time, three years ago, when everything had been in upheaval. When he'd been terrified of losing Riley *and* Landry *and* Mo. But he hadn't. Things hadn't turned out like he'd expected, like he'd *wanted*, but in all the ways that counted, he still had all of them.

Even Morris, who'd told him unequivocally that they were still friends. That they'd always be friends. No matter what.

"You're really fucking smart, you know that?" Aidan finally said.

Riley beamed. Like his older brother's approval was all he'd ever wanted. And maybe that was true. He patted Aidan on the knee. "You're gonna get through this," he said.

And between what Riley said, and Levi last night, Aidan was beginning to believe that was really true.

CHAPTER 3

THE SUN WAS FALLING behind the tree line when they piled back into the boat and headed back to the house.

Levi was warm and toasty around the edges, pleasantly relaxed, except for the buzzing under his skin.

He'd spent the afternoon trying not to watch Aidan and mostly failing.

Aidan had always been attractive, but Levi had never been particularly interested in doing anything about it before. Of course, he hadn't thought he *could* do anything about it before.

And you still can't, Levi reminded himself. *Not til next year.*

When Aidan pulled the boat back to the dock, Riley was already complaining about how hungry he was, even though they'd decimated the enormous amount of food they'd brought out.

"We should order pizza," Landry suggested, and Aidan sighed.

"One cheat day isn't going to kill you," Riley said, like he already knew what Aidan was going to say. "And the best place in town *finally* delivers out here."

"That was all Charlie," Aidan said. "That kid could charm anyone to do anything. He spent the last few summers convincing them to deliver out here."

"Charlie?" Levi asked.

"We're gonna get you to watch hockey, at some point," Landry said, ruffling Levi's hair. "Charlie Barnes? The Barnes brothers?"

"Oh, right. And Charlie's charming, eh?"

"Could charm the paint right off a house," Aidan said.

"He cute? Single? Into guys?" Levi asked. Not that he was actually interested, but spending the whole day trying to pretend that Aidan wasn't the best-looking, most mouth-watering option he'd seen in awhile was killing him.

Landry rolled his eyes. "Calm down, bro."

"Not sure about the middle one, but one and three? Yeah," Riley said, shooting Landry a knowing look. Landry just groaned.

"And Charlie's practically a baby," Aidan complained. "He's what . . .twenty-one? Twenty-two?"

"You get drafted at eighteen and go straight to the NHL, you're not a baby," Riley said staunchly. "He's a good guy. Even better for finally batting his baby blues at Gio, down at the pizza shop, and convincing him to deliver out here."

"I heard he did a lot more than just bat his eyes," Aidan said. He was frowning now as he parked the boat and turned it off. Was he jealous of Levi wondering if Charlie Barnes was single? No way, he couldn't possibly be jealous. Not when he was still in love with Morris Jeffries.

"I like him already," Levi joked. "Knows how to get the job done."

Aidan's frown deepened. "I need a shower. Ri, you wanna order?"

Levi half considered doing something stupid and wandering into Aidan's bathroom. Joining him in the shower.

It would be a good time. No question about that. But after it was over, Aidan would probably wish he hadn't done it, and Levi could deal with a lot, but he never wanted, with anyone, to be something they regretted.

"Levi—you want your regular?" Riley asked him as Landry piled shit into his big arms—damp towels and empty bags and the cooler with only the remnants of melted ice rattling around inside.

"Yeah. Pepperoni mushroom."

"Make that two," Aidan said.

"Another pepperoni with ham and pineapple and jalapenos," Landry said.

"Ew gross," Riley said. "You'd better be eating that one by yourself."

"Riley, I hate to break it to you," Aidan said, slinging an arm around his brother's shoulders, "you're not only dating the man, but his excruciating taste in pizza toppings."

"Kinda like whoever ends up finally taking Levi off the market has to tolerate his ugly shorts?"

Levi snorted out a laugh. His shorts were *great*, thank you very much.

"Exactly," Aidan said. "You'd better hope they're colorblind."

They trooped up to the house, bags and cooler divided among them, and went their separate ways, Riley's voice echoing in the living room as he put in the order with Gio.

Levi didn't wander into Aidan's shower. Kept to his own, even though he let himself drift off as the cool water flowed down his body, cock taking more than a healthy interest once he let his mind wander in Aidan's direction, again.

His orgasm was satisfying, but the moment he walked back into the kitchen and saw Aidan's throat working as he swallowed half a bottle of Gatorade, backlit from the fridge light, it was like he hadn't even bothered to touch himself.

Levi tried to ignore it. No, *scratch that*. He *did* ignore it. Nothing had changed. Aidan was still Aidan. Annoying and the most big brother to ever big brother. Hot yes, but what a holy pain in the ass.

And Levi was still Levi, someone who just wanted to have fun whenever he could, with whoever he could.

"Hey," Aidan said, setting the bottle down. "Food should be here in about fifteen. Riley and Landry went up to shower."

"Together?" Levi slipped around Aidan and pulled a bottle of beer from the fridge, popping the top off with a twist of his fist, a trick he'd perfected over the years.

"Uh, yeah. They might be awhile." Aidan lifted his eyes heaven-ward, like he was praying for patience.

Levi took a long sip of his beer but it didn't help. That thirst still lingered.

Probably because Aidan was still damp, an old Thunder T-shirt clinging to his pecs and biceps. Hair falling in soft blondish-brown waves from his face. Looking, honestly, just about good enough to eat.

"Hey," Aidan said quietly, "I wanted to talk to you."

"Yeah?" Levi felt a frisson of something work itself up his spine as he leaned back against the kitchen counter. Not worry, not exactly. But there was an awkwardness in Aidan's stance, and he had a feeling last night's conversation—and possibly last night's promise—was about to come up again.

"I . . ." Aidan wet his lips and glanced away. "I was drunk last night."

"Oh, I know," Levi said. But if Aidan tried to claim he hadn't known what he was doing, what he was agreeing to, Levi would strongly disagree with that. There'd been heat and want in Aidan's gaze. In his touch, when he'd slipped his fingers under the hem of Levi's shorts.

"And well. Sad, too, and a little desperate." Aidan gave a self-dep-recating laugh, still not meeting Levi's eyes. "You caught me at a really down moment, dude."

"I know that, too."

Aidan flushed. "I was thinking about that, and not thinking through what we talked about. If I had, I just wouldn't have agreed to . . .well, what I agreed to."

Levi nearly asked him if he was going to say something that Levi didn't already know. But if he did, this train wreck might end, and there was a perverse part of Levi, who had been suffering, at least a little, all day, at how fucking good Aidan suddenly looked to him. It only felt fair that Levi wasn't alone here.

"Sure," Levi said.

"So we can forget it?" Aidan asked hopefully. Like he really thought Levi would let him off the hook. Levi would, possibly, but he didn't really think Aidan even wanted to be let off. Aidan wanted to *get* off. Levi was ninety-nine point nine percent sure he was just freaking out.

Time to make sure.

"No," Levi said, pushing off from the counter. He took a few steps closer, right into Aidan's space. He held his ground, which didn't surprise Levi at all. Aidan wasn't a person who was easily intimidated.

"No?" Aidan squawked.

"Why do you want to forget it?"

Aidan's gaze went shifty, looking right over Levi's shoulder. Aidan might be a lot of things—a football god and a pain in the ass and suddenly painfully, ridiculously hot—but he was a shitty liar. Always had been. Landry had been making fun of him for it, forever.

And because Levi had been around forever, too, he knew exactly how Aidan always gave himself away.

He was definitely lying now. The only question was why.

"I just . . .it seems so stupid and impulsive," Aidan claimed. "Who even knows what I'm going to be doing in a year. What *you're* going to be doing in a year."

"So you're wanting to forget it for my sake, then?" Levi asked archly.

"Well. No. Yes. I . . ." Aidan trailed off. Looking flustered and annoyed. "I just think it's a bad idea."

"No, you think it's a great idea, which means you want to believe it's a bad one." Levi took another step closer. He was near enough now that he could smell Aidan's shampoo. Something strong and masculine, with a hint of citrus. Sweeter than lemon. Orange, maybe?

It smelled good. So good, Levi kind of wanted to wreck him.

Not now. Not yet.

"That's not how it works." Aidan frowned.

"With you, yeah. I know you, remember?"

Aidan didn't refute that. Didn't say anything. Levi tried again.

"How about this," Levi offered, "we'll try . . .an experiment of sorts, just to check if it's still a good idea."

"Are you joking?" But Aidan didn't let him even answer the question before he was already plowing ahead, looking nervy. *Aidan* looking nervy. If Levi wanted evidence that this was the right call, there it was. "What kind of experiment are you talking about?"

"Kiss me," Levi said.

Aidan's jaw dropped. "Are you freaking—you're *actually* serious."

Levi shrugged. "If you hate it, if it doesn't do anything for you, sure, then, we'll forget it."

"And if it *does*?" Aidan challenged, then looked like he regretted asking. Clearly he hadn't really thought about what the alternative meant. That he enjoyed it. That he *liked* kissing Levi. That he might want to do it—and more—again.

"Then in a year we'll both come back here and it'll be us together in the shower upstairs."

Aidan licked his lips. Like he was already thinking about it.

"This is a bad idea."

"If it was such a bad idea, you wouldn't be so worried about it," Levi pointed out dryly.

Aidan made a face. "Fine, *fine*." Then suddenly he was the one in Levi's space, leaning all the way in.

The last thought Levi had before Aidan kissed him was that it was *definitely* oranges he was smelling.

Then Aidan's mouth was on his, tentative and gentle, softer than he'd imagined Aidan Flynn would kiss.

Not that he'd ever imagined what kissing Aidan Flynn would feel like before this, but now Levi wasn't sure he'd ever be able to forget it.

Aidan tilted his head, lips firming and kissing Levi more intently. Like once he'd hesitantly tried it, he couldn't help but give it his best effort.

Levi couldn't help it either. Or the little groan he made in the back of his throat as Aidan's tongue slipped between his lips. The kiss turned suddenly hungry, Aidan no longer taking gentle little sips of his mouth, but starving gulps.

It was going to have to end. Levi was going to have to pull them back, because Aidan had proved the point, a little too fucking well, and it was becoming obvious they were both getting carried away by it.

You can't do this. Not for a year.

It had been very stupid to suggest this. Because how was he supposed to pretend he didn't want it again for a whole fucking year?

Aidan spun them and pressed Levi—who was *bigger*, thank you very much—into the edge of the counter, and if Levi had needed more evidence he was into this, there it was, pressing right into his hip. His dick, hard and undeniable.

Gasping, Levi wrenched his head away.

Aidan's lips were red and wet, and his eyes wild.

For a long drawn-out moment, neither of them said anything. Levi knew what he *should* be saying. Something like "Ha, see? You proved it! You liked it, bro!" As for Aidan, he looked shocked into silence.

Was it better or worse that he'd kind of done it to himself?

If this wasn't . . . well, *like this,* Levi might have even tried to blast right past any awkwardness by asking him that. But that wasn't going to help right now.

Might even make it worse.

Levi kept expecting Aidan to move away. To attempt some kind of joke. But instead, Aidan lifted a hand up to his cheek. Cupped it briefly before his hand dropped back to his side, again. He still looked shell-shocked.

After an effort, Levi found his voice. "Was that your first kiss with a guy?" he asked quietly.

Aidan nodded.

Okay, so he hadn't kissed Mo.

Levi shouldn't be happy about that. Shouldn't feel some kind of vicious satisfaction that it had been *him*, and not Morris.

But if he'd known that, maybe he wouldn't have suggested it.

Lie, Levi's subconscious yelled, *you're a fucking liar.*

"Uh, good?"

Aidan's cock was still pressing into his hip. Still just as hard as it had been when they'd been kissing, so obviously it had been. Levi had been there. It had been a really fucking good kiss. But maybe even more than that for Aidan.

This—and all the whiskey Aidan had drunk last night—was exactly why he'd said a year. Why he'd let Aidan go to bed alone last night.

Because Mo was still lingering between them, unmentioned, but still very much present.

Levi didn't want to hear that Aidan had been saving his gay kissing virginity for Mo. Or that he'd settled for giving it to Levi, instead.

"Guess you showed me." Aidan's voice was rough and dry around the edges.

"Actually," Levi said, "I think *you* showed *me.*"

Aidan laughed and finally took a step back. The awkwardness—or that weirdly quiet intimacy—hadn't dissipated entirely, but it was beginning to.

Logan was always telling him that leaping without looking was going to bite him in the ass someday, and it seemed like that had finally happened.

If only it hadn't happened with *Aidan.*

The doorbell ringing sent Aidan even further away, his eyes darting in the direction of the front door. "That's gotta be the pizza." Aidan took off, and Levi nearly wanted to grab his T-shirt, haul him back.

But he didn't let the desire take hold. Pushed it away, instead.

There was no fucking point in wanting it. Not yet, anyway.

By the time Aidan came back with the pizza, Landry and Riley had arrived in the kitchen, and they were chattering loud and insistently enough that the rest of whatever had just happened between him and Aidan was swept away, like smoke.

Landry was pulling more beers out of the fridge, and suddenly it was easy again. Their brotherly camaraderie back in spades. Riley poking sly fun at Aidan, and Aidan rolling his eyes. Landry slinging an arm over Levi's shoulders, like he'd been doing their whole lives.

Everything back to normal. Exactly what Levi had been hoping for.

That should have made him feel better. More settled, anyway.

But the truth was, the thought lingered all through dinner, and the movie they put on in the living room, sprawled out with bags of popcorn, completing their cheat day.

What did it mean that he and Aidan could have the hot, almost intense passion of the kitchen and the ease and familiarity of the Banks-Flynn connection?

It shouldn't be fucking him up that he *could* experience both, that they could share both sides of a coin, but it kind of was. Why should it even come as a surprise? Riley and Landry had done it. Did it every single day.

But it was different for him, somehow. For him *and* for Aidan.

Levi thought about it, still on the couch, as he watched Aidan heave himself up and head off to bed.

"Come on," Landry said to Riley, "we should head up, too."

"I wanna finish watching this," Riley said, gesturing at the baseball game they'd put on after the movie. "Then I'll be up."

Levi made a noise of agreement, even though he could give a shit about baseball generally or this game specifically.

He didn't want to go up to his empty bed. He wanted to slip into Aidan's bedroom. Wondered if Aidan would tell him to get out, or would wave him in.

In his pocket, Levi's phone buzzed. Then buzzed again. It was nearly ten, and he couldn't imagine who was calling him. But they did it again.

Riley shot him a look. "You dodging someone, bro?" he asked.

The only person Levi could possibly be doing that to currently was Riley's older brother, and he was asleep upstairs. Levi didn't think there was a chance in hell Aidan was the one calling him right now.

He yanked his phone out of his pocket, and as he'd figured, it wasn't Aidan. It was his agent, Alec.

"Actually," Levi said, worry suddenly making his heart and stomach clench, "it's my agent."

"Oh, you're working on that new deal, yeah?" Riley said casually, like it wasn't a big deal. Like it wasn't a big deal to get a call from his agent at nearly ten at night.

"I better take this," Levi said. Riley nodded at him as he lifted himself off the couch and headed outside, settling down in one of the Adirondack chairs before accepting Alec's call.

"Hey, man," Levi said.

"Levi," Alec said, sounding tired.

Also not a good sign. Levi tried to tamp down his apprehension but wasn't sure it worked. Alec had told him before the bulk of the negotiation with the Seahawks began that it was possible they wouldn't give him the kind of deal he wanted. The kind of deal that Alec agreed that Levi deserved. That they might be better off exploring other options.

Levi hadn't liked the idea. He'd been drafted by Seattle six years ago. The two-year deal he took to extend his rookie contract had been a bridge, but Alec had reassured him that they'd figure out something long-term after that.

"I take it it's not going well," Levi said hesitantly.

He wanted to stay in Seattle, but then Logan hadn't stayed in Minnesota and Landry hadn't stayed in Buffalo either. Watching his brothers end up happy playing for different teams had given him a different perspective. If Seattle didn't want to give him what he needed, then he'd find a team who would.

"I'd like you to come out to LA," Alec said, not really addressing what Levi had said. "Tomorrow? Can you make that happen? I think I can get you a flight out of Dallas."

"I'm not in Texas," Levi said. "I'm in Michigan. With Landry and the Flynns."

"Okay, Detroit, then." Alec paused. "Seahawks won't budge on the long-term part of the deal. The money's good, but it's not as many years as we wanted. It's . . .at *best*, another bridge. There's some GMs out here, taking some meetings, and I think it'd be easier if you were here in person. I don't want to drag you away from your offseason—"

Levi didn't want Alec to drag him away from his offseason either, especially not after the kiss he'd just shared with Aidan. But he didn't need anyone to tell him that it would be a mistake if he stayed in Michigan and kept kissing Aidan. Or that if he did stick around, despite his best intentions, he'd probably keep doing it.

"It's okay," Levi reassured him. Reassured himself that this was better, anyway. "I was leaving soon anyway."

It wasn't true, but Alec didn't need to know that.

"Alright. Good. I do think we can make it work with one of several other strong possibilities, Levi. Teams that might even be a lot closer to a ring, even."

That had been the one downside about Seattle. They hadn't made the playoffs the last two years, and based on how the team was building next year's team, Levi could see that trend continuing.

Logan had left Minnesota and had won a Super Bowl. Landry had done the same thing, two years later with the Condors.

Levi could do that, too.

"If that's the best path forward, then we'll explore it. I told you I'd be willing to leave Seattle," Levi said.

Alec sighed. "I didn't want you to *have* to. But they won't budge. One of the new draft class is someone they seem convinced can take your spot in a year or two, and he'd be a lot cheaper. It comes down to money, honestly."

"Do you think he could?" Levi wasn't offended by the possibility. Okay, he wasn't *much* offended by the possibility. A rookie being good enough to take his spot? *Yeah fucking right.*

"Honestly? No. They're vastly underestimating his upside, but the point isn't if *I* think he can. *They* think he can, and they're all about saving money, because their new QB is going to get a huge deal in two years and they need the cap space."

Levi muttered a *fuck* under his breath. Why did teams only care about the quarterback and not the guys who kept him upright long enough to throw the fucking ball? It had never made sense to him, but from what he'd seen from the Seattle front office, this shortsightedness was not entirely unexpected.

"I know," Alec said. "It's really fucking stupid. But what can we do about it? There's teams that want you, Levi. A whole lot."

Levi knew it. "Yeah. And I know it happens. Landry and Logan both did it."

"Yep. So, I got you a flight out from Detroit tomorrow morning. It's early-ish, which means you're going to have to leave even earlier for wherever you're at."

"Ugh," Levi groaned. "Yeah, we're an hour and a half out from Detroit."

Alec chuckled sympathetically. "Better get some rest, then. I'll send a car to pick you up."

"Oh shit," Levi said suddenly. "All I brought with me are lake clothes. Swimsuits. Shorts. T-shirts. I think I might've thrown a golf polo in . . ." He couldn't remember exactly what he'd packed. Landry had told him about the trip at the last minute. "I honestly can't say for sure though."

"We'll figure it out," Alec said reassuringly. "You might not even end up in any meetings, I just want you here. We *could* do this over the phone but . . .I think this'll be easier, for now. I'm sending your flight info now, it should be in your email."

"Thanks," Levi said. Carter had told him that Alec was the best agent in the business, and that recommendation seemed to be paying off in dividends now. Everything was unsure, except that he knew Alec would take care of him.

"I'll see you tomorrow. Rest up, kid," Alec said and hung up.

Like Alec promised, the flight info was in his inbox. And it *was* early. So early he was going to have to leave to drive to the airport in a few hours. Shit. *Shit.* He was gonna need to talk to Riley and Landry. And Aidan. God, *Aidan.*

Riley was still flopped on the couch when he walked back into the living room.

"Everything all good, bro?" Riley asked.

"I'm leaving soon," Levi said, trying to stay calm. "Like really soon. Probably in a few hours. Gotta catch a flight out, go to LA, meet with some people and my agent."

Riley shot him a sympathetic look. "Not gonna stay with the Seahawks, then?"

"Not looking that way."

"Sucks," Riley said.

"Yeah, maybe. But might be okay, too. I'm trying to keep an open mind."

"Good. You should just take the rental." And that was right, *shit,* he and Landry and Riley had only rented one car to drive out here. "We'll get Aidan to drive us to the airport."

Aidan would probably not love that, but he'd understand.

"Thanks," Levi said gratefully. "I need to get like a couple hours of sleep."

"Yeah, get some rest," Riley said, nodding. "I'll let Landry and Aidan know the deal."

It felt kind of shitty to ghost Aidan like this, but only because of what they were in the middle of. If he'd never suggested the sex pact and they'd never kissed in the kitchen of Aidan's lake house, it wouldn't have been a big deal for Levi to have to take off without saying goodbye.

And that's what it's going back to. At least for the next twelve months, Levi reminded himself.

"Tell Aidan thanks for everything," Levi said. He'd text Aidan himself in the morning, when he got to the airport. "And tell Landry I'll keep the family group chat up to date."

"Sure thing," Riley said. He yawned and stood. Pulled Levi into a big hug. "Good luck, bro."

CHAPTER 4

At least, Aidan thought as he stared at the ceiling, weak morning light dappling the white paint, he wasn't *hungover* and freaking out this morning.

Just plain freaking out.

He'd kissed Levi yesterday and he'd liked it.

He'd *known*, of course, that he was queer. His feelings for Mo, while unrequited, were clear enough. Thinking about touching Mo had made him hard lots of times. He had a nice stable of fantasies involving his best friend that he couldn't help but reach for when he wanted to get off. He'd even done his time with gay porn, figuring out what he liked. What he wanted.

But he'd sort of assumed that for him, it wasn't all guys, or even *some* guys, it was *only* Mo. That he was bi, maybe, but very selectively. That was a thing. The internet said it *could* be.

And obviously whatever the internet said was true.

Except then he'd kissed Levi yesterday, and it turned out that it *wasn't* just Mo who lit him up inside.

Levi definitely did it too.

He'd felt his hard cock, and he'd wanted it. Bad enough that there was no point in pretending any longer that he didn't.

For a second, Aidan just lay there, breathing in and out and letting the idea that he'd never know if kissing Morris felt the same way kissing Levi had. It hurt, but the hurt was slowly beginning to ebb away. The tide coming in and taking it out, little bits at a time. Until he imagined that one day he'd wake up and it would be mostly gone.

He'd thought kissing Mo would feel good; that it would feel *great.* But he'd never know, now.

He'd only know how kissing Levi felt.

Frankly it had been good enough that he'd seriously considered, more than once, sidling up to Levi and offering, under his breath, that they could really forget the year part of the pact and go upstairs to his nice big bed right now.

Levi had said no the first night, but Aidan had been drunk and they hadn't kissed yet. And Aidan might be new to gay kissing, but he was not new to kissing and that had been a damn good one.

The kind of kiss that haunted you later.

Well, Aidan knew he had at least a couple of days to work on Levi. To convince him that he wanted *him,* not just as a stand-in for Mo.

Because how could Levi be? He was so different. Everything about him was different. And that, too, felt like kind of a blessing.

Aidan lay there for one second longer, feeling the hurt, and then pushed it away.

He didn't need it. Not today.

Today, he didn't bother showering before he took the stairs downstairs. He smelled coffee and sausage. Could hear fat sizzling in the pan before he walked into the kitchen.

When he did, Landry was at the stove again, Riley back on the counter.

"Geez, guys," Aidan teased, rolling his eyes. But he was smiling. It was hard not to. Not this morning.

"Morning, bro," Riley said. "I made coffee."

"Knew you were my favorite," Aidan said, ruffling Riley's hair as he grabbed a mug. Poured himself a cup as he tried to come up with the most casual way of asking where Levi was. If he was still in bed. Oh, he could go wake him up. That could be fun.

"Breakfast ready in a few," Landry said, gesturing to the stove with the spatula in his hand. "Gonna make some eggs too."

"Where's Levi?" Aidan finally just did it. It wasn't that weird. It was only weird if he made it weird.

"Oh, bro, you didn't hear? Levi said he was going to text you."

Aidan sipped his coffee. "Didn't hear what?"

"He had to go to LA. Early this morning."

"Really fucking early," Landry agreed.

"Was meeting with his agent. I think he's going to end up signing somewhere that isn't Seattle," Riley said, making a face.

"Wait." Aidan wasn't sure he understood. "He left, *this morning*?"

Riley nodded. "Had to, I guess. The call came in after you and Landry went to bed, and he thought about waking you up—"

"Thank God he didn't. I was *wiped*," Landry said. Aidan frowned, because yeah, he didn't *like* being woken up, but he didn't like this either.

He didn't like that Levi hadn't bothered to wake him up. Like Aidan was just the same as his brother, cool with the way they just casually slid in and out of each other's lives.

"Did he text you, bro?" Riley asked.

Aidan hadn't bothered to check his phone this morning, because he'd been stupidly working under the assumption that the most important people in his life were currently under his roof, just down the hall.

"Uh," Aidan said. Pulled his phone out of his pocket. And sure enough, there wasn't just a text from Levi, but three.

Hey, the first one read, **I gotta dip early. My agent wants me to get to LA and meet with some people. Thanks for having me at the house. We're gonna have to do this again.**

The second: **Really mean that, actually. Next year, I'm there.**

And the third: **Thought for a hot second about waking you up at four AM, when I left, but I thought if I did that, I'd miss my flight.**

Aidan's mouth went dry.

"See?" Riley grinned at him when Aidan glanced up, suddenly afraid that the messages—and the hot, liquid pulse of desire at the base of his stomach—were written all over his face. "Told you he'd texted you." Riley's expression was very fond. "Idiot."

"He doesn't think so now, but getting out of Seattle would be good for him. The best thing for him," Landry said, flicking the stove off.

Aidan tried to get his brain together. He was still reeling from the fact that Levi wasn't here. Then there were the messages in his text thread with Levi. Then apparently that he wasn't going back to Seattle, after all.

"Really," Riley agreed. He nudged Landry with a foot as his boyfriend detoured to the fridge, pulling out a carton of eggs. "You're a hell of a lot happier in Charleston than you were in Buffalo."

"And that's got nothing to do with you?" Landry teased back, eyes sparkling as they gazed at Riley.

God, Levi had really left. And left him alone with these two, a situation designed to make him feel like the most third wheel of all time.

He knew Riley and Landry understood what that felt like, because they did try to go out of their way to usually bring others with them. Case in point: they'd dragged Levi along this time, and up until the point where Levi had to leave early, it had worked out great.

Could've worked out even better, Aidan's uncooperative mind supplied.

"Oh, it's got everything to do with me," Riley retorted, pressing a quick kiss to Landry's mouth.

"You guys are gross," Aidan said. He took a long drink of coffee and wondered, stupidly, again, if it was too early to add a slug of something stronger to it.

"We know," Riley declared happily. Proudly.

Gah.

"Who do you think's interested in Levi?" Landry wondered as he cracked eggs into a bowl.

For a split second, Aidan nearly dropped his mug. Then he realized what Landry was asking. Not *who* was interested in Levi, as in what guys wanted to fuck him—Aidan was definitely not going to raise his hand and volunteer himself—but *what teams*.

"Condors would be great," Riley said wistfully. "But I don't know if we've got the cap space."

"And you've got Ferguson already on that side. He's solid. You don't need a superstar in your right tackle slot, baby."

Aidan cleared his throat and tried to get his mind together enough to join in the conversation. "You know Logan would push for Levi to play with him."

"Not sure the Piranhas have the cap space either," Landry said. "But it would be cool, for them to play together."

"You wouldn't feel left out?" Riley asked Landry.

"Nah. I've got lots of good guys. And you." Landry kissed him again.

Aidan held back his groan of disgust.

His brother and his best friend were hard enough to deal with when there was another person present to exchange suffering looks with, but when it was just him? It really fucking blew.

"What about the Thunder?" Riley asked.

"What about us?" Aidan asked.

"I mean, you could always use a better piece on your line," Riley pointed out, not unkindly. "You're not getting any younger and more mobile, bro."

Aidan made a face. "I'm sure if the brass thought they could sign him, they'd make a run at him."

And wouldn't *that* be a trip?

Both he and Levi had assumed the next time they'd be around each other would be a year from now, football season long over, sitting across from each other in Aidan's kitchen, again.

What if that wasn't true though?

What if Levi ended up in Toronto? On his team? On his offensive line? Watching his back, every practice and every game? Deeply meshed with the rest of his guys. Always around in his ugly shorts with his broad smiles. Giving Aidan those knowing looks. The ones that only Aidan would be able to decipher.

"He'd be good on the Thunder," Landry said, so casually it was clear he really didn't suspect what had gone on the last two days.

"Good on a lot of different teams," Aidan pointed out. It was true, as well as being a more comfortable proposition.

Because while it might be great, Aidan didn't know if he really wanted it.

Did he *want* Levi watching him in that way he did? Like he could see right through Aidan? All fucking season? Aidan wasn't sure he could handle that. He'd barely handled it for two days.

He tried not to think about it as the conversation segued into a discussion of their training schedules as Landry finished scrambling the eggs and they loaded plates up.

After breakfast, Riley left to take a shower as Aidan was washing the dishes. On his way out of the kitchen, Riley glanced over at Landry, still lingering at the table and then gave Aidan a look that said, *tell him now.*

Aidan was already planning on it. He didn't know how he felt about this new Riley who was going around telling everyone, including him, what to do.

It wasn't bad, but it *was* different and taking some getting used to.

"So uh," Aidan said to Landry as he washed the frying pan Landry had made their eggs in, "I talked to Riley."

"You talk to Riley every day," Landry said.

Aidan made a face. "I mean, I talked to Riley about *Mo.*"

It was annoying how Landry didn't even look even the tiniest bit surprised. "Yeah?"

"I guess you figured it out, too," Aidan said.

Landry shot him a look. "Dude, you literally *held out*, not for your own contract, but for Mo's. That's not like you."

"So everyone keeps saying," Aidan muttered. "And that was *three* years ago."

"Yeah, and you pined for him for awhile. Probably took awhile to figure out why exactly you missed him so much, yeah?"

Aidan expected to feel another pulse of annoyance at how well Landry knew him, but instead, all he felt was seen and heard and *understood*. A warm and cozy feeling, like a fuzzy blanket, enveloping him.

"Yeah," Aidan said. "And when I figured it out, it wasn't like I *wanted* to feel that way."

"I felt that way too about Riley at first. Like, what do you mean I want him? I shouldn't want him."

Aidan considered agreeing with that assessment, but the truth was, he'd left those feelings behind a long time ago. "It's a mind fuck, for sure."

"Worse even, 'cause it didn't turn out for you the way it did for us," Landry said gently.

"Ugh, how do you even know? It could have been great. It could have been awesome. Mo could've told me he loves me too."

"He probably did," Landry said. "He probably told you he loves you as a friend."

Aidan grimaced. It hadn't been fair. It still wasn't fair.

"As for how I knew, it was obvious, dude. You tried to pretend you weren't fucked up when we got here, but it was pretty obvious."

Aidan finished rinsing off the pan and set it on the rack to dry. "Why didn't you say anything?"

"Would you have actually talked about it?" Landry raised an eyebrow.

I told Levi. I talked about it with Levi.

"No," Aidan agreed. Because it wasn't like he'd wanted to talk about it with Levi. Levi had practically harassed him into it. He'd ended up doing it only because it was the best worst choice.

"Well, I'd imagine you still don't want to," Landry said, and yep, bingo, he was right there, too. "*But* Riley would kill me if I didn't say that we're here for you, no matter what."

"Thanks," Aidan said, discovering he actually meant it. He'd tackled so much of this alone. Sure, he'd *known* he could talk to Riley and Landry about it, but the thought had never occurred to him. The first person he was going to tell was always going to be Morris, even if it didn't turn out the way he'd hoped it would.

"And *I'd* kill me if I didn't add that it's okay to be whatever you are. That you don't have to always know right away about who that is," Landry added.

"Was it weird for you, realizing it so late?" Aidan asked. Because it had been weird for him. He'd lived in denial for several additional months because he'd been sure that if he was actually queer, that he liked men *like that*, because if it was true, he'd have known before he was in his thirties.

"Oh yeah. Threw me for a huge fucking loop. Kept thinking, was I just believing it was okay for my brothers to be gay but not me? Fucked me up for awhile."

"Yeah. That thought crossed my mind, too." He told himself not to ask but then he couldn't help himself. "How early did you know about Logan and Levi?"

Landry sighed. "Logan took longer; he was mid-teens when he finally came out to the family. But Levi proudly declared it at eleven."

"Of course he did."

Landry grinned, pride radiating from every pore. "Levi's never bothered fucking around. He wants something, he wants to do something? He just does it."

He sure had. And apparently what he wanted now was Aidan, and Aidan couldn't even pretend it wasn't mutual.

When he'd finally come to terms with what he felt for Mo, he'd promised he wouldn't live in denial any longer.

Pretending that he wasn't attracted and interested in Levi would be lying. Even if it was only to himself.

"Pretty admirable," Aidan said.

"Yeah," Landry said. "I hope that attitude serves him through this contract mess."

Aidan found himself hoping for the same.

And hoping a little, despite his discomfort, for Levi to end up in Toronto.

Later that day, he texted Levi back.

It was honestly my pleasure to have you, he sent. **And you'd better put me on your schedule. A solid week. And next time, you won't have to debate about waking me up.**

Aidan hoped his meaning was clear enough—Levi wouldn't have to, because he'd already be in Aidan's bed—and he couldn't help the smile when Levi sent a whole string of emojis, including the blushing smile, the dancing man, *and* the fire.

Yeah, Levi was right about that. It *would* be hot.

Riley and Landry left a few days later, extracting promises that if Aidan needed them, they'd be booking the next flight out from Charleston.

But Aidan knew they wanted to get on with their offseason training program, and he could hardly blame them for that. He was working hard, too, putting in long hours in the gym he'd added to the house. Riley had made him promise not to be such a loner, and he'd actually made good on his promise, texting Avery Barnes.

One night, he'd invited the Barnes brothers over and they'd showed up with some of their hockey friends in tow, and it had been a good night. Another night, he and Avery had just shared a beer around their firepit, his brothers out of the house at some party he hadn't wanted to go to.

"It's just a bunch of younger kids, a lot of guys Charlie went to the development program with," Avery had explained.

They'd had a chill night, sharing stories about football and hockey and their college days. Avery had gone to Michigan for two years before he'd joined the Mavericks, and so had Aidan, once upon a time.

"Ethan went to Portland U. Wanted to be his own man," Avery explained, back against one side of his chair, legs dangling over the other side, his brown eyes full of dry humor. "Where did Riley go?"

"Stanford." Aidan sighed. "He wanted to do his own thing too. Always has." He'd spent enough years mourning that, and now there was nothing to do but accept—and actually embrace—it.

They'd had a nice big-brother chat and discovered a lot in common despite the ten-year difference in their ages.

So he hadn't been totally alone.

But Aidan had been alone enough. Alone enough to really think. To start letting the truth of the situation with Morris really sink in.

It sucked. No question about it. He'd had his low points. Cried about it, even. One night he'd railed against the unfairness of the situation, how cruel life and fate could be, to put the one man—possibly the only person he'd ever really loved—in front of him and then made sure Mo didn't return his feelings.

But even though it didn't feel great, Aidan did believe he was slowly beginning to work through it. Riley, Levi, and Landry were all right; now that he'd learned the truth, the bare facts of the situation, every day was a little better than the last.

He worked out and worked some of his feelings out, too. Feeling like every drip of sweat that fell was changing him, too.

Aidan couldn't say he didn't think about Levi. He did. On purpose and also in passing, whenever his ongoing contract situation came up on ESPN. When it got too hard to use his stable of Mo fantasies for jerking off, he thought about that kiss in the kitchen and imagined if neither had pulled away. And *that* thought kept him fueled for a whole bunch of jerkoff sessions.

Three weeks after Riley and Landry left, he was chilling in bed, exhausted after a harder than usual afternoon workout, TV turned down low, and his phone dinged.

Rolling over, Aidan grabbed his phone, glancing at the screen. He'd kept expecting that at some point he might hear from Levi. Maybe even Levi making an offer to come back to Michigan. But he'd been quiet, apparently laser-focused on his contract negotiations.

Aidan knew he wouldn't be hearing from Morris. Not anytime soon, anyway. The way they'd left things in Vegas, Mo had said he'd give Aidan as much time as he needed. And while Aidan did feel like he was getting somewhere, he wasn't ready to open that wound back up again. Not yet. Not until it was a little more healed over.

It wasn't Levi and it wasn't Mo.

It was Landry.

I told Levi to tell you, but he's being weird about it. Levi signed with the Thunder this afternoon, so I'm pulling a classic Aidan overprotective-big-brother move. You'll let him stay with you, right? At least until he finds his own place in Toronto?

Aidan took a breath and then another, trying to calm his suddenly racing heart.

Levi was coming to Toronto.

Levi hadn't wanted to text Aidan to tell him.

It was impossible not to wonder what that meant.

When Levi had left to go meet with his agent, had he known that Toronto was a strong possibility? Was that why he'd left? So Aidan couldn't overhear and talk him out of coming to Toronto? Talk him *into* it?

Did he think Aidan wouldn't be happy about it? That he wouldn't welcome him?

Fuck, this was going to be *weird*.

Good, but weird.

Aidan exhaled, slowly, fingers hovering over his screen. Unsure what he wanted to say. Knew what he *should* say. Three years ago when Riley had signed with the Condors, he'd called Landry and essentially demanded that Riley move in. Insisted that Landry needed to become Aidan's extension in Charleston.

Thank God his best friend had been too smart to do that.

He wanted Levi to know he was welcome. That Aidan was glad he'd be there to watch his back. He really was a fantastic tackle and would solidify the offensive line. He even really liked the guy. He was chill and funny and always himself; he'd slot into the locker room like he'd always been there. There were no downsides to this, except for the fact that the last time they'd seen each other, they'd been kissing in Aidan's kitchen.

Except for the other fact that they'd promised they'd have sex in a year.

The next time they'd see each other, it would not be next year, not in Aidan's kitchen, or on Aidan's patio, and he wouldn't be sharing this exact bed with Aidan. It would be in six weeks, and it would be in Aidan's condo in Toronto, which was big as condos in Toronto went, but not really *big* when you compared it to just about anything else.

Aidan hesitated just long enough he felt absolutely shitty.

Landry didn't know about the kiss or the sex pact. He only knew Levi was his younger brother and Aidan was his best friend.

Aidan was going to do the right thing, if it killed him. And considering what he'd spent a fraction of the last month fantasizing about, it *might*.

Sure, he texted back to Landry, **of course he can stay with me.** Aidan hesitated some more. He should switch over to his convo with Levi and ask *him* this directly, but he wanted to come armed with more info, if he was going to talk to Levi.

When he was going to talk to Levi.

Why was Levi weird about talking to me? he sent to Landry. **Did he not think I'd be fucking thrilled to have him on my team?**

Something about overstepping, Landry texted back. **But I'm gonna let you work it out.**

It was right there, between the lines. Landry being a fucking adult, just like Aidan knew he could be—mature and full of honest communication—telling him without telling him, *you'd better work this out, bud.*

And Aidan was going to goddamn try.

First, he gave himself a very firm talking-to.

You will be normal. You will be friendly. But not too friendly. No mentions of beds, other than the guest room bed at your condo that he's going to sleep in, alone.

No flirting. No kissing. And definitely, not under any circumstances, any mention of sex. Now or a year from now.

Then Aidan opened his texts with Levi. Ignored the last thing he'd sent. Ignored the last thing *Levi* had sent. That string of emojis that made it so clear they'd both had the same thing on their minds.

Hey, he said instead, calling on his many years of NFL captain behavior, **I heard the great news that you're coming to Toronto. Couldn't be more excited. My guest room is all yours for as long as you need it.**

Aidan decided that was clear enough. The last thing he'd sent Levi had hinted that the next time they saw each other, they'd share a bed. But now? It was not happening.

Not now, anyway.

Levi replied almost immediately. A single thumbs-up emoji. That was it.

Aidan flopped back on the bed. Annoyed and additionally annoyed with himself for being annoyed.

He had enough shit on his plate, he did not need Levi to twist him up in circles.

If that was even what he was doing.

But before Aidan could work up a good head of steam, another text arrived.

Camp is gonna be so sick. Flynn-Banks FTW!

It made him feel better and somehow also worse.

Because the other Flynn-Banks was Riley and Landry and they totally kicked ass on and *off* the field, and Aidan didn't want that, of course. He was still in love with Mo. But he *knew* that wasn't what Levi meant.

He shouldn't even want Levi to mean it that way.

But he was afraid he kinda did.

Aidan rolled over, groaning.

The next six weeks were gonna pass way too slowly.

CHAPTER 5

Six weeks later

Of course Aidan lived at the top of this enormous building. In the fucking penthouse, no less.

Most of his stuff was in a pod, heading to a storage facility outside Toronto, for when Levi figured his shit out and found a place of his own.

Until now, all he had with him was two big duffel bags, sitting at his feet in the elevator as he and Peter, the concierge for the building, watched as the floors ticked by.

"Anything you need, anything at all," Peter said, tipping his head towards Levi, "you just let me know. Any guest of Aidan's is a guest of ours." He winked then. "And you're also a *Banks*. The best one, too, if you want my opinion."

Levi laughed. "Don't let Landry or Logan hear you say that."

Peter just shrugged, his kind brown eyes gleaming.

"I thought y'all were more hockey fans up north," Levi said.

"Oh, we are. But football's come a long way. Aidan's been a big part of that."

That was something he and Alec had discussed. It wasn't that the Thunder went under the radar here in Toronto, but compared to the intense microscope that the city put the hockey team under, anything would seem like less. There'd be less pressure, no question, than if Levi went to one of the more impassioned football cities, like New York or Philadelphia.

In some ways, Seattle had been chill, but not so much in others. It was a small-ish city, really, not like Toronto or New York or Los Angeles.

Hard to really work and live under the radar.

"We're looking for you guys to bring us another championship," Peter said. And yep, that had been a big part of Levi deciding he was coming here, to Toronto. Aidan had won two back-to-back Super Bowls early on in his career, but the Thunder had been coming up short the last decade. But Levi didn't need Aidan to bluntly say he was nearing the end of his window. If he wanted to win another Super Bowl, it was going to need to be soon.

And Levi intended to be right there, lifting it with him.

"Planning on it," Levi said. The elevator door dinged open, revealing a narrow white hallway, a door at the opposite end.

"Now, your keycard will get you to this floor—you'll need to use it, like I showed you, to be able to get up here—and then it'll get you into the main apartment," Peter said, gesturing towards the door, with its discreet black electronic panel next to it.

"Alright, thanks, man," Levi said, shaking his hand. "I appreciate it."

He lifted his bags and walked over to the door, hearing the elevator close behind him. He could use his keycard, of course. Aidan had called down to Peter specifically, asking him to make sure Levi knew how to get into the building, where to park, etcetera. But it felt weird to just let himself in.

It wasn't the first time Levi had felt weird about this new situation—actually, it was the second. When he and Alec had narrowed down his offers and options and Toronto had emerged the unlikely frontrunner, Levi had deliberately not let himself think about who the Thunders' QB1 was. Didn't want to let Aidan's presence there be a pro *or* a con.

But after he'd made the decision, Levi had felt a sudden jolt of awkwardness. He'd kissed plenty of teammates over the years. Fucked them, too. But Aidan was different. Levi couldn't pinpoint why exactly—maybe it had to do with how intricately and closely they were tied together, before they'd ever made the stupid sex pact.

Before he could parse exactly what was different about Aidan, and why he suddenly felt so weird about the whole Toronto situation, Landry had been pushing into his space. Making demands and suggestions and generally being the sort of oldest brother that he rarely was.

Yeah, Levi had never played for a team that wasn't Seattle, but he could do this. Landry had been worried about him fitting into a new environment, though, that much was clear. So he'd shoved himself into the middle of it, texting Aidan before Levi could even figure out what he wanted to say.

Then Aidan's response had been perfectly Aidan: straightforward and succinct. Cutting right through the awkwardness.

No, Levi realized now, as he stared at the door. He hadn't cut through it. He'd pretended it didn't exist at all. Like they'd never kissed. Like they'd never promised to fuck.

It was a very Aidan thing to do. Didn't know how to deal with something? Act like it just wasn't there, like through sheer force of will he could shape the world to suit him.

But that wasn't Levi's way at all. He wasn't going to pretend. He didn't think he *could*.

Because even though he had no intention of fulfilling his half of the pact now, he had every intention of showing up at Aidan's house next summer and doing it.

And until then? Well, he could think about it and jerk off about it and flirt with Aidan about it.

Decision made, Levi pulled his key from his pocket. Aidan had wanted him to have it, so he was going to use it.

He pressed it to the sensor and twisted the doorknob.

The first thought he had wasn't Aidan. But *light* and *blue*.

Over the years, he'd seen pictures of Aidan's place. Knew it was floor-to-ceiling windows and an open floor plan. Relentlessly practical and modern. Riley liked to say it was soulless, and it was, a little, but why would you want to dim this view?

Lake Ontario spread out in a great blue swath in one set of windows. On the other side, sunlight reflected off the glittering skyscrapers.

Aidan was sitting on a big navy blue sectional in the main living space, sprawled out next to another guy.

Glancing up, Aidan gave him a friendly smile. "There you are," he said.

"Hey, bro," Levi said. Kind of annoyed that now Aidan had made it weird a *third* time.

He hadn't anticipated that Aidan would have anyone over. After all, Aidan had known that Levi was showing up around now. Did he think he could find a way for them to never be alone together? That was ridiculous and impossible.

"This is Dawson Hall, our kicker. He's new to the team, too, but we played together at Michigan, with Landry."

Dawson nodded at Levi, and now Levi realized he looked vaguely familiar.

"Dawson not like Asa or Beau Dawson, right?" Levi asked, referring to the Piranhas' famous head coach and his son.

"Nope." Dawson shook his head. "Just happened to be my name."

"Dawson and I are just catching up," Aidan said, like this somehow explained why they were sitting in Aidan's living room.

"Ah," Levi said. He wanted to pull Aidan aside and tell him to *be cool, dude,* but he'd forgotten one important factor in all this: Aidan had never been cool a day in his life.

"Here, I'll . . .uh . . .show you the guest room," Aidan said, getting to his feet.

Now that Levi was looking, he recognized Dawson for more than just his stint at Michigan. The guy had put together a whole string of great seasons, but last season had been a disaster. He'd missed a bunch of field goals, and even a few extra points. The Ravens had released him, and after, a bunch of stuff about his ugly divorce had come out.

He'd clearly been distracted—which, for a kicker, who relied heavily on their mental focus, was a big problem.

"Thanks," Levi said, picking up his bags.

The living areas in Aidan's apartment were spacious, but the hallway leading to the bedrooms was not, and Levi's shoulder brushed Aidan's. Aidan didn't exactly spring back but he didn't look over either.

He didn't need to tell Levi he was pretending nothing had ever happened in Michigan, because it was obvious that was the tactic he was going with.

"I'm right over here," Aidan said, pointing to a closed door. Like he thought physically closing a door might be enough to send a ragingly obvious hint that Levi wasn't supposed to show up in his bedroom. "And you're over here. Attached bathroom. There's a closet, I made sure it was empty, and there's a dresser, and stuff. If you need more space—"

"I shouldn't," Levi said, setting his bags down and doing a quick survey of the room. It was nice, basic maybe, but big enough, the bed taking up almost the entirety of the space.

"Oh. Okay. Good. I want you to make yourself at home." Aidan had stayed in the doorway. Like he wasn't about to enter a room with Levi and a bed.

Again, Levi was possessed by a strong desire to tell Aidan to chill. But he already knew it wasn't going to change anything, so why bother? It would only make things even more awkward than they already were.

Clearly, Aidan didn't want to talk about it, so Levi wasn't going to force him. *Yet.*

"It's great of you to offer," Levi said. "I could've found another place, probably."

"Are you fucking joking? Of course you were staying here," Aidan scoffed.

Please don't tell me you did it because of Landry.

Funny enough, Levi might not have cared before, might have brushed it off as big bros being big bros, but he didn't want Aidan to have invited him *only* because Landry had butted in.

"You could've asked Dawson," Levi said, because he was very stupid and apparently couldn't leave this alone.

Aidan shot him an incredulous look. "I could've, sure. But you're practically family." He made a face then, like he realized how bad that sounded. "But *not*, of course."

"Of course," Levi said, nodding vehemently in agreement. He was still jerking off, thinking about that single kiss. He did not need Aidan to decide, somehow, that they were *family*, despite their brothers being madly in love.

"And," Aidan added, dropping his voice and taking a step closer, like he'd finally forgotten that he wasn't supposed to be going into the room with Levi and the bed, "Dawson's feeling sorta . . .well, he's prickly about help."

Levi had only really followed the bare bones of Dawson's situation, but it had sounded bad.

An acrimonious divorce was bad enough, but then there'd been rumors Dawson's ex-father-in-law, a financial advisor, had stolen a lot of his NFL cash.

"I get it," Levi said. He suddenly wondered if Aidan hadn't *only* invited Dawson here today because Levi was scheduled to arrive. After all, this was Aidan they were talking about. The guy's motives had motives. Riley was always complaining about how he liked to arrange everything.

Levi wasn't sure how he felt about being arranged.

On one hand, that was kind of hot.

On the other, it was annoying that Aidan was going to do it and not be transparent about it.

"Honestly, I'm trying to distract him." Aidan grimaced, like he was bad at it. He probably was. Even when he was providing prime jerkoff fodder for Levi, he wouldn't have called Aidan Flynn *entertaining*.

"Want me to help?" Levi asked.

"*Yes*," Aidan said, looking intensely grateful.

"Alright." Levi rubbed his hands together. "No problem."

Aidan looked suddenly worried. "What are you gonna do?"

"*Bro*, stop looking so constipated," Levi teased, smacking him on the arm. It was good to get the casual touching out of the way. He touched everybody. He wasn't going to keep his distance just because Aidan was pretending that they'd never kissed.

"What do I have to do to get you to stop calling me bro?" Aidan asked, pained, as he trailed after Levi, heading back into the living room.

"Dawson, my man," Levi said, flopping down on the couch right where Aidan had been. He held out his hand for a fist bump. Dawson hit it back, after a long confused pause. "How's it hanging?"

Aidan shot Levi a look and settled into the big armchair kitty-corner to the couch.

"Well, uh . . .it kinda sucks." Dawson made a face. "I'm sure you've heard."

"Some of it, yeah, but not really any of the details." Levi reached over and patted Dawson on the knee. "Sucks, tho."

Dawson shrugged, awkwardly. "I should've known better."

"No, you shouldn't have," Aidan argued. "How were you supposed to know not to trust him with your money? He was your fucking father-in-law."

Dawson looked like he wanted to bury his head in the couch and not come out. Levi internally sighed; no wonder Aidan was struggling here. The point wasn't for Dawson to keep talking about how he'd been screwed over, literally *and* figuratively, but to *distract* him from it.

Levi hefted himself off the couch and walked over to the entertainment center. It was sleek and streamlined, and to Levi's complete lack of surprise, contained no gaming consoles. He glanced back at Aidan. "No PS5? Seriously, bro?"

"You really want to play *games*?" Aidan asked self-righteously.

God, he was kind of the worst. Levi couldn't believe this was the guy he had a boner for, no matter how hot he was.

"Yeah, for sure, bro," Levi said. He looked over at Dawson. "You got a system?"

Dawson shot a half-apologetic look at Aidan. "It's packed . . .somewhere. I don't even know what I got in the divorce, honestly."

"Same with mine. Stupidly assumed that *some people* would be locked and loaded." Levi pulled his phone out of his pocket and texted the only other guy he knew on the team—Nate Bishop, a linebacker and a friend of Landry's who'd played with him initially on the Condors but had been traded to the Thunder two years ago.

"Hey," Aidan complained, but Levi ignored him in order to compose a text to Nate. **Hey, man, it's Levi. Just got into town, staying with Aidan. Turns out this guy is a freak and doesn't have a PS5. You wanna bring yours and come hang out with us and Dawson?**

Levi's mom would've had his head for inviting someone over to a house that wasn't his, but Aidan *had* told him to make himself at home. That was all he was doing.

And, of course, saving Dawson from a fate worse than death: spending an entire afternoon with Aidan, who'd probably inadvertently make him relive every horrible moment of his divorce and defrauding.

Nate, the great guy that he was, didn't leave Levi hanging long. **Oh, yeah, sure. Give me half an hour. Warn Aidan. He kind of hates me. Something about a bad tackle at practice last year.**

Levi was extra proud of himself now. It was always funny when Aidan got annoyed—and snooty—about something. Even better when it was a someone.

Landry would tell him to be nicer, but Riley would tell him to go for it.

"Hey, good news," Levi announced. "Nate's coming over with his."

Aidan looked like he'd just sucked a lemon. "Seriously? How do you even *know* Bishop?"

"Are you kidding? He was drafted by the Condors. He and Landry are tight. You should know that, bro."

"*Bro*," Aidan muttered under his breath.

"You're gonna pry that out of my cold, dead hands," Levi said.

"Probably along with your neon shorts," Aidan said.

"Probably," Levi agreed. He wished he'd worn his brightest pair today, but the ones he'd picked for moving in were just a very standard blue. Not even an eye-searing blue. Clearly, a tactical mistake.

"You don't like this Bishop guy?" Dawson asked, directing his question towards Aidan.

"I don't *dislike* him," Aidan said, which was just like him. "There was a practice last year. Let's just say he got a little enthusiastic."

"Dude," Dawson said, chuckling, "you used to be able to take it."

"I still can," Aidan complained. "I just don't *want* to."

"That's why I'm here," Levi said. None of his siblings would argue that he was particularly good at smoothing anything over, but if he wanted to have a nice chill afternoon, he was going to need to make an attempt.

"What, to protect my honor at practice?" Aidan asked, the corner of his mouth quirking up.

Levi tried to pretend that didn't sound absolutely fucking awesome. "To keep you *upright*, bro."

Aidan looked at him, meeting Levi's eyes, and for a second, everything else fell away. They weren't in Toronto, they were back in Michigan, in Aidan's kitchen, and they were a breath away from each other, again.

The silence drew out, taut and loaded with anticipation. Then Aidan looked away, fingers drumming on his knee.

Dawson glanced between them, curiosity blooming on his face, and it was obvious he wanted to ask, but he didn't.

Probably smart, Levi thought, because he wouldn't have known how to explain that away. Or rather, he'd probably say something that was close enough to the truth, because he hadn't bothered with circumspection in years. But Aidan was trying to pretend like Michigan hadn't happened at all, so he'd probably get all awkward and self-righteous about it.

Besides, everyone knew Levi was into dudes but *nobody*, just Levi and Morris and maybe Riley and Landry, knew about Aidan.

So even if he'd wanted to, Levi couldn't come right out and say, *hey, bro, it's all good, we just made a sex pact, and clearly Aidan's still thinking about it. I know I sure as fuck am.*

"I guess if Bishop's coming over, I could order some food," Aidan said reluctantly.

"You mind if I invite my rookie?" Dawson asked.

"Your rookie?" Levi wondered.

Dawson nodded.

"The new punter. Cam Greene. He's . . .well." Aidan hesitated and shrugged. "There's rookies, and then there's *rookies*. Dawson's rookie is a *rookie*."

"He's from Montana. Grew up in a town of like a couple hundred people. Went to Western State. Toronto's been . . .well, we'll say it's an experience for him."

"He's cool, though?" Levi asked.

"Oh, yeah. Yeah. He's cool." Dawson looked like there was more he wanted to say, but he didn't.

"The first time I had him over, he literally spent the whole time staring out my windows and saying *golly gee, look at that view*." Aidan chuckled.

"He did not," Dawson said, but he was laughing now. "I was here! He didn't."

"Okay, he looked like he *wanted* to," Aidan amended.

"He's a good kid," Dawson said bluntly, clearly feeling like he should defend Cam. "Inexperienced maybe. Naive for sure. You should invite Wes, too, if we're inviting people over."

"Wes?" Levi asked. He couldn't think of anyone he knew on the Thunder roster named Wes.

Aidan sighed. "My backup. Wesley Matthews."

"Dude, he's not just gonna be your backup," Dawson reminded Aidan. "You told me Coach said he wants you to teach him. Mentor him, like."

No big surprise that Aidan didn't like the defensive guy who'd laid him out in practice, even accidentally, or his potential replacement.

"Right. Mentor him." Aidan didn't sound like that was any better than *backup*.

Levi got up and elbowed him hard in the side. But not *that* hard. It *was* his job to keep him upright. Keep Aidan in one piece. Keep him safe.

Even when he was being an ass.

"Invite him," Levi said.

Aidan rolled his eyes, but he pulled his phone out of his pocket.

"You're pretty bossy for someone who's been here less than an hour," he said to Levi after he sent the text.

"Hey, I'm just trying to get to know my teammates," Levi said.

Aidan didn't look convinced, not even a little bit, and then of course, Dawson actually started laughing.

"Flynn," he said, "you have *not* changed, dude."

"Nope," Levi agreed, and he and Dawson high-fived as Aidan continued to look disgruntled that his afternoon chat with his old college buddy, regurgitating every bad thing that had happened to him in the last year, was probably permanently on hold.

Aidan had planned this and he had also *not* planned this.

He *had* gone out of his way to make sure that when Levi arrived at the condo, there would be a buffer person here. Dawson was an easy invite, because he'd also been wanting to get some one-on-one catch-up time with his old friend, and he knew Dawson probably had a lot to talk about, with the divorce and the criminal proceedings against his ex-father-in-law.

Dawson also didn't make him feel old or washed up or like he was in the twilight of his career, the way that Wes sometimes did.

Of course, Aidan hadn't been dumb enough to think that he could have a buffer at the house *all* the time. He and Levi were going to be living together, at least in the short-term. They'd be alone sometimes. But Aidan hoped at least that it wouldn't be right away. That he'd have some time to recalibrate his brain first. To think of Levi as a teammate. As his best friend's little brother. Not as a guy he'd kissed. Not as a guy that he'd like to do more than kiss.

But he hadn't planned that his living room would be full, hours later, with a bunch of teammates, Levi in the middle of them, cheering and yelling as Wes got annihilated at *Mario Kart* yet again.

"You should take a turn," Dawson said to Aidan, nudging him with his shoulder.

"Nobody wants to see that," Aidan said.

"I know you know how to play video games. You played in college."

"That was a long time ago." It felt like a lifetime ago, honestly. When things had been so different, his life and his career stretching endlessly and optimistically in front of him.

"Not that long," Dawson said bluntly. "I'm the one who's divorced and washed up. So you can't act like that's you too."

Maybe Aidan wasn't divorced, but he'd never gotten close enough to anyone to marry them in the first place. Except Morris. And *that* had turned out so fucking well.

"No," Aidan agreed.

"Come on," Dawson said persuasively. "Do it for me. Remind me what you were like ten years ago."

"Making me feel old," Aidan retorted, but he leaned over the couch and considered tapping Levi on the shoulder. He had one of the controls. Had yet to lose, in fact. But instead, Aidan tapped Wes, who *had* been losing, regularly.

"My turn," Aidan said and Wes glanced back at him, nodding.

"Sure," Wes said, because he was not stupid. He knew his place here, on the team, and also in Aidan's condo. He moved off the couch, handing Aidan the controller as he went.

It was probably a mistake to take Wes' seat, because he'd been pressed right up next to Levi—practicing that good team bonding, Aidan told himself firmly, *nothing else*—but it would look weirder if he didn't. He was going to have to get used to touching Levi, anyway, and existing in the same close bubble with him.

It should've been easy, like he'd adjusted to everyone else he'd ever played with, but he kept thinking of that kiss.

And how much he'd like to do it again.

Aidan dropped down on the couch, ignoring the thrill up his spine as their legs pressed together. The shorts today weren't eye-searing but they *were* short, and Aidan specifically did not think about how toned and muscled his exposed thighs were.

"You ready to go, Flynn?" Levi turned to him, wild grin on his face.

Aidan had never thought he was handsome or even cute. To him, Levi had always been the youngest Banks. Landry was objectively the most attractive of the three, but Levi had grown into his face and his looks the last few years. He was wearing his hair a little longer than he had been, and it curled in dark brown tufts over his head, his much lighter eyes speckled with hazel flecks warm and affectionate as they gazed at Aidan.

"Born ready," Aidan retorted.

He'd wanted Levi to go back to the way they were before, but he experienced a flash of annoyance that Levi could look at him just the way he always had. Especially when Aidan wasn't sure he could perform the same radical recalibration.

Levi started the game.

And Aidan *was* out of practice. He felt every one of those ten years since he'd picked up a controller, and the fact that he'd never played this particular game before and everyone else clearly had.

"Geez, bro, you suck at this," Levi teased as he half fell into Aidan on the couch, their race finally finished. Levi had won again. Cam made a noise of annoyance as he came in second again, and Aidan pulled in at the very end, way behind everyone else.

Aidan let out a frustrated huff. "It's been a few years," he admitted.

"You're as bad as Logan," Levi complained. "I spent two weeks last summer teaching him to play *Call of Duty*, and I'd have claimed it was the toughest thing I'd ever done, but you might be even more of a project." Levi knocked their shoulders together, still grinning. "But I'm willing to tackle it, if you are, bro."

"Sure, *bro*," Aidan retorted. He didn't *like* losing. He didn't like the fact that Levi might have to fucking tutor him *more*.

He lost two more rounds, relinquished his controller back to Wes, and retreated to the bathroom.

He peed, then stared at himself in the mirror as he fixed his hair, shoved his cap back on. His cheeks were flushed no matter how much cold water he splashed on them.

And he wasn't thinking of Morris, hadn't thought of him once, not since this morning, when he'd woken up and realized, with a pressing finality, that Levi would be arriving today, and when he did, Aidan couldn't deal if it was just the two of them.

That was good though. Aidan told himself it *had* to be.

Better that the thoughts of his new teammates and camp, starting tomorrow, pushed the painful, pointless thoughts of Mo and the frustrating unfairness of the whole situation out of his mind.

Except that Aidan couldn't quite believe that it was *just* the teammates and football that had superseded Morris. It was undeniable that a good chunk of those thoughts were owned by Levi, and as much as Aidan wished they were, they hadn't been very platonic thoughts. Maybe if Levi had worn longer shorts, he'd have had a chance in hell of keeping his mind above the belt.

Aidan pushed open the bathroom door, kind of wishing that everyone else would leave, and hoping they would stay forever.

Of course, Levi was right there, leaning against the wall opposite the bathroom, like he was waiting on Aidan. Not to vacate the bathroom so he could use it, because he had his own bathroom, attached to his bedroom.

So he was just waiting for Aidan, *period*.

Aidan pretended his breath wasn't coming a little faster and that flush wasn't right back on his cheeks like he hadn't just tried to cool himself off.

"Hey, bro," Levi said.

God, Aidan was going to throttle him if he didn't stop saying that stupid-ass nickname. He wasn't Levi's *bro*. It didn't even matter that Levi called pretty much everyone bro. Because when he called Aidan *bro,* it always sounded different. Flirty and pointed. Like he was trying—and succeeding—to get a rise out of Aidan.

"When are you going to stop calling me that," Aidan complained. He should head back into the living room, where he could hear the raucous yelling of another round of *Mario Kart* happening. But instead, he stayed, lingering in this quiet dark hallway, alone with Levi.

"Never," Levi said, and this smile was slower, more deliberate. Like he knew what calling Aidan that in that particular voice did to him.

Aidan told himself not to flirt back. Failed, immediately. "Is this how it's gonna be, then?"

The problem was Levi's irrepressible smile. "God, I kinda hope so. Don't you?"

Aidan, who had been very sure two months ago what and who he wanted, didn't know how to answer now. He swallowed hard, painfully aware of how each second ticking by that he didn't answer made it even more obvious what he *did* want.

"And," Levi said, leaning a little closer, but not so close there wasn't plausible deniability they were still being friendly bros, "you were even nice to Nate."

"Nate's a nice guy. Why wouldn't I be nice to him?"

Levi chuckled. "You were *just* complaining about him. He hit on you?"

He knew Nate was gay. Just like Wes. Like Levi. Dawson was bi, had dated a guy in college. They were living in a brand-new world, full of acceptance and rainbows.

It wasn't like Aidan *hadn't* accepted himself. He *had,* or else he'd have had no business telling Mo he was in love with him or kissing Levi in his kitchen.

"No, of course not," Aidan said. Nobody knew about him, though. Just Mo and Levi, really. Landry and Riley barely counted—they were family. "Did Nate hit on *you?*"

Over the years Landry had been full of stories about what players Levi and Logan had hooked up with. Carter Maxwell was the most infamous of those stories, because he'd made no secret out of the fact that he'd wished he'd gotten the whole Banks set. But Landry had never been into anyone but Riley.

It was not out of the realm of possibility that during an offseason workout or a Pro Bowl party, Levi had hooked up with Nate Bishop.

It had never occurred to Aidan before. Okay, it *had,* and he genuinely hadn't given a shit.

Unlike now, when he wanted to know so badly if Levi demurred, he didn't know what he was going to do about it. Maybe stomp, pouty and sulking, into the living room, yank the power cord from Nate's gaming system, and send him on his way.

"Did Bishop hit on me?" Levi laughed, like Aidan's embarrassing jealousy was actually amusing. "He's not my type."

"That didn't answer my question," Aidan said, taking another step closer.

This was not plausible deniability. This was not keeping his distance. This was definitely not teammate recalibration.

"Maybe, maybe not." Levi grinned. "Lots of guys hit on me." He shot Aidan a knowing look that said, without a single word, *and you're one of them, dude.*

Embarrassing, only because it was true.

"What about—"

Levi raised a hand and let it drift down to Aidan's chest. Pressed into his T-shirt. "I'm gonna stop you right there, bro. How about this, I've *never* kissed anyone in this condo, except—"

"Okay, message received," Aidan said hurriedly. He didn't need Levi to *say* it, not when he was trying so hard to pretend that it hadn't happened.

"Wes is cute, but as I'm sure you know, he's still torn up about his ex." Levi shot him a frank look. "I know I told you my stance on that."

"You did."

Levi nodded. "Anyway, is that what you wanted to know?"

He shouldn't be so humiliated about his blatant jealousy but it had been obvious. He hadn't liked the idea that Bishop or Wes or, God forbid, Dawson, somehow between his marriage and his divorce, had hit on Levi.

"Yeah," Aidan said shortly.

Levi let his hand drop, and straight-up winked at Aidan. "Good chat, bro."

"Ugh," Aidan groaned as he followed him back into the living room.

He'd just grabbed another water from the fridge, thinking he'd watch them play a few more rounds before kicking the lot out, when Nate intercepted him. "Flynn."

"Bishop." They'd greeted each other with the bare minimum when Nate had showed up with the gaming system. Aidan had a feeling this was going to be more than a bare-minimum convo.

"You ready for camp tomorrow?"

Aidan nodded. "You?"

Nate sighed loudly. Dramatically. "You're kind of an ass, you know that?"

"What? I asked you the same question," Aidan defended.

"And looked like you were annoyed the whole time," Nate pointed out.

He was probably not wrong. Aidan knew he had a bad case of resting bitch face. He was not *always* so pissed off. "You just always look so serious, so intense," Riley always complained. "And I know for a fact that you don't need to be."

Aidan wasn't sure Riley was right. But Nate had a point, too. They were teammates. It was a new season. He should at least try to make nice.

"Sorry," Aidan said. "I *did* mean it. You ready for tomorrow?"

Nate looked like he relaxed a bit as he leaned against the counter. "Yeah, I guess so. Is anyone really ready for the first day of camp? Even if you put the work in?"

"Let's hope you didn't put in more work than my linemen," Aidan joked. It wasn't a very good one but he was *trying*. This would be Nate's second season in Toronto, and yeah, he should be better. He wouldn't have this, forever. At some point, there wouldn't be any more preseason camp. No more teammates. And then he'd have to figure out how to have friends, not just the friends he'd always had, like Landry, or people who were forced to like him because they were family, like Riley.

Like Levi.

Except Levi wasn't family.

He definitively was *not* family, despite his love of calling Aidan bro.

But Nate smiled, no matter how stupid the joke was. "Can't make any promises," he said seriously. "But I'll try not to lay you out, first day."

"Thanks," Aidan said dryly.

"You're old, man. Not sure you'd bounce back from a real good hit," Nate teased lightly.

Aidan forced himself to smile, going along with the friendly nature of the conversation, but there was no question Nate's comment rankled.

He'd taken good care of himself. He still had a couple more good—or at the very least, *decent*—years under his belt.

He wasn't going to get taken out, not yet, no matter how many times he was reminded about mentoring Wes.

"Sure, dude," Aidan said, clapping him on the back. And now, *God*, he sounded like Levi.

Which was worse: *sounding* like Levi or being forced to listen to him? Aidan wasn't sure.

Nate shot him a questioning look but thankfully didn't call him on it.

"It was nice of you to invite Levi to stay with you," Nate said.

And okay, maybe he had. Just not in the way that Aidan might've expected.

"Well, I'm a nice guy." Ironically, the same thing he'd said about Nate to Levi.

Nate's dark brown eyebrow rose even higher. "Oh, yeah? That's new."

"Dick," Aidan retorted, rolling his eyes.

"Hey, I'm just telling it like it is," Nate said. "You're a great quarterback and a pretty dang good teammate. But a *nice* guy? I don't know."

That shouldn't have bothered Aidan. Who aspired to be *nice*?

What was the saying? *Nice guys finish last.*

Aidan had no intention of finishing last. In fact, he had every intention of raising the Vince Lombardi trophy again before he called it quits.

"Nice guys finish last. I'm gonna remind you of that at the end of the season," Aidan said casually. He wasn't ridiculously superstitious, not like some other guys he knew, or like *hockey* players, God forbid, but he wasn't going to make promises now that he couldn't keep to teammates.

Just to himself.

"Sure," Nate said, chuckling under his breath. "But you could *try* the nice-guy act, maybe?"

Aidan sighed. "Believe it or not, I *am*. Maybe that's why I invited Banks to live with me."

"No, you invited Levi to live with you because Landry probably told you it was happening, and you didn't want to argue with him *or* with Riley if you said no."

"It would be a lot easier if you didn't know them," Aidan said. Ridiculously, at one point, he'd even lorded it over Riley when Nate had ended up in Toronto.

Nate snorted a laugh. "You mean, easier if I didn't know enough to call you on your bullshit?"

"Exactly."

"You're gonna be okay," Nate said, clapping him on the shoulder and Aidan wanted to ask him what he was supposed to be recovering from—though of course, *he* knew exactly what he was recovering from, even if Nate couldn't—and how Nate knew, somehow better than anyone else, that he was going to be okay.

He wanted to, but he didn't.

But the thought lingered, anyway.

Instead, he watched the two other games in silence, then as Nate and Wes packed up the gaming equipment, Levi making jokes the whole time about how he was going to start digging through his boxes in storage right away, to make sure he wasn't gaming system bereft.

Aidan had originally invited Dawson over because he'd wanted-slash-needed a buffer, but to his surprise, it was pretty chill after everyone left, quiet falling over the condo as the sun finished setting, the last of its light shifting across the Toronto skyline, before finally dipping everything in a dusky blue.

Levi retreated wordlessly to his room, and Aidan heard him unpacking.

His meal service dropped off his box for the week. He'd ordered double his normal amount, and after putting them away in the fridge, poked his head into Levi's room, letting him know.

Levi raised his head, as he sorted through clothes on the bed, three of the dresser drawers open. "Thanks," he said. "You didn't have to do that."

"Yeah, see how you feel about it when you eat their quinoa bowl for the third time in a week," Aidan joked weakly. "Obviously if you want to make other arrangements after, it's totally cool."

Levi nodded. "Thanks, bro."

After that, Aidan retreated to his own room, shutting the door behind him. They had an early call in the morning for the first day of camp, and he wanted to get a good night's sleep.

But as he lay in bed, he picked up his phone after a long moment and ordered the same system that Nate had brought over, and any games that looked decent. Aidan hesitated for a second and then added a few more controllers to his cart before checking out.

When he got the confirmation, he took a screenshot and texted it to Levi. **Now you don't have to tackle your storage boxes, just Nate,** he added as a caption.

Levi didn't leave him hanging for long. He texted back almost immediately. **BRO, you're the best.**

You ever gonna give that up?

What do you think? Levi texted back.

Aidan's fingers hesitated over his screen. Maybe it would be easier to bring it up now, over the relatively bloodless arena that was texting, even though Levi was technically in the next room over.

He could say it. It would be easy. *Bro,* he could say, *you ever think about when we kissed? Bro,* he could also say, *I can't stop thinking about it.*

Instead, he should say something like, *bro, I can't stop thinking about it, but I need to.*

But Aidan didn't send anything at all. Chickened the fuck out and left it all unsaid. He could deal with it tomorrow. Tomorrow he'd be more recalibrated.

CHAPTER 6

LEVI HAD BEEN PLAYING in the NFL for six years now, but he still felt like a rookie every time he stepped out onto the practice field for the first time at camp.

That feeling, like he still didn't quite know what he was doing, was exacerbated by the fact this wasn't Seattle, and all the guys he was currently heading towards were new to him.

He'd already been added to the lineman group chat, and he'd met a handful of them, in passing and at different NFL events, including the center, Griff Michaels, and the starting left tackle, Ross Acker, at the Pro Bowl last year.

"Hey, guys," Levi said, jogging over to where they all stood together in a loose circle, weak sunshine shining on him. He'd say this about Toronto—so far, the weather wasn't *that* much different than Seattle. But everyone kept warning him that the fake summer would, in a few months, give way to some truly shitty and cold weather. That *would* be different than Seattle.

Landry had already texted him twice, making sure that he'd brought his small stock of winter gear with him to Toronto.

Like he was going to leave it at home when he was moving to *Toronto*?

"Banks, good to see you," Griff said, pulling him in for a quick hug. Levi made the rounds, greeting all the guys, including Ross, who, as Levi expected, gave him a bit of a cold shoulder.

Levi could play both sides—but he personally thought he was better at left tackle, even though he'd spent most of his time in Seattle on the right side.

The coaching staff, while giving him the standard greetings when he'd signed, hadn't said anything about him taking Acker's spot on the left, but he'd watched some film, over the summer, and that had told him at least part of the story on why he was here.

Acker was fine, maybe even serviceable, but that side *could* use some shoring up, especially considering it was Aidan's blind side.

Ned Johnson, the offensive line coach, showed up a minute later and put the group through their stretches, then some basic drills.

"We're going to go through a few different formations," Ned said when they were warmed up. He listed off names, and so far, on both lines, he was on the right side, so Ross could rest easy, at least for now.

They ran some basic plays, getting a feel for each other, Ned standing off to the side, next to the guy that Levi was pretty sure was the offensive coordinator.

"Great pulling move there, Banks," Ned said, clapping his hands as they finished up the final drill before lunch.

Levi had worked hard in Seattle. He thought he'd been a pretty decent lineman in college, but in the pros, everyone was bigger and faster and just plain *better*.

He'd had to learn to take his natural skill and his bulk and how to move more aggressively.

In Seattle, they'd had a progression of mobile quarterbacks, and he'd had to adjust on the fly. If they decided to run, Levi was going along for the ride, blocking as they sprinted downfield.

Aidan wasn't particularly mobile—he hadn't even been that way when he'd been younger—but he could run. He occasionally did, still. But mostly, he was going to sit back in the pocket and throw his picture-perfect passes.

"That *was* a really good move," Griff said to him as they walked into the building for lunch. It was supposedly midday, but the sun was still weak, hiding behind a haze of clouds.

This was definitely way better than sweating his brains out in Charleston or Miami, which was what his two brothers were currently doing.

"Thanks," Levi said, meeting Griff's low five.

"I was stoked as shit when I saw the Thunder signed you. You're gonna really bring some fire to this line." Griff paused, his expression melting into a more contemplative look. "But what do *you* think? You glad you came here?"

That was a really fucking good question.

"Uh, yeah, I think so. Don't know if Acker's too happy I'm here," Levi said, glancing around first to make sure that Ross wasn't in hearing distance.

Griff rolled his eyes. "Don't let him throw you. He's just a fucking diva."

Levi nodded. He'd been around guys like that his whole career. They always thought they were better than they really were. And often that attitude hid the fact they *knew* they weren't as good as they pretended to be.

"You played left some in Seattle," Griff pointed out. "What are you gonna do if they want you to do it here?"

"I just want to keep Flynn's jersey clean. So if they ask, I'll do it," Levi said.

Griff gave him an approving nod. They'd reached the cafeteria, and they split off, Griff heading towards the sandwich station, Levi for the salad bar. He'd spent his offseason bulking up, and now he wanted to make sure he was lean and fast for camp.

As he loaded up his plate, he thought about what Griff had asked—and not for the reason he'd asked.

For half a second yesterday he *had* worried that he'd chosen wrong, coming to Toronto. Maybe Aidan would never get over his awkwardness, and he'd never be able to slot back into the place he'd always occupied in Levi's life, comfortable and familiar.

But in the end, Levi thought he'd gotten over his awkwardness, even if Aidan *hadn't* exactly slotted back into that previous position. It was just different now, an awareness simmering between them that hadn't been there before.

Levi wasn't against them enjoying that low-level simmer all season and then acting on it next summer.

After all, they *had* promised.

He was still surprised when he headed towards the table Griff and a few of the other linemen had taken and realized that sitting right smack in the middle was Aidan. Wes was next to him.

Levi had seen him today, of course. They'd woken up in the same condo. He'd seen Aidan shuffle into the kitchen, not much different than he'd been in Michigan, wearing threadbare old shorts and no shirt, his gold chain gleaming dully against the tan skin of his neck, his hair curling wildly around his head.

His eyes had been sleepy when he'd glanced up at Levi. Maybe the awareness had spiked a little then, going from a simmer to something stronger, but it had calmed back down again as they'd shared Aidan's car, heading in to the practice facility, joking as Levi had made fun of Aidan's shitty music choices.

It had been normal enough that he'd told himself that this would all be fine.

But seeing him again, now, hair curling damp under his hat, against his neck, made Levi want to duck down and nibble the tanned curve of it.

"Hey," he said in as normal a voice as he could manage as he slid down onto the bench seat. "How's it going?"

He was normal; he could *be* normal. Levi had never imagined that demanding Aidan tell him what was bothering him would lead to *this*. And even worse, he'd never imagined that even finding out the truth and offering to have sex with him would churn him up like this.

Sex never had before. Especially sex that he wasn't currently having.

Aidan shrugged as he chewed around his wrap.

"Really good," Wes chimed in. "Offense looks good, already."

Aidan shot him a look.

"What?" Wes said. "It does! Trev, the rookie tight end? He's got some hands on him."

"You might know Trevor's older brother," Griff said to Levi. "Lane Robinson. Think you played with him in Seattle for a year or two?"

Levi swallowed his bite of chicken and nodded. "Yeah, he's cool. I didn't realize he had a brother—"

"It's a *step*brother," Wes said. "Trevor's his stepbrother. And they're not really close, so like . . .I don't know, tread carefully."

Aidan looked put out by this comment. "I told you, I'm not treating anyone with kid gloves."

"Not individually," Wes hastened to add, "but you know . . .collectively."

"Collectively. Seriously?" Aidan set his wrap down.

Levi could see that Aidan was gearing up for one of his big-brother coded lectures, which could be fun—especially if Levi could needle him about it—but he was more curious why Lane and Trevor didn't get along, so he said, casually, "So what's the big deal, anyway? Do these guys not like each other because they're stepbrothers or what?"

Griff groaned under his breath. "It's just stupid. They're both tight ends. Both on the same team. They should be *helping* each other, not giving each other shit."

Levi had been pretty sure he'd like Griff, but now he knew he would. He and Griff seemed to have similar opinions on things. Unlike him and Aidan—which made this whole hang-up on Aidan confusing. Levi shouldn't care about what he thought, and he *hadn't* cared about what he thought. Until now, seemingly, he did.

"For real. My brother Logan and I are always giving each other tips. Trading lineman secrets." Levi looked over at Aidan, pointedly. "And I *know* you and Riley do that now, too."

"Now?" Aidan raised an eyebrow.

"Well, before you were just talking *at* him. I'm assuming that now that you realize he's a grown man and a pretty decent QB1 in his own right, you listen, too."

Aidan had the nerve to almost look ashamed, which then made Levi feel bad for bringing up Riley's first season, when they *hadn't* seen eye to eye. Back then Aidan had still been determined to control him because of some misplaced idea that Aidan needed to protect him still. But Riley very clearly didn't need it, and at least Aidan had realized that.

"Pretty decent?" Wes commented. "Riley Flynn's more than pretty decent."

"Watch out, Levi," Aidan said dryly. "You've managed to stumble on a guy who's even more of a Riley fan than me or Landry."

"Dude, I didn't think that possible," Levi said.

Wes gave a happy sigh. "He's just . . .*ugh*. So fucking good."

"It's a good thing your ego is so well-developed," Levi told Aidan, nudging him with his shoulder.

Aidan rolled his eyes. "He also thinks Riley's hot. Don't tell Landry."

"Riley *is* hot," Levi said.

Aidan looked half annoyed, half disgusted. "Ugh, really, not you too?"

For a brief moment, Levi considered telling Aidan that he was *also* hot. In fact, Levi found him much hotter than Riley. Always had. After all, Aidan wasn't the copy, he was the original, and Levi didn't think even Riley could beat him in this particular contest.

"Sure," Levi said casually.

Aidan looked even more disgruntled, and that was payment enough for not telling Aidan the whole truth. He was always so cute when he was being deliberately thwarted. Levi lived for the way his mouth tilted downward and his blue eyes narrowed intently.

"Back to Lane and Trev—I think we just need to encourage them to communicate," Wes said firmly.

"I thought I was supposed to be taking it easy on them *collectively*," Aidan retorted.

"*You* are," Wes said.

"This is like the team for wayward dogs," Aidan mumbled under his breath. "Next I know, we're going to be adopting someone with separation anxiety who howls all night."

Wes elbowed him. "Be nice," he said.

"Why should I be? You're nice for all of us. Like, *collectively*, the QB room is nice because of you. You can keep being good cop and I'll be bad cop."

"You're not actually bad cop," Levi argued. "You just want to win."

Aidan smiled then, and that was worth all the annoyed looks put together. Aidan had a fucking great smile. Levi didn't know why he hadn't been stuck on it before, but he was now. "You got it," he said.

And it was fair, because they *all* wanted to win, but it was pretty much a given that nobody wanted to win as badly as Aidan Flynn did.

Levi, who never wouldn't have claimed he didn't want to win, who'd actually spent his six seasons in the NFL working his ass off to get even close to a Vince Lombardi trophy, discovered that he had a new depth of desire for winning that he hadn't had before.

He wanted to see Aidan's eyes light up in satisfaction and glory.

He wanted to make it happen.

And he wanted to be right next to him when it did.

It had been a long day. Aidan was tired—bone-tired, really—but his brain was still buzzing, working through all the options and ideas and permutations of the team they'd have during the upcoming season.

He should go to bed, but instead, after taking a long, hot shower, he headed to the couch. Picked up one of the controllers he'd purchased and Levi had set up and flipped on the TV and the system.

He was halfway through the race and losing horribly, tongue stuck out of the corner of his mouth as he tried to concentrate and work the stupid controller faster, when a voice behind him said, "God, you actually do suck at this."

Aidan risked looking back at Levi, because it wasn't like he could finish this round any worse than last place. "Hey. Sorry if I'm keeping you up."

"Couldn't sleep either," Levi said and flopped down on the couch next to Aidan. No space between them, Levi's bare thigh pressing against his sweatpants. God, did Levi *own* shorts that didn't expose fucking everything? That didn't make Aidan want to lean over and get his mouth on all that bare skin?

"You wanna play?" Aidan asked, handing him the controller even though the round hadn't ended.

Levi shot him a skeptical glance. "No, bro, don't take this the wrong way, but you *need* the practice."

"Ouch," Aidan retorted.

"Hey, just the voice of truth here," Levi said. "You really don't play." He sounded surprised by this, like Aidan's lack of gaming system hadn't been enough to give him away.

"I don't," Aidan said. "I've been a little busy."

"You're gonna make me say it, aren't you?"

"Say what?"

"All work and no play makes you a *very* dull boy," Levi teased, nudging him with that ridiculously bare thigh. Even worse, he didn't even move it away after, the line of it hot even through the fabric of his sweatpants.

"I'm not dull," Aidan argued, even though he kinda was. Boring and over-focused and over-serious. Maybe that was why Mo didn't—no, *no.* Aidan cut that thought off fast and ruthlessly. Mo *did* love him, just not the same way he loved Mo.

Levi looked over at him as the round finally ended, and he came in so far behind the other little cars he should be embarrassed, except that he'd essentially given up halfway through.

"Sure, bro. Not dull. No games for you." Levi reached out and snagged a second controller. "Come on, I've decided I'm gonna take pity on you."

"Pity?" Aidan squawked.

Levi's faux frown deepened. "I'm deeply, *deeply* concerned for you, dude. You *need* to be better than this. It's my duty to make that happen."

"Whatever," Aidan said, rolling his eyes, but he pressed the button to restart the game.

This time, he didn't give up halfway through. Levi was way better, no question, but he was slowly getting his feet under him again, remembering how to work the controller. The one thing he didn't have to worry about were his reaction times. Those, after a lifetime playing football, were stellar.

He just had to figure out how to apply those instincts to the game in front of him.

Second time around, he got closer to beating Levi. Not *close* but a lot closer.

Third time, he got really fucking close, and it was Levi's turn to squawk about it.

"Goddamn it, *were* you faking me out?" Levi demanded as he mashed the shit out of his controller, leaning over and falling halfway into Aidan, which wasn't distracting at all or anything.

"No, of course not!" Aidan practically yelled back, and a second later after the race ended, Levi barely squeaking out a win, mentally shot a half-hearted apology to his neighbors.

It wasn't *late* necessarily, hardly late enough for them to be pissed, but Aidan was sure this was probably the loudest he'd ever been since moving into this building.

"Shit, shit," Levi said, breathing heavily. He looked over at Aidan, way too close, his eyes sparkling with enjoyment. "Were you seriously having me on?"

"Are you really gonna claim I can't figure out how to get better? *Me*?" Aidan questioned.

Levi shrugged, still grinning. "Bro, you were so bad."

"I'm still not good. Maybe you're just taking it easy on me."

"Hardly," Levi scoffed.

It was dangerous. Aidan could feel it, the pitfalls lighting up in his brain, but it was easier than it should've been to pretend they didn't exist. To lean into what Levi had just claimed he *couldn't* and play a little. He pressed the button to restart the round.

This time he had Levi's number the whole way; how the controller felt in his hands, the way his fingers moved, all gelling again like he'd never stopped.

"Holy shit," Levi said when the race ended, and Aidan had won by a healthy margin.

Aidan couldn't resist turning to him. "Eat shit, *bro*."

Levi's jaw dropped. "Are you fucking joking? You must have . . .*no.*"

"No?" It was impossible to not be a little smug. He was Aidan Flynn, after all, and Riley had claimed more than once that he'd come out of the womb smug.

Contrary to predominant belief, he didn't lean into that smugness as often as everyone claimed, but he leaned into it now. It felt good, and it felt even better when it lit Levi's face up with an irresistible combination of indignation and enjoyment.

"You must have . . .*ugh*. Did you cheat, dude?"

"Cheat?" Aidan laughed, not even offended like he might've been, because it was so obvious that Levi didn't really mean it. "No way. I didn't need to cheat to beat you."

Levi choked out a laugh. "Fuck you, bro. *Fuck you, bro.* Give me another round."

The planets and stars had aligned during that last one, Aidan finding a Zen-like zone that had guaranteed his win. He wasn't sure that would happen again, but at least it had happened *once.*

Aidan restarted the game, and this time it was more neck and neck, Levi clearly making a real effort to win. Aidan couldn't say he *wasn't* trying hard, either. In fact, he could probably say that he was working even harder than he had during the race he'd won.

Then he finally, *barely,* pulled away, right before the finish line and Levi yelled. Before Aidan could brace himself, Levi was pushing them both off the couch, landing with a breathless gasp-slash-laugh on the ground, cushioned by the plush rug over the hardwood.

"Oh shit, shit," Aidan gasped, another chuckle escaping him. "*You* cheated this time."

Levi stared down at him, licking his lips, and it hit Aidan like a truck. Levi was on top of him, his body blanketing Aidan's own, his arms braced on either side of Aidan's head. He was big and solid and warm, those strong thighs pressing into Aidan.

Aidan's breath caught in his chest. "Cheater," he repeated, because he was playing, and it felt so good, he didn't know why he'd stopped. Or *when* really. After that first Super Bowl win? Before, even?

When he'd lost the constant presence of Landry after college, because he'd apparently relied on his best friend to regularly yank him out of his own ass?

Levi was smiling down at him, like he'd gladly taken his older brother's mantle. Maybe he didn't even realize he'd done it. Didn't even know there *was* an open position, or that Landry had once slotted in there, as easy as breathing, and there was no question it was going to be Levi, now.

"I had to do *something*," Levi claimed. Then his head dipped an inch lower, eyes slipping down to Aidan's mouth.

Suddenly, Aidan's tongue was too big for it. Dry and unwieldy.

He'd certainly never wanted to kiss Landry before. The thought had never crossed his mind, not once, but he couldn't stop catching strays when it came to Levi.

Aidan half expected Levi to finally say something about it. Oh so casually, of course, like, *hey, you thinking about Michigan too?* Because Aidan was sure as fuck thinking about Michigan.

About what it might've been like if he'd drunk like two and a half glasses of whiskey less on the night they'd made s'mores, or if his stupid brother and his even stupider best friend hadn't been in the house when they'd kissed in the kitchen. Or if Levi hadn't had to go to LA so unexpectedly to deal with his contract.

But Levi didn't say anything. Just kept gazing at him like he was merely enjoying the heat between them and wasn't particularly wedded to the idea of *doing* anything about it.

It made Aidan feel insane. Feral. He wanted to push himself up and bite Levi's bottom lip.

It made him want to do all the things.

But he wouldn't, because while he *felt* insane, he *wasn't* insane.

Instead, he gathered his strength and pushed Levi off.

If Levi was disappointed, it didn't show. He just laughed again.

Meanwhile, *Aidan* was having trouble hiding his own disappointment. Why else push him off the couch and full-body tackle him to the ground if Levi wasn't interested in doing anything about it?

Levi rolled over onto his side and just looked at Aidan, like Aidan was supposed to know what the fuck that look meant. He was a quarterback, not a mind reader.

"Why am I not surprised that you *doing something* was tackling me off the couch?" Aidan asked, raising an eyebrow.

Levi just shrugged. Like it wasn't a big deal. Like the last time they'd been this close they hadn't been kissing. Except they had been.

"What else did you want me to do?" Levi was talking around it again, and that made Aidan want to grind his molars in frustration.

Don't say kiss me, don't say kiss me, don't say kiss me.

He really wanted to say *kiss me*, but Aidan didn't. Barely.

"I don't know." If Levi could be nebulous, then so could Aidan.

"You really hate losing, don't you?" Levi seemed amused and maybe even surprised by this. And he shouldn't be. Aidan was Aidan. He could say a lot of things about himself—and plenty of other people had said their share, too—but at least he was consistent about it.

"Even at *Mario Kart*, sure," Aidan said. *Also when you act like you want to kiss me and then don't.* That definitely felt like losing.

"You're ridiculous," Levi said, getting to his feet then, like *Aidan* was the one who was letting this thing hang in the air between them without actually naming it.

Aidan could name it, no problem. It was sex, plain and simple.

But then, hadn't they said a year in their pact? They had, but that was before Levi had ended up in Toronto. He couldn't really believe that Aidan would need a year to think about Levi and only Levi in his bed.

He knew for a certainty that was not going to be a problem.

Levi didn't say anything, but he didn't leave either. Instead he flopped himself right back on the couch, where he'd been sitting before losing and then almost losing again.

For a second full of intense contemplation, Aidan actually considered saying it. *I know we said a year, but I've changed my mind. Let's make it sooner. Way sooner.* But he didn't. It was going to be so awkward—like he was practically begging for Levi's dick; like Levi's dick was freaking *life-changing* or something—if he said it first.

An annoyingly perverse part of Aidan wanted *Levi* to be the one to stick his neck out, even though he already had. Even though he wasn't sure that hooking up was even a particularly good idea. But it was impossible to deny that it was also the best goddamn idea that anyone had ever had.

Instead, he picked up his controller and looked over at Levi. "Wanna go again?" he asked, swallowing down everything else he wanted—and didn't want—to say.

Levi's glance over at him was knowing and mischievous. "You really want to take me again?"

Oh boy, did he.

Aidan took a deep breath. "Sure," he said. "What did you say? It was your *duty* to help me get better?"

"Oh yeah, bro. For sure." Levi was laughing again, now, and Aidan did not remind him—because he was apparently a fucking saint—of what else Levi had decided it was his duty to do.

"I swear to God I'm going to get one of those buzzers and smash it every single fucking time you call me bro," Aidan said.

"Aw, you love it!" Levi crowed.

Aidan didn't know which was worse: that it was true or that Levi had guessed the truth.

"Don't worry," Levi said, leaning over, his lips practically brushing Aidan's neck, "I know when to use it and when not to."

Aidan *knew* what he was talking about. Levi for sure knew what the fuck he was talking about. So why didn't he just bluntly say it? *I know not to use it when we're in bed together. Like we're gonna be. Soon.*

He wanted to scream. To throw his controller down and say, *I give up, actually. I will totally say it first. Screw looking desperate and pathetic.* But he didn't.

He calmly and reasonably nodded and restarted the game.

And beat Levi, again.

CHAPTER 7

"Bro, I'm so glad I caught you," Levi said to Logan, his phone tucked into the corner of his shoulder and his ear as he turned the corner from the neighborhood coffee shop that he'd started visiting in the mornings. Aidan had a coffee machine, but it was kind of shitty drip coffee, and he couldn't care less about it because he was apparently insane and "above caffeine" and "his body was a temple." *Whatever.* Moments like that made Levi wonder why he was so hung up on the guy.

Why every time they got close, his heart felt like it was in his throat and his dick was about to bust out of his shorts and he wondered why the fuck he had said a year, when right now seemed like such a better idea. He was trying to play it cool, and he thought he was doing an okay job of it, too, because Aidan seemed to be on a similar page.

"Yeah, you're some big shot now, with that huge contract," Logan teased him.

Levi took a long sip of his latte. It was still iced but Blaize at the coffee shop kept teasing him that soon he'd need it hot.

"Like yours is any smaller," Levi retorted after he'd swallowed.

"But it's going good, yeah? Aidan treating you well?"

Levi didn't really want to touch the subject of Aidan Flynn with a ten-foot pole. Which was why he had ignored Landry's offer to talk this morning with a quick *sorry I'm busy* text and taken up Logan on his instead.

"Yeah, of course," Levi said, hoping that generic answer would smooth over any of Logan's concerns.

"Good, 'cause he can be kind of an ass," Logan said. Levi could hear a hint of his brother's disapproval even over the phone. But then, Logan had never made any secret of how much their eldest brother's best friend annoyed him sometimes.

"Come on, he's not that bad," Levi said. Part of him couldn't quite believe he was defending Aidan, because before he'd never have done it, and surely that would make Logan think something was up. But the other part of him actually believed what he was saying, because now that he'd had the privilege to get a bit closer to Aidan, he could see what Landry had always seen: his loyalty, his protectiveness, and even his bone-dry sense of humor.

Then there was that he was screaming fucking hot, too. That didn't hurt.

"Are you okay?" Logan asked, sounding mystified. "Aidan's not that bad?"

"He's mellowed," Levi argued, even though he thought the opposite might actually be true. Sometimes Aidan reminded him of a polished diamond, all deceptively sharp edges, working harder than everyone else on the field while still attempting to look like he wasn't. Levi didn't want to be dazzled by Aidan's facade, but it was hard not to be.

"Sure." Logan didn't sound convinced, but at least he'd accepted it.

"Things all good in Florida?" Levi changed the subject before Logan decided he had more to say about Aidan.

"Oh yeah," Logan said. "We're kicking ass here. Taking names. Dylan says hi, by the way."

"Your boyfriend's hot," Levi said, because he knew it would annoy Logan.

He huffed out a breath. "You're just saying that to get under my skin."

Levi chuckled. "Or maybe he's just hot."

"But you don't have to *say* it," Logan complained.

"Sure I do. What, do you not think Dylan's hot?" It was too much fun to wind Logan up like this. Made it hard to resist.

"You know I do," Logan said flatly. "*Anyway*, he says hi. He's doing good too."

"If everyone's doing so good, why did you want to chat?" Levi wondered. He pressed his keycard onto the outside door to the apartment tower, letting himself into the lobby. A glance at his watch told him he had five minutes with Logan before Aidan had said they were leaving.

"I'm worried about *you*," Logan said, annoyingly self-righteous. "You fitting in okay there? How're the other guys on the line? I know Griff some, he always seemed like a stand-up guy."

"Never gonna stop worrying about your baby brother, huh?" Levi joked, but his heart was warm as he hit the button to the elevator that would take him upstairs so he could grab his bag from the condo before practice.

"Something like that," Logan said.

"The guys are good. You're right about Griff." Levi paused. Wondering if he should say something. Logan was his brother, sure, but he played for the Piranhas, who didn't need any advantages to be competitive.

"You sticking at right tackle?" Logan asked before he could say something.

Damn, it was like Logan knew him. That wasn't so surprising, but it was amazing and also kind of frustrating to be known like this, inside and out. "You saw the speculation."

"Kind of hard not to," Logan said.

Levi hit the button for Aidan's penthouse floor hard, swiping his keycard on the reader so it knew he was allowed to go up that high.

They'd had an open practice two days ago, and the media had seen Ross Acker struggle on a few plays to protect Aidan's blind side, and since then, there'd been approximately a hundred articles about how their newly signed blockbuster right tackle, Levi Banks, had played left tackle more than adequately during the handful of opportunities he'd had.

Levi sighed. "The guy already kind of hates me."

"Is it gonna be a problem?" Logan asked.

He hadn't bothered saying anything to Ross about his own abilities, because there was no way that wouldn't break bad. He'd only reassured Ross that Ross himself had skill to make it happen.

Secretly he wasn't sure that was true, and he only intended to be loyal to Ross as long as he got the job done. If he didn't—if he let Aidan down—then Levi knew exactly what side he was coming down on.

"I don't think so," Levi said optimistically. The guy knew his starting job was riding on his performance; he'd bring it today. If it were Levi in Ross' position, he'd make sure of it.

"If you think so," Logan said dubiously. Clearly he was siding with Levi here. He'd probably already watched the film from practice half a dozen times and seen the issues just as clearly as Levi had. Ross was a hair too slow to react to the rush, and not as agile as he needed to be to stick with the coverage.

"Yeah," Levi said. The elevator dinged open. Another look at his watch told him he had two minutes to grab his bag. "Hey, we're heading into practice. I gotta grab my stuff and make sure I don't make Aidan late."

"Sure, that would be a nightmare," Logan said.

"Hey, *you're* punctual," Levi said, keying himself in one more time to the main door to the condo. "No judgment."

"I'm gonna judge all I want to," Logan said stubbornly. "But as long as you're happy, baby bro, that's all that matters."

"I'm happy," Levi said automatically.

"Good," Logan said. "Don't be a stranger—to Landry or Lyla, either, okay?"

"Yes, *Dad,*" Levi said, only because he knew it would annoy Logan.

It worked perfectly, Logan squawking in outrage as Levi hung up the phone. Sometimes Levi thought Logan had gotten the majority of the big-brother genes even though he wasn't the oldest.

He had approximately thirty seconds to grab his bag from his bedroom and meet Aidan at the front door.

Aidan was already waiting, hat turned backwards, old Thunder T-shirt on, the fabric clinging to his biceps and stomach in a way that Levi found incredibly distracting.

"Ready to go?" Aidan asked and Levi nodded.

He was quiet as they rode down to the garage level, where Aidan's Range Rover was parked, thinking about what Logan had asked and how he'd answered.

He hadn't considered the question before he answered it, not really anyway, because it was always a mistake to be too honest with any of his brothers. They tended to get fiercely protective and over-involved—though he'd give them credit, because they'd never, ever been as bad as Aidan had been with Riley—and make trouble when Levi could handle his shit just fine. He was twenty-seven. A full-grown fucking adult. He didn't need to be bailed out from tricky situations.

He'd done it with his contract, hadn't he? Lyla had told him when they'd talked about it that she'd been sure he'd settle for less, just to stick where he'd always been, and she'd been proud of him for branching out. For refusing to accept less than he was worth. For going to a team, even a team new to him, that had a real shot at winning it all.

Levi had rolled his eyes, annoyed at his sister, even as he was a little touched by her concern.

He tossed his bag into the backseat and was just buckling up, watching out of the corner of his eye as Aidan hooked up his phone to monitor the traffic to the practice facility, when Aidan said, "All good?"

"Yeah, bro, of course."

Aidan shot him a long-suffering look as he pulled out of the space. The practice facility was further out of town than the stadium, which was nestled right in the heart of downtown, forming a sports triangle with Scotiabank, which the Maple Leafs and the Raptors shared, and the Rogers Centre, where Canada's only baseball team played. But the practice facility was at least a thirty-minute drive, if traffic cooperated, and even though Levi had only been in Toronto for just over a week, he'd begun to realize that traffic rarely cooperated.

"You're being super quiet," Aidan pointed out. "That's not like you."

Levi tried not to feel suddenly self-conscious that he was spending the drive into practice every morning chattering Aidan's ear off.

Aidan hadn't seemed particularly annoyed by it, and Levi knew he hardly held back offering his opinions when something *did* annoy him.

"Talked to Logan this morning," Levi said, which was not really the change of subject Aidan probably thought it was. "He asked me if I was happy, and I just told him yeah, sure, because . . ." Levi slid a glance over at Aidan, suddenly unsure if he should say everything.

Aidan was Landry's best friend, after all, and the original card-carrying member of the Overprotective Brother Club.

"Because?" Aidan prompted.

"Because if I said no, one of them would be on the first flight out here, fuck their own responsibilities," Levi said.

Aidan hummed under his breath. "You really think so?"

"Oh, I *know* so," Levi said.

"'Cause they've done that before?"

Levi laughed, because of course Aidan knew they hadn't. That he was only trying to make a point.

"They've threatened it enough times," Levi said.

Aidan merged onto the freeway, already full of barely moving cars, and slid between a Lexus and a Camry, flipping off the Lexus when the driver tried to box him out.

"I'm only saying this because I have some experience with this phe-nomenon," Aidan said dryly, "but threatening and doing are two very different things."

"Huh?"

"Threatening is just their stupid-ass way of showing you without actually saying the words that they're here for you, no matter what. They're not actually gonna do it."

Levi raised an eyebrow. "That what you did with Riley?"

"I didn't—" Aidan broke off his sentence with a curse under his breath. "I only ever wanted Riley to know I had his back. Went about it in the worst fucking way ever, which is why I'm telling you so you'll understand the difference."

Levi considered this for a long moment. "That's really fucking stupid," he said finally.

"It sure is," Aidan agreed. "Never claimed that any of us have more than shit for brains."

"You ever explain this to Riley?"

"Had to understand it first," Aidan said. He flopped back against the seat as the traffic came to a complete standstill. "But once I did, yeah. Took me a year or two. Think it's why he's still talking to me. If he hadn't known that I wasn't trying to overstep, just show him that I cared, without using the actual fucking words."

"What's wrong with using the words?" Levi had never understood how masculinity, especially toxic masculinity, claimed you couldn't communicate worth a shit. Emotions weren't scary; even talking about them wasn't as ball-shrinking as so many guys claimed. You still had them long after you finished talking about your feelings.

But then Levi also understood that he was possibly more evolved than the regular straight white guy. Touching dicks regularly could do that for you.

Aidan wouldn't be that enlightened, as he hadn't actually touched another dick yet.

Yet.

Now Levi was thinking about it, again. That simmering heat between them was enjoyable, no question about it, but while Levi might have normally enjoyed the tingling anticipation for any amount of time, he felt weirdly impatient with Aidan. Kept wondering why time wasn't passing any faster.

"Nothing's wrong with using your words, if you're any good at it," Aidan admitted.

"Nobody says you have to be *good* at it to do it, bro," Levi said.

Aidan laughed. "Good point. Anyway, I did do it. Badly, probably, but I did it. That's probably why Logan's always asking you if you're okay. If you're happy. He's trying to communicate with you that he cares."

"He touches Dylan's dick *all* the time. You'd think he'd be better at it."

Aidan had just been taking a long drink from his water bottle and choked. "What, *what*?" he questioned. "What about Dylan's um . . .dick?"

The flush that crept up Aidan's cheeks at saying the word *dick* was adorable. Levi couldn't even make fun of him for it.

"There's a certain kind of enlightenment in communication skill when you regularly touch dick." Levi reached over and patted Aidan on the knee. Wanted to let his fingers linger, but he pulled back.

He'd only been trying to offer an understandable sympathy that Aidan wouldn't be familiar with this turn of events, yet. Besides, Levi was trying not to torture himself anymore, because he was already suffering enough.

"That's just something you made up," Aidan said, but he was chuckling under his breath.

"No, it's really not," Levi said.

"Then how come Landry is so shitty at it?" Aidan cut a glance over at Levi. Levi wondered if Aidan wanted to claim *he* was too, even though he regularly touched dick.

But Levi was great at communication. He'd been the one to pull Aidan out of his sulking spiral in Michigan. He'd gotten him to lighten up several times since then. Even though Aidan didn't talk about it, Levi knew the Morris situation had to be rough on him.

"Great question," Levi said. "My theory is the big-brother thing gets in the way. Kind of obscures any advances you can make on the dick-touching front."

"And Logan?"

"Still technically a big brother," Levi pointed out. "Sometimes I think he's attempting to outdo Landry there."

"So really only the youngest is free from this?" Aidan cocked his head, like he was considering the situation. "I guess Riley's pretty good at communicating. At least recently."

"And he's touched a lot of dick, recently."

Aidan smacked him on the chest. "That's my brother you're talking about, dude. And *your* brother's dick."

"Just stating facts," Levi teased.

Aidan changed lanes, the traffic finally lightening up a bit. "If we're going with your theory, then I'm pretty much fucking hopeless."

"Never hopeless, just needing a lot more . . .um . . .practice." Levi didn't want to say, *you need to touch a lot more dick. Specifically mine.* It wasn't time for that, as much as he was beginning to realize he wanted it to be.

But that was the whole point of a sex pact, wasn't it? You weren't supposed to have the sex before the time limit was up.

It shouldn't have bothered Levi, but it did, even considering that Aidan might get naked with him and be thinking about Morris Jeffries the whole time.

"Practice, huh?" Amusement was rich in Aidan's voice. He shot Levi a hot look. "Is that what we're calling it?"

"You're the Super Bowl–winning quarterback, I didn't think I needed to lecture you on how practice makes perfect, bro," Levi said.

"Not so much. Just wasn't sure if you thought there was hope for me and my shitty communication skills."

Levi did *not* bring up how Aidan had done one of the toughest communication challenges in the world, which was to tell someone he loved them without having any idea if they loved him back the same way.

He was *not* going to bring up Mo. Not right now.

Not when his own cock was half hard in his shorts, just contemplating Aidan touching it.

"There's always hope for you," Levi declared optimistically. "And you wouldn't ever want to give up before you gave it a real go, right?"

"Never, bro," Aidan said, half sarcastically, half earnestly.

It didn't give Levi whiplash. Not exactly. But it made Levi think that maybe Aidan didn't even know what he wanted.

Exactly why you told him next summer, Levi reminded himself.

"Awesome, dude," Levi agreed, but still thinking that somehow he'd lost control of this conversation too. That didn't make sense. He'd touched way more dick than Aidan. Exponentially more. Aidan shouldn't have a leg up on him here. But suddenly, he seemed to.

Levi shook off his worry.

Aidan must've agreed, because he thankfully changed the subject from dick to something else. The something else being Ross Acker.

Levi might've changed it again, but he supposed they *should* talk about it.

"You saw the articles about Ross?" Aidan asked.

"Yeah," Levi said.

Aidan sighed heavily. "I'm gonna get asked about this today during media availability. No question."

"Sorry?" Levi wasn't sure if he *was* sorry. It was better for everyone, but most of all Aidan, for the team to find out now if Ross Acker couldn't cut it at left tackle.

"You're not sorry," Aidan retorted. "Don't tell me you don't want that spot for yourself."

"I . . ." Levi huffed out a breath. "Actually, bro, I came here to play right tackle. I *can* play left, but I didn't come to Toronto to steal Acker's spot."

Aidan shot him a look. "But you're a Banks. I know you all way too well. If you need to step up—"

"It's not ever gonna get to you asking me. I'll already be there," Levi said.

"Of course," Aidan said.

Silence fell between them—Levi estimated they only had about ten minutes before they reached the practice facility—and Levi couldn't help himself. He thought about how Aidan had so easily assumed that he wanted a challenge, even craved it, like his brothers. But he couldn't say that he'd been that way when he'd played in college or even when he'd gone to the NFL. He'd always wanted to do the best he was capable of. That was never the question. But in Seattle, the offensive line coach had talked to him more than once about how he'd thought with some additional work, he could be a starting left tackle. That he'd command more money, more respect, etcetera, if he made the leap.

But he'd never wanted to. Never felt the need.

Yet here he was, already thinking about how he could play that position way better than Ross currently was. Had already decided that if Ross couldn't, *he* would.

Levi didn't know if it was because he'd grown up and was ready to take a leap into the unknown or if it was because the idea of grass stains on Aidan's jersey made him want to howl.

Maybe it was both.

As Levi got ready for their first practice of the day, he realized it didn't *feel* like only one thing.

Still, he didn't know for sure.

Then they got out onto the field, and after warmups, Coach Ned let them know they'd be running some plays. He listed off the formation, and Levi wasn't surprised to hear he'd be playing right tackle. The coaching staff had to know if Ross could do it.

Aidan needed to know if Ross could do it.

They set up, Aidan's expression relaxed beneath his helmet, but Levi could see the tenseness of his shoulders, even under his pads.

Zane, the Thunders' offensive coordinator, blew his whistle, and Aidan called out the snap count, Griff hiking the ball back a moment later.

Levi braced against the turf, hitting the defensive end who launched himself in Levi's direction. It was a solid defensive move, even if the guy was slighter bigger than Levi. But Levi was stronger and faster, and he managed to shuck him off.

But it didn't matter.

He heard a grunt behind him, and the moment Levi had taken care of his assignment, he turned back, and sure enough, Aidan's ass was on the ground. Ross was looking at his quarterback and Nate, the edge rusher, who'd just taken him out before Aidan could even get rid of the ball.

Sure, Bishop was a killer defensive player. He gave lots and *lots* of teams fucking headaches during games. He was never going to be an easy assignment to block.

Except the whole point was to learn how to block guys like Nate Bishop every single week. Guys like Watt and Garrett and Henrickson and Parsons.

Before Ross could do it, Levi extended a hand and helped Aidan up. "You okay, bro?" he asked.

Aidan nodded, but there was a white tenseness around his mouth.

"Yeah, you good?" Nate asked, his casual touch lingering on his shoulder.

"Sure, yeah. It was a good clean hit," Aidan said, patting Nate back.

Right. Of course Aidan would be sensitive to that, after last year. But when he squinted his eyes and looked around, Nate wasn't who his eyes locked on to. It was Ross.

Levi half expected Aidan to say something to Ross. He'd be absolutely within his rights to do it, because he'd been the one who'd ended up on the ground.

But he didn't. Instead he just gave Zane a nod, and they went to run the play again.

This time Aidan didn't end up with his ass tackled to the turf, but he had to throw the ball away too early, hitting Jaden on the outlet route, instead of Trevor deeper.

"That would've been a first down if you could've hung on to the ball," Coach Zane pointed out.

Levi gave Aidan a fuck ton of credit. He didn't argue. He didn't blame Ross. He just nodded, and then ran it again, and again, and then again.

Once out of eight runs, Aidan hit Trevor on the deep crossing route. That was it.

For an offense that was going to be structured around their two tight ends—Trevor and his stepbrother, Lane—it was not a stellar beginning.

As they walked into the locker room, breaking for lunch and their afternoon meetings, Levi stared at Aidan's sweaty neck.

He wanted to say something. Not just to Aidan but to Coach Ned. Suggest that they try that same play again, but after rearranging the line. Swapping him and Ross. He wasn't one hundred percent sure he could block Nate Bishop but he did think he was a better player than Ross.

"Hey," Levi said, hurrying up to catch up with Aidan, nudging him with an elbow in the side.

Aidan glanced over at him. He looked tense, still, and Levi wasn't sure he could blame him. Offensive line problems would doom an entire team. Make it hard for them to score. And if the offense couldn't hang on to the ball, there was way too much pressure on the defense, not to mention inflating their playing time.

The best football teams—the ones who made it to the playoffs and then won—were the ones who kept everything in balance.

The Thunder were not in balance right now. There was always time. Teams could find it during the season, but it was harder if the pieces weren't already there.

"What's up?" Aidan asked.

"I could ask you the same question," Levi said.

Aidan sighed. "We're gonna get there. We've not run many two tight end formations yet."

Right. Because Trevor was a rookie. They'd had more tight ends than Lane on the roster last year, of course, but it took a higher quality player to run the kind of plays that Zane had designed. Lane and Trevor were perfect for them, if Aidan could get the protection he needed.

"I can see the vision," Levi said, trying to be optimistic. The vision was there. But if they couldn't move the vision to the field and execute, there was no point how fucking good it was.

"Me too," Aidan said, frustration leaking into his voice. They turned a corner, heading into the locker room.

"Maybe this afternoon'll be better," Levi said.

Aidan shot him a look that spoke volumes. He didn't think it would. Levi didn't really think so either.

They cleaned up. Ate lunch. Went to meetings. Levi filmed a fun segment for the social media team, introducing himself and sharing some of his likes/dislikes to help the fans get to know him better.

Then they were back at it on the field, Coach Ned looking resigned as he listed off the line assignments. He didn't shift Levi to the left, but he did adjust the play. Trevor—the bigger of the two tight ends—wouldn't be running a route but staying back to help Ross block Nate.

It was an erosion of the original vision, but worse than that, it actually worked.

Levi never had trouble taking extra blocking help in certain games. Some teams rushed more reliably and had better quality pass rushers. A tight end on the line could mean the difference between a clean game and allowing a bunch of sacks.

But to have to do it in practice, just because they were trying to work on running plays?

Fucking embarrassing.

After practice, Levi caught Coach Ned's arm as he was picking up a bunch of cones from the last set of drills they'd run at the end.

"Hey, Coach," Levi said.

"Banks." He looked like he knew exactly why Levi was talking to him. Everyone probably knew why. Levi could see Ross walking slowly towards the locker room entrance, eyes still on the field. He probably knew it too.

Levi half expected some muttered, under-his-breath comment when he got into the locker room himself. But he'd take Ross' anger if it meant they could fix this problem.

"You know I can play left tackle."

Coach looked over at him, finally meeting his eyes. "Yeah."

"Move me over tomorrow." It was hard to know, being new to the team and new to Coach Ned's leadership, just how to broach the subject. How to correctly pitch the suggestion so it had the most chance of landing right. Levi had debated all during the last drill and had finally come to the conclusion that the most blunt way—cutting through all the crap—was the best tactic here.

It'd let Coach know, also, just how serious Levi was.

Coach Ned shoved his hat off, and set it back in place only after he'd finished running a hand through his hair. Levi was pretty sure he was doing it to give himself a minute to think. But Levi also knew there was no way he hadn't already considered this option.

"Banks." Coach sighed. "This isn't a small thing you're asking."

"I know." He knew. It wasn't as simple as tossing him to the other side and letting Ross take the right tackle spot. Maybe Ross had no experience playing right tackle. Plus, there was the delicate balance of winning football games and your players' egos. None of the coaching staff wanted to go scorched earth on Ross. Hell, *Levi* didn't even want to go scorched earth on Ross.

"I'm not quite ready to try it yet. Tomorrow we're going back to drilling fundamentals. Work on everyone's basics."

Levi stifled a groan. What Coach meant was that they wanted to work on *Ross'* fundamentals and everyone else was going to suffer as a result.

"We'll see if that makes a difference," Coach said, sounding like he was trying for optimism. Levi couldn't dredge up the same. He'd looked Ross up during lunch. The guy was thirty-three now and his speed and reaction time probably weren't something that could be fixed by drills. Age had come for him, the way it came for all of them, eventually.

"Sure thing."

"Expect you to help set the tone, Banks," Coach said, patting him on the shoulder.

"You got it, Coach," Levi said.

Griff cornered him when he got into the locker room. "So?" he asked.

Levi glanced around. Ross was already gone—probably in the showers.

"No dice," Levi said. "We're drilling tomorrow."

"Fuck," Griff said earnestly.

"Pretty much my thought." Levi gave him a supportive slap on the back. "Tomorrow's gonna suck."

CHAPTER 8

"ARE THEY TRYING TO kill them out there?" Wes asked Aidan, as the second offensive lineman broke ranks and went to a knee, retching onto the grass.

Aidan shrugged. "Levi said they were drilling basics today. He didn't sound very excited about it, but they gotta get better."

Wes shot him a look.

"Okay," Aidan amended, "the protection's gotta get better. How can we run the kind of game we want if it doesn't?"

"That just looks . . .rough." Wes winced.

Aidan shot the group another glance. Zane had already informed them that they wouldn't be running plays this morning—that the offensive line coach had said they were running drills instead, which jived with what Levi had told him on their way into practice this morning.

"Good news, we've got a day off tomorrow," Aidan said.

"Hey, speaking of that. And speaking of *that*," Wes said, gesturing towards the offensive linemen, "we should get a group to go out. Celebrate not dying today, or something."

"Or something," Aidan said dryly.

"Seriously, I know a great place. New bar that's been open for a few months. Friend introduced me to it."

"You have *friends*?" Aidan retorted fondly, smacking Wes on the back of the head.

"Hey, shut up. More friends than you."

"Here I thought you were too busy sulking over—" Aidan cut himself off. It had been one thing to tease Wes over his ex, but it was another to tease him when he knew how that felt. At least Wes had *had* his guy. Aidan hadn't even gotten that far.

Wes shot him a look. "Yeah, sort of am. That's why the friend took me out. Said I needed to get my head out of my ass."

"Well, *that's* true," Aidan said. "Dawson could use it too. He's seriously angsting over the whole father-in-law-stealing-all-his-money shit."

"Kind of hard not to," Wes said sympathetically.

"Who's this friend?" Aidan wondered. "Do I know them?"

"Uh, no. He's actually not a football player. Hockey player. He's on long-term injured reserve though. No idea when he'll be off of it. Bad concussion."

"Sucks," Aidan said.

"Yeah, I told him to come up here, stay for a bit on my couch so he wouldn't just be alone in Buffalo. Bored. Feeling sorry for himself."

"I know weirder things have happened but I *also* know a few hockey players," Aidan said. "Hockey's no football, but it's pretty decent to follow."

"Don't let him hear you saying that." Wes tossed him the ball and Aidan tossed it back. They were still waiting on the receivers to finish their warmups. Over on the other side of the field, the only linemen still upright were Levi and Griff.

Aidan decided that probably didn't bode well for his protection this season. Maybe he *could* use a drink tonight.

"Maybe you know them too. The Barnes brothers? Avery plays on the West Coast, but Charlie's in New York," Aidan said. "They're from Michigan. Own a house on the lake a little bit down from me."

"Oh yeah. I do. I think . . .yeah, pretty sure my friend knows them. Knows the youngest anyway. Played on his team in college when he was a senior. Ethan?"

"Oh yeah. That's the youngest. Haven't met him yet, though. Only Charlie and Avery."

"Well, you'll like my hockey player. Everyone does," Wes said wryly.

"Let's get a count together of who's in during lunch," Aidan suggested, and Wes nodded.

The receivers were trickling over, finished with their warmups, and Wes threw a long pass to Trevor, who snatched the ball out of the air.

"Come on," Aidan said, gesturing towards him. "Let's get some plays going."

They worked on timing routes for over an hour, both the receivers and the cornerbacks getting a good workout.

"Trev, you gotta break a little sooner," Lane yelled over at his stepbrother on the very last set of passes.

Wes and Aidan exchanged concerned looks when Trevor ignored Lane, brushing off his concern.

"You wanna deal with this?" Wes asked Aidan.

"Hell no. I'm supposed to be . . .how did you put it? Being nice to them *collectively*. And we already established I'm no good at it. You're the good cop, Matthews, so you're on it. Consider this part of my mentorship. Gifting you the demon twins."

Wes shot him a look. "Calling them the demon twins isn't really being nice—collectively or not."

"Nope. Just being honest." Aidan nudged him again as twenty yards down field, Trevor and Lane had started exchanging words. "Come on. Get down there, before they start doing something *collectively*."

"You're the worst," Wes groaned. But he jogged down there anyway.

Aidan watched as he defused the situation, and, deciding that Wes had it under control, he headed towards the locker room to get cleaned up for lunch.

Levi cornered him while he debated between a buffalo chicken and a turkey ranch wrap for lunch.

"Wes told me we're going out tonight," Levi said, looking too excited considering he'd spent the morning being dragged to hell and back.

"You sure you're up for it?" Aidan said, pulling the turkey ranch wrap onto his tray.

Levi made a scoffing noise. "Those guys just aren't conditioned right."

"Yeah?" Aidan raised an eyebrow.

"Okay, well, there were a few rough moments, but I'm still here," Levi said, chuckling under his breath. "And nothing better than a few drinks to medicate the pain away."

"Alright. I'll add you to the list. Or um, to Wes' list."

Levi nudged him. "I didn't think you *had* a list, bro."

"Is this your way of saying I'm boring?" But he knew he was. That he'd ground down all his hard edges, ages ago. Anything that could compromise him winning had been eliminated.

"*Bro*, you don't even drink coffee." Levi shot him a sad, pathetic look from his brown eyes. "You need to lighten up. Not a lot, just a little."

Aidan huffed out a breath. Half embarrassed, half annoyed, but entirely interested in lightening up if Levi was involved.

"I'll take that under advisement," Aidan retorted. He wasn't about to tell Levi how attractive that idea sounded, but only if *he* was the one specifically doing the lightening up.

"That right there? That's it, *right there*." Levi leaned right into his space, looking and smelling better than he had any right to, especially after the morning he'd had. "*Advisement*."

"What?" Aidan asked, suddenly even more self-conscious.

"Bro. We get it. You went to college."

"So did you," Aidan said dryly.

"Well, *some* of us don't go around advertising it all the time," Levi teased, like somehow that was a bad thing.

Aidan had worked like hell for his degree. He'd been in school, going to classes, QB1 for a major NCAA program, and he'd been basically raising Riley on his own, since his parents had been too busy squabbling to bother doing it.

He wasn't ever going to apologize for getting it done and for actually graduating.

"Am I . . ." Aidan trailed off. He rarely experienced a crisis of confidence, but it was becoming obvious that, at least to Levi, he was a boring, pompous stick-in-the-mud.

No wonder he hadn't brought up sex since he'd gotten to Toronto. Who would even want to have sex with him? Not Levi. And apparently not Morris either, though Morris' disinterest was at least because he wasn't interested in having sex with *any* guy.

"Are you?" Levi questioned. He was still grinning, like he was actually enjoying this conversation.

Aidan, on the other hand, wanted to sink through the floor. If this was what losing your confidence felt like, no wonder he'd spent his life avoiding it. "Am I . . .*ugh*. That awful? A boring, pompous ass?"

Riley had called him an ass on multiple occasions, and even Landry had, once or twice. That had felt earned. He'd overstepped his bounds. Out of love, for sure, but in the end, did it matter how much he cared if the way he showed it was by being an overbearing dickhead?

The answer: *no*.

Levi, however, looked floored. "What?" he exclaimed.

"I said it," Aidan mumbled. God, he was embarrassing. If Landry was witnessing this, he'd never let him forget it. Riley, either. And Mo? Well. Aidan rarely thought it was good he'd been traded, but right now? It was humiliating enough that Levi was here. That he'd actually *asked* Levi.

"I just . . ." Levi looked more than floored now. He looked dismayed. "Aidan, I was *teasing* you. I wasn't serious. You're . . ." His voice dropped even more, so low Aidan could barely hear it and they were practically on top of each other. "You're not boring, and you're not pompous and you're definitely, well, *most* of the time, not an ass. And when you are? Well, these days it's kind of hot, if I'm being honest."

Aidan couldn't believe it. "But you just—"

Levi groaned under his breath. He'd flushed red, too, which Aidan couldn't say he'd thought was attractive before, but he was rapidly changing his mind on the subject. "I was an idiot, okay? You just . . .you fluster me. And I like flirting with you. I'm like a snotty-nosed stupid kid, pulling your pigtails."

"Seriously?"

"The idiot part? Or the flustered part? Or the snotty-nosed part?"

Aidan was barely keeping up. "Um. All of them?"

Levi leaned in even closer. Aidan's pulse jumped, even as he told himself to keep calm. Or maybe it didn't even matter. Aidan was flustered. Well, according to Levi, he was too. "Newsflash, I *like* flirting with you. And I wouldn't do it if you were boring or pompous."

Aidan swallowed hard. Maybe right now was when Levi would bring up the sex pact. *Next,* he'd say, in that matter-of-fact, teasing voice that was hotter than it had any right to be, *I wouldn't have agreed to have sex with you in a year if you were boring. Or pompous. Or kissed you right there, in your kitchen and enjoyed every second of it.*

But of course, he didn't.

He just didn't.

Aidan kind of wanted to yell it, right there, in the middle of the cafeteria. *Why aren't you saying it? Why are you pretending like it didn't happen?*

Instead, Levi took a step back, giving Aidan a very cute wink. God, he even thought *that* was cute. He actually *was* embarrassing. "So, don't worry about that, okay? Promise me?"

It was not a hard promise to give. "Uh, sure. Yeah. Of course."

Levi patted him on the cheek, the touch fleeting, but Aidan felt it all the way down, deep in his stomach.

"Excited about tonight," Levi said.

For a split second, Aidan almost imagined that Levi was talking about something else. Not a trip out to a bar or a club, but just the two of them, circling each other in his condo.

But that wasn't what this was. Despite the flustered comment and the admission Levi had made about flirting with him, he didn't seem to have any interest in pushing it any further.

"Me too." Aidan tried not to be disappointed. Levi patted him on the cheek again.

"It'll be lit," Levi told him.

Aidan almost said what he was thinking, which was that he hoped it wouldn't be *too* lit. But he was trying to loosen up a little. *Just a little*, Levi had said. And he could do that.

He *could*.

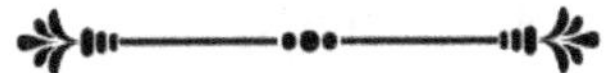

"Oh my God," Levi exclaimed as Wes led them down a dark-ish Toronto alley. "It's like a *secret* bar."

"Oh yeah," Wes said, glancing back. "It's called Vault. Some kind of play on the old-fashioned speakeasies. There's no sign or anything." He looked down, consulting something on his phone as they walked deeper into the alley.

Aidan shoved his hands into his jeans pockets and wished he hadn't worn his Patek Philippe watch. They were probably going to get mugged and his lawyer would give him a look like, *what the fuck did you expect?*

"Is this the kind of place you guys normally go?" It was the rookie punter, Cameron, his voice wavering a little, apprehension clear on his baby face, even in the dim light.

"No, which makes it better," Dawson said, reassuringly.

"Hell yes," Lane agreed.

"This better be worth all the fucking theatrics," Nate muttered under his breath.

"It's worth it," Wes reassured them. "It's just down here."

He guided their group further in, then down a set of stained concrete steps set into the ground.

"It's like we're descending into hell." Lane sounded delighted by this.

"Only you," Trevor muttered.

There was a black wooden door, shiny with lacquer, at the bottom of the stairs. To the right of the door was a gold key, shining in the murk of the alley.

That was the only sign.

"We're gonna get killed," Cam whispered behind him. "Our organs harvested. That happens in big cities, right?"

"Rook, I promise you, I'm gonna personally make sure your organs stay unharvested," Dawson murmured back.

Wes knocked on the door—a distinctive knock, even; two long knocks punctuated by one short one—and a hidden window in the door opened.

"Holy shit," Lane exclaimed.

"We're with Andresen," Wes told the set of eyeballs framed by the tiny opening.

A second later, the door opened, not grinding open like Aidan half expected, but swinging open smoothly, the hinges clearly oiled.

Then they stepped into another world.

The ceilings were low and the room was dim, but that was the last depressing thing about it. There were low chairs and couches scattered around, all upholstered in thick, rich fabrics. Blues and purples and dark turquoise greens. The walls were covered in midnight blue, with a subtle gold pattern picked out.

An oval bar dominated the space, dark wood shining even in the low light. And spinning out from the central room, like spokes on a wheel, were various doorways, each accentuated in a slightly different color of wood. Like they'd descended into an underworld, and these were portals to different fantastical universes.

"Holy shit," Lane exclaimed again, but hushed this time. Reverent. Like this was the coolest thing he'd ever seen. And Aidan wasn't sure he'd disagree. Wes had said it would be worth the trip, and so far, ten out of ten, no notes.

Leaning against the bar was a tall guy, solid muscular build, with curly hair the color of a shiny gold coin and a face that could probably make anybody on earth do anything.

"Oh, hey, there he is," Wes said, gesturing towards the guy and leading their group over.

"This," he said, waving at the hot blond guy, "is Ramsey Andresen. He's a hockey player for the Buffalo Sabres."

A brief, very complicated emotion crossed over Ramsey's face. Aidan barely caught it before it was gone, smoothed over in a cover-model smile.

"Hey," he said. "Welcome to Vault."

There was a collective lull that fell over the group. Aidan supposed he wasn't surprised. Ramsey didn't seem that surprised either, like he was used to going around, just living his everyday life, having that effect on people.

"This place is so sick, isn't it?" Wes said excitedly. He greeted Ramsey, tugging him into a bro-hug. "Here, let me introduce you to the team."

Aidan stepped forward first, used to being the leader. "Aidan Flynn," he said, offering Ramsey his hand.

Ramsey's handshake was brief but firm. Up close he was even more attractive. Maybe before Aidan wouldn't have noticed, but it was difficult *not* to notice.

"You're the QB, huh? Mentoring Wes here?" Ramsey asked.

Aidan nodded. But he didn't really want to talk about mentoring Wes. He knew he'd be good at it, and Wes would even be a good mentee, frankly. But the thought of calling it that made something uncomfortable and horrifying crawl up his spine. He wasn't *old*. He wasn't washed up. Not by a long fucking shot.

"Hockey, huh?" he said to Ramsey. He didn't think hockey produced these kinds of pretty boys. Though to be honest, Ramsey didn't seem like a boy at all. He was clearly all man.

Aidan wondered which of his teammates he was going to have to drag off this guy by the end of the night.

"Dawson." His friend approached next, holding out his hand.

Okay. Well, there was something to be said about getting over someone by getting under someone else. And Aidan had known Dawson was bi since their college days.

"Oh my God you're hot," Cam said, then clapped a hand over his mouth, looking horrified that he'd actually said that out loud.

If Aidan had worried about how this guy would react—because he would absolutely throw down and protect his rookie, no questions—Ramsey only grinned crookedly, more real than the cover-model smile and said, "Hey, so are you, kid."

"Holy shit," Lane mumbled behind him.

Trevor nudged him. "Dude, please tell me you have something else you can say to this guy other than *holy shit*."

"That's Cameron, we like to call him Cam," Wes said, nodding towards their rookie. "Then there's Levi. Lane. Trevor. And Nate."

Aidan watched as Ramsey greeted all the guys. His gaze didn't linger on any of them, but they all seemed half ready to slobber all over him. Nate seemed to be the exception, hanging back, barely giving Ramsey a nod.

Aidan supposed he shouldn't be surprised that Levi looked, though Aidan could hardly blame him for it. *He'd* looked, hadn't he?

But Levi didn't bother trying to muscle his way to Ramsey's side as he started talking about how he'd reserved them one of the private rooms.

"There's different private rooms?" Dawson asked as they spread out at the bar.

"Oh yeah. Several different gaming rooms. Pool tables and darts. A poker room. A library. And the vault."

"There's an actual vault? Holy shit." Lane seemed to still be stuck on *holy shit.* "That's so fucking cool."

"Next time we'll try that one out," Ramsey said with a wink.

"This place is pretty awesome," Levi said to Aidan. Somehow they'd ended up next to each other at the bar, both glancing over the same cocktail menu. It was in the same midnight blue as the walls, thick rich paper, almost like velvet to the touch, and all the text embossed in gold.

"Yeah, Wes said it was, but Wes is pretty enthusiastic about most things," Aidan admitted. "Or else he tries to be."

Levi shot him a look. "Oh, you noticed that too, huh?"

"There's no point in asking him about it. He doesn't talk about his ex," Aidan said.

"Not that you actually tried," Levi pointed out gently.

"Hey, I *did* try," Aidan said. Last year he'd made several attempts, when it had become obvious that his new teammate was going through it. But Wes had never wanted to talk about it.

Aidan hadn't entirely understood back then, but he got it now. When Riley had shown up at the lake house with Landry and Levi in tow, and Levi had demanded to know why Aidan was sulking, he hadn't wanted to talk about Mo, either.

But he couldn't deny that it *had* helped.

"*You* tried," Levi stated, voice edging with disbelief. "You, Aidan Flynn, attempted to talk to someone about feelings."

"Hey, you keep insulting me, I'm gonna get a complex." And when it came to Levi, he really didn't want to get even *more* of a complex than he already had. He'd already embarrassed himself once today.

"No, your ego is just gonna be normal-person sized," Levi teased, foot nudging Aidan's, smile on his face.

How had they gotten so close together?

Levi's eyes were bright with amusement and joy, the color of the best whiskey Aidan had ever drunk.

"Sure," Aidan said.

The bartender stopped in front of them. "What can I get you two?" he asked. The vests the staff were wearing were velvet too—but a deep dark purple, almost black, with a tiny gold key pin on the open collar of his black shirt.

Aidan glanced over at the bottles of whiskey subtly lit and displayed in the center of the bar. "I'll have a Lagavulin," he said.

"Make that two," Levi said.

When Aidan shot him a questioning glance, Levi just shrugged. "Not gonna watch you get wasted on whiskey by yourself this time."

"I'm not going to—"

"Chill," Levi said, nudging him again, but this time he didn't move his shoulder or his foot, leaving them pressed against Aidan. "It's all good. I'm teasing, remember? Flirting with you." He paused. "Please for the love of God tell me someone has flirted with you before."

"Obviously." Aidan rolled his eyes. But he couldn't say that anyone had ever done it like Levi Banks had. Gently poking fun at him, laughing at him but also *with* him. Hoping Aidan would laugh, just because Levi was laughing. There seemed to be no ulterior motive, no hidden agenda, and none of the mercenary crassness that a lot of the women—and occasionally men—employed when they approached him.

To Levi, he seemed to be just Aidan, the older brother of the guy *his* brother was dating. Not Aidan Flynn, QB1 of the Toronto Thunder and two-time Super Bowl MVP winner.

"Not enough, though, if this is how you take it," Levi said. "Or is it 'cause I'm a guy?"

Aidan made a face, but he was amused. "No. Don't mind that you're a guy."

"*Obviously*," Levi said.

He nodded to the bartender as he set their glasses down.

Aidan was surprised to see Levi pull out a hundred-dollar bill from his clip and slide it across the counter. "Keep the change," he said.

"Oh, but Mr. Andresen told me everyone's drinking on his tab," the bartender said apologetically.

Levi shrugged and stuffed the bill into the cut-glass tip jar on the bar.

"What do we know about this guy?" Aidan asked under his breath.

"Ramsey?" Levi sounded unconcerned.

"Wes told me he's a hockey player. On long-term injured reserve," Aidan said, "but that's it."

Aidan realized he should have spent a minute googling this guy they were hanging out with. He trusted Wes—who apparently knew him well—but he should have done his research anyway.

Instead he'd spent the two hours after practice before they met up getting a haircut and agonizing in front of his closet trying to figure out what shirt made him look more laid-back than he actually was.

He shouldn't have worried honestly, considering that Levi was in some egregiously neon-bright patterned shirt. Nobody was even going to notice he existed when he was next to Levi.

Except—Levi might notice, and that was the only person Aidan wanted to look at him anyway.

When they'd all grabbed a drink, Ramsey led the way to their private room. As promised, it had dark green walls, faintly embossed with a wavy leaf pattern, and at the center of the room, a pristine dark wood pool table. To one side were the dart boards, closed up in their matching wood enclosures. The music was lower here, and there were at least two big NFL player–sized couches and a number of comfortable-looking chairs scattered around the space.

"This is a pretty sweet setup," Levi said.

"Told you," Wes said a little smugly. "Ramsey's the best at finding places like this."

"And you're not even from Toronto," Aidan said a little pointedly.

Ramsey just shrugged. "No, but Buffalo's so close. And Wes is here, so we've met up a bunch." He hesitated. "Especially last year."

Wes made a face, clear pain flashing across it before it was covered up by exasperation. "Don't," he said.

"Chill. I wasn't going to mention Marcus," Ramsey said.

Aidan hadn't even known that Wes' ex was named Marcus, so it seemed like Ramsey was a *very* good friend, if he knew that much.

"Wes said you were on injured reserve," Levi said.

Seemed like he and his new right tackle were on the same page—they both wanted to know more about this friend of Wes'.

Aidan hoped that it wasn't because Levi wanted in his pants, but then, Levi wasn't flirting with him. Not the way he flirted with Aidan, anyway.

"Yeah," Ramsey said. "Concussion syndrome. Had a bad one last year, right after I signed my extension. but I'd had a few before, in college, and this one lingered." The way he said it made it clear that he'd had to repeat this information many times, in a lot of different situations.

"Didn't know you could drink with concussion syndrome," Nate said casually, nodding at the drink in Ramsey's hand. It might have been the first time Nate had said anything since being introduced to Ramsey and Aidan thought that was surprising. Nate wasn't the most social guy on the planet, but he wasn't exactly quiet, either.

Ramsey raised an eyebrow, giving him a pointed look. "This? This isn't vodka. It's just sparkling water, dude."

Nate's mouth thinned into a hard line. "Ah."

It was surprising how annoyed Nate seemed; he was usually up for a good time, and from all angles, it seemed like both this bar and Ramsey were a good time.

"Hey," Dawson said, "who's up for a game?" He grabbed a cue from the rack and rolled it between his palms.

"I'll play," Cam said immediately.

"Count me in too," Lane said, and Trevor nodded too.

"Flynn? Banks?" Dawson asked them.

"I'm good," Aidan said and Levi shook his head.

"My balance isn't what it used to be. I can usually make do with darts, but not pool," Ramsey said wryly.

"Dude, that sucks," Levi said sympathetically. "So what's it like, long-term injured reserve? Know what it's like in football but not hockey."

"Get paid. Do nothing. Try to recover so I can play again. That's what it's like," Ramsey said. "Hardest part is staying busy. Which is why I'm up here. Wes was tired of me whining about being alone in Buffalo."

"He was so depressing," Wes said earnestly. "And we're there for each other." They exchanged glances, loaded with some kind of emotion—Aidan was pretty sure it wasn't sexual or romantic, but then, he was shitty at figuring out feelings anyway. There was a reason he was struggling with the whole thing with Levi.

"Adorable," Nate said dryly.

"We've known each other a long time," Ramsey said, jaw jutting out a bit. Aidan had a feeling he wasn't really defending himself but Wes.

Honestly, what was Nate's problem? Aidan was naturally kind of suspicious of new guys—especially new guys who weren't football players—entering their circle, but Ramsey was a pro, too. *And* Wes was vouching for him.

"Yeah?" Aidan asked casually, but sending a pointed look in Nate's direction. He wasn't Nate's captain—that was Sterling. But he was a veteran and a leader on this team, and usually his teammates listened to what he was laying down.

"We went to Portland U together," Wes said.

"Hockey player and football player becoming friends? That's unusual," Dawson said, as he finished racking up the balls.

"Not *that* unusual," Ramsey said. "We've got friends who ended up together. Dean plays football for the Riptide and Brody *could've* gone pro as a hockey player. Was drafted and everything but he decided to go to med school, like the fucking overachiever he is."

"You're still torn up about that," Wes teased. "Brody picking science over hockey."

"Well, *yeah*," Ramsey said flatly. Like he couldn't imagine anyone picking *anything* over hockey.

Coming from a guy currently not playing, it hurt. It hurt to look at him, and not just because he looked like the kind of guy who belonged on the cover of *GQ*.

"You're gonna get there, bud," Wes said, patting him on the arm. He pulled him over to the dartboards a moment later, along with Nate, and Aidan and Levi were left to their own devices.

Aidan settled down on the end of one couch, where he could see both the pool game and the dartboards, and he wasn't surprised at all when Levi joined him.

He *was* surprised that Levi settled down right next to him and then slung an arm across the back of the couch, his fingers brushing Aidan's shoulder. He didn't pull Aidan against him, but he might as well have.

Aidan swallowed hard and glanced around the room but nobody was paying attention to them. Maybe they'd already noticed and just assumed Levi was touchy-feely like that.

And Levi *was*. Aidan had seen him hugging Griff and the other linemen. Pulling Trevor into an embrace. Casually resting a hand on Nate's back or Wes' arm.

With him, though, it felt like more. Especially when the tips of Levi's fingers lingered along his shoulders. Practically stroking him.

"You good?" Levi asked, leaning in a fraction closer.

Aidan told himself to stop overthinking—to stop thinking, *period*—and just enjoy it, like it wasn't a big deal. Because clearly, Levi didn't think it was a big deal.

"Yeah. Should probably be asking you that, after today's practice." Aidan took a sip of whiskey. It was warm and smokey on his tongue.

Levi chuckled. "Told you, Flynn. I'm tougher than that."

And he was tough, for sure. No question about that. But he wasn't just tough; he was soft, too. Not just good at putting people at ease, but caring enough to do it.

"Bet Ross wishes you were a little less tough," Aidan said.

Levi sighed. His fingers stroked with more purpose, like it wasn't just an incidental touch, but entirely on purpose.

"It might get ugly, at some point," Levi pointed out carefully.

"What's gonna be ugly is if I spend the next twenty weeks with my ass on the turf," Aidan said, trying to keep his voice light, but it was impossible to keep the dread out of it. If that happened, they wouldn't win very many games. They definitely wouldn't be going to the Super Bowl, never mind winning it. It might even cut his career a year short.

"I promise you that isn't going to happen," Levi said.

Aidan almost said that was impossible; there were too many factors to consider besides Levi's sheer fucking will, but when he looked over, he could see the certainty shining in Levi's eyes. He believed it, and that made Aidan want to believe it, too.

He felt Levi's whole hand cup Aidan's shoulder. It comforted, but it also sent a spike of longing through him.

"Okay," Aidan said, and Levi smiled. It was that same camaraderie that he'd learned over the years you could share with a teammate, but it was more too. Because the smile wasn't just a smile. It made Aidan's insides heat up until they felt sizzling hot. Practically caramelized.

"I got you, baby," Levi said under his breath, squeezing Aidan's shoulder.

He had teammates, of course, that he could rely and depend on. That had always been true. But before Mo had left for Vegas, he'd been that extra-special support. The guy that Aidan could trust more than he could trust himself.

Aidan had told himself so many times that nobody could ever take that spot. And Levi wasn't, not really. It was like he was in the middle of carving a *new* one, right next to Aidan. Not just next to him, but slightly angled to the front. Ready and prepared to take the hit before Aidan even registered it was coming.

That was new.

The *baby* was also new.

Aidan wanted to crinkle his nose and demand that Levi never call him that again. But if he did, he'd probably call him something worse. Like *sweetheart* or *honeybunches.* Or God, *bro.*

They finished their drinks in silence, watching as Cam cleaned everyone out at pool, and surprisingly, Ramsey owned Nate and Wes at darts.

"Hey, I said I was better at darts," Ramsey said as Nate bitched about him cheating.

"Yeah, if you don't like losing, don't play him at cards," Wes said seriously.

"Noted," Nate said, shooting Ramsey an almost dirty look. Nate was a bad loser, sure—they *all* were—but Aidan still wasn't sure what Nate's big issue was with the new guy.

"Hey, it's almost like I'm in trouble for being awesome," Ramsey said, laughing. The almost dark look in his eyes that had been lingering before was gone. He slung an arm around Wes. "We better get you home, get you to bed. Big day tomorrow."

"It is?" Wes questioned. "I thought we had the day off."

"Yeah, exactly. You have the day off before the run-through for your first big start."

Aidan wasn't going to say it, but Trevor said it anyway. "Dude, it's a *preseason* game."

Ramsey smacked him upside the head as Wes made a face. "*Dude,* I'm being a supportive friend, even though football sucks."

Everyone looked at him at the same time. "What?" Ramsey asked, shrugging. "It does. It's not hockey, that's for damn sure."

"Can I get pissed at him *now*?" Nate muttered under his breath.

"No," Aidan said firmly.

A harder hit or a landing that wasn't quite as smooth as it should've been, and he'd be Ramsey. Haunting someone else's house, just so he didn't have to be alone and contemplate the pointlessness of his existence.

It would probably be Riley's house, and as much as he loved his brother, that would've been hell on earth.

"I like you," Ramsey said, moving his arm from Wes to Aidan. "You're not what everyone says you are."

Aidan raised an eyebrow. "What does everyone say I am?"

"Don't listen to him, bro," Trevor interrupted earnestly. "You're the best."

"No, no, I really want to hear this," Aidan said. It couldn't be any worse than the teasing comments Levi directed his way regularly. Even if those did sting less, delivered in that flirty voice like Levi always used. Knowing that, despite all his flaws, Levi *liked* him. At least as a friend.

It suddenly occurred to Aidan that he wanted Levi to like him *more* than that, though.

Shit.

Shit, shit, shit.

"Hey," Ramsey said, glancing at him, because Aidan had clearly tensed up, "are you alright? I don't have to—"

"No, tell me," Aidan said forcibly. Maybe absorbing Ramsey's semi-offensive opinions about his reputation would distract him from Levi.

Ramsey shrugged. "Nothing bad. Just serious. Intense. Works hard. Never takes a break. No fun." He grinned then. "But you're kinda fun, actually."

"Don't tell him that. It's just gonna go to his head, and his ego's already big enough," Levi said.

Aidan wondered if he was imagining the way Levi's gaze narrowed at Ramsey's arm rested so casually around Aidan's shoulders.

He shouldn't want Levi to be jealous. That would be petty and childish and ridiculous.

But he wanted it, anyway.

"My ego's the perfect size," Aidan said, adopting the smug tone that everyone believed came easily to him, but didn't quite sit as comfortably on him as they thought. *Fake it til you make it*, or something.

"Oh, it is, baby," Levi teased.

Ramsey's eyebrows crept up, and for a second breathless moment, Aidan thought maybe he'd figured it out. Not that there was *anything* to figure out. He and Levi were teammates. Friends. Co-stepbrothers-in-law or something like that.

But Aidan caught Ramsey's knowing look as they headed out towards the door, and Aidan wasn't quite sure that *was* all they were. Not anymore.

CHAPTER 9

Preseason was a pain in Levi's ass.

He liked *playing*. He liked being on the field, actually affecting the outcome of the game. He also liked game outcomes *mattering*, and this one was totally fucking meaningless.

But then, that wasn't entirely true.

To Wes, who was starting the game. To Ross, who was fighting for his fucking life out there, in the trenches. To all the other guys struggling to make the fifty-two-man roster, this game was everything.

It was just nothing to Levi, and he was *bored*.

That seemed like a good enough reason to bother Aidan. Especially because every single time he did it, his golden-brown eyebrows slammed together and he looked like he wanted to pin Levi to the bench behind them and shut him up with his mouth.

Obviously Aidan wouldn't do that. He *couldn't* do that. But the fantasy was stimulating and distracting, a nice hot departure from watching this boring-ass game.

Aidan said something into the headset he was wearing—he wasn't even dressed for the game, wouldn't play until the second game, and then probably only a single series—about the coverage.

"Wes is playing great," Levi said, nudging him.

Aidan looked over at him. Covered the microphone on his headset. "Can I help you?" he asked, sounding half fond, half exasperated, which Levi had discovered was the perfect Aidan-balance.

Levi shrugged. "He *is*."

"Yes," Aidan said, pursing his lips. "Lucky Wes. Ten years younger and a hell of a lot more able to run for his life."

Wes had made more than a handful of great throws on the run, because as Levi had expected, the hard work and going back to basics had not magically turned back the clock on Ross' skills.

"You could do that, still," Levi said. He'd seen Aidan work out. He'd seen Aidan practicing, now. Was intimately familiar with what he was capable of.

"Yeah, sure, but I don't *want* to be doing that," Aidan said.

"I'm gonna fix it," Levi said confidently. He was going to corner Coach Ned after the game and tell him to put him on left tackle. Especially for the next game. Surely Ned had seen everything he needed to with Ross.

He wasn't getting the job done; he wasn't *going* to get the job done.

Aidan shot him a sideways look—full of doubt. "Yeah, Acker's just gonna move to the right, no big deal."

"You'd be surprised," Levi said. Aidan shrugged, like he would be.

But Levi had been doing his homework. At night, when he lay in bed and sleep felt elusive, because he was trying not to think about Aidan, just one room over, he watched film of past Thunder games. He didn't have Coach Ned's twenty-plus years of coaching experience, but he felt reasonably sure that Ross could move to the right without too much trouble.

The next most obvious question was could Levi move to the left without much trouble? It was a lot more high-pressure spot on the line. Arguably the *most* important spot, though Levi thought Griff might argue that the center was more vital, considering he was responsible for the ball.

He'd tried to talk himself out of it, half a dozen times now. He was getting paid the big bucks, now. He didn't *have* to put his neck out there, especially on a brand-new team. He could just keep playing under the radar, making the coaches happy with *his* performance. He didn't need to make these waves. But why else had he come to Toronto if it wasn't to take the next step?

If it *wasn't* to stick his neck out? To make himself *the guy*.

The game ended, a 38-to-10 win for the Thunder, even though the score really didn't matter. Wes had played well, and Levi patted him on the shoulders, telling him so, in the locker room after the game.

Then he went to look for Ned.

"Put me in at left," he said again, once he'd found his coach in the equipment room, helping some of the staff pack up to head back to Toronto.

Ned looked up at him. He was sixty if he was a day, with these dark eyes that pinned you right in your place. Maybe if Levi was less sure, he might be intimidated by the guy, but he wasn't.

There wasn't any room inside him for intimidation, not if he was going to get this done. Not if he was going to get himself his first ring.

Not if he was going to get Aidan another one.

"You again," Ned said with resignation. "This week didn't cure you of this crazy idea, did it?"

Levi shook his head. "I can do it."

Ned raised an eyebrow. "Seem pretty sure about that. Left tackle's no walk in the park."

"I can do it," Levi repeated.

Ned didn't look convinced. It made Levi really want to get it done. To prove to him and to Aidan and to *himself* that he didn't just skate by in his life and his career, doing the bare minimum. Being the spoiled and indulged and adored youngest. The one that nobody ever pushed, because Levi had always just been enough.

He'd never questioned if that was true, not until now.

He could hear Logan in his ear, telling him not to push the issue. To take the spot he was given.

But Logan was just as protective as Landry, both of them being two big brothers. Then he heard Lyla, in his other ear, telling him how proud she was that he'd fought for something more, when he'd decided not to re-sign with Seattle.

This was like that. Bigger, almost.

Of course, if it didn't work out, if he sucked at left tackle, he'd go back to the right side, but coaches would remember.

His reputation wouldn't be as unblemished as it was right now. Especially since one of his signing points—giving him those extra dollars—had been because of his possible flexibility.

"Just try it," Levi continued. "Give me one practice to show you. You want to try those two tight end formations with Lane and Trev? You *know* those are gonna win games. If we don't fix the left tackle, we'll never be able to run those plays effectively."

Ned sighed. Shoved a hand through his hair. Put his hat back on. "You really are a Banks through and through, aren't you?"

Levi wasn't sure before this watershed moment if he'd have agreed with that. He was a Banks, sure, and had the work ethic and the drive and the sheer size.

But he hadn't seen the same things in himself that he always saw in his brothers.

Maybe he could see a little glimmer of it now.

"Guess so, Coach," Levi said.

Ned gave him a reassuring pat on the shoulder. "We'll try it out. But—let me tell Acker. He's not gonna take it well, especially after getting lit up this week."

Levi nodded in agreement. It never felt good to be benched, but after you already knew you played like crap? It cut you when you were already down.

"Rest up, Banks. We'll be back at it in two days."

"For sure, Coach."

It wasn't a guarantee, or quite as good as Levi had promised Aidan, but it was an opening. And all Levi needed was the opening.

He found Aidan in the locker room, lounging against the wall next to Wes. They were discussing the game.

"Hey," he said, as Aidan glanced over, "that thing we talked about? It's happening. Next week."

"Seriously?" Aidan said. "You just asked and Coach was like, sure! We'll let you decide the offensive line formation?"

"Shhh," Levi said, glancing around. But Ross was already gone. Probably licking his wounds in the training room or the shower. "Ned wants to tell Ross himself."

"I can't believe you just told him and he said okay," Aidan said, disbelieving tone out in full force.

"He said he'd let me *try* it, and frankly, after today he was already thinking he might, but I can't imagine me taking the initiative hurt."

Aidan rolled his eyes, but the corner of his mouth was lifting into a smile. Like he just couldn't help it.

Levi couldn't help how much he loved it.

"Hey, you said you'd make it happen, and you did."

"Manifested that shit," Levi teased.

"Anybody gonna tell me what's going on, or are you two just going to stand there and flirt about it?" Wes asked.

Levi watched as Aidan froze and then forced himself to relax. On the other hand, it was hard to be bothered when he pretty much owned up to it. He was flirting with Aidan, no question.

"Levi's getting himself moved to left tackle," Aidan said under his breath, just loud enough for Wes to hear.

Wes nodded. "About fucking time," he said.

"Yeah, I can't run for my life the way you can," Aidan pointed out dryly. "So you can imagine how I feel about it."

"Good work, man," Wes said, clapping Levi on the shoulder, tugging him into a quick bro-hug.

"Hey, don't get too excited about it. Maybe he'll suck worse than Acker," Aidan said, but he was still smiling, like he couldn't stop.

"Bullshit," Levi said, smiling right back. "I *promised*."

"Yeah, if that was all it took," Aidan retorted, but Levi could see he didn't mean it.

He'd known that it would feel some kind of way to stick his neck out for himself, but he hadn't known that it would feel *this* kind of way when it came to Aidan.

And as much as he kind of hated that he'd set the terms of the sex pact a year out, it occurred to Levi that maybe it was better this way. Maybe he needed some distance. If Aidan landed in his bed right now, it might not stay a friends-with-bennies situation for Levi. He just *liked* the guy.

Yes, some distance would be a good thing.

"You gonna tell me what's going on with you and Banks?" Dawson asked, tone blunt, as they waited in Aidan's favorite sushi restaurant for their rolls to arrive.

Aidan choked on a bite of his seaweed salad. "What?"

"What's going on between you and Banks?" Dawson asked again, leaning forward and setting his elbows on the table. "You forget I know you."

"*Knew* me," Aidan corrected, but Dawson brushed the reminder off.

"Don't be stupid," Dawson said. "You haven't changed that much. Really at all. You pretend to be chill, but we all know you're not. It's not even a surface-level fake-out, dude."

"Ouch," Aidan said.

"It's not a bad thing. You're an intense guy. Driven. Successful. Why should you hide it?"

God, so many reasons.

Because it drove everyone away, eventually? Because he'd constructed this vision of himself when he was too young to know any better—when it had felt like the only way he could get through the shit hand he and Riley had been dealt—and he'd only realized later that this version of himself pushed everyone he cared about away?

He was fucking lucky Riley was still willing to have him in his life, after he'd almost epically fucked *that* relationship up. The fact that they were still close was probably due more to Landry's loyalty than any forgiveness tour Aidan could perform.

"Why do you think something's going on with Levi?" Aidan asked, changing the subject. It wasn't necessarily better, but it was different, and right now that felt better than explaining that sometimes when you fucked up, it was too late to really fix it.

"He flirts with you, pretty much nonstop, and you actually seem to like it. You don't even brush it off, not like I've seen you do to legions of, well, pretty much everyone else over the years."

It was hard to explain that without telling Dawson everything. And Aidan wasn't sure he was ready to say Mo's name out loud, yet. He thought he might be, but what if he wasn't? What if he broke down in the middle of one of his favorite lunch spots and he could never come here again?

"Levi's a fun guy. Fun to have around. Is he flirting?"

Dawson rolled his eyes at Aidan's fake obliviousness. "Dude. You know he's flirting with you. You even welcome it. And—" Dawson paused now for dramatic effect. "And you even fucking like it."

"How do you know that?" It was bad enough to be really seen by Levi; he didn't know if he wanted to be witnessed by Dawson too.

"Because you flirt back." Dawson tossed it out like his final argument-winning volley. "And I didn't even know you *could* flirt."

"Wow," Aidan said flatly.

"I'm just saying. You've always been above it. But you look at Levi, and it's like you're suddenly not."

For a split second, Aidan wondered what he'd been like with Mo. If he'd been this obvious. If all their teammates had known, had watched him pathetically panting after his friend for ages and just never said. Maybe if they had, he'd have realized it sooner. But as it was, he'd never understood what that feeling was, not until Mo was gone and everything had suddenly been so terrible.

"I . . ." Aidan licked his lips. He still didn't know how much he should say. But maybe that meant he should tell Dawson everything. The whole goddamn pathetic story. "How long do you have?"

Dawson raised an eyebrow, slumping back in his chair. "I got all day, bro."

"Uh, so turns out I'm not straight."

Dawson didn't look surprised.

"Really? You can't tell me you knew that. *I* didn't know that," Aidan complained.

"Honestly, who's straight anymore?" Dawson asked.

"You're ridiculous."

"But probably right," Dawson argued. "Anyway. So you're what . . .bi?"

"Does a label matter?" If Dawson was going to be slightly dick-ish about Aidan's coming out, then Aidan could be slightly dick-ish back.

Dawson grinned. "No way. Course it doesn't. Anyway. So you figured that out. You wanna tell me how it happened?"

"Not really but I have a feeling you're not gonna let it go if I don't."

"It wasn't Levi, then," Dawson said thoughtfully.

"Nope. It was . . .well, an ex-teammate. I didn't even realize how I felt until he left, went to another team—"

"Oh, *oh*, are we guessing who it is?" Dawson interrupted. "I can totally get this one right."

Aidan leveled him with the most brutal look in his arsenal. "Really?"

"Totally Morris Jeffries. I can't even blame you for that one. He's hot as fuck."

It was weird, hearing Mo's name come from Dawson's mouth. It didn't hurt as bad as Aidan had expected. The gaping hole inside him didn't feel quite so bottomless these days. Like it'd finally begun to fill in, and it wasn't just endless pain but the manageable ache of a bruise when you pressed on it. Still a wound, but a healing one.

"Yeah, well, it didn't change anything," Aidan said. He sounded more resigned than bitter these days, and it was hard not to take that as a win.

Dawson's mouth fell open. "Not really? *Really*? He turned *you* down?"

Aidan decided Dawson's shock was flattering. "Yes."

"Wow, dude. I'm sorry."

"Me too," Aidan said. He was, even if he could safely say he wasn't as sorry as he might've been, once. Eventually, he did think he and Mo could be friends again—*just* friends, this time around, without any unrequited feelings getting in the way.

"Huh. So where does this leave the Levi thing?"

"Funny that." Aidan sighed. "He figured it out. Or convinced me to tell him. I'm still not sure. There was a lot of whiskey involved."

"'Course there was," Dawson said, chuckling.

"And somehow in the middle of that, he uh . . .promised me. Or I promised him?" Aidan paused, hesitating. Saying it out loud made the whole thing sound more ridiculous than he'd anticipated.

"What did you promise him? Don't leave me hanging, bro," Dawson complained.

"I wanted . . .I wanted some practical experience with a guy. And he promised me that if I was still single in a year, he'd do it."

Dawson's jaw dropped. More than when Aidan had admitted that his feelings for Mo hadn't been returned.

"You made a sex pact?"

Aidan crinkled his nose. "Would you call it that?" *Bro,* he could imagine Levi saying, *you'd absolutely fucking call it that.*

Dawson shot him a look that echoed Levi's voice in his head. "Uh, yeah, I absolutely fucking would. So you made a sex pact with Levi Banks. Huh. Interesting. I can see that."

Aidan didn't immediately demand to know why that was. Or if they were *that* obvious. He wasn't sure he could deal with the truth.

"Not for *right now*. It's for a *year* from now," Aidan stressed.

"You sure he got that memo?" Dawson asked.

There it was. The question that haunted him at night. During the day. Every spare moment when he wasn't at practice or watching film or breaking down plays, he was wondering when and if Levi would bring it up again.

"The year from now was *his* idea," Aidan said.

"Really?"

"He was all about it. Said that . . .uh . . .he didn't want me thinking about someone else if I ended up in his bed."

"That's fair. But . . .dude, I have to ask. *Would* you?" Dawson paused. "From where I'm sitting, yeah, you're still getting over Mo, but I look at you two, at the way you flirt *back* with him, and I wonder."

"Uh." Aidan didn't know how he felt discussing this. Even with Dawson, who he'd known for a long time. The only other people he could imagine doing it with would be Riley and Landry—and they were *obviously* off-limits in this particular situation.

"You can tell me," Dawson said persuasively. "Though maybe the one you should be telling is Levi."

"He just acts like that," Aidan said uselessly. Maybe it was better he couldn't talk about this with Riley or Landry, because he was crappy at even identifying his feelings. And talking about them? Nearly impossible.

"Does he?"

"Well, *yeah*," Aidan said. "You see him."

"Maybe with you, sure. Not with anyone else. You see him the other night? He didn't even try to flirt with that Ramsey guy, who was hot as hell. It's just you."

Aidan finally broke down and said the thing out loud that he'd been thinking for over two weeks now. "I just keep expecting him to *say* it. Like bring it up. Even just refer to it. Like casually. But he *doesn't*."

"Hmmmm. But he *did* say a year, and *you* haven't brought it up, either, I'm assuming."

Aidan huffed. "No. Of course not. When we agreed—he was still in Seattle. I didn't expect him to come here. I don't think *he* expected to come here."

"Okay, so he showed up in your vicinity early but . . .I don't get it. Just say something." Dawson grinned. "Or are you allergic to making the first move?"

"Hell no. *I* kissed *him* in Michigan," Aidan retorted and then realized a moment after he'd said it that he hadn't meant to divulge that much info.

"Oh, *oh,* now we're getting to the good stuff," Dawson said, rubbing his hands together.

"It was just . . .it didn't mean anything."

Dawson didn't look convinced. *Aidan* wasn't convinced.

"Sure it didn't, Flynn."

Aidan sighed. "I invited you to lunch to talk about *you*," he said. "Your whole situation. I thought you might want to unload, and instead we're gossiping like teenage girls about the guy I kissed."

"Uh, *yeah*. So much more fun to gossip like teenage girls than to break down my hellhole of a life," Dawson said. "I'd rather talk about you, ten times out of ten."

Except Aidan didn't want to talk about Levi. It made everything a shade too real, and he couldn't help but worry that Dawson might talk him into doing something drastic he wasn't ready for.

"Well, that's all there is to say. We kissed."

"When?"

Aidan rolled his eyes. "You want me to break the whole thing down?"

"Well, now that you offer it so nicely, *yes*." Dawson looked delighted. "Give me a whole timeline. Draw a fucking diagram."

"It was the morning after we uh . . .agreed to the—"

"Sex pact. The morning after you agreed to the sex pact," Dawson interrupted. When Aidan glared, he just shrugged. "You were *not* gonna say it. Call it what it is, at least."

"Okay, fine. Yes. The morning after the sex pact."

"And what else?"

"Nothing. My brother and his boyfriend—you remember Landry, I assume—were there. And they didn't interrupt but it was um . . .close. And after, I wanted to talk to him about it. I was *going* to talk to him about it."

"The kiss was so good you were gonna invite him to your bed early." Aidan glared again. But Dawson was undeterred. "Dude, it's obvious. It's written all over your face. You totally were."

"Maybe," Aidan said. He'd thought about it, for sure. Hard not to.

"So what happened?"

"He left. He had to go, like all of a sudden, for his contract situation. One minute we're texting about him waking me up in my bed and the next thing I know, he's signing a contract with the Thunder and coming to Toronto. *Living in my house*."

Dawson nodded sagely. "Now I get why you wanted me there when he showed up."

"I . . .God, was it *that* obvious?" Aidan winced.

"Only because I know you," Dawson said reassuringly. "But the vibes that day were . . .not *weird*, not even close to that, but definitely off from what I expected, coming in."

"I bet." He'd been an unexpected nervous wreck. Still wondering how they'd gone from texting with definite sexual intent to not just becoming teammates, but roommates too.

"Aidan, you gotta say something to him."

"No way," Aidan scoffed. "No fucking way."

"He's waiting for you to make a move, again," Dawson said persuasively.

"If he is, he's going to be waiting a whole goddamn year," Aidan said even though the thought of that sounded like sheer fucking torture.

"I'm just gonna say this once. You know what this last year has taught me?" Dawson said, suddenly looking very serious.

"Don't trust your father-in-law with your bank account?"

Dawson kicked him under the table, gently but with definite intent. Aidan shrugged, because okay, yes, he'd probably deserved that.

"I mean, yeah, that too, for sure. But also, that life is short. Happiness doesn't last forever. You gotta take what you can get, while you can get it. Clearly Levi makes you happy. He makes you forget, even for a minute, that you're Aidan fucking Flynn. And that's a blessing."

"Is it?" Aidan questioned, even though he *knew* it was. Just like he knew that if he'd actually been able to talk to Riley or Landry about this, they'd be saying the same thing.

"Don't bullshit me. You know it is."

"I just . . . I don't know how much I want to put myself out there again. We said a year. I don't want to make him uncomfortable by pushing him for it sooner. Maybe he's got other stuff going on . . ." Aidan trailed off as Dawson shot him a frank look.

"Maybe he does. Maybe he doesn't. But you'll never know if you don't ask."

"I could just wait the year. Meet up with him in the offseason, in Michigan. That'd be a hell of a lot simpler. Keep him in sort of that box, you know? It complicated everything when he came here."

"You don't want to do that, though," Dawson guessed correctly. *Annoyingly.*

He didn't. It would have been easier, and absolutely simpler, if Levi had stayed in the Michigan box. If he'd never come to Toronto. Aidan could have waited the year, no question, and if it had still felt right, hooked up with him mid-summer. Where there were no consequences and no additional connections.

But that wasn't how things had turned out.

"I'll think about it," Aidan said. Because it was true; he was already having difficulty thinking of anything else. Only football distracted him these days, and not even that. Not that well.

"I guess that's probably the best I'm gonna get," Dawson said.

"You know it is."

Dawson let out a heavy sigh. "You're a piece of work, dude."

Aidan knew it. He'd been knowing it for thirty-three years now. Even if he wanted to, he couldn't forget it.

"Does that mean I'm allowed to ask about you now?" Aidan asked.

"Seriously?" Dawson barked out a laugh.

"We talked about *me*," Aidan said. And he hadn't even wanted to.

"Oh look," Dawson said, gesturing towards the waiter who was coming towards them, arms full of plates. "Our sushi's here."

Aidan was nice. He let Dawson get half a roll in before he circled back around.

"We really *should* talk about it," Aidan said reproachfully. "I'm here to listen. Anything you want to say."

Dawson glanced up. "Oh yeah? You wanna hear how much it sucks to find out your wife cheated on you and then, when you go to get divorced, your lawyer figures out that your father-in-law's been siphoning money out of your investment accounts for years? And *then*, if that wasn't the worst fucking set of events you could imagine, it fucks you up so bad mentally, so you can't even do the one thing you're good at and you get fired?"

"Uh."

"Exactly," Dawson said. "It fucking sucks and there's not much else to say about it."

"You don't want to rant about it? I'm happy to listen if you do."

"Did you want to rant about it when you realized you were in love with Mo and he didn't love you back?"

Aidan wanted to be annoyed that Dawson had brought that up, *again*. It wasn't like he enjoyed thinking about it. But then he really listened—repeated back in his mind what Dawson had just said—and realized that no, he hadn't wanted to talk about it. He'd railed at fate plenty, sure, but he'd done it alone, after everyone had left the lake house.

A lot of nights out on the patio, in front of the fire, staring at the flames, moodily sending so many *fuck you*'s to the universe.

"Not really," Aidan admitted.

"There you go," Dawson said. "Now eat your sushi and let's talk about something else. *Anything* else."

"How's Cam handling things?"

Dawson groaned under his breath. "He's too damn cute. All naive and shit. So fucking young. Were we ever that young?"

Dawson might've been, but Aidan hadn't been. He'd never had that privilege.

"Do I need to give *you* a shovel talk?" Aidan asked, raising an eyebrow. He hadn't expected Dawson to say Cameron was "too damn cute." He hadn't noticed any non-platonic vibes between them, but then he hadn't been paying that much attention, either. He'd been too wrapped up in football and Levi.

"Nah. He's just . . ." Dawson sighed, pushed his empty plate away. "He's a cool kid."

"I gotta warn you about using that nickname, unless you wanna get your ass kicked on the regular," Aidan said.

"How so?"

"I used to call Riley that, and it absolutely came back to bite me in the ass. How many times have the Thunder beat the Condors in the last three years? *Zero*, that's how many. It's embarrassing. And every time it happens, and we meet mid-field to shake hands after, he gives me this look and calls *me* kid."

"Ouch," Dawson said, wincing.

"What I'm saying is that we better fucking win this year," Aidan said. "*And* don't call Cam that unless you want to live to regret it."

"Probably better if I don't, anyway." Dawson looked like he was hesitating, and a warning bell pinged at the back of Aidan's brain. "Might be creepy. Riley's your younger brother but Cam's not my bro. He's my . . .my . . .*you know.*"

Aidan shot him a warning look. "Your *rookie*?"

"Exactly."

It occurred to Aidan then, as they finished up their lunch, that he needed to be paying a little closer attention to what was going on with the team. He wasn't the special teams captain—that was actually, ironically, Dawson—but he was the de facto leader on the team. And if this shit was going on under his radar, that could be a problem. Cam *was* young, and definitely on the naive side, and Dawson was not. While he was licking his wounds, some hero worship and blown-out-of-proportion admiration might look real good to him.

Aidan wouldn't begrudge him the distraction, but the fallout could be ugly.

The Levi thing *had* distracted him. He needed to either decide, once and for all, to let things play out next summer, the way he and Levi had originally agreed to, or *do* something about the sexual tension simmering between them.

CHAPTER 10

LEVI WAS EXPECTING FOR Ross to make some kind of comment to him on Monday morning when they showed up for practice.

If he was being honest, he was dreading it. He'd talked to Logan *and* Landry about it over the weekend, and they'd both reassured him he was doing the right thing. That even if Ross was pissed, it was *still* the right thing to do.

He and Aidan hadn't talked about the switch more, but he'd sensed Aidan's gaze heavy on him more than once, as they'd been driving into the practice facility, in the locker room, and even now, with the offensive linemen gathered on the opposite side of the field from the skill players.

But so far Ross had been silent—sullen, more like—but that was better than dealing with any unnecessary bullshit or passive-aggressive comments.

"We're gonna make a change," Coach announced to their group. "Gonna try Banks out at left tackle. Acker—you're gonna move to right."

It was clear from the annoyed resignation on Ross' face that Ned *had* told him ahead of time, at least, but he still didn't look happy about it.

"Sure thing, Coach. Sounds good," Griff said, clearly trying to smooth things over. He gave Ned a solid nod and then shot Levi a reassuring smile.

Still, despite Griff's clear support, Levi found he was nervous as they got lined up for the first set of plays.

He could sense Aidan behind him, a distinct presence in the pocket. When he raised his gaze, he met the eyes of the defensive guys in front of the line. They weren't playing first team on first team—which Levi was profoundly grateful for, at least for this first attempt—so the defensive players didn't necessarily have starter skills, but they were hungrier to prove themselves.

Ned blew the whistle, Griff yelled out the snap count and Levi had a single breathless moment to brace himself before the defensive tackle was pushing into his space, pulling a tricky spin move that Levi knew he'd been working on in practice.

Levi knew how to deal with something like that, he *did*. Had been dealing with it for years, because in the National Football League, you couldn't just block and call it good.

But he'd been unprepared for it and his weight was shifted wrong. It took him a second to adjust, and that single second was all it took for the defensive end to get the upper hand, pushing him back with a sudden burst of strength and speed.

Levi retrenched, painfully aware that the pair of them had probably pushed deep into Aidan's pocket of space. At any moment, he might collide with his quarterback before he could throw the ball, and that wasn't *worse* than a sack, but it sure wasn't good either.

Breathing hard, Levi mustered a last burst of strength and tried to muscle the guy off to the side, more out of the way, but he was three-fifty if he was a pound, and had the upper hand.

Levi managed to get him only half as far as he'd hoped.

The whistle blew.

"Shit." Levi exhaled sharply as he finally looked up from his play to downfield. The play had been a double tight end pattern, Trevor running short and Lane running deep.

The hope was that Aidan could hit Lane, but Trevor was there as a backup option—hopefully at least a first down, but probably not much more than a ten-yard gain.

Trevor was holding the ball as he jogged back to the huddle.

Levi looked over at Aidan, who just shrugged. "I had to get rid of it faster than I wanted," he said.

He gave Aidan credit for honesty. They weren't making this switch for shits and giggles. Everyone needed to be better, to give Aidan the time he needed.

Including Levi.

As they gathered together for feedback, Ross looked right over at him, his lip curled in a sneer beneath his helmet's grill. "Harder than you thought, huh, Banks," he muttered under his breath.

Levi didn't smile as much as he bared his teeth. "No, just about as hard as I expected," he retorted.

Ned shot him a look, obviously telling him to cool it. He was probably right; they didn't need a brawl breaking out in practice. Levi was going to need all his energy and focus to deal with this positional change. He couldn't—*shouldn't*—waste it on Ross.

"Better—but we need to give Flynn another five seconds," Ned said. "Let's run it again."

And then they did. Over and over. Until Levi's legs and arms were burning with exhaustion, but he pushed himself hard and then harder.

By the time practice ended, he couldn't say it had gone *bad*, but he also didn't want to give himself a gold star he hadn't earned.

He *would* earn it, no question about it, but he hadn't earned it today.

Ned patted him on the shoulder as they headed into the locker room. "Not good yet," he said thoughtfully.

"No," Levi agreed, even though he was afraid that would be the end of the experiment. The coaching staff knew what they had in Ross Acker. He was a proven entity at left tackle, which was one of the most impor-tant pieces on the field. Levi was still getting up to speed. It had been years since he'd played left. He'd *never* played it consistently. It wasn't that much different, but there were enough nuances that it took some getting used to.

"You're gonna get there," Ned said optimistically.

"You're not pulling me?"

Ned shook his head. "There's something there. You've got the chops, kid. Just need more reps. More experience."

"Isn't that what Acker's gonna tell you?" Levi wondered.

"He already tried," Ned said. "Argued with me for an hour when I told him we were gonna try this out. He's not happy."

"Yeah," Levi said. That much had been obvious.

"But he's good on the right. Not as good as you, obviously, but Aidan's not left-handed, so it's kind of a moot point."

If Aidan *had* been left-handed, then Levi playing right tackle would've covered his blind side. But Aidan wasn't left-handed, and so he needed a dynamite left tackle.

Levi nodded.

"Don't let it get you down. It was a decent first practice," Ned said, clapping him on the back, despite his sweaty pads. "And don't let him pull you into any posturing bullshit, okay?"

"Sure, Coach," Levi said.

He'd been planning on ignoring Ross' comments anyway, but it gave him a little bit of extra motivation to do it as Ross sat two lockers down from him and kept muttering insults under his breath.

They weren't surprising or honestly very creative. Levi had heard way worse.

Griff stopped in front of him as he was finishing getting dressed after his shower.

"Great effort today," Griff said.

"Thanks, dude," Levi said.

"Don't listen to him, okay? He's just pissed. He'll get over it."

Levi rolled his eyes. "Even if I thought he was right, I wouldn't listen to him."

Griff nodded. "You're gonna get there."

Levi hadn't needed the reminder that he wasn't there yet, but at least Griff had been nice about it.

When he finally climbed into Aidan's car at the end of the day, dusk rolling over the city, Aidan apparently wasn't going to be the same.

He was quiet for a long time after they pulled out of the parking lot. "You should tell Ned you changed your mind," he said, when they were more than halfway home.

Levi wished he was surprised. But of course, Aidan had zero fucking patience for the time it would take for him to get up to speed. He wanted to be pissed off. Offended, even, that Aidan had no faith in him. It didn't feel great, that was for sure.

"No way," Levi said. "I know today wasn't as good as it needs to be, but, dude, you're kind of being a dick."

Aidan's hands clenched white around the steering wheel.

"I'm not, I'm being realistic. You are *lock down* at right tackle. And Acker will get better. It makes the most sense to go back to what we did before."

"He's not getting any better, and I *know* this is gonna work." Levi frowned.

Aidan didn't say anything.

"I really took you for someone who doesn't just try something for a day and then give up 'cause it's too hard," Levi continued, because now he *was* a little pissed. Had he read all this wrong? Was Aidan actually the unrelenting perfectionist that the world had made him out to be for all these years? He'd seen something more, lurking under the surface, and assumed he was right about what that something more was. But what if he'd actually been wrong?

"That's not—" Aidan broke off. "I'm not *giving up* because it was too hard. We tried it."

"For one fucking practice!"

"Yeah, well, one was enough. I . . .you're *new* to this team, Levi. You don't have the automatic goodwill you had in Seattle. There aren't unlimited fuckups available to you."

Levi's jaw dropped. He couldn't believe this.

"I'm trying to keep you upright, you idiot." Levi couldn't believe this needed saying. "I don't need your protection, but the opposite is sure as fuck true. It's why I'm here. That's my *job*."

Aidan had known when he got into the car what he needed to say to Levi, and even though he'd been dreading it, because he knew how it would sound, he'd felt like he needed to do it anyway.

He was in meetings that Levi wasn't in. Meetings with Zane and Robertson, their head coach. Meetings where everyone was bluntly honest about how the line and the whole offense was coming together and clicking. Nobody bothered to sugarcoat things for Aidan anymore. He wouldn't have wanted them to.

But no matter what Aidan said to defend Levi, Zane wasn't happy about Levi demanding the switch. He wasn't happy with Ned for giving in to it either. Even if it was only on a trial basis.

Aidan knew how shitty life could get if your coach didn't have any faith in you. It hadn't happened in the NFL, but for a year at Michigan, there'd been a coordinator who'd wanted his handpicked QB to be the starter, and he'd done everything he could to topple Aidan from his spot.

He hadn't won then, but Aidan wasn't stupid enough to think that if Zane wanted Levi gone, he wouldn't eventually be gone.

"I don't need your protection, but the opposite is sure as fuck true. It's why I'm here. That's my *job*," Levi said, sounding wounded and offended.

He didn't even know it, but he did need Aidan's protection, no matter how good his contract had been. No matter how aggressively the Thunder had pursued him during this summer, all it took was getting on the wrong person's bad side, and suddenly, Levi would be traded before the deadline.

Lots of teams would salivate over getting a lock down tackle.

Right *or* left.

"Levi," Aidan warned. He didn't want to tell him about what he'd heard.

Maybe if Levi had over-performed expectations, Zane would've shut up and dealt with it. But Levi hadn't. He'd done well—but basically exactly as expected, playing the way anyone would if they were being switched to a slightly different position.

"I don't get why you're being a dick about this," Levi complained. "I'm not gonna just roll up tomorrow and tell Coach, sorry, that was just too tough for me. I'm a *Banks*. We don't do that shit. Neither do Flynns. You should understand, better than anyone else."

Aidan understood all too well. But he also understood that this year, which might've been hellish for him, yet another without Mo on the field with him, and now, not even in his inbox or over the phone, had been better than he'd ever imagined, because of the guy next to him.

And he wasn't going to let that guy go without a fight.

"I do understand that, but you gotta trust me here," Aidan argued.

"I do but, bro, I am literally on the field to protect you. That's my whole job, my whole existence."

Aidan made a face as he pulled into his parking spot in the garage. "I can see we can't be reasonable about this."

"I'm not the one being unreasonable," Levi continued as they got out of the car, pulled their bags from the trunk. "You're being ridiculous."

Aidan wanted to yell at him that he wasn't disposable. He couldn't just use himself up and then be okay with being tossed away. *Aidan* wasn't okay with that.

"Not the first time I've heard that," Aidan muttered. Riley had said it to him plenty, but back then he'd deserved it. He wasn't being overprotective of Levi. He was just plain fucking protecting this good thing he'd *just* gotten.

God, two months ago, he'd never have even imagined he'd be in the trenches, fighting for Levi Banks, but here he was, and he wasn't going to stop, not anytime soon.

"Maybe sometime you'll actually listen," Levi retorted. They stepped into the elevator, and he crossed his arms over his chest.

Aidan's temper flared. "*Me* not listening! I'm fucking telling you . . .you know what? Never fucking mind. Just ask yourself if Toronto feels like Seattle. The shit you pulled on the regular in Seattle isn't going to fly here."

Zane was good, but he was tough and liked having things just the way he wanted them.

Levi elbowed him as they stepped off the elevator onto their floor. "Are you fucking joking? I wouldn't have *ever* pulled this shit in Seattle." He dropped his bag on the floor just inside the living room. Aidan wanted to complain that wasn't the right place for his shit, but Levi was still going and didn't seem like he was going to stop anytime soon. "It wouldn't have ever even occurred to me to say anything. I'd just have showed up, every single fucking day, and done the job I was given. But here—but *you*—it's different."

Levi looked at him then, and something in his face reminded Aidan of that morning in his Michigan kitchen. A wanting he'd kept trying to find there and hadn't ever seen since then.

"What do you mean?" Aidan asked, licking his suddenly very dry lips. He should go into the kitchen, find some water. He was probably dehydrated. But he was rooted to this spot on the floor. Staring at Levi like he was about to hear all about the shape of the missing puzzle piece.

But Levi just rolled his eyes. "You know what I fucking mean, bro."

Aidan really didn't. He wouldn't have asked otherwise. He never asked questions he didn't already know the answer to. And he really didn't know the answer to this one.

Anger flared to life inside him. Hot and molten, lurching through him in waves, in a way that he never got pissed off anymore. Because he never let it. He certainly never let it overtake him, not like this. But it was doing it now, places inside him flaring to life, and his hand shook as he ran it through his hair.

He wanted to push Levi. He wanted Levi to tell him the fucking truth, for once.

He wanted him to stop flirting so meaninglessly and flirt with *purpose*. With *him*.

"You can't be this dense," Levi said again.

Oh, he wasn't dense. But Levi hadn't ever *said*. He'd just shown up here in Toronto with his easy smiles and teasing little asides and ridiculous short shorts and *what*? Expected Aidan to understand?

Well, Aidan didn't fucking understand.

One second they were standing apart and the next Aidan's temper, already boiling, snapped. He pushed Levi right up against the entryway wall, the way he'd been thinking about, the way he'd never expected to actually *do*, and Levi, built like a tank, just *went*.

Gazing at Aidan the whole time like Aidan should've been in on the joke the whole fucking time.

Newsflash, he *hadn't* been.

If he had been . . .*well*, Aidan couldn't say that he'd have ended up in Levi's bed or vice versa much sooner, but who was he kidding? It would've happened.

One word from Levi, and he'd have been there, panting and eager.

"Bro," Levi said, voice breathless now.

"God, you keep fucking *saying* that," Aidan bit off. "I'm not your *bro*. I'm not related to you at all. I don't *want* for you to be related to me. I want—"

He couldn't finish.

He *needed* to finish.

"You should've said," Aidan said finally. He swallowed hard. His hands were still pinning Levi's shoulders to the wall, but Levi had never looked less bothered in his life. In fact he looked like, well, he looked like he was waiting for Aidan to close the last few inches between them and kiss him.

But Aidan wasn't fucking doing that. Not before he understood what the hell was going on.

"*I* did say," Levi said.

"No, you came here, and you didn't say anything. Like no big deal that we . . .that we . . ." Aidan swallowed hard again. He couldn't seem to get a breath, and his mouth was *so* dry. He should've detoured into the kitchen for water. But it was too late for that now.

It was too late for everything now.

"And here you're getting mad at me for not saying it," Levi teased softly, fondness radiating out from his expression.

"I can say it," Aidan argued. But that was the biggest problem, wasn't it? He wanted it so bad, but the words weren't enough anymore. He had to just *do* it.

Levi raised an eyebrow. "Can you though?"

Aidan kind of hated him. But that didn't change anything either. He still craved Levi so much it physically hurt to not just lean in and take exactly what he wanted.

"We kissed," Aidan said, tongue too big for his mouth. "We kissed, in Michigan."

"Yeah, we did," Levi said, nodding.

But Aidan knew he wasn't done. Levi had said he couldn't do it, but he *could*. He could force the words out from between his uncooperative lips, even though the whole stupid exercise had started because *Levi* wouldn't say it.

He could make Levi do it. He *could*. But he wouldn't.

"And, we promised we'd . . ." God, his throat was *so* fucking dry. "We'd have sex. You'd have sex with me. Um. Yeah. We would. In a year."

"It hasn't been a year." Levi's tone was gentle but pointed.

"No, no of course not." God, he hadn't lasted even two months. Embarrassment curled through his stomach. Scorching. Dizzying.

Humiliation that he was this into it—into *Levi*—shouldn't be this hot.

He curled his fingers into Levi's shoulders. He was so big, so solid. Aidan could push him over and over, and he'd never budge.

"I didn't say it because you didn't seem like you wanted me to," Levi said. "I thought maybe . . . maybe I pushed you too hard, in Michigan."

Aidan laughed, even though it wasn't funny. Nothing about this was funny. He was going out of his fucking mind. Would he have been this unhinged if he and Mo had actually ever gotten to this point? It felt impossible. Nothing could feel bigger.

"I thought I made it pretty clear you didn't," Aidan said, when it felt like he could speak again.

Levi still hadn't pushed him away. Still looked like he wanted to do the opposite—pull him close.

So why didn't he?

"I wanted . . . I wanted you to say something. I was afraid you would, and I still wanted it so fucking bad," Aidan murmured finally. "I thought you didn't—"

"Stupid," Levi said, smiling now. That was all the warning Aidan got before Levi wrapped an arm around his waist and pulled him flush against him, and a second later, they were kissing.

For a second, Aidan wasn't sure who'd kissed who first, like that was actually a question that needed answering. But then Levi tilted his head, and he was *God*, a really great kisser, better than anyone Aidan had ever kissed, and the question evaporated like smoke.

Turned out it didn't matter who'd moved first.

It only mattered that Levi wanted it, and there was no question that Aidan wanted it just as much. Maybe more.

Aidan heard a groan, and a second later, realized it was him.

Not so much a *maybe*, then.

But before Aidan could get too far into his own head about *that* realization, Levi tensed and a second later it was Aidan against the wall, Levi's strength moving him so effortlessly he'd barely seen it coming even as it was happening.

He groaned louder then, Levi's mouth slipping to his neck, to his jaw.

"God, so fucking hot," Levi murmured into his skin.

And yes, some people thought so. He knew that was true. But Aidan had never looked in a mirror and seen what they saw. What *did* Levi see when he looked at him? When he touched him?

Levi tilted his head and kissed Aidan harder, deeper, tongue slipping into his mouth. It was a really fucking good kiss. Nothing like kissing a woman. Levi's mouth was firmer against his own, lips thinner, more insistent, much harder to deny. Even if Aidan had wanted that, and he didn't.

The scratch of Levi's stubble against his skin. The breadth and strength of his body. Aidan had never been pinned down in a sexual way before, and he hadn't thought he'd like it.

But it was lighting up a part inside him that he'd never imagined even existed before this moment.

Levi's hands slipped down from his shoulders, coasting down his sides, tucking into the waistband of his shorts, under the fabric of his T-shirt. Aidan gasped into his mouth. He hadn't even known someone just touching his skin could feel like that. But it *did* feel like that, when Levi touched him.

"Good?" Levi murmured against his mouth.

It was so fucking good, but Aidan wanted it to be even better. Aidan wanted it to be so insanely good it turned his brain off. Short-circuit it so epically he could stop *thinking*.

"More," Aidan demanded. Because it was too much to say all that. Levi didn't need to know it, anyway. Even with the way he felt now, coherency sluggish, he knew it would expose something that nobody had ever seen. Not Mo. Not Levi. *Not yet*, his brain whispered.

"You're sure?" Levi asked.

Aidan no longer trusted he could answer in words. But he aligned their hips, Levi gasping at the feeling of their hard cocks brushing together and Aidan swallowing the sound into his mouth.

It felt like, off the football field, he was barely soft around Levi anymore. He didn't just want it; he *needed* it. The promise from Michigan tangible in the space between them, so close to becoming actual reality that Aidan felt breathless with it.

But then Levi pulled back. "Aidan," he said, voice rough, "I gotta know."

Levi had always seemed so self-possessed. Back in Michigan and then when he'd showed up in Toronto. Easy and confident, flirting like it was second nature, never particularly bothered.

But he seemed bothered now—*hot* and bothered.

"What is it?" If Levi wanted them to stop now . . .Aidan would do it, but he'd be in his room in five seconds, hand on his cock, coming his brains out probably another five seconds after that.

He wasn't proud of it but that was just the blunt reality of the situation.

"Do you—are you . . ." Levi shook his own head like he was desperately trying to clear it. Aidan sympathized; there wasn't much blood—or thought—in his brain right now. "You're sure?" he asked for the second time in the last five minutes.

Aidan realized what he was really trying to ask.

If we do this, way earlier than we promised, are you gonna be thinking about me? Or is Mo the one on your mind?

Aidan reached up, framed Levi's face with his palms. His stubble was rough in the best way against his skin. He wanted to feel it all over. "It's . . .it's you, I promise."

He hoped it was enough. Words were never his strong suit, even on his best day, and right now, he was at a serious disadvantage. But hopefully Levi understood.

Levi grinned at him, wildly, and a second later, dropped to his knees right in Aidan's foyer, tugging at the waistband of his shorts.

"Yeah?" Levi asked, gazing up at Aidan. His pulse was rabbiting out of control, just at the way Levi looked like this.

Comfortable and easy and *hot*.

Aidan swallowed hard. "Yeah."

He'd had blowjobs before. You couldn't be a professional athlete and not have it offered ten times or a hundred times or even a thousand. It was a surefire way to never get a girl pregnant, and Aidan had heard guys say over the years, in too many locker rooms, how a good bj could be as good as fucking.

Aidan liked them for none of those reasons. They always felt less . . .close. A good way to get off that didn't require the kind of intimacy Aidan had never liked sharing.

But this blowjob felt radically more intimate than any other he'd ever gotten.

Levi's face pressed to his thigh, tongue tracing the muscle there as it tensed and then he forced it to relax.

His dick was hard and leaking and twitching, so turned on he had to curl his fingers into his palms, nails digging in, so he didn't reach down and drag Levi to where he wanted him most.

It was so tough to let Levi take his time and set his pace, but by the time Levi's tongue wrapped around him, the blood was pounding in his ears and his mind was only one long litany of *please, please please*.

He wasn't going to last. He'd wanted this too badly, and now that it was finally here, it was more overwhelming than he'd ever imagined.

Aidan wasn't a blowjob expert, but while Levi definitely seemed experienced, it wasn't like he was doing anything special. That didn't matter at all. Had never mattered less. Pleasure fizzed just under his skin, like bubbles popping, and the back of his head hit the wall.

Levi hummed in approval around his cock, and Aidan couldn't even help the noises that spilled out of his mouth.

It would be so easy to close his eyes. Let that fizzy pleasure envelop him.

But then he'd miss the fact that this felt different than every other sexual experience he'd ever had.

Because it was a guy, sure, that was part of it. But it was more than that, too. It was *Levi.*

And he never wanted to forget it was Levi.

Levi had worried, justifiably, if they ever ended up here—Aidan's cock in his mouth—he'd be thinking of Mo first and Levi second.

But there was no way Aidan wasn't thinking of him and *only* him.

Some guys closed their eyes. Wanted to lose themselves in the sensation. But Aidan didn't look away. Kept his gaze on Levi and his eyes open, barely blinking.

Like he never wanted Levi to think he wasn't one hundred percent aware of whose mouth was on his cock.

Aidan was big, more girth than length, a pleasant weight on Levi's tongue. The act had been a turn-on forever, ever since he'd done it the first time. But it had never felt like this before, urgency rolling through his blood as he sucked harder, deeper.

"Fuck," Aidan muttered under his breath, voice rough. "Fuck, that feels so fucking good."

Levi's knees ached. But his cock ached more. He was never particularly impatient to get his own, but he found he couldn't wait. Pressed a palm against himself, groaned harder around Aidan's cock.

He wasn't doing anything fancy yet, spit-slick mouth meeting his hand, wrapped around the base, building up a decent rhythm, but that didn't seem to matter. Aidan got noisier, surprise widening his eyes, like he'd never expected to like it so much. Or expected for any of those sounds to escape him.

If Levi had a brain cell to spare, he'd think it was probably both.

But between losing himself in the act and the hot wash of bliss as he ground against his hand, he wasn't thinking at all.

"You're so fucking hot like this," Aidan said, his voice sounding as fucked out as if he was the one giving the blowjob. "I can't stop looking. I wanted it so much."

Levi hadn't realized. He'd felt Aidan's eyes on him, sure, but his desire hadn't felt immediate or pressing. Except he'd been wrong. Aidan had buried it. Hid it. Wanted in silence.

But he wouldn't be able to any longer. Levi knew what to look for now.

Knew how to take him apart.

Aidan's hips stuttered and he groaned, low and insistent. "I want—"

"Yeah," Levi said, guttural, breaking off. "Come on." He pumped his hand and tried to hold off on his own orgasm so he could make sure Aidan got his.

Aidan cried out, and finally, his eyes did squeeze shut, like staring at Levi then was a step too far. Stripes of come fell across his tongue and Levi swallowed.

"Goddamn," Aidan ground out when he was done shaking apart.

Levi was barely hanging on to his self-control. Wanting more than anything else to shove his hand, wet with spit and come, into his own shorts so he could get himself off. But if he did, he'd be stealing that first time—that first orgasm Aidan ever gave a guy—from him.

There'd be plenty of other times. They were attracted enough to each other to know *that* was true. But there'd never be another first.

Aidan leaned over and tugged him to his feet. He'd probably need to ice his knees after this, between practice and Aidan's insanely hard floor, but it had been worth it.

"Fuck," Aidan murmured and then kissed him, tongue finding Levi's again, like he didn't care where his mouth had just been. Levi gave him props for that. He might be new to guy-on-guy action, but he wasn't shying away from it, either.

"I'm—" Levi didn't even get the sentence out, though he hadn't been entirely sure he knew how it ended.

I'm horny. I'm hot. I'm desperate for you.

Any of those would've worked.

But Aidan interrupted. "I got you," he said and, without hesitation, pulled Levi over to the living room. At first Levi wasn't sure why, and then he got it.

Aidan's thirty-three-year-old knees wanted the cushy rug there. Because even though Levi could barely believe it, he was sinking to the floor in front of him, pulling his shorts down.

Trailing his fingers up the hard length of his cock in his boxer briefs. Rubbing in the wet spot he'd formed on the front of them.

"I don't know what I'm doing," Aidan said in a low voice. Not apologizing, just stating the bare truth.

"Kinda figured," Levi teased. "I don't care what you do, just do something. I'm so—"

"I got you," Aidan said again.

And he did, pulling his underwear off and ducking his head down.

It was mostly a handjob, and a *good* handjob at that, Aidan's hesitancy disappearing with each stroke. But then he tipped his head down, tongue wrapping around the head, curious and exploratory, and Levi had to muffle his groan into his arm.

"I wanna hear you," Aidan ordered.

Really, he shouldn't be the one giving the orders right now, but of course, it was Aidan, so that he'd still try didn't come as a surprise.

"It's good, though?" Aidan asked when Levi gave a particularly throaty moan. He'd *said* he wanted to hear, and it felt damn good. Levi figured there was no point in holding back.

"Fuck yeah," Levi said and muttered another *fuck* under his breath as Aidan slipped more of him into his mouth. He wasn't small, but Aidan didn't seem intimidated. Instead, his confidence seemed to grow.

And it turned out that was incredibly sexy. Already riding the edge, Levi knew he wasn't going to last very long.

Then Aidan rolled his balls in one hand, thumb brushing up the back, and Levi knew he was going to come *very* soon.

"I . . ." he gasped out. "Yes. Please."

"I got you," Aidan repeated, dark blue eyes intent and serious, and Levi had the insane and wild realization that he'd follow this man anywhere. Onto any football field. Into any sexual exploration he was even remotely into. Into the depths of hell. Aidan only needed to say they had to go, and Levi would go.

It was that thought that tipped him over.

His orgasm fell onto his thighs, his abs, and Aidan worked him through it as Levi panted.

If that look in Aidan's eyes as he came wasn't overwhelming enough, after he'd finally wrung every bit of pleasure out of Levi's body, he tugged his T-shirt off and used it to wipe up the mess.

Tossing the dirty shirt in the direction of his bedroom, Aidan lifted himself up and slumped down on the couch next to Levi.

They weren't cuddling necessarily but they weren't *not* cuddling either.

They had good post-nut vibes, Levi decided.

"Bro, that was crazy," Levi said, more to fill the silence than because it had been. It had sort of been the opposite, actually. Maybe the most inevitable hookup of all time. Levi had imagined this attraction had come out of nowhere, when they'd been in Michigan together, but now he was beginning to think maybe not.

Not for him, anyway.

Aidan's gaze slid over to him. His bare chest was still golden brown from the summer, his skin looking like it was lit from within.

"Was it though?" Aidan asked.

Levi shrugged. Aidan kept his secrets, and Levi was going to keep a few of his own, too. Aidan didn't need to know how deeply attracted he was. Not when Aidan had literally started them down this road by telling him he was in love with someone else.

"I guess," Aidan said with a sudden, fierce grin, "I should at least be grateful you didn't call me bro while we were doing . . .um . . .that."

"You asked me not to."

"Yeah, well, I didn't think you'd actually *listen*," Aidan teased. And that was new too. The *Aidan teasing* part.

"Maybe next time," Levi said. With the proper motivation, he could be a little bit of a brat. Aidan might enjoy that. There were so many things Aidan might enjoy, honestly, and Levi had half a mind to try them all.

There was no reason they couldn't. Mo wasn't going to magically fall in love with Aidan now and Levi didn't have interest in hooking up with anyone else in Toronto.

Even though he'd come here with the assumption he and Aidan weren't going to be making good on their sex pact anytime soon, he'd had trouble imagining anyone else in his bed.

"There's gonna be a next time?" Aidan sounded hopeful.

Levi raised an eyebrow. "You want there to be?" He didn't think there was a question—it was obvious Aidan had enjoyed it—but he thought it was good to make sure they were on the same page.

"Obviously," Aidan said wryly, a shy sort of smile emerging onto his face.

It made him look younger. A little vulnerable. It occurred to Levi that he didn't hear much from Landry about Aidan hooking up. Or that he'd had more than a series of casual, not-serious girlfriends.

Obviously he'd been caught up in Mo for awhile, but even before that had probably materialized, Aidan hadn't exactly gotten around, even though he *very* much could've.

"I just want to make sure you're getting your needs met," Levi said.

"Trust me, they're met. Exceeded?" Aidan looked like he was actually considering this. "I don't think I've ever enjoyed sex that much."

Levi realized then that he hadn't been considering anything—except if he should tell Levi the truth about it.

It shouldn't have made Levi like him even more but there was no question about it: getting to see a faint glimmer of Aidan Flynn's sensitive side made him hotter for the guy than ever.

"You're welcome," Levi said, keeping his voice light. He didn't need an Aidan Flynn manual to know if he got too serious, it would freak the guy out.

Aidan nudged him with an elbow but didn't move it after, like once they'd been touching in another place, he realized how much he liked it. "I guess you being a little smug about being able to suck a dick that good isn't the most ridiculous thing you've ever done." He sounded sleepy and relaxed. And *happy*.

Levi would suck his dick every single day if he never got that painfully uptight edge to his voice. That pained look in his eyes that said *nothing is going right and I can't do anything about it.*

"Not even close, bro." He paused. "And thanks."

He considered telling Aidan that he hadn't even pulled out any tricks yet. That, properly motivated, he could do a hell of a lot better. But he was still unpacking that Aidan had been essentially overwhelmed by the bare minimum and Levi wasn't ready to bring *that* up yet. At least not until he could wrap his head around that fact better.

Aidan hummed. He hadn't made any move to get dressed or even to pull his shorts back up. But then he had absolutely nothing to be ashamed of. He probably wanted Levi to look, and Levi was sure as hell looking.

"You ever gonna tell me what had you so freaked out earlier?" Levi asked.

Aidan sighed, clearly resigned. "You don't want to get on Zane's bad side."

Levi was undeniably relaxed. But he still half tensed up. "You know this from prior experience?"

"Not from Zane, though he has an ego, like these dudes always do," Aidan said. Then frowned. "Back in Michigan, I had an offensive co-ordinator try to remove me from QB1 just because I wasn't his favored choice or whatever. The guy he'd personally recruited. I was better than that guy. Could throw circles around him. But that didn't matter. I only barely held on to my starting spot." Aidan looked over at him. There was worry and affection in Aidan's blue eyes. "I don't want that to be you."

"You don't know that it will," Levi said.

"I *still* don't want it to be you," Aidan stressed again.

"And I *still* don't want you to spend the next twenty-some-odd weeks with your ass on the turf, running for your fucking life," Levi said. "You think we're gonna win games like that? Let me piss Zane off now. He's gonna be glad we made the change by week three when you're lighting up defenses."

Aidan made a frustrated noise. "You assume we're gonna do that."

That feeling, the one he'd had fifteen minutes ago, when he'd looked at Aidan, who'd just said, *I got you,* and he'd known Aidan did, no questions, no hesitation, *nothing,* was back. But even stronger this time.

"You still Aidan Flynn?" Levi asked.

"Yes." Aidan's reply was cautious. Confused.

"Then we're gonna do that," Levi said. *Case closed.*

CHAPTER 11

Levi was prepared for Aidan to continue acting at practices that Levi moving to left tackle was a bad idea.

But when they lined up for their first play of the day, the day after they'd argued and then hooked up, Aidan only gave him a nod of approval as Levi took his spot to the left of Griff.

Like Levi had expected, it went better than it had been yesterday. He was more prepared, slightly more at ease in the new position. Everything he'd hoped from the additional reps.

On the fourth run-through, Aidan got a full five count before he had to throw, and he hit Trevor on a deep crossing pattern, the guy sprinting the ten remaining yards to the end zone.

"Well," Aidan said to Levi when they returned to the huddle, "can't argue with that."

Levi only grinned. "Told you," he said.

It wasn't perfect. There were still kinks to work out, problems to fix. But they were smaller. Less impactful. More the regular kinds of problems that every football team had in the preseason, when they were still trying to find their chemistry and gel on the field.

Levi wasn't surprised when after two touchdowns on two successful series, Zane subbed Wes in to get him some reps with the first team offense.

Levi watched as Aidan retreated to the sideline, setting down his helmet, pushing his hair back.

He had great hair. Levi wished he'd gotten more of a chance to touch it last night. But he hadn't wanted to scare Aidan away or freak him out. He'd been trying to be careful, to not put *too much* on Aidan, even though there was so much he'd wanted.

It had killed him, a little, to pull back, but he'd done it because that was preferable to Aidan deciding they were never going to do it again.

"Something over there look good?"

Levi jumped a little and turned to find Wes smirking at him.

"No," he lied.

Wes shot him a knowing look. "Yeah, okay, dude. Keep your secrets."

"Like you keep yours?"

Wes' expression turned almost melancholy. "You've not been around long enough to know anything about them," he said primly.

That was true. But Levi did know that around a football team, secrets didn't tend to stay secret very long.

"Give me some time," Levi promised, but Wes only rolled his eyes.

"How did we end up talking about *me*, when I wanna talk about *you* and QB1 over there?" Wes asked. "'Cause don't think I haven't noticed you've got your head on a swivel when it comes to him."

"We're weirdly related," Levi said.

"Yeah, okay," Wes scoffed. "That's what you're going with?"

Levi wasn't going to out Aidan to his team. Even to his backup quarterback. Aidan deserved to have the coming out that he wanted—if he wanted it at all.

"Hey, you have Flynn as your older brother's boyfriend's older brother and see how you feel about it," Levi retorted.

Wes frowned. "That's . . .no. You're actually *not* kidding."

"I'm not," Levi said. That much was the truth.

"Huh. Well." Wes seemed lost for words.

"Exactly," Levi said smugly. "Hey, I *was* thinking something though."

"What?"

"Don't let Aidan push you off, not give you the mentorship you need, okay?"

Wes did not roll his eyes again, but Levi could tell it took effort. "Are you actually serious?"

"Hey, you gotta demand what you want from the world. Don't wait for it to come to you," Levi said.

"Is that your life philosophy?" Wes cracked a smile, but he seemed genuinely interested. Levi liked Wes; could imagine that it probably wasn't easy being Aidan Flynn's backup.

"Yeah, usually," Levi admitted.

He went after things he wanted. And he usually got what he wanted. He'd decided a long time ago those things were probably related.

Except two months ago in Michigan, Levi had realized he wanted Aidan and he'd *not* taken him. He'd wanted him the night he showed up in Toronto, and he'd taken a step back instead. Not invited Aidan to his bed, the way he'd been thinking about.

He'd wanted every day since then, too, and only made a move when it was clear Aidan was actually on the same page.

It wasn't the only time Levi had waited for someone else to decide, but it was unusual enough, it felt prickly under his skin, still.

Like it meant something. Levi just wasn't quite ready to face quite what that was, yet.

Zane came up then, ready to restart practice, and Levi turned towards him, pushing the pesky annoying thoughts of Aidan out of his head. He didn't need the distraction, especially not now.

They got through practice and headed in for lunch. With preseason games well underway and everyone's conditioning sufficiently tested, they didn't have an afternoon practice—just positional meetings and film study.

Which meant Levi didn't see Aidan until they met up late in the afternoon at the car for their drive back to the condo.

"Hey," Aidan said, patting him on the shoulder. Levi had noticed that he was slowly becoming a little more touchy-feely. Like it took him some time to warm up to the idea of casual touches. And knowing what he knew about Aidan, that wasn't really much of a surprise.

"Hey, bro," Levi said, grinning. Specifically hoping that maybe dropping Aidan's least favorite nickname might rile him up enough to guarantee more orgasms at home.

Aidan did roll his eyes. "You keep thinking that's gonna piss me off, huh?"

"Not even," Levi said. It was probably good Aidan hadn't figured out yet that Levi was doing it on purpose. That teasing Aidan had its own reward system built in.

"I was thinking," Aidan said as he slid into the driver's seat, "we could grab some dinner on the way home."

It was a very casual invitation. They were both still in shorts and T-shirts. Levi decided after a fraught half second that it wasn't a date. Nothing about this screamed date, the least of which was Aidan's own entirely relaxed expression. It didn't mean anything. Just dinner.

And maybe if Levi got him worked up enough during dinner, orgasms *after*.

"Sure, that sounds like a plan," Levi said. "Where're you thinking?"

"Oh, I got a place." Aidan shot him a sideways look, which might have been normal for everyone else but was downright playful for Aidan.

"You do?" Levi would teach this guy to flirt with him if it killed him in the process.

"Dude, I've lived here for ten years. Yeah, I've got a place."

It turned out that he did.

Levi was still trying to get his bearings in Toronto—he was lucky that up until now, he'd had no reason to take his car out of the parking space in the condo's garage—but he was getting more familiar with the drive to and from the practice facility just outside of downtown. He noticed when, about ten minutes away from the condo, Aidan took an exit off the freeway and, after winding through some residential neighborhoods, pulled down a side street and parked.

The pizza parlor was small, and while not on the trendiest-looking street in the world, the front window was sparkling clean, framed in red-and-white checked curtains.

Moretti's, the gold script on the door declared.

"You eat pizza?" Levi joked as Aidan led him inside the restaurant. It smelled incredible—the richness of tomato and roasted garlic, cut through with the acidic freshness of herbs.

"On special occasions," Aidan said, the corner of his mouth tilting up.

And Levi had to suddenly wonder if this *was* a date, and somehow he'd missed all the signs. Of course Aidan wouldn't date like anyone normal. Normally Levi liked that Aidan didn't go about anything in a remotely standard way, but not being sure of where exactly they stood made him nervous.

They'd said they'd have sex. They'd had sex. What was next? Obviously more sex, and Levi had assumed they'd keep hanging out as friends, like they had been, but now that the line was crossed, everything felt murky and gray.

The restaurant was cute but simple. Straightforward. Half a dozen tables, all covered in the same red-and-white check as the curtains, shakers of parmesan and red pepper flakes on the tables, a wine rack on one side, the scuffed wood making it clear it was actually used and not just here for decoration.

"Yo, Aidan's here," a voice from the back called out as Aidan walked them deeper in. No Italian accent—in fact, they didn't even sound particularly Canadian, either. American, too, if Levi had to guess.

"Hey," Aidan called back. "I'm gonna grab a table." It was still early—barely five—and only one of the six tables was occupied, by an older couple who didn't seem to recognize Aidan.

Aidan picked a table towards the back and sat with his own back towards the rest of the room. Not surprising.

Even at the end of his tenure in Seattle, Levi hadn't been very easily recognized on the street. He'd understood that was a piece of luck, because he knew how often Landry—and now Riley—were stopped by fans and non-fans alike.

Levi sat down opposite. "So what's the scoop?" he asked.

Aidan regarded him steadily, the look in his blue eyes easy and not too serious for once. "What do you mean?"

"I mean," Levi waved around the room, "what's the deal with this place? Not the kind of dinner spot I'd imagine Aidan Flynn eats at."

"Exactly," Aidan said wryly. "But no, it's seriously the best pizza in town, and even better, the guy who runs it is chill. My old backup used to come here all the time and got me coming here too."

A tall dark-haired man with a gorgeous face sauntered over, white T-shirt clinging to pecs and biceps and, ignoring Aidan, gave Levi an up-and-down look. "Hey, who's this?" he asked.

Aidan chuckled. "Hey, Dom. This is Levi, a friend and a new teammate. Had to bring him to try the best pizza in town."

Dom's dark eyebrow arched. "Then why'd it take you so long to come see me? You've been back in the Six for ages, dude."

"Training. You know how it goes. If I thought I could get away with it, I'd be here every week, you know that."

"You athletes," Dom said with a resigned sigh. "Depressing."

"You can't tell me Jones and Reynolds or, God forbid, Matthews or Marner come here regularly," Aidan said.

"No, and they know better. *They* get recognized." Dom shook his head. "Can't believe more people don't recognize you."

"It's a blessing," Aidan said, sounding like he meant it.

"Good thing you're not a hockey player," Dom said wryly. "What can I get you two? Your usual?"

Aidan looked over at Levi, who was in the middle of trying to figure out if Dom might be gay—and even more, if Dom somehow had a crush on Aidan and that was why he'd immediately demanded to know who Levi was.

Then, of course, Levi wondered, because he couldn't fucking help himself, if Aidan had ever brought Mo here. He wasn't going to ask though, because obviously he must've. Mo had been one of Aidan's best friends. His best friend on the Thunder, for sure.

"I always get their supreme pizza, and the garden salad to start. You good with that?" Aidan asked.

Levi nodded.

"Glass or two of chianti, too?" Dom asked hopefully.

Aidan just laughed. "I wish, but no. We'll just stick with water."

Dom made a face but disappeared a second later behind the swinging kitchen door.

"Been coming here for awhile," Levi observed.

"Yeah. Dom's a . . .well, a friend. He comes to Thunder games sometimes. I get him tickets to my suite. He's originally from California, and don't tell anyone, but he says hockey just isn't the same."

Levi was not going to ask. He was absolutely *not* going to ask.

"Just a friend?" he asked anyway.

Aidan's expression morphed from shock to astonishment to amusement. "Are you for real?"

Levi wanted to tell him he was just joking. That he hadn't meant it. But he kinda had. "In my defense, bro," Levi said, painfully aware at how un-casual he sounded, "you *are* Aidan Flynn."

"Yeah, okay, but you know—well, you *know*," Aidan retorted without much heat.

He did know. Aidan had been in love—*was* in love?—with Morris Jeffries. And two months ago, he'd told Levi that he'd never done anything with a guy before.

But that didn't mean Dom didn't wish that things were different.

"I promise," Aidan continued dryly, "I'm not *that* much of a prize."

That was a complete fucking lie. Aidan was hot and funny, in a lunatic, overachiever, dry sort of way. He was rich and a famous quarterback in the NFL, even though he was doing it in a city that cared way more about the Leafs and their never-ending quest for a Stanley Cup.

"The craziest part of that sentence is that I think you might actually mean it," Levi said, shaking his head in disbelief. Because Aidan was a lot of things but he wasn't the kind of guy who pretended not to be awesome so someone would argue with him.

"Of course I mean it," Aidan said, shooting Levi a confused look.

Levi *almost* told him that just because Mo hadn't wanted him didn't mean nobody else did, but he'd done a very good job of keeping the guy's name out of his mouth so far and he wasn't about to break now.

"Besides," Aidan added, "Dom's got a boyfriend."

"Ha," Levi said. His gaydar had never been wrong yet.

Except, of course, when Aidan had told him that he was into guys and he'd been floored.

Another waitress—young, with a sweet smile—showed up with their waters, a bowl overflowing with salad, and two plates.

"You ever look at guys?" Levi asked as Aidan heaped salad on their plates.

Aidan glanced up at him. "Seriously?"

"What, it's an understandable question," Levi said. "Your best friend's Landry, and even though he's *my* brother, I can say objectively he's damn good looking. Best-looking person in our family by a mile."

"Hey now, don't sell yourself short," Aidan said, sounding honest to God a little offended.

Levi didn't particularly need the ego boost—he was intimately aware of his pros and cons, probably even more than Aidan was—but Aidan's easy retort still felt really good.

"Aw, thanks," Levi teased, like Aidan hadn't been as serious as he'd been.

Because Aidan being *that* serious about it sort of threw him.

Made him wonder, before he shoved the thought down, if this *could* be a date.

"To answer your question though . . .I don't *think* so, but then, I didn't think I was into guys at all. I think . . .sometimes I think I wasn't even paying attention. Like just too caught up in everything I was doing, to wonder about what I *wasn't* doing."

"Yeah, I get that. I had Logan—but then, I think I came to terms that the fact I was gay a lot sooner than he did, even, so I'm not sure he really helped all that much."

Aidan smiled. "Why do I think you probably helped him more than he ever helped you?"

"Maybe. I've just . . .I just always knew."

"Lucky," Aidan said, a little wryly.

"Hey, you got there eventually."

Aidan had the nerve to look sulky. Levi hated it. Wanted to wash the look off his face, but he knew he couldn't. Not here, not now.

"Eventually," Aidan added quietly.

They ate their salad in silence, Levi mentally searching for a way to cheer Aidan up that wasn't just grabbing him and kissing him in the middle of this little neighborhood restaurant.

Knocked his foot against Aidan's casually, but other than a brief curl of his lips, Aidan didn't really react much.

Aidan's plate was almost empty when his phone dinged. Levi didn't think he'd actually heard it make a noise since he'd arrived in Toronto, and Aidan had to get a shit ton of messages, so he was surprised to hear it actually notify him.

Aidan glanced over at it, and whatever it was, *whoever* it was, was enough to drive that look off his face entirely.

God, what if it was Mo? Levi suddenly felt sick to his stomach. Jealous, even though he didn't want to be, and guilty because of it.

Dom had been bad enough, with his curly dark hair and his handsome, friendly face.

But before Levi could figure out how to ask who it was that had put that smile on Aidan's face, Aidan murmured under his breath, "It's Riley. Just wants my advice on something. I'll text him back later."

"Oh yeah? How's the kid doing?" Levi said it, knowing it would pry some kind of reaction out of him.

Aidan shot him a glare. "Don't call him that."

"Chill, it's a joke," Levi said, smiling.

"He's just . . . *I* just . . ." Aidan took a deep breath. "I screwed up a lot and I'm trying to be a better brother."

"I don't know, dude, from what I've seen, you've always been the best kind of brother." Landry hadn't told him everything, but he'd told Levi enough. Enough for Levi to know that while their parents had been intricately and intimately involved in their lives and that he'd always felt the warmth of their love, Aidan and Riley hadn't been the same. They'd only really had each other.

Aidan made a scoffing noise. "Yeah, well, even the best of intentions don't mean anything."

"Still. I know you basically took care of him. Raised him. Made him into the quarterback he is today."

Aidan's mouth clamped down into a tight line. "Riley made himself into the quarterback he is today."

"Bro, take a little credit. Riley gives you plenty of credit. He's always talking about it."

Aidan's smile emerged again. Soft and sweet. Now Levi recognized it as his Riley smile. How had he missed it before? Probably because he'd been too busy being stupidly jealous.

"Yeah, he is. Kind of loudmouthed about it, if we're being honest."

"He loves you."

"Yeah." Aidan leaned back in his chair. "I love him too. We only really had each other for a long time. Forever it felt like."

Kind of like Mo, Levi had always felt like Aidan and Riley's parents were sort of a banned conversational topic. Aidan *never* brought them up. Riley hadn't used to, but slowly over the last few years, as he'd become the Condors' starting quarterback and found success, he'd started not discussing *them* more openly but at least the fact that Aidan had been largely responsible for his upbringing.

Still, he felt like he should ask. Get the truth out of Aidan's own mouth, anyway.

"What was up with that?" Levi wondered.

Aidan looked surprised, like he hadn't expected Levi to ask.

"Uh, well, long story short, 'cause nobody wants to hear the whole ugly thing—"

"Never said I didn't," Levi interrupted casually. He kind of *did* want to know.

Aidan shot him a look but kept going. "They got divorced," he said simply. "You know when you hate something so much you want to hate it more than you want to find something you actually love? That was them. They got so occupied hating each other it was like they forgot about us."

Levi had thought it was something like this. Landry had mentioned a few things, over the years, even if it was never the details. But that didn't mean the details didn't hit hard, when they hit.

"Oh shit. *Shit*. Bro."

"I mean, not entirely." Aidan shrugged. "Maybe if they had, it would've been easier. But like, I'd arrange everything for Riley. Make sure he was taken care of and stuff, you know? And then they'd remember oh shit, yeah, we have sons. The next day, the whole schedule would be fucked up, because they suddenly thought they knew best."

"No wonder you're a control freak," Levi said softly.

"I'm . . . don't say it like it's a good thing. It's not a good thing. It wasn't a good thing."

Levi was surprised by the fierce note in Aidan's voice. "No, well, maybe not to the extent you were with Riley, but, dude, you did right by him. At a time when nobody else wanted to."

Aidan looked even tenser then, and Levi felt desperate to say some-thing, the *right* thing to get him to understand. But not just that, to *relax* him, too. To realize that out of everyone, Levi was the last person who'd judge him.

"You guys are good now, though," Levi added. "I saw you together this summer, and it seemed good."

Aidan nodded. "Yeah. Of course. But I nearly screwed it up—"

"No, you didn't," Levi argued. "I mean, *maybe*, but is it really screw-ing it up when it comes from a good place? Landry told me you'd do all this film study not just for *you*, but for *him*. Time you probably didn't have, just to help Riley out, help make him successful in the NFL."

Aidan relaxed a fraction. Not a lot. Not enough. But some. "Landry told you that?"

"Listen, *bro*, you thought his dream could hurt him, and you were *still* out there, helping him make it possible. That's . . .I don't even know what that is. Like fucking unselfish behavior."

"I didn't know Landry had told you that," Aidan said. He didn't seem upset, only surprised.

"You know we've always talked a lot. And while Logan tends to handle most of the overprotective-brother shit in our family, Lyla and Landry will do their share, too." Levi hesitated, unsure of how much of this he should say. How much Landry had *already* said. "He worried, too, when he and Riley started dating."

Aidan frowned, but the waitress appeared then with their pizza, and Levi thought maybe that part of the conversation was over.

But after he'd demolished his first piece of pizza, Aidan shot him a look. "What do you mean?" he asked. "What was Landry worried about?"

Levi had a sudden, inexplicable fear that maybe Landry *hadn't* ever told Aidan about this, but of course he had. He *had* to have. That was just the kind of person Landry was. Generous and loyal, to a fault. Not just to Riley, but to Aidan.

"It was just tough on him, at first. Trying to figure out the balance between being *your* friend and being *Riley's* boyfriend."

"I'd have told him to pick Riley every time," Aidan said which was not only ridiculous, it was the most Aidan thing ever.

"Fucking please," Levi complained. "Like he'd even do that."

Aidan sighed. "I *did* tell him that when he got all angsty about it. I want Riley to have someone who puts him first."

"And he probably does. Like ninety percent of the time. But like . . .you're one of Landry's best friends. Have been, forever. I don't think even Riley could change that."

Aidan thoughtfully chewed on his second slice. "True," he agreed. "Probably easier too when I finally figured out my shit with Riley. Stopped putting him in the middle."

"Hey, Riley could've told you that you were overstepping. He didn't."

Aidan looked up, shock widening his eyes.

"What?" Levi shrugged. "It's true. You're not a fucking mind reader."

"But I should've—"

"Nah," Levi interrupted.

Aidan shot him a pointed look.

"Riley's got Landry and *you* looking out for him in this. Who's looking out for you? Seems like I'm gonna have to do it."

"Nobody says you have to do anything," Aidan said, contrary. Because of course he was. Couldn't even take a fucking compliment.

"I'm telling you I *want* to," Levi insisted. "You're a good guy, Aidan."

Aidan rolled his eyes, but Levi could see that he was pleased, under all that.

"It's so weird you can take a compliment when it comes to football, but give you any other kind of praise and it's, like, you automatically reject it."

"Do not," Aidan argued.

"Do so."

"You're ridiculous," Aidan said. But he sounded amused and was giving Levi that fond look that Levi enjoyed putting on his face so much.

186

CHAPTER 12

THE PIZZA WAS, AS promised, really fucking good, and Levi ate too much, groaning a little as Dom came to collect the empty plates.

"I take it you enjoyed that," Aidan said. He was smiling again, like he was finally ready to take the win.

That was the thing Levi was learning about Aidan; he always wanted to know he'd worked hard for the win, before he let himself enjoy it.

Levi considered this as they drove back to the condo.

Dusk was falling, and the view out the living room windows, right over the lake, was second to none.

He sank down on the couch, listening to Aidan puttering around the kitchen. Every moment, Levi expected Aidan to round the corner of the couch and settle down next to him. It was still early-ish. Maybe they could watch a movie. But then it would be hard to pretend that this hadn't felt like a very date-ish evening. At least Levi had managed to keep his lips and his hands to himself so far.

But then Aidan didn't show up.

"What are you doing back there?" Levi finally called out.

Aidan was silent for a long moment. "Unloading the dishwasher?"

Of course. "Dude, get over here. We can do that anytime."

"You mean, *I* can do it anytime," Aidan said wryly.

Ouch. Okay, so he wasn't great about chores. That was fair. But then, Aidan had a housekeeper who showed up twice a week and did things like load and unload the dishwasher.

"How about I do it tomorrow morning before we leave for the walk-through?" Levi suggested sweetly. He deserved a medal for not bringing up that Lora was coming tomorrow afternoon and could do it then.

Aidan didn't say anything. That was when Levi was one hundred percent certain that he was procrastinating and not actually worked up about who was going to unload the dishwasher.

Maybe the dinner *had* been a date. Or was Aidan just realizing that now? Was that the reason for the sudden burst of housewifely-ness?

"Seriously, man, get over here. They're just dishes."

Aidan dawdled, even as he rounded the corner of the couch, and he made no move to sit down, his eyes flicking up, past Levi, to the view.

"Uh, nice view tonight."

Levi patted the couch, feeling a little like a seductress. Except he was wearing old ratty shorts and one of his brand-new Thunder T-shirts. "Come on. Dude. Sit down."

Aidan eyed him nervously. Trying to hide it but not even coming close. Levi had begun to recognize his tells. "Maybe I'm tired. Maybe I need to watch some film."

"So we'll watch it together," Levi said. He wasn't ready for the evening to end. It had been unexpectedly good, and he felt reasonably certain he could convince Aidan to bridge the distance between them if he was out here on the couch. If they were in their own rooms? Much less likely.

Aidan still didn't sit down.

Levi sighed. "Dude, I don't bite." He paused. "Unless you want me to, and then I'm totally down for that."

Aidan flushed. "Is that . . .do you . . ."

"I get it," Levi said. "You're probably used to the kind of girls that I know hang around. Who make all the moves and make it obvious they want you. They probably climb on your lap and just say, *take me, Aidan, I'm yours*. I can do that, too. You want me to do that?"

Aidan's jaw dropped. "Do I? Um. I don't know." He sat down on the couch, but he looked so unsure, so completely unlike the normal confident Aidan, that Levi *didn't* crawl over to him, the way he desperately wanted to.

He deserved major props for self-control.

"Well, it's up to you." Levi hadn't thought it needed said, but maybe Aidan had been waiting to hear it.

On one hand, Aidan didn't look surprised. But on the other, he didn't immediately say, *okay, take me, I'm yours* either.

Hard not to be disappointed, but Levi schooled his expression into neutrality. The last thing he wanted to do was scare Aidan away with his enthusiasm.

Instead, Aidan pulled out the remote, and just when Levi had resigned himself to watching film for the next hour, he found a movie, something with Tom Cruise and lots of brainless explosions, and settled back against the couch.

Still a frustrating few inches too far away, but every five minutes he seemed to relax even further, until Aidan's shoulder was almost touching Levi's.

It was enough of a green light that Levi pressed his thigh to Aidan's. Waited a breathless moment for Aidan to move away again, but he didn't. Instead, he pushed up against it. Like he'd been waiting for Levi to do it.

Tom Cruise had just blown up a huge building—Levi wasn't sure if it was on purpose or not, he was only paying about a quarter of attention. The rest of his focus was on the man next to him. The way he breathed. The way he smelled. The solid warm feeling of his leg against Levi's.

Levi was not going to pull the *need-to-stretch, put-my-arm-around-your-shoulders* move, but he was tempted. At least another twenty-five percent of his brain power was currently being used up in the debate about whether that would be too obvious. The answer: *yes*.

But just when the dick part of his brain was lodging its appeal on that stupid-ass decision, Aidan turned to him.

"Are you following this?" he half asked, half demanded.

"Uh." Levi really hoped that Aidan was not going to ask for a run-down of the plot, because his understanding consisted of *Aidan's hair; Tom Cruise stabbed someone; Aidan's thigh; motorcycle chase; Aidan's mouth against his last night; some incomprehensible bad-guy speech.*

"Are you?" Aidan repeated.

There was no point in pretending. "No," Levi admitted. "I think Tom Cruise is . . .um . . .trying to stop that guy from destroying a space station." He gestured towards the screen.

Aidan frowned. "That's Tom Cruise's partner. He's trying to *prevent* them from destroying the space station."

Okay. Well. He'd made a good effort, at least. Somewhere Landry and Logan were poking fun at his total lack of game. Lyla would pat him on the cheek and tell him he'd do better next time. None of them would be wrong.

"Maybe you should explain it to me," Levi said, finding it hard to not be at least a *little* sulky. Aidan was driving him out of his mind—the majority of his brain was in Aidan's pants right now—to the point he couldn't even figure out who the bad guy was in this terrible Tom Cruise movie. But Aidan knew. It was kind of a blow to the ego.

Maybe it hadn't been as good for Aidan last night as it had been for Levi.

And if that was true, then Levi needed to remedy that *immediately.* He could do better; he *would* do better.

He'd blow Aidan's mind into tiny little smithereens, Tom Cruise–style.

"Wait," Aidan said.

"What?"

"Do you really think *I'm* paying attention?"

It was a perfectly legitimate question. After all, *Aidan* had put the fucking movie on.

"You *just* explained the plot to me."

Aidan laughed and then poked him in the side. "You idiot," he said, making it sound like the sweetest pet name in the world, "I only know that 'cause I've seen this before."

Levi opened his mouth and then snapped it shut again. Hoping he understood what Aidan was getting at, but totally unlike him, not sure how to ask if he was getting this right.

Before he could, Aidan was suddenly moving, and it was *him* swinging a leg over Levi's thighs and settling down lightly into his lap, hands on the back of the couch, framing Levi's head.

He didn't dip his face down to meet Levi's. There was still a whisper of apprehension written there, like he was actually unsure that Levi would like this.

Aidan was clearly being his normal neurotic self because Levi *loved* this.

"Hey," Levi said warmly, settling a hand on Aidan's hip. Making sure Aidan knew, from every bit of his body language and his expression, just how into this he was.

Aidan still looked like he was half a second from squirming away. "Hey."

He was beautiful all the time, but he'd never been more gorgeous than he was like this, dusk shadowing his face, blue eyes torn between desire and restraint, biting his lower lip like it might physically stop him from closing the rest of the distance between them.

"Do you want to talk about it?" Levi asked.

He figured that was fair even though the last thing he wanted to do was have a conversation. He just wanted to *do*.

AKA strip Aidan naked and make him moan.

"Talk about—" Aidan broke off, shaking his head. "No. No. I . . ." He tucked his face away in his shoulder, so Levi could only see a sliver. "I want this." A shuddering breath went out of him, making him tremble. "I want this so much."

Levi could ask why he'd pretended like he didn't. Why he'd tried to unload the dishwasher. Why he'd sat so far away on the couch. Why he'd put on the stupidest Tom Cruise movie in existence.

But Levi didn't. He'd known before tonight that Aidan's head could be a bramble of complex, tangled-together emotions, but after Aidan had shared more of his past, it was obvious how much he fought even things that were good for him.

Instead, he reached up and tangled his other hand in Aidan's hair. It was soft and curly around the edges, burnished gold in this light. Levi had only thought about touching it hundreds of times since he'd gotten to Toronto, and it felt even better than in his fantasies.

Aidan went easily, settling more completely in his lap, mouth brushing up against Levi's. It seemed that was all it took because the last of the tension relaxed out of Aidan's shoulders, and he was kissing Levi like he had last night. Intense and passionate. Focused.

Not even like last night though. This kiss wasn't tinged with frustrated desperation, but instead it was sweet and almost tender.

Lush, Levi's mind supplied, as his tongue stroked Aidan's. His fingers tightened on Aidan's hip and even though they were already pressed together, he brought them impossibly closer. And it was still not close enough.

"Thought about this all day," Levi murmured, breaking the kiss to slide his lips down Aidan's neck. The angle was tricky, but he didn't mind, because he wasn't going to be stupid enough to move Aidan right now.

He was perfect just like this, loose and boneless and wanting.

"All day?" Aidan had the nerve to look surprised, even as he kept shifting, like he was trying to get his hips better aligned to Levi's.

Levi wanted that too. His cock was hard and aching in his shorts, and he didn't just want the friction of Aidan's body, he *needed* it.

"Yeah," Levi breathed out. "Of course."

"I thought . . ." Aidan licked his bottom lip again, and Levi didn't just need Aidan's body, he needed his mouth too. So many desperate cravings; so little time. "I thought it was just me."

That was so ridiculous he had to kiss Aidan about it. Press their mouths and their dicks together and just grind it out. Make sure that Aidan would never think that kind of stupidity ever again.

He wasn't Aidan's, and Aidan most definitely was not his, but in this moment, it felt neither of those things were true.

"God, this feels so good. Like . . ." Aidan gasped into his mouth as Levi curled a hand around his ass, encouraging him to move harder, faster. "Best sex ever."

It was really good. There was no question of that. Nobody was even naked, and it was great despite that. Levi wouldn't have said it was the best sex he'd ever had though.

But a moment later, Aidan gasped into his mouth and Levi realized he'd just come in his shorts like a horny teenager who couldn't control himself a second longer.

"Shit," Aidan exhaled unsteadily. "I didn't—"

"That was hot," Levi said, before Aidan could do something stupid like apologize for liking it that much.

Aidan looked straight at him. Blue eyes hazy and pleased, lips red and swollen. He looked so good like this Levi never wanted to let him go, but if he didn't—and didn't get himself off soon, the desire a heavy and insistent beat in his blood—there was going to be a real mess to deal with.

"Come on," Levi said, carefully sliding Aidan off his lap, even though the last thing he wanted was space. So he didn't give him any. Not really. After standing up too, he reached out and took Aidan's hand in his, tugging him in the direction of their bedrooms.

He could've taken them to his room. His bathroom. That would be the safest choice, but Levi was way past *safe*.

He knew Aidan had a gorgeous big shower with room for the two of them and plenty to spare, and he wasn't ready for this to be over yet.

Aidan didn't protest once as he took him in that direction, the corner of his mouth tilting up as Levi took them right into the bathroom with its enormous glass enclosure.

"Been wanting to try this," Levi said, leaning against the counter and finally letting go of Aidan's hand. Gestured towards the shower. "You wanna show me all the bells and whistles?"

Aidan licked his lips as he looked Levi up and down.

"Yeah," he said, "but first . . ." He trailed off, and to Levi's astonishment, he reached over and pulled Levi's T-shirt off. Then went to his knees, doing the same with Levi's shorts and briefs, until he was totally naked.

Levi's breath caught in his throat. He hadn't expected this. A hot, sexy shower in Aidan's fancy facilities? Sure? Ogling the guy when ogling was not only allowed but encouraged? Absolutely.

But he hadn't expected Aidan to drop to his knees.

"Aidan," he exhaled sharply. "God, that's so hot."

Aidan shot him a look from underneath his eyelashes, singeing Levi around the edges. Making it clear that Levi wasn't the only one enjoying this.

Aidan knew he could have his neurotic moments.

But funny, face to face with a cock for the second time in his life was not one of them.

He knew what he wanted, and with the lassitude of his own orgasm lingering, he wasn't even anxious about this, the way he'd been last night. When he'd been worried he'd try it and not like it.

Well, he'd tried it, and the opposite had actually been true.

Shuffling a little closer, it was impossible not to feel a surge of smugness when Levi's cock twitched, hard and curved up towards his abs.

He clearly wanted Aidan, and he wanted him despite the fact that Aidan couldn't possibly be good at this—no matter how much he craved competence, he was also a realist.

Aidan pushed that thought, that sudden anxious worry, away and leaned in, swiping his tongue up Levi's cock.

It was warm and the skin surprisingly soft despite its hardness. Aidan had wondered, late last night as he'd lain in bed, thinking about what they'd finally done, if he'd hallucinated how good it had been. How much he'd liked it.

But it turned out that it wasn't a fantasy or a dream or even a misre-membered echo of the truth.

Aidan groaned in the back of his throat. He liked it *so* much. Slipped more of it into his mouth, enjoying the weight of it against his tongue. Sucked harder and loved the way Levi's thighs tensed under his palms.

It was like learning a new play. Figuring out what worked, and what didn't. Untangling the necessities for success from the fancy optionals.

He took Levi too deep once, too fast, and choked a little. Levi soothed the back of his head with a soft touch, but Aidan realized he didn't even hate that. He disliked more that he'd lost sight of quality in pursuit of enthusiasm.

"God, baby, so good," Levi babbled above him. His hand hadn't strayed from his hair, and he wasn't tugging, but he was gripping firmly. Turned out that was hot too, like it was grounding both of them in this moment.

Aidan didn't even second-guess that Levi was gassing him up. Maybe it wasn't the best blowjob he'd ever gotten, but he seemed lost to the pleasure of it anyway. Mouth caught open in a perpetual moan, making the kind of noises that Aidan was pretty sure might actually make him hard again.

"I'm—" Levi broke off, groaning. "God, I'm so close."

Aidan knew the standard for success, but it wasn't just the inevitable conclusion he wanted. He didn't *just* want to win. This felt different.

Intimate, yes, and like it existed in a whole other category from other things he'd strived to become good at.

He wanted it not for himself. But for the man in front of him.

"Yeah," Aidan said breathlessly, nodding as he took Levi's cock as deeply into his mouth as he dared. Hoping the way he couldn't help convulsively swallowing around the head would push Levi over the edge.

His fingertips dug into his scalp and a second later, with a breathless moan, Levi came down his throat, every muscle in his body shaking as Aidan coaxed him through his orgasm.

As he fell back on his heels, Aidan had only one overriding thought—besides the fact that his cock was rock hard again, just from sucking dick—that sex had never, in his thirty-three years, felt that incredible.

Had he been having the wrong kind of sex?

Or was it more like he'd been having sex with the wrong people? The wrong *sex*?

The thought was mind-boggling, and Aidan wasn't ready to unpack it yet. To even consider if it was true.

Not when Levi was pulling him up from the floor, hands still in his hair, mouth meeting Aidan's in a fiercely hungry kiss.

"Come on," Levi murmured against his mouth. "Shower time."

Aidan broke away for just long enough to get the water going and pull out additional towels. Thinking—and maybe for the first time in his life, *hoping*—that they might make a mess.

"That was so good," Levi murmured against his sensitive column of his neck. "Can't believe you're real."

It was incredible Levi said that because if Aidan was looking at this situation objectively, the only really special one here was Levi.

He'd seen what almost nobody else had. He'd witnessed the shards of Aidan's broken heart, but he hadn't pushed. At first had only put his arms around him, warming him up from the cold, and then he'd slowly, gradually, helped Aidan up.

Three months ago, Aidan would never have imagined he'd want to do any of this with anyone but Mo. But there was no denying he wanted Levi so bad it felt like he was going out of his mind with it.

Not just for sex. Though the sex clearly had some life-altering qualities to it. He wanted to treat Levi right. As a friend, but also . . .well, whatever they were. He'd taken him to Moretti's because he wanted to share with Levi the good parts of Toronto. The little niches of good things and good people he'd found.

Of course, then they'd come back to the condo and he'd sort of freaked out.

That had been, for all intents and purposes, a date, and Aidan didn't even date *women*.

He didn't know how to date men. And he definitely didn't know how to date Levi.

But is that true? Seems like you're doing just fine. That was Levi's voice in his head, calm and funny and poking holes right where he needed his bad assumptions deflated the most.

"You're thinking hard here," Levi said, his fingers still loosely tangled in Aidan's hair. He tugged his head around so Aidan could meet his eyes.

"A little, yeah," Aidan admitted. "But not overthinking. I promise."

He'd done that before. But Levi had pushed him right out of it, easy as breathing.

Kind of like he did, right now, tangling their fingers together and tugging him into the shower.

The shower had been one of his few indulgences when he'd had the condo remodeled a few years back. The contractor had given him a knowing grin when he'd talked about how big he wanted it. Like he'd be packing the girls in, two or three or four at a time. But it had never been about that. Sometimes Toronto—his condo—his *life*—felt so small. He'd wanted room to breathe.

And even though he hadn't known it at the time, turned out he'd also wanted room for him and Levi in here together.

"Well, if you do," Levi said, tipping his head back into the waterfall spray, "just say the word, bro, and I'll pull you right back out."

Aidan didn't know if he should be embarrassed that Levi had seen through him so easily, but he wasn't, actually.

Maybe Levi's matter-of-factness was rubbing off on him.

Levi's hand settled hot and intent on his hip, squeezed. It lit Aidan up inside, in a way he swore he'd never felt before.

"You want it?" Levi asked softly. Aidan's cock twitched, still hard just from the residual taste of Levi's cock and the ghost of the feeling at the back of his throat.

It shouldn't be so hard to just say it. Levi said things he wanted all the time. But every time it was the moment for Aidan to echo that desire, he clammed up. He'd known he was in love with Mo for almost three years before he'd even found the balls to tell him.

Not because he hadn't *felt*. But because it had felt sometimes like he felt too fucking much. The emotions overwhelmed him. Stole his breath, then snatched the words right out of his throat.

But he wasn't stupid enough to think Levi would be satisfied forever with nods, and so, ignoring the way his brain was screaming, he snatched the words right back.

"Uh, yeah. *Yeah.*"

"Bro," Levi said, gazing at him amused and fond.

Aidan rolled his eyes, that same feeling blooming inside him and unsure how that had even happened. "I thought we agreed the *bro* stays out of the bedroom."

"We're not *in* the bedroom," Levi said.

He was ridiculous, and Aidan never wanted him to stop being ridiculous.

The only way he could tell him that was just to kiss him. To kiss him and kiss him, warm water cascading over their bodies, until Aidan wasn't sure where he left off and Levi began.

Levi slid a hand around his cock and it felt like it only took a few strokes before he was gasping into his mouth, overwhelmed and overwrought with the pleasure surging through him.

"God, so good," Aidan murmured into Levi's shoulder. It was wide and broad, rippling with muscle. Strong enough to hold him up, even though his knees and his heart were wobbly.

They dried off slowly. It felt natural for Aidan to make sure Levi's back was dry in a move he knew was more tender than he was ready to talk about. But after that, it didn't just feel weird to send Levi to his own room, but *wrong*. Even though he'd never wanted to share his space, ever, with *anyone*.

But Levi wasn't just going to stay here, unless Aidan spoke up about it.

"You . . . uh . . ." Aidan hated how uncertain he sounded. After hanging up his towel, Levi glanced over at him. Aidan cleared his throat and started over. "Don't go back to your room tonight."

Levi's eyebrows skidded up. It was a sudden, messy, painful realization that sleeping in the same bed might not fall under the umbrella of a hookup. Because that was what a sex pact was, right? It was right there in the name—*sex* pact.

But before Aidan could take it back, Levi was leaning back against the counter, gloriously naked and apparently completely unashamed of that fact. Frankly, Aidan couldn't blame him.

"Are you saying that because you feel like you should or because you want me to stay?" Levi asked. He added, the corner of his mouth quirking upwards, "Remember, I'm only going across the hall."

Aidan knew that.

"I know," Aidan said, licking his lips. "I want . . ." There was that hiccup again. If this had been football and he kept running into something that tripped him up, he'd work on it until he could do it without a single moment's hesitation. Why was this any different?

He plowed ahead. Kept it simple. "I want you to stay."

He ignored the voice inside him that shrieked that he was going to push Levi past his comfort zone. That he was going to end up pushing him away entirely. Logically, Levi didn't look like he was going anywhere, but then Aidan had already figured out that voice was wrong more often than it was right.

Still didn't mean it wasn't loud.

Levi didn't leave him waiting. "Okay," he said, just as straightforward. "I'm gonna go grab some things. My phone charger."

Aidan pulled on a pair of boxer briefs and the old ratty T-shirt he slept in and, while he waited for Levi to come in, paced in front of the bed.

He was being weird. He knew it, and he couldn't even stop it.

He *wanted* this.

He wanted to keep this good feeling going, the heat he felt inside when Levi looked at him with those warm honey-brown eyes. He wanted to feel it when he woke up, too. It was the best thing he'd felt in ages. He was beginning to wonder if it was the best thing he'd felt, ever.

But no. That couldn't be true. *Mo* was the best thing he'd ever felt, even though it had never ever, not once, been like this between them. They'd never shared a bed or a shower or their bodies.

That was the only reason it felt different now, Aidan justified. All that intimacy.

"Are you freaking out yet?" Levi asked as he reappeared in the doorway.

Aidan did not jump. He *did* stop pacing, at least. "What? Are *you*?"

Levi rolled his eyes. "No." He climbed right onto the bed, stretching his long legs out, like it was nothing.

That tracked. The only freak here was Aidan.

Gesturing to the bed next to him, Levi said, "If you ever want me gone, you just have to say the word. I won't take it personally."

Levi wouldn't. It wasn't like he didn't care about *anything*—he very obviously did, though Aidan was uncertain where he fell on that particular list. It was more like he wasn't struck down by the same affliction Aidan had: caring about all the wrong things, way too much.

Being neurotic, Riley would tell him, poking him gently in the side. *Stop that, before you break your brain.*

It was that thought that got him on the bed. They slipped under the covers. They were both big, but the bed was bigger, and there was still room between them. At least until Levi turned over and slung an arm over Aidan's waist.

Aidan must've tensed—with surprise, more than anything else—because Levi asked in a quiet murmur, "Is this okay?"

He nodded.

"Good. 'Cause I like it." Levi's smile was soft, and that warmth in his eyes was flooding Aidan's insides.

"Me too." There, he'd said it.

Levi looked pleased. "That's the idea. I set an alarm."

"What time?"

Levi shot him a look, but told him, and Aidan frowned. "That's too early," he said. "We don't have to be at practice until nine."

Moving closer, Levi nudged his mouth with his own. It was so easy to slip into another kiss. Not heated, this time, but quiet, intimate. Kind of like falling asleep in the same bed and then waking up the same way. "I know," he said, when he finally moved back. "But that gives us an extra half an hour."

"For what?"

Levi chuckled. Kissed him again. "Turn off the alarm tomorrow morning and you're gonna find out."

CHAPTER 13

"Are you sure you're okay?" Wes asked Aidan late the next afternoon. They'd already gotten through practice—Levi was slowly but steadily making progress at the left tackle position and that pinched look on Zane's face was slowly beginning to smooth out—and lunch and several hours of video study in the QB room.

"What? Why?" Aidan had thought he'd been in a pretty damn good mood all day. More than once, he'd actually caught himself smiling at nothing at all, thinking of how the alarm had gone off this morning, Levi's arm warm and heavy along his body, his cock hard against the back of Aidan's thigh. How Levi had pulled the covers back and sucked the two brain molecules he usually had in the mornings right out of his dick.

He'd been so loose and relaxed it had actually been easy to tell Levi just how right he'd been.

And when Levi had glanced over at his phone charger, plugged into his side of the bed, raising an eyebrow—asking without asking if he should leave it—it had even been doable to tell him he wasn't sick of him yet.

Levi had grinned then, and Aidan knew he'd gotten what he'd meant. It was good; *he* was good.

But Wes was frowning at him right now like he was being even more nuts than usual.

"I'm just saying. You smiled at that Rams coverage like it was nothing."

"Been a hell of a lot easier to handle since Donald retired," Aidan said, because that was better than saying, *I'm happy. I didn't know what that felt like, really, but now I do, and I don't want to let it go.*

He and Wes didn't really talk about personal shit. But then, Aidan didn't talk about personal shit with *anyone*, usually.

Wes didn't look convinced. "Something's up with you. I can't figure out what it is, but it's *something*. Like you're actually . . .I don't know . . .relaxed. It's kinda freaking me out."

Aidan wasn't going to get offended by this. He was *not*.

"I can relax," he insisted.

Wes shot him a dubious look. "In theory, sure. Not sure if I've ever seen it in action, though."

That was probably fair. Wes probably hadn't. But then Wes wasn't Aidan's favorite person. Wes was the living embodiment of *the clock is ticking*.

Aidan just shrugged. Still not sure if he wanted to discuss any of the particulars of why that might be true. Before they'd met Wes' hockey friend at Vault, he hadn't even known what Wes' ex's name was.

They just didn't have that kind of relationship.

You barely have that kind of relationship with anyone, Riley chimed in. *Just Landry. And me.*

He was going to need to call Riley, and soon, with the way he kept worming his way into his brain in the last twenty-four hours.

"You get laid or something?" Wes asked casually, but the look in his eyes made it clear he thought he was right.

Aidan told himself not to flush but went bright red anyway.

You're thirty-three years old, he told himself firmly, *sex is not a bad word.*

"Okay, yeah, that's cool," Wes said. "You wanna talk about it?"

"Absolutely not," Aidan ground out. But even now, he wasn't actually annoyed. The good mood that had buoyed him all day was still keeping him nice and toasty inside.

The thought that when he and Levi climbed in the car to go home, it would be just them. Just them on the couch, Levi giving him shit for how terrible he was at *Mario Kart*. Levi in his shower. Levi in his *bed*.

"It's not Ramsey, is it?"

"Ramsey?" Who was Ramsey again? Was that a player new to the team whose name he'd already forgotten? *Shit*. He was usually better about that stuff. Levi had him a little distracted. *Understandably*, but still. Aidan prided himself on being better than that.

"Ramsey," Wes said slowly. "My friend? The hockey player? We met him at the bar."

"Oh yes. Yes." That guy.

Wes looked appalled and then Aidan realized he thought that *yes*, Ramsey was the person Aidan was sleeping with.

"No," Aidan said forcefully. "No, definitely not. Not that I give a shit about that. Not that I don't . . ." He'd come out to so few people, he wondered if it would ever be easier or less awkward. Today was not that day. "I do, actually. Uh. Like guys, that is."

Wes raised an eyebrow. "Okay," he said. "You do realize I'm gay, right?"

Aidan knew, which made his awkwardness even worse. "Yeah."

"Then it's all good, man," Wes said, patting him on the shoulder. "Not that Ramsey wouldn't show you a real good time, but I always got the impression you want more than a hookup, and that's all he's ever interested in."

How was that possible when Aidan had only had fleeting hookups in his life, and in the last few years, while Wes had been around, none at all?

Well, that was probably why. There'd been none at all, because he'd been too busy pining for Mo.

"Uh, well, yeah. I guess so." Because it wasn't like hookups *had* ever done it for Aidan. But then, he wasn't entirely sure if this thing with Levi *was* a hookup. They hadn't defined it; they'd only both grabbed for it.

Maybe that meant something. Maybe it didn't.

"It's really all good, Flynn. Glad it's going good." Wes patted him again, absently, then gestured at the screen. "You wanna go over these coverages again?"

"Yes," Aidan said with certainty. He'd probably only play a series or two—if Zane felt they needed more to look at—but Wes was going to be in the rest of the game.

They finished up in the next hour, and when Aidan glanced at his phone, he saw that Levi had finished up early and had caught a ride back downtown with Lane and Trevor.

Aidan ignored the spike of disappointment and sent a thumbs-up response to Levi and then another text to Riley. **You free in a few?**

Riley sent back a response almost instantly. **Yeah, give me ten.**

That was just about perfect. Aidan gathered his bag, picked up a chicken caesar wrap he'd supplement with a protein shake when he got home, and headed towards his car.

Riley called six minutes into his drive back, just after he'd finished cramming the last of his wrap into his mouth.

"Perfect timing," Aidan said, a little garbled as he chewed and swallowed.

"Yeah?" It was only a single word but Riley sounded good. Happy and upbeat. Typical Riley.

Sometimes Aidan was slightly envious that he could be like that, but whenever he was, he remembered that Riley *could* be like that. That he'd protected him from the worst of their parents' bullshit, and Riley's sunshine had never been dimmed.

"Yeah, just finished eating. Well, part one anyway."

"I've never heard anyone sound so happy about a protein shake," Riley teased.

"It was a good day," Aidan said, and because he didn't say it enough—and he *hadn't* said it enough, before, which meant he always went out of his way to say it now—added, "Even better now."

He could practically hear Riley beam through the phone. "Yeah, you guys kicking ass this year? How's Levi on your line? Landry's been weirdly close-lipped about it."

"Not sure Levi's been telling him much," Aidan said. Levi had told him over dinner last night that he'd decided to be more circumspect. It was one thing to play for teams on opposite sides of the country that played each other maybe every few years. It was another thing entirely to be in the same division.

Landry wouldn't take advantage, but Landry wanted to win the same way that Levi did. That Aidan did.

"Makes sense," Riley said. "We never had that problem, though."

"I think it's just gonna take some getting used to. You want me to talk to him?"

Riley was quiet for a moment. "No, no. It'll work itself out. Landry's just neurotic about it. Worried about Levi, even though he shouldn't be."

"Good news is you're a pro at dealing with that." Even a year ago, Aidan didn't think he could've made that joke, but the shame crawling up his spine when he thought of how he'd acted—and how Riley had tolerated it and endured it and then finally snapped over it—felt less pressing than it had back then.

"True." Riley's voice was wry. "So you're on friendly terms, then?"

Of course Riley was digging. Gently, in a very Riley-like way, but still digging. Aidan experienced a momentary fear that he was only doing it because he suspected something. But how could he?

"Ri, he's living in my guest room."

Riley chuckled under his breath. "I know. I *know*. But you two have never been close. You gotta forgive a younger bro for looking out for other younger bros."

Riley wouldn't be Riley if he didn't—not because he needed to. Aidan reminded himself that Riley knew that.

"We're doing good," Aidan said, hoping that would be the end of it.

"No details? Just 'we're good'?" Riley still sounded playful but the intent was there. Aidan knew him too well not to hear it.

"You know how it is," Aidan said. "We're at the practice facility twelve-plus hours a day. Putting in the work. He did . . .uh . . .we've been playing some games. He finally got me to get a new gaming system."

"Oh yeah?" Riley asked brightly. "Good work, Levi."

Aidan rolled his eyes. "Maybe I'll even get one for the Michigan house."

"You better, bro."

Before Aidan could change the subject, Riley continued, "You know it was awesome when he came with us this summer. Only a bummer he couldn't stay longer."

Aidan told himself for a second time that Riley couldn't know anything. They'd been careful and Riley had been, as usual, totally distracted by Landry. Besides, the last personal development he'd told Riley was that he was trying to get over Mo.

"For sure," Aidan said. What else could he say? He couldn't demand Riley tell him what he knew—or what he suspected.

"You talk to Mo?"

Aidan let out a frustrated sigh. "Why don't you just come out and ask, Ri?"

"Ask what?"

Aidan growled, but Riley only laughed.

"I'm not sure what you want me to ask? I'm just trying to figure out where your head's at," Riley said.

"My head's at—" Aidan broke off. He and Levi hadn't discussed what they were doing. Not recently anyway. It didn't seem like whatever the definition was, it still fell under the sex pact umbrella. But he wasn't going to say anything to Riley before he'd even talked to Levi about it.

And he was totally okay leaving it undefined for now. Things felt delicate and new, and he was *happy*. Why would he want to fuck with that?

"What?" Riley asked. Kindly. Gently.

"It's good. I'm . . .I'm good."

"So you've talked to Mo, then."

Of course Riley was not going to drop it. It would be ridiculous to assume he would. Maybe Riley had never been in the running for the Overprotective Brother of the Year award, but he was a Flynn all the way through.

"Actually, I haven't." He'd thought about texting him, though. More than once. Maybe in a few weeks, he might. It wasn't just because of Levi, though that was part of it, too.

It just felt weird to be starting a season and not talk to him at all.

A few years ago, Mo was in the passenger seat next to him and there'd never have been a need to text him.

"Bro," Riley said earnestly, "that is so good. I'm so proud of you. I know it probably wasn't easy to take the time you needed to move on."

Aidan didn't really want to go into it, but almost three months removed from the whole mess, he'd begun to realize that the crux of the matter was that he'd never really believed he'd get the things he wanted from Mo. Even when he'd gone to Vegas and asked, he hadn't really believed it would go his way. He'd only done it because it *had* to be done.

"No, but it's okay . . .I mean it."

"Good." He could hear the smile in Riley's voice. "You seem like you're doing good."

Riley babbled for a few minutes longer, about Carter and Beck and Micah. Landry was in there, too, affection rich in his brother's voice whenever he came up.

But the whole time, Aidan was turning over what he'd said—and what Riley had said in return.

It *was* okay. He hadn't thought it ever would be, but he'd been wrong. Telling Mo and then finding out he hadn't been wrong about it had felt more like an end than a beginning.

That had hurt. Of course it had. Aidan would've had to feel nothing for it not to. But over time, the hurt was fading.

Distraction was good, of course. The football season starting helped. And Levi in his bed, too.

But Levi was far more than a distraction.

He wasn't just *using* him to not be miserable. He'd known even back in Michigan that he wouldn't, that he *couldn't*. And he wasn't.

Aidan wanted him exactly where he was at—just to the left of him, protecting his blind side. Reminding him he wasn't alone. Filling the condo with the comfortable, easy noises of living. This morning, waking up to the warmth in his eyes, filling him with heat.

By the time Riley was talked out, Aidan was only a few blocks away from the condo.

"I gotta go," he told his brother. "I'm nearly home. And I'll lose you in the underground garage."

"Don't be a stranger," Riley lectured. "And hey, say hi to Levi for me. A big hug, even."

Aidan's pulse skittered. Still half convinced with the way Riley kept bringing Levi up and what he kept freaking saying that he knew *something*. "Ri," he warned.

Riley just laughed though. "Oh, dude, you hug people. Don't even try that with me."

He was doing a hell of a lot more than just hugging Levi these days.

"Okay, fine. Sure." He didn't mind promising. Hugging wasn't really something he and Levi were doing, but it would give him an excuse to close any distance between them when he stepped through the front door, and Aidan was taking every single one of those opportunities these days.

"Good luck in your game. You're playing, right?" Riley asked.

"Yeah. A series. Maybe two." Riley had already played in his preseason game and wouldn't be taking the field again.

"You're gonna kill it," Riley said with the upmost confidence.

"Thanks," Aidan said dryly.

He hung up the call right before he turned into the garage. After parking, he grabbed his bag and headed towards the elevator.

When he opened the front door, he heard the sound of a blender in the kitchen, and when he walked in, Levi was in there, no shirt and only a ratty pair of Seahawks shorts that looked like he'd had them for twenty years, not seven.

"Hey," Levi called out. "Made you a protein shake."

Aidan hadn't texted Levi that he was on his way home, but apparently Levi was psychic that way.

"You a mind reader now?" he asked, walking into the kitchen. Levi had just finished pouring the shake into a glass and had turned towards the sink to rinse out the pitcher.

It was so easy—especially because he'd promised Riley he'd do it—to put his arms around Levi. Tug him back against his body.

Levi made a surprised but pleased noise. "No, but I think you must be. Knew I wanted you."

Hooking his chin over Levi's shoulder, secretly glad he was just tall enough he could do this, Aidan said, "You did?"

"Don't sound so surprised, bro," Levi teased.

"I'm not." But he was, kind of. He knew he wanted Levi. Badly, in fact. But Levi was more chill, less intense all around about everything. He could want Aidan and he could want a bunch of other people too, and Aidan wasn't sure he'd ever know the difference.

That thought didn't feel good, so Aidan pushed it away.

"You ever gonna tell me why you knew I was on my way home or is that a Levi secret?"

Levi chuckled. Turned in his arms. Pressed a kiss under Aidan's jaw. "I texted Wes to ask him a question and he said you'd just left. Thought I'd have your shake ready for you, 'cause I know you like it right when you get home, especially if you didn't eat dinner."

"I had a chicken wrap," Aidan said, but Levi wasn't wrong.

"Oh, yeah, like that's gonna be enough." Levi grinned. "I know you, dude, you're a hungry guy after a long day like that one."

"Walkthrough tomorrow. Should be chiller," Aidan said. After that, they'd take the long flight to California. And then back right after. It sucked to have to travel so far for a preseason game, but Aidan was sadly used to the way the NFL schedule liked to fuck with them.

"Yeah," Levi said. "About that. I'm sort of counting on it."

A spike of worry speared through Aidan. He tried to tamp it down with no success. "You okay? You nursing an injury?" He hadn't seen Levi on the injury report, but vets could be cagey. Afraid to report things, afraid to be held out, especially if their playing time was up in the air.

Levi's wasn't, but he was still pushing through the last of Zane's reluctance to make him the starting left tackle, and Aidan could imagine that right now, Levi wouldn't want to draw attention to himself or rock the boat in any way.

Levi just laughed though, tucking his face into Aidan's neck, arms winding around his waist. Somehow he was even closer then. Aidan knew he should drink his shake—Levi had made it for him, after all—but that would mean letting go of Levi and he really, really didn't want to.

"No, bro, I'm good. I'm so good. I just . . .thought we could take advantage of the light day tomorrow."

Levi shot him a knowing look, but Aidan wasn't sure what that meant or why Levi was being so cagey. He typically had no issues asking for what he wanted, now that they were doing this.

It was Aidan who had all the neuroses about expressing his desires. "I'm not sure what you mean."

"Bro." Levi sighed with exaggeration. "I forget you're new to this."

Aidan decided he was going to take that as a compliment. "Yeah."

Levi nudged his hips flush against Aidan's. "Want you to fuck me tonight."

Maybe he shouldn't have been surprised. Of course that was a thing queer guys did together. Aidan had watched enough porn with fucking during his own sexual awakening to know he'd be into it.

He'd always imagined it with Mo. Kind of imagined that maybe Mo might want to do it to him, and Aidan wasn't against that at all.

But the thought of fucking Levi filled him with heat.

"Uh, yeah. *Yes.*"

Amusement bloomed across Levi's face. "You'd be into that?"

"Yeah," Aidan said. "And um . . .maybe someday, the other way too? If you are."

Amusement melted into pleased astonishment. "Oh yeah. I didn't think—"

Aidan flicked his shoulder, then smoothed his palm over the muscle there. "Shouldn't be making hetero-normative assumptions, Banks."

"No, I really shouldn't. Yeah, we can do it that way too. I just . . ." Levi's eyes went dark, heated, and Aidan's cock twitched in his shorts. Okay, he *really* wanted. Hadn't even thought about it really, not until now, because what they'd been doing had already been so good. "I just really want it tonight."

Aidan was having trouble thinking of any good reason to not immediately drag Levi to his bedroom. His whole brain had short-circuited and practically gone offline, just at the thought of it.

His hands tightened on Levi's skin. "Yes, yes, let's—right now."

But Levi just laughed. It was such an easy, effortless sound. Every time Aidan heard it, it felt like it sucked out just a little of his hurt and his anxiety and his worry. Even the pain of Mo turning him down, diminishing little by little.

"What?" Aidan couldn't believe he'd suggest it and not want to go to the bedroom *now*.

"Dude, at least drink your shake." Levi fluttered his eyelashes. They were dark and surprisingly long. "Gotta keep your energy up if you're gonna keep up with me."

"Fuck," Aidan said.

Only the thought of what was waiting for them when they did finally make it to the bedroom allowed him to let go of Levi and slide the shake over.

He took a big gulp and swallowed. It was perfect. Exactly the way he liked it. He hadn't thought Levi was paying that much attention, but his thoughtfulness—though not exactly obvious—was doing things to Aidan. Things he couldn't define. Things he couldn't deal with.

"You eat too?" Aidan asked, changing the subject and burying the *things* way down. He could pull them out and look at them later. *Much* later.

"Yeah, dude. You don't gotta worry about me. Heated something up from the meal service." Levi was still sending that twinkly-eyed look in his direction, and it was making Aidan feel unhinged.

Like go all caveman-style kind of unhinged.

Maybe Levi would even enjoy that. There was a part of Aidan that thought *he* might even enjoy it, if the tables were turned.

Aidan took another big drink of his shake. "Thanks for this, by the way." He gestured towards the cup. "You didn't have to."

"Of course I didn't, but I wanted to." He paused. "Maybe I thought making your shake might butter you up. Might make you more likely to agree."

"What, to agree to *fuck you*?" Aidan's jaw dropped. "You thought I'd need buttering up for that?" The concept that Levi wasn't sure he'd go wild for it, wild for it like he was already doing even though they hadn't even started yet, was difficult to comprehend.

Levi just shrugged, like it was no big deal.

But it was a big deal to Aidan, and he wasn't going to let that stand. Maybe he was shitty at expressing himself, but he could do this, at least.

"Listen," Aidan said, "you don't have to butter me up or bribe me or any of that shit. I want to. I *really* want to. I don't want you to think you're pushing me into any of this." Truthfully, it felt like most days he was holding back from everything he suddenly craved. Or was it sudden after all? Aidan wasn't sure.

Levi shot him a knowing look. "It was a joke, bro. I know. You're into . . .this."

There was enough of a hesitation that Aidan thought he might have been about to say *you're into me*, instead of *you're into this*.

Just into the gay sex, generally, instead of being into Levi, specifically.

Before, two months ago, Aidan would've said he was right. He'd wanted to experiment, safely. He'd wanted to know what he was doing, before it really mattered.

But there was no way he could stand here now and say it didn't matter at all, with Levi.

It mattered, a *lot*.

Way more than he'd ever expected it might.

Aidan swallowed the rest of his shake. Turned to the sink to rinse it out, so he didn't have to look at Levi when he said it.

"I am," he said quietly. He should add on, *I'm into you, too*. But the words stuck in his throat. Reminding him, a little painfully, of the moment he'd told Mo how he felt.

The shock and then the sympathy on his face as he'd gently let Aidan down. *I just don't think of you like that,* he'd said.

Levi liked Aidan's body. Liked sex with him, sure. But maybe he didn't think of Aidan *that* way, either.

The one thing Aidan was sure about was that he couldn't say it again and have it turn out the same way.

"Now that I know the truth—that you're easy for me—see if I ever make you another protein shake again," Levi teased. Like he knew Aidan needed to be tugged back out of his head, again. More than that—like he knew and he didn't even mind.

"Bro," Aidan drawled, and Levi cackled in delight before moving in closer, nudging one thigh against Aidan's.

It was so easy to lean in the rest of the way and kiss the laugh right off his mouth.

Levi's body was so hot and big and *there*—so strong he could manhandle Aidan anyway he wanted, but this time, he let Aidan press *him* into the counter. Aidan groaned in the back of his throat as he pressed them together. Feeling Levi's cock, hard and ready, against him.

He felt lightheaded with desire, like he could barely take a breath.

"Come on," Levi said in a low, rough voice. "Bedroom."

Aidan expected Levi to drag them to *his* bedroom, where they'd slept together the night before, Levi's phone charging cord in hopefully semi-permanent residence on his side, but Levi didn't.

He took them to the guest bedroom instead, Aidan falling on the mattress, Levi crawling over him, their mouths barely breaking apart, even for a moment.

"God," Levi groaned. "Want you so bad." He pulled Aidan's T-shirt off, hand trailing down his chest. "Want every bit of you."

Aidan almost told him *You can have it*, but before he could work up the nerve, the words were gone, lost in the sensation of Levi's palm pressing against his hard cock.

Digging his fingernails into the meat of Levi's shoulders, his head fell back against the bed.

Levi hummed, looking and sounding smug and satisfied. "I'm gonna ride you into oblivion," he told him.

Aidan choked on his breath.

"Is there anything—" he tried to ask but Levi just cut him off.

"You want to?"

Of fucking course he wanted to. He wasn't just a pretty face and a convenient dick.

Levi was big, but Aidan was strong, too.

It took effort but, squeezing his thighs around Levi's hips, he got them flipped. "Yeah," he said, and this time it was him who sounded smug.

Smiling, Levi gazed up at him. "There's . . .uh . . .lube in the drawer. If you want to—if you—"

"If you ask if I know how, I'm gonna smack you," Aidan grumbled under his breath. Yeah, he was a rookie at this, but he wasn't *stupid*. He could fucking google. He had a right hand and an incognito browser, same as everyone else.

Crawling over Levi, he found the lube, but no condoms.

"We were both tested, when we got to camp," Levi explained, when Aidan lifted an eyebrow. "I'm not sleeping with anyone else. Are you?"

It was impossible not to laugh. There'd been a time he wouldn't have been able to. "Please tell me you're joking," Aidan said.

A smile broke over Levi's face. He'd said, completely subconsciously, that Landry was the most attractive of his brothers, but there was no denying that Levi turned Aidan's head, all the time now. So hard and so earnestly, it felt like he could barely look away.

And when he was smiling up at Aidan like that? Like Aidan was both the most ridiculous person he knew and also like he couldn't quite believe he was lucky enough to be here, in Aidan's condo, in Aidan's bed, Aidan hovering over him? He was fucking breathtaking.

"Maybe, a little," Levi admitted, gasping out at the end of his sentence as Aidan tugged his shorts down.

Aidan shot him a pointed look as Levi spread his bare legs open, inviting Aidan inside.

"Kind of desperate, huh?" Aidan wondered as he opened up the lube. "To be freeballing it in the kitchen, making me a protein shake?"

"You say it like it's a bad thing." Levi let out another sharp gasp as Aidan brushed his hole with the pad of his thumb, spreading the wetness around.

"And," Levi added, "maybe I am, a little. Desperate, that is."

He wasn't the only one.

Aidan felt like he was going out of his mind not just with want, but with *need*. He needed to be inside Levi, *yesterday*.

Maybe he'd never done this before, but he knew what *he'd* like, and he went with that. Slow and deliberate, no matter how much Levi tried to beg and plead for him to go faster. One finger, then two, and then when Levi was writhing on three, he leaned over him, Levi panting into his mouth as they kissed and asked, "Are you good?"

Aidan realized *he* was panting, too, his cock aching with how desperately hard he was.

Levi nodded. "Like *yesterday*, bro."

Aidan was so out of his mind with it he didn't even tease Levi about the *bro*. In fact, it felt just right for him to say it, intimate and knowing like that. Like he couldn't be referring to anyone else but Aidan.

"Okay." Aidan breathed in and out. Suddenly nervous, even though he shouldn't be. He'd had sex before. This was not *that* different from other sex he'd had. But deep down, it felt incredibly different.

And when he finally pushed in, still trying to be slow and careful, no matter how Levi's heels nudged at his back, trying to urge him to go faster, it *did* feel different.

So tight and so hot, yes, but so much more than the physical.

Levi let out a long drawn-out groan when he bottomed out. "Fuck, that's so good." He batted his eyelashes at Aidan. "Fill me up so good, baby."

Aidan huffed out a breath. Furiously trying to hold on to his control, even though it was slippery and it felt like he couldn't get a grip on it. "Yeah?"

"Oh yeah." Levi winked at him, and Aidan couldn't help the laugh he choked out. He'd never imagined laughing during sex before, but with Levi it felt natural. Easy. Like for the first time in his life, he wasn't pretending to be someone he wasn't. Occupying a persona the rest of the world had created for him.

Tucking Levi's knee against his chest, he began to thrust, still carefully at first. But the pleasure was fraying at the reminders to be gentle, and Levi was certainly begging him enough to go harder, faster.

It hit him suddenly: he didn't *have* to be careful.

Levi could take it. He *wanted* to take it.

When Aidan gave a hard thrust for the first time, Levi's head flopped back against the mattress and he let out a sound that Aidan would be hearing every time he jerked off, from now until the day he died.

"There, *there*," Levi pled, and Aidan did what he did best: physically perform.

Hips moving like pistons, Levi squirming on his dick. Maybe it shouldn't have been so good, but it was. Life-changing, really.

There was a point where Aidan thought he might've blacked right out, the sheer *feeling* of rightness pushing out everything but the pleasure and the man underneath him.

"Come here," Levi breathed out, voice fucked out and rough, and Aidan leaned over, kissing him. Feeling the precome-slick head of Levi's cock rub against his abs, and a second later, everything tightened around him as Levi groaned out his orgasm right into Aidan's mouth.

Aidan couldn't hold on a moment after that, Levi's body clenching around him, and he followed after, everything in stark black and then white, like a spotlight had just flashed bright in his head.

"Fucking hell," Levi said as Aidan carefully pulled out and then collapsed on the bed next to him.

He didn't know what the standard behavior was, not after sex like that, but he wasn't moving.

Levi turned to him, fingers twitching against his sweat-damp chest. Stroking his skin. Like it was normal. Like it was allowed. And maybe it was.

"Good?" he asked after a long moment of silence. Aidan just trying to catch his breath; trying to remember what he'd been like half an hour ago, before they'd ever done that.

"I feel like my brain just melted out my ears," Aidan admitted. Apparently his caution had gone the same way, evaporating in the white-hot supernova of the best sex he'd ever had.

"Yeah," Levi agreed, smiling. He didn't look patronizing or like he was just going along with whatever Aidan said. "That was . . ." He sighed, happy and satisfied. *I did that*, Aidan thought.

Normally, Aidan might not have asked, but he wanted to know. "That was?" he wondered.

Levi nudged him. Knowing twist to his lips. "Fucking unreal, you know it was. You were there, bro."

"And you were trying to *bribe* me into it, with a protein shake."

Levi gave a groan. "You ever gonna let me live that down?"

"You ever gonna stop calling me bro?" Aidan was beginning to really understand why people let their lives and careers get burned down by really good sex. If someone said he had to give this feeling up, like he'd just been filled with helium and set free, just floating above the bed, he'd fight them.

"Nope," Levi said unapologetically.

And Aidan smiled. "Exactly."

CHAPTER 14

"How was the game?" Logan asked Levi as he lay in bed.

Aidan was gone, at brunch with his agent, who'd swung up to Toronto on a trip to the East Coast to check in with his players before the season started.

Usually he and Logan FaceTimed, but Levi had specifically told his brother he was naked in bed, so he wouldn't have to additionally explain that he was naked, in *Aidan's* bed.

Because the big bed, the room, the decor, the floor-to-ceiling windows with the sunlight streaming in, told the whole story and Logan wasn't stupid. This wasn't the guest room, and Levi didn't want to lie to his older brother and tell him it was.

"It was fine," Levi said. "I played like, a series. I don't know, like ten plays? We scored a TD. Beautiful fucking slant to Trev. Don't know if you saw it."

"Sure did," Logan said. "Flynn looks strong."

Strong and gorgeous and confident.

Levi had never been more proud to block for a quarterback in his life, and he knew that meant something, but he was feeling a lot better about it if he *didn't* look at that too closely.

"Yeah, for sure," Levi agreed.

"And you at left tackle." Speaking of pride, it was practically leaking out of Logan's voice. "Didn't think you'd ever want to make the switch."

Another bit of motivation Levi didn't really want to examine too closely. But it was bone-deep in him at this point. He wanted to protect Aidan and shield him and make him smile, too. Relieve even just a fraction of the weight he carried around on those capable shoulders.

And not just because the sex was great, though it was, but because Levi had begun to see that nobody had ever done that for him before.

"It was the right choice," Levi said simply.

Logan's silence was telling. "Oh yeah? Just you volunteering to move over? To deal with a whole new set of problems?" His voice was arch. He'd clearly been reading the media chatter surrounding Levi's switch. Levi didn't know if he was flattered by that, or annoyed.

Or maybe it was more fear that Logan would assume all the right things.

"Like you've never done that," Levi muttered.

"Yeah, I sure have, but you? I can't say *never*, 'cause you're a Banks, through and through. Never saw a challenge you didn't want to meet. But mostly, you just didn't see them."

It was an uncomfortably accurate assessment. Typical Logan. Levi wished he was slightly less observant.

Before he could drop any more truth bombs, Levi changed the subject. "And how was the sideline for you yesterday, bro?"

Logan groaned. "I had to watch Dylan suit up. It sucked. I hated it."

"Dude, you're never even on the field at the same time as your guy. Not in preseason. Not in a regular game, either." Logan played center on the offensive line and Dylan, his boyfriend, was the Piranhas' kicker.

"I know." Logan still sounded frustrated. "It still sucks? Like he was involved and I was just…*there*." He echoed all the things that Levi didn't like about the preseason, either.

They really *were* both Bankses, through and through. Levi had a feeling if they got Landry on the phone, it would be the same for him. He'd whine about how he'd had to watch Riley throw to some other tight end that wasn't *him*.

"Season starting soon, though," Levi promised.

"Yeah," Logan agreed.

Levi wet his lips. Wondering if he should say something about what was really on his mind. Why he'd really called his brother. Even if he was nebulous, Logan might guess—but then, why should he? He didn't know about Aidan.

Landry did, which was why it was Logan he'd called. There was a slightly better chance Levi might be able to talk about this and not give it all away.

"So um, I gotta ask," Levi said, "I know you're crazy about Dylan—"

"That's nothing new," Logan said.

"No, I know. Which is why I gotta ask. How did you *know* you wanted him to be more than just a hookup?"

Logan went deathly quiet. Unfairly, Levi thought. Logan had had his hookup phase, just the same as Levi had. He'd never made any secret about it and had never had any shame either. Sure, Levi's had lasted a year or two longer, but they weren't *that* different.

It wasn't like Levi was allergic to relationships or emotionally stunted. He'd never just looked at someone and wanted and wanted and wanted. Wanted so much he didn't think he'd ever find the bottom of it.

But he was beginning to think that was the situation with Aidan.

"Are you serious?" Logan asked. "Who is it?"

Levi rolled his eyes. "Yes, and why am I not surprised that's your first question?"

"Well, bro, you haven't been in Toronto *that* long."

Levi almost told him it had started before that. This summer, even.

Maybe it had started a long time before that.

It wasn't like he'd never looked at Aidan and thought, *holy fuck he's hot*. He'd just never believed he could do anything about it, not until Aidan had come out to him.

"No, but isn't that what people say all the time?" Levi wondered. "Time doesn't matter. Like when you know, *you know*."

"If that was true, you wouldn't be calling me up about it, asking how I was sure I had feelings for Dylan and didn't just want to get into his pants."

"I don't want to be wrong." Levi didn't know if he wanted to be feeling this at all, if he was being honest. Aidan might never feel the same. After all, this whole thing had started because he'd told Levi he was in love with Morris Jeffries.

Aidan might still be in love with Morris Jeffries. He might be in love with Morris Jeffries *forever*.

That did not bode well for Levi's potential feelings.

"You're not stupid," Logan said, which was shockingly unhelpful.

"Duh," Levi retorted.

"I'm just saying, the fact that you have to ask me how I knew I didn't want to just hook up with Dylan? Well, that tells you something right there."

Levi was afraid of this, which was why he hadn't brought it up before now. Not *only* why he'd been cautious about it, but no question it was a factor.

"And," Logan added, his voice growing kinder, "you know what just wanting someone feels like. When you've nutted, you're kinda done, you know? With Dylan, I never feel like I get enough. I want him around all the time. Just to talk. Or laugh. Or whatever."

Yeah, Levi knew. Sure, they were living together, so they'd be together anyway, but Levi looked forward to pretty much every moment they hung out. Even if it was as stupid as sitting together on the plane back from California, with three-quarters of the team asleep in the cabin around them, as they watched their touchdown drive on Aidan's tablet and broke down every single play they'd run and how they could run it better next time.

Normally, that would be work. An obligation that Levi did because he had to, not because he wanted to.

But he'd enjoyed every single moment of it, because it was Aidan he was doing it with. Aidan he could poke gentle fun at. Aidan he could make smile. Aidan he could knock his knee against and watch as his blue eyes grew just a little smoky with barely banked heat.

"You gonna tell me who it is?" Logan asked again.

Like hell he was. If he told Logan, there was no way Logan wouldn't tell Landry—and that would be yanking open a whole can of worms.

Levi hesitated.

"I get it—it's probably someone on the team," Logan said.

"Yeah," Levi said. He could admit that much. It would at least keep Logan off his back, because Logan would assume that they weren't out publicly yet and that was why Levi was being close-lipped about their identity. That was *also* true. But that wasn't really the reason Levi wasn't saying.

"I never thought you'd be the one asking these questions," Logan said.

There it was again. Just because Levi enjoyed hooking up and had never really felt like he needed *more* from someone, he was never going to want more. Levi made a face, glad again that Logan couldn't see.

"What is that supposed to mean?"

Logan clucked, like the eighty-year-old grandmother he wasn't.

"Hey, you got around plenty pre-Dylan," Levi said, before his brother could make any more disapproving noises.

"Sure," Logan said.

"Then why the judgment?" Levi demanded to know.

"I just . . .*we* just . . .we worry about you."

Logan didn't need to go into detail about who the *we* consisted of. Landry and Lyla, no doubt. All uniting against him and his perfectly understandable desire to have a good time. "God, I'm almost jealous of Riley. Only one older sibling to worry about."

"Come on," Logan chided. "I'm just saying. I've been telling you that sex that isn't just sex to get your rocks off is pretty damn good."

He *had* been saying it, for literal years now, but then Levi was also sure that was because he was head over heels with and completely, entirely dickmatized by Dylan.

"Yeah, 'cause you found the right guy to have that sex with."

Levi couldn't blame him; Dylan *was* a great guy and also happened to be perfect for his brother. Hot and funny and smart. Easygoing and easy to get along with, with none of Logan's dramatics. And a damn good kicker, too.

Competency porn was totally a thing.

Levi might've gotten a little hard watching Aidan throwing that touchdown to Trevor. The soft touch with the ball. The accuracy and how he'd put it where only Trev could catch it. Fifteen years of college and NFL experience condensed into one single throw. It was easy to see why Aidan had two Super Bowl rings, looking at a throw like that.

"And," Logan said bluntly, "maybe you've finally found the right guy, too."

God, Levi almost hoped that wasn't true. He liked Aidan so much, but dating him would be complicated.

There was the Flynn connection. Then the fact they were teammates. And of course, the most complicated part of all: that three months ago, Aidan had told him he was in love with someone else.

"Don't get carried away," Levi said, snorting. Easier to make it a joke. Easier to do that than to try to figure out how to take it seriously. Even though there was a part of him—a part he was increasingly concerned wasn't his dick—that wanted to.

"Hey, you're the one who called me. Asked me how I knew Dylan was the guy." Logan exhaled, a happy, contented sigh that Levi was not jealous of. Not one bit.

Levi had a fierce mini internal debate and finally gave in. "The guy told me he was in love with someone else," he said.

It seemed like he'd shocked Logan into silence.

"For real?" he asked after that long fraught moment.

"Yeah. When I found out, it didn't feel like a big deal. Like it told me he was queer, right, 'cause it was another guy he was into, and he was hot and I was like, well, why not give him a taste if he's into it. He was. He *is*. But . . ."

"But?" Logan prompted.

Levi made an exasperated noise. "You fucking know what, Logan. But now I'm probably into *him*, and he's not into me. Not like that. Likes the sex, sure, but what about anything else?"

"You *could* ask, you know," Logan said.

"Yeah, 'cause if he doesn't feel that way, that wouldn't be awkward or anything." It would be awful. He'd have to move out, but it wouldn't matter, because he'd still see Aidan all the time. Every day, really.

And Aidan would feel bad—despite his reputation, Levi had discovered he had an unexpectedly soft heart underneath it all—because he'd just gone through the other side of this. But it wasn't like feeling bad actually changed anything.

"Might not be."

"Yeah, I don't think so," Levi said, feeling more sure than ever that he couldn't.

"Levi," Logan said softly.

"It's a bad idea," Levi said firmly.

"Alright," Logan agreed. "But think about it, okay? Things always change."

"Things *might* change."

"Who are you and what have you done with my optimistic brother?" Logan teased, but the words hit home.

He didn't want Logan to think he was sitting here crying about it. Aidan was in *his* bed—or he was in Aidan's—and he couldn't see that changing anytime soon. Maybe Aidan would never feel the same way about him, but as long as he had that, did he *need* more?

Levi didn't think so.

"Actually, it's good, I'm actually totally fine with how things are," Levi said firmly. "He's in my bed—or I'm in his. He's not leaving for anyone else's. So it's cool."

"How does Aidan feel about this guy being in your bed?"

Levi choked on air. Hoped that Logan didn't hear it. "Uh, well. He's um . . .he's cool with it." Cooler with it than Logan even realized.

"I was sort of surprised you didn't find a new place right away," Logan said, like he had no idea the shit he was currently wading into. And Levi really, really hoped he never figured it out.

"Uh, well, I'm pretty happy here. Settled, now. Aidan's pretty decent to live with."

"Sure." Logan did not sound convinced. "I'm trying to figure out how you used to bitch about him, and now you're like *Aidan's cool!*"

Ever since I started thinking about getting him naked.

Levi wanted to defend the shift—wanted to defend Aidan, if he was being honest—but he couldn't go too hard. Not without raising Logan's suspicions. "Dude, he's really kind of great."

"You said that before," Logan said. "Last time we talked."

"Well, it's true." *Don't sound defensive, don't sound defensive.*

"Huh. Well. I suppose that makes sense, since you didn't move out the moment you could."

Levi hadn't even thought about moving out. Especially not now, not since he'd started sleeping next to Aidan every night. Waking up in the morning to his bed head, to the sleepy heat in his blue eyes. He enjoyed it so much he couldn't imagine leaving it for a bland, empty apartment.

"Yeah, well, if it works, it works." And it *worked.*

"Guess so." Logan still sounded incredulous but at least he wasn't pushing it. Or suspicious.

"You gonna play in the next game?" Levi asked, changing the subject.

Logan made a frustrated noise. "No idea, but probably not. Coach is pissing me off."

"Are you even allowed to say that?" Levi joked.

"Hell yes," Logan grumbled. "He's sitting a bunch of us. Resting up, I guess. Pax is really pissed, too. Wade and Tris, too. Sebastian's been whining at Beau about it all week."

Pax was the Piranhas' starting quarterback, and Wade and Tristan played tight end and wide receiver for them, respectively.

"Wait, isn't Sebastian *dating* Beau?" Levi asked. Sebastian was the Piranhas' Pro Bowl safety, and Beau was the assistant coach—and *son*—of the Piranhas' head coach, Asa Dawson.

"Yeah, you *know* that, Levi. That's why he's trying to use his influence."

"I take it it's not working."

"Not really."

"Sucks, dude," Levi said, though it wasn't like he was going to play again. Coach Zane had made a few offhand comments about running him again at left tackle for a few plays next week, but Levi wasn't sure if he had a decent week of practice if those reps would even materialize. Especially if they wanted to spend the field time figuring which backups would be making the final fifty-three-man roster.

"I just wanna play," Logan complained.

"You're gonna get there," Levi soothed. Sometimes Logan could be so bitchy. "Week one isn't that far off."

"Fair," Logan agreed. There was a sound on his side of the call. "Hey, I gotta go. Dylan's home."

"Can't keep your man waiting," Levi joked. Even though Aidan would be home soon, too. Aidan wasn't his man. Not in the same way Dylan and Logan belonged to each other, but he still wanted to be off the phone by then.

"Yeah, yeah," Logan said. But he sounded distracted already, and that was par for the course whenever Dylan was involved.

"Talk to you later, bro," Levi said and hung up.

He groaned and slid out of bed after plugging his phone in to charge and got into the shower.

By the time he was done, pulling on only a pair of shorts, he headed into the main living area, and sure enough, Aidan was back, putting stuff into the fridge.

"Oh hey," Aidan said, straightening up, the beginnings of a pleased smile emerging on his face. "I brought you some food. Put it in the fridge 'cause I didn't know when you'd want it."

"Now. Obviously now," Levi said, detouring towards the kitchen. Aidan had pulled the takeout container out, setting it on the counter, and Levi popped the top.

Wherever Aidan had gone to brunch looked incredible. That had to be brisket, sliced thick, with a decent-looking smoke ring, nestled under two poached eggs, on top of biscuits, with a little cup of sauce on the side. And alongside, an enormous pile of delicious-looking breakfast potatoes, full of crispy crags.

"Damn," Levi said, unable to resist popping a potato in his mouth. "I think I love you."

He said it without thinking, and he told himself not to freeze when Aidan flushed red. "Just thought you'd enjoy it. Hope it's good. I know you've got feelings about brisket and biscuits, being from Texas."

"Hard to find good barbeque outside of it," Levi agreed. "But this looks great. Thanks."

He slid the whole mess on top of a plate for reheating, even though he'd already had a protein shake this morning.

"Just don't tell the nutritionist," Aidan said, flushing.

"Please tell me you had something that was at least this good," Levi said as the food spun in the microwave.

Aidan winced. "Avocado toast and egg whites?"

"Dude. *Dude.*" Levi pulled a fork out of the drawer. "That's so fucking disappointing."

"I did splurge a little. Got a mimosa. Felt like celebrating."

"Oh yeah, why?" The microwave beeped and Levi pulled his food out. Didn't even bother moving to one of the barstools—just leaned over the counter and dug in. The brisket wasn't quite as good as his favorite from Austin, but this was still pretty damn good, especially considering they were in *Canada*.

"Told my agent I was . . .well, that I was *something*," Aidan said. He sounded so matter-of-fact Levi had to look up and try to read his face.

"That you're queer?" Levi questioned between bites of biscuits and brisket.

"Yeah," Aidan said. "I didn't give him a label, because I'm not sure I *know* the right one."

"Makes sense," Levi said.

Aidan looked surprised. "You're not . . .you really think that?"

Sometimes Aidan was an idiot. A *cute* idiot, sure, but an idiot all the same. "I said it, didn't I?"

"I mean . . .shouldn't I know?"

"No?"

Aidan sighed. "Okay. Well. Anyway. I told him. First person outside of um . . .family and close friend circles I've told."

"Who *have* you told?" Levi wondered. Then realized he probably didn't need to ask that. Didn't need to *know* that.

But before he could tell Aidan that, Aidan just shrugged and said, "Well, you, obviously. Riley. Landry. And um . . .Dawson, too. Wes knows. And now Carson, my agent."

"Cool," Levi said, nodding.

He couldn't make the argument these biscuits were as good as the ones his mom made, but they were close enough that he was going to have to get the name of this restaurant out of Aidan. Maybe a bit of sexy bribery might work?

And next time Aidan went, Levi would go with and make sure he didn't get freaking *avocado toast*.

"I'm not really thinking of coming out, not publicly," Aidan said, "but I'm not against it either? I don't talk about my personal life much, anyway . . ."

"Bro, you *have* a personal life?" Levi joked, smile fond.

He wasn't ever sure what would be a step too far for Aidan—he could be so painfully serious, often caught up in his own head—but he only grinned. "*Bro*, see if I ever bring you the good stuff again."

Levi laughed. It didn't surprise him anymore when Aidan was funny. He sort of even expected it now. He imagined that Logan might tell him that Aidan's sense of humor was still shit, but that when you were down bad, objective judgment on what was actually funny went right out the window.

"Oh, you will," Levi boasted. Maybe Aidan loved Mo and not him, but who was he here with now? Who had he brought brunch to, just because he'd seen a dish on the menu he thought might be in his wheelhouse? Levi, that was who.

"Probably," Aidan grumbled, but the corner of his mouth was tilting upwards, like he couldn't really help smiling—even when he didn't want to give Levi the satisfaction.

"So what did he say?"

"Who? My agent?" Aidan pulled a bottle of water out of the fridge. Toyed with the cap. "Oh, all the right stuff. The league's more accepting these days, the public barely even blinks at a coming-out party now, etcetera, etcetera. He's right, I'm sure, and I didn't think he'd say anything else."

"It's a brave new world," Levi said. He finished his food. Patted his stomach happily. "Now I'm gonna go flop onto the couch in a food coma."

Aidan shot him a sideways look. Tried to be all subtle about it, but he was looking. "You wanna play some *Mario Kart*?"

"Thinking you're gonna win because I'm full of brisket and biscuits? Bro, I'm from Texas. We were raised on this shit. I'm still sharp, food coma or no."

"No, no. Just . . ." Aidan half grimaced and Levi couldn't figure out why he'd made that face. Not until he finished his thought. "I just thought it might be fun."

"Fun? *Fun*? Who are you and what have you done with Aidan Flynn?" Levi crowed, smacking him on the shoulder.

Aidan's smile was slightly self-conscious, but Levi loved every bit of it. "You're the worst."

You love me. Levi almost said it, but he stopped himself just in time. Thank God for small miracles, at least.

Levi hadn't been lying. No matter what he'd stuffed himself with, he was still sharp, beating Aidan so many times in a row Aidan actually lost track.

He was distracted, more than he wanted to admit to, by Levi's big warm thigh, exposed in another pair of shorts, bright magenta this time, and the way it pressed against his own.

He was in jeans, but he could feel the heat of Levi's skin through the thick fabric. It reminded him of sleepy, slow mornings, and how Levi had spent the last few nights in his bed.

How he was already wanting to coax Levi into it, even though it was the middle of the afternoon.

Finally Aidan tossed his controller down. Frustrated but not particularly surprised. "I do not have it today," he said with a frustrated grimace.

Aidan knew he wasn't particularly good at taking time off, even on scheduled days off, but he was pretty sure that wasn't why he felt so antsy, tension crawling under his skin.

It was because Levi made him feel things when they were together that he'd long since dismissed as fantasies straight from bodice-ripping romance novels.

Sex couldn't possibly be that good, because sex had never been that good for him.

"Bro, you really don't," Levi said, turning to him. He looked concerned, which was actually embarrassing. "I thought your meeting went okay?"

"It did." Of course Levi thought him being tense was about his agent. It was cute he was worried, but that didn't change how Aidan wanted to sink through the couch and die.

"Well, it's a big step," Levi said, touching his knee. "It's okay to be stressed about it."

Aidan wanted to scream. Especially when Levi's hand lingered on his thigh.

Was it worse to admit he was not stressed about his sexuality—at least not in the way Levi seemed to think—than to come clean about what actually had him worked up? Aidan didn't know.

"But I'm not really," Aidan admitted.

Levi flashed him a confused look. "No?"

He told himself not to do it. It was not chill. They were hanging out like regular bros on the couch, playing video games. Like he'd do with Dawson or Landry. Or one of a dozen teammates over the years. Doing it now would be blurring some lines that hadn't been blurred yet.

Aidan did it anyway, leaning over and pressing his mouth against Levi's. Levi seemed surprised for half a second, but then he melted into the kiss.

Levi tasted like brunch, and underneath it something so distinctly Levi—a flavor it felt like he'd been chasing for months now.

It barely took a minute of increasingly deep kissing and heavy breathing for Levi to get the picture.

He pulled back, Aidan wanting to chase his mouth with his own, but he held himself back, *barely*. "That's why you were worked up and distracted. You were *horny*."

It was still embarrassing. Even more now that Levi had said it out loud, in that soft delighted voice.

Aidan didn't answer. Didn't trust himself not to word vomit all about it onto Levi's bare thighs.

Just sank to his knees, tugged down Levi's micro-shorts and took his half-hard cock in his mouth.

Every time he did this, he liked it more and thought he got a little better at it. He wasn't entirely sure those two things weren't somehow intertwined. But then Levi sank his fingers into Aidan's hair, and he couldn't think at all.

There was only the weight of Levi's dick in his mouth, sliding deeper and then deeper still. The bitterness of his precome coating Aidan's tongue.

He felt lightheaded with it. With how good it was, and he wasn't even the one squirming with pleasure.

Levi's thighs tensed and the grip on Aidan's hair increased, and he moaned in the back of his throat. Needing to feel Levi's orgasm.

It hit a few seconds later, and Aidan swallowed.

"God damn." Levi exhaled hard as Aidan rocked back on his heels. Admiring the way Levi had melted right into the couch, sleepy satisfaction in his eyes. "Guess you were horny."

"Still horny," Aidan whined, pretending his voice didn't waver over the second word. It was still weird to be this into sex. To want it so much. To *admit* to wanting it so much. He kept half expecting Levi to make fun of him for it, but Levi only kept looking blown away by Aidan's obvious desire.

Even now, he just gave Aidan a steady look and said, "I got you."

Pulled Aidan back onto his lap, unbuttoned his jeans, and shoved his hand into Aidan's underwear. It probably should have been additionally embarrassing how quick he got there, or all the noises he made as he came all over Levi's hand. But it felt so good it was impossible to feel bad.

Jeans still undone, Aidan flopped back on the couch. Levi's arm snaked around his shoulders, pads of his fingers brushing against the sensitive column of his neck.

"So you can say the word," Levi teased.

"I can say horny," Aidan said, but even he could hear the waver. It was even harder now, now that he *wasn't*. Well, actually, he still kind of was. A low-level hum of desire that he'd had to learn with live with—though it wasn't like he'd been doing a particularly good job of that.

Levi shot him a look. "It's cute," he said, like he'd jumped right over that Aidan *barely* could and settled instead on how much he liked it.

"Alright," Aidan said, rolling his eyes, even though he was pleased, deep down.

Not worrying about being stupid or out of touch or even *bad* at this was more enjoyable than he'd even imagined it could be. He could be his complete dork, un-cool self with Levi, without ever having to put up the *I'm-a-quarterback-in-the-NFL* front.

A lot of people, even teammates, often expected the front. The *act*.

Levi looked at him weird when he even attempted it, and it was so much fucking easier to just drop it completely in these quiet moments.

To just be Aidan.

"Do you want to talk about it?" Levi asked.

"Sex?"

Levi laughed. "I hate to break it to you, but I'm not eighteen still. We're gonna have to wait some more time for that. I mean, whatever's bothering you."

Aidan opened his mouth to argue that nothing was—at least nothing that he wanted to talk about, but Levi kept going. "I know something is. I can see your mind going, behind your eyes. You're always thinking, analyzing, but this is more than that. Something you're wrestling with. If it's not your sexuality—"

"It's not *not* my sexuality," Aidan said, before he could stop himself.

That was the problem with relaxing around Levi. Aidan was actually, in fact, *relaxed,* and shit he didn't mean to say or do kept happening.

"Then what is it?" Levi asked gently. His fingertips stroked Aidan's neck. He'd never thought he'd like such a delicate touch, either. Thought he'd been above that since he was twelve and his parents' marriage had imploded so spectacularly.

"I . . .I've never liked sex as much as I like it with you," Aidan admitted.

He knew Levi by now. Should be sure that Levi wouldn't freak out at that kind of confession, but Aidan tensed anyway.

He shouldn't have worried; Levi grinned, huge and overjoyed. "I'm trying not to fist-pump here, bro."

"I'm only surprised that you're holding yourself back."

Levi turned soulful brown eyes on Aidan. "I'm trying to be supportive. Don't doubt that."

"I don't," Aidan said and meant it.

"So, that's fucking you up, then? What it means?"

Trust Levi to get right to the heart of the matter. "Yeah. Basically. Like maybe . . .if I never understood why people went crazy for sex, because the sex I was having was only mediocre, clearly there was something that wasn't working for me. And what is that? Well, it's pretty obvious what it must be."

"Yes and no," Levi said.

"Oh come on, man, you know what it is. It's that you're a *guy.* Here I thought I was straight my whole life. And first there was . . .well, you know, and now *you.*"

"That could be it, for sure," Levi agreed. He didn't look particularly shocked by how Aidan would—or actually, *wouldn't*—bring up Mo. "But I'm not convinced."

"What?"

"First, I just wanna say labels don't matter."

Aidan shot him a look. "Seriously?"

"*Seriously*, bro. What does it matter what you call yourself as long as you know what you want?"

"You mean, as long as what I want is you," Aidan said flatly.

Levi burst out laughing, delighted. "Yeah. Duh. Of course. But it's more than that. More than just me. Bigger than just us, Aidan."

"Right." Aidan didn't like that. He didn't want it to be bigger than just this moment right here, side by side on his couch. Because if it was, then Aidan might have to find someone else who fit him like Levi did. And he really fucking didn't want to.

"I'm just saying, labels are for other people. Not for you. You know who *you* are." Levi squeezed his neck now, like he was reminding him. "But also, I thought you might be gray or demi, too."

"What's that?"

Levi swallowed hard. He'd been very self-assured during this entire conversation, but now he looked concerned. Like whatever he was about to say might cost him something he wasn't quite ready to pay.

"Like, to be interested sexually in someone, your emotions have to be engaged first. And you've never had a serious relationship, right? Only hookups?"

"I guess. Yeah." He'd never met anyone he wanted to know better. And sex had always felt like a whole other subject, completely removed.

"Well, maybe that's part of it too."

Aidan noticed that Levi had skipped right over the vital part of that explanation: that he'd been sexually attracted to Mo because he'd loved him, and that he enjoyed sex with Levi because he had feelings for him, too.

Well, if Levi didn't want to talk about it, Aidan was okay not talking about it either. He wasn't sure he was ready; wasn't sure he'd *ever* be ready. Not again. Not the way he'd been, before.

But even as he thought it, he knew that was a lie. Another few weeks or months of having Levi like this, and he'd be more than ready. Fear gone. Ready to jump all in. Because this was so much more than he'd ever gotten with Mo? Or was it something else?

Aidan didn't know, but he could feel it, growing sure and firm, beneath his breastbone, reminding him it existed every single time he took a breath.

"That's . . .helpful, actually," Aidan said.

Levi nodded, gaze serious.

"I'm gonna look that up."

"Not really very surprising that you might," Levi said. "And it's just a guess. A hunch. I could be wrong. Again—labels don't matter when you're talking about yourself, about who you are."

"You're smart," Aidan said, because he could see exactly what Levi was saying.

"Shhhh," Levi said, the corner of his mouth quirking up. "Don't say it too loud, bro."

The laugh bubbled up out of Aidan, before he'd even known it was coming. And after, long after, after he'd lost three more games to Levi and actually managed to win one, he realized how much lighter he felt.

Settled, almost.

And he knew it wasn't the conversation—though that had helped, *so* much—it was just Levi.

CHAPTER 15

When Levi finished folding his laundry, he poked his head into the living room. Aidan had been reviewing tape—obsessively, even, to the point where Levi was a little over it, which was why dealing with the laundry had seemed appealing—but now he was clearly talking to someone. Had he switched to *Mario Kart*? Was he letting someone else beat him?

That was totally unacceptable. The only person allowed to trounce Aidan at video games and then make him feel better about it was Levi.

But when he glanced in the living room on his way to the kitchen, there was still game tape, paused in the middle of a play, on the TV.

As Levi reached into the fridge, he heard the voice again. It was Riley, and, Levi realized as he shuffled items around the shelves, he and Aidan were actually breaking down game tape *together*.

"I see what you're saying," Riley said. Levi could practically hear him nodding.

"I'd have handed it off to your running back—I forget who it is now," Aidan said, and Levi had become familiar enough with his various tones that he could pick out just how careful Aidan was being.

"Yeah," Riley agreed. "What about on the next one?"

As Aidan hit the play button, Levi gave up the pretense that he was actually looking for something in the fridge, straightening up as he watched the TV over the tops of the barstools.

It was a QB read play—otherwise known as the run-pass option—and Riley had passed to Landry, a nice little slant throw that hadn't gone far but *had* gotten the Condors the eight yards they needed for the first down.

"Honestly," Aidan said, after he'd watched it twice, "I think that was your best call. They were stacking the line. You got the first down. Is it sexier to get twenty, thirty, forty yards? Hit your speedy receiver with a TD? Sure. Always."

Personally, Levi thought it was the sexiest when Aidan talked this way. If he wasn't currently on the phone with his brother, he'd be tackling Aidan to the couch. Kissing him and grinding their hips together until Aidan couldn't take it anymore.

Riley gave a self-deprecating laugh, but Aidan kept going. "No, seriously, Ri. You made the right call. You nearly *always* make the right call, and nobody does all the time. You're doing a stellar job, and your instincts are spot-on. Trust those, okay?"

Riley said he would and a minute later the call was over.

Aidan glanced behind him, meeting Levi's eyes. "Sorry," he said, "Riley just wanted some advice on some plays from their last game."

"Didn't you get in trouble with Landry for doing that?" Levi asked.

Aidan pursed his lips as Levi came around the kitchen island, then sank onto the couch next to him.

"Yeah," he said. "Before. But a lot's changed since then. I learned my lesson. If Riley wants feedback, I'm always happy to give it to him, but I wait til he asks."

"Does he?"

"Ask?" Aidan pondered this. "Yeah. I mean, not right away he didn't. And I get that. We needed that reset time. More me, to see how Riley had grown up and changed. But him too, to tell me when I was being too overbearing." Aidan laughed, a little self-consciously. "We just both love each other too much, you know? Too many years of it being just us against the world. I love him so much I want to coddle him, and he loves me too much to tell me I'm fucking it up."

"But now he does, 'cause he trusts you." Levi wanted Aidan to see that—that yes, he'd fucked it up before, maybe, but that he'd become a better person, so he could be a better brother. Sometimes Levi thought Aidan only saw his initial flaws. Not the changes he'd made with blood and sweat and tears to turn things around.

"Yeah, he must," Aidan said. He paused and shot Levi a look. "You're not that sly, you know."

"Hey, I wanted you to see it and you do. Did you fuck up before? Sure. But you don't anymore, so stop mentally beating yourself up, okay?"

"Easier said than done," Aidan said wryly, but still, he'd seen it, which was all Levi was after.

"I'll just have to keep reminding you." Levi was not only willing to do it, he *wanted* to do it.

Maybe that should've scared him, but it didn't.

"I'd like that," Aidan said, and it felt like more than a friend thing. Felt like more than a "sex pact" thing, for sure. But Levi didn't want to push. In July, Aidan had been heartbroken over Mo. Maybe he was still heartbroken over Mo. There was a part of Levi that wanted to ask—*needed* to ask, nearly—but he didn't, because what if he was? What if Aidan was in love with Mo and Levi was in love with . . .

He cut that thought off hard and fast.

He wasn't. He *wasn't.*

He absolutely could not be.

That would be insane and very, very stupid, and after witnessing his siblings be both of those things regularly, Levi had done everything he could to avoid following in their footsteps.

"Good," Levi said, nodding, faking a confidence he didn't quite feel. "'Cause it's happening."

There was a faint vibration noise. Levi dug his phone out of his pocket, but it hadn't been his. He glanced over at Aidan, who was staring at his phone, sitting on the coffee table, with an inscrutable expression on his face.

"Who is it?" Levi asked. He stretched out on the couch, wondering if he could bait Aidan into playing some video games before they went to bed.

Before they went to *bed*.

"It's . . .uh . . .Mo."

Everything inside Levi clenched hard and tight. A cold ball of dread formed in the base of his stomach, even though he tried to ignore it.

Levi understood that straight people *did* exist, and it was very possible Morris Jeffries was one of them, but the deeper into this thing he got with Aidan, the more outrageous it seemed that you could know Aidan and *not* want him desperately. Maybe Mo had changed his mind.

"Oh." Levi didn't know what to say. Wasn't sure he could keep up the casual pretense.

"It's nothing," Aidan brushed off. He stood up and headed towards the bedroom. Every single one of Levi's muscles clenched. Should he follow? Should he ask if Aidan was okay? Should he ask what Mo had said? *Could* he ask what Mo had said?

He wanted to, desperately, even though he wasn't sure he should.

But a second later, Aidan emerged. "Had to plug my phone in to charge," he said. His face had returned to normal. Levi might've worried it was that mask Aidan put on sometimes, but he was fairly certain he could see past it at this point, and he seemed . . .genuinely fine.

"Oh. Alright." Levi still wanted to ask. But maybe it was nothing. If it had been *something*, surely Aidan wouldn't be out here with him, acting normal.

"Wanna play some *Mario Kart*?" Aidan asked.

"We're going to have to teach you another game at some point," Levi said. If Aidan could be normal, so could he.

"Yeah, let's get me good at this one first," Aidan said wryly. "You still beat me like seventy-five percent of the time."

"Weak," Levi teased. "It's more like ninety."

Aidan's glance over was full of heat. "Exactly." He grabbed a pair of controllers and tossed Levi one.

And okay. Even if Mo *had* texted, this was Aidan saying nothing between them had changed. They were still going to play video games. Levi was still going to beat Aidan. Aidan would still pout in a way that shouldn't have been sexy and cute, yet *was*. And after, Levi would drag a very willing Aidan to bed. After their orgasms, they'd curl up together and everything would be normal.

Would be *right*.

You're fucked, Logan's voice echoed in his head.

But Levi pushed the thought away. He didn't need his brothers chiming in—didn't matter if it was real or not—not when he already felt acutely how fucked he actually was.

Aidan booted up the game, and it was a testament to truly how fine and normal everything was, because he played just as shitty as he usually did. But this time, Levi didn't have his own head screwed on straight and he played even worse. Aidan beat him twice in a row before he finally managed to pull out a hard-fought victory in their third game.

"Ha!" Aidan crowed smugly. "See! Ninety percent, my ass."

"You just lost," Levi reminded him. But then he'd won twice before that. Aidan didn't need to remind him of what one out of three actually came out to percentage-wise.

"Still," Aidan said, grinning obnoxiously. It was evidence of his fucked-up mental state that even *that* was doing it for him.

"And you cheated," Levi pointed out. He nudged Aidan's thigh with his own, where it had pressed hot and insistent the whole fucking game.

Levi's thighs were bigger. Just about everything on him was bigger. That wasn't bragging; that was just facts. But Aidan's thigh was still gorgeous. Slim but firm. Rippling with muscle. Muscle that Levi wanted to lean down and bite. Just nibble right along the tendon until he reached the hem of Aidan's shorts.

"Did I cheat though?" Aidan looked very proud of himself.

Levi glanced down. Aidan's shorts might not have been nearly as short as Levi's. It would take some work and Levi would be very happy to dedicate himself to the task, no matter how long it took.

"*And* you still lost."

Aidan grinned. "Not sure I did, bro."

"Bro!" Levi squawked and rolled over, pressing Aidan to the couch.

Aidan's forehead tipped against his, and it was so easy, so right, the most natural fucking thing in the world to kiss him then.

He was fine.

He was fine.

Aidan had told himself when Mo's text came in that he was, thinking something along the lines of *fake it til you make it*, but the weirdest part was that he *was*.

Not just because Levi had just sucked his soul out of his dick, either. He'd been fine before that, too. Fine enough that he'd played better at *Mario Kart* than he could remember doing before.

He'd come back out of the bedroom, after putting his phone on the charger, and just seeing Levi on his couch made him feel better. Even though the thought Mo had texted did still bug him, a lingering annoyance in the back of his skull that still faded the longer he and Levi sat together.

Until now, when he'd practically forgotten it until Levi turned to him, eyes sleepy and relaxed from his orgasm and asked, "Are you sure you're okay, bro?"

His first instinct was to say, *yeah, I'm fine,* even if he wasn't fine.

But in fact, he was fine.

Totally fine.

"I'm good," Aidan said instead, hoping the alternate word choice would in fact convince Levi that he was.

"You seem good," Levi said, sounding surprised.

Nobody was more surprised than Aidan. But that was reassuring, right? It was a positive development he'd seen Mo's name on his lock screen, was able to look at the text—God, of course the only thing Mo had sent was *hey dude, what's up?*—and not spiral.

Not only *not* spiral, but come back into the living room like nothing was wrong.

Because nothing *was* wrong.

"Yeah. It's . . .well, it is what it is. He's probably just checking in before the season starts. It's still weird he's not here," Aidan said.

Something complicated flashed across Levi's face, but before Aidan could figure out what it was, it was gone.

"Right. You guys played together a long time," Levi said.

"Seven years," Aidan said. It hadn't ever felt that long; had felt like seven seconds, honestly. He'd woken up and blinked and Mo had been gone, despite all his efforts to keep him in Toronto.

"Yeah, no wonder," Levi said. "You wanna play again or . . ."

"No, let's go to bed," Aidan said, hauling himself off the couch after he turned all the electronics off. He wanted to believe what he'd told Levi was the truth—that Mo had only texted him because it was the beginning of another season and they were still used to having each other around—but Aidan wasn't entirely sure that was true.

Because he'd asked Mo to give him some space, and for the last three-ish months, Mo had respected that.

They were nearly in the bedroom when Levi casually pressed him against the wall next to the doorway and kissed him. It was an intense kind of kiss, not a kiss he'd expect, not after the sex they'd just had, but Aidan couldn't help but sink into it. Levi's hands framed his face and his body caged him in, and it was so good to just not think at all. To just glory in the feel of Levi against him.

They stumbled into the bedroom a minute later, Aidan flopping down onto the bed, Levi crawling over his body after him.

They made out for so long Aidan lost track of the minutes. Floated in the bliss of Levi's mouth moving against his own, alternatively passionate and gently sweet, until Aidan's cock was definitely getting hard again.

They weren't playing in the preseason game in two days—Aidan wasn't even dressing, though Zane had made some noise about Levi taking at least a series to continue fine-tuning his new position—and Aidan thought maybe Levi might suggest they fuck again. Or maybe Levi could even fuck *him*.

He'd totally be down for that.

Sure, they had the walkthrough, but it wasn't like they wouldn't be careful.

Levi pulled away, and Aidan fully expected him to bring it up. Was looking forward to turning the tables on him by suggesting they try it the other way, but instead of saying anything, Levi pulled his phone out of his pocket.

He glared at the screen. "It keeps fucking buzzing," he said with frustration. "Doesn't it know I'm trying to go two for two?"

Aidan laughed. "Put it down, then, and come here." He let his legs fall open in invitation, but instead of following instructions, Levi just kept staring at his phone.

He was trying not to get a complex, but it was tough when Levi was not as into this as he absolutely should be.

Finally Levi looked up at him. "Why," he asked slowly, carefully—too carefully—"is everyone asking me if I'm excited? What should I be so excited about?"

An anxious sensation spiraled through Aidan. He wanted to be happy—it sounded like he should be, whatever it was that had just happened—but it was hard to be when he was still so in the dark.

He scrambled for his phone, and there it was, on the screen.

A *lot* of texts. So many texts. Fifty-four in the Thunder group chat. Two from his agent. Some from other players he knew. Texts from Riley. Texts from Landry. And then the damning ones. Four more texts from Mo.

Aidan opened those first, heart in his throat.

There was the first one.

Hey dude, what's up?

Then, twenty minutes later, probably when he'd been in the middle of creaming Levi at *Mario Kart,* **I really meant to give you the space you wanted, swear to God.**

Another seven minutes after that: **But things are moving quick here. I thought I'd get a say, and I don't. But I still can't say I'm pissed this is happening.**

Then the last, probably when he'd been rolling around with Levi on the bed, not even five minutes ago: **Gonna be sweet to play with you again.**

There it was.

Mo was coming back to Toronto.

Aidan's phone slipped from his suddenly nerveless fingers.

He didn't know what to say. Only that he should say something, at least when Levi looked at him in confusion.

"What is it?" Levi asked.

He had to say it. He only had to get the words out. Just the actual thing that had just happened. He didn't have to say how he felt about it yet—because he didn't fucking know. Or how this would change anything with him and Levi—theoretically nothing, because it wasn't like Mo had suddenly changed his mind on the whole *interested in guys* thing generally or the whole *interested in Aidan specifically* thing.

"Mo just got traded back to the Thunder."

Eight words. Aidan counted them back in his head as he watched Levi struggle to get his expression under control.

There was a part of him that wondered if it was just sex, if they were just doing what they'd promised in July, why Levi would look like he was being marched to death row, but he shut that question down. Aidan only had the bandwidth to deal with the fact Mo was back. After he'd acclimated to that idea, he would try to figure out what the fuck this meant for him and Levi.

Was there even a him and Levi? Aidan couldn't be the one to decide that. *Fuck.*

"Wow. Okay. Wow." At least Levi didn't seem to know what to say either.

"Yeah."

Aidan opened Landry's texts next. They were all variations of *are you okay?* He didn't know what he was, so he moved on to his convo with Riley. Riley had only sent one message, but it was a fucking solid paragraph of text. God, Riley was the worst texter. Aidan could basically sum the whole thing up in two sentences: *That's crazy, but great. I hope you're holding up okay.*

He looked up at Levi and realized a second too late that Levi was still staring at him.

"Do you want to talk about it?" Levi asked.

If he did, Aidan wasn't even sure what he'd say. There were the things he was expected to say, first as the starting quarterback of the Toronto Thunder, along the lines of, "We're excited for the opportunities this opens up in the passing game." And then as the long-time friend of Mo, something like, "I'm thrilled he's back."

But then there was the secret Aidan—the Aidan he'd buried back deep down, in July, and that was quieter, that hurt less, but still existed, somewhat.

The Aidan that had hoped and maybe even dreamed a little that something like this could happen. After all, it was the NFL, anything could—and did—happen.

The *real* Aidan.

The Aidan that had stood in front of Mo just last June and had told him the truth. Had accepted even through Mo's surprise and sympathy that nothing was ever going to happen.

The Aidan that had sulked through that weekend in early July, and the Aidan that had told Levi the truth to first. The Aidan that was here with Levi now. That wanted him so badly he shook with it.

"I don't even know what to say," Aidan said, finally. He couldn't be the first Aidan. The QB Aidan or even the public-friend-to-Mo Aidan. Levi had already long since slunk his way under those walls. He could only be who he really was—the Aidan who'd only shown himself to a handful of people he trusted.

There was no question Levi was one of them.

Maybe the one he trusted the most.

Less than ten minutes ago, he'd been wild for Levi to fuck him. If that wasn't trust, Aidan didn't know *what* that feeling was, pressing hard and fast up against his breastbone.

"Talk to me," Levi persuaded in a soft voice. He relaxed on the bed and actually managed to coax Aidan down. He settled half on Levi's chest, Levi's arm stroking up and down his back in a comforting, reassuring way that he didn't think he'd ever experienced before.

"I'm freaking out," Aidan said finally.

"Yeah, no shit," Levi said, voice rumbling underneath him. "Which part?"

"All the parts?" He knew, of course, what the public Aidans needed to say. That was never a question. "No, that's not true. I know what I'm supposed to say about it. What I should feel about it."

"Bro," Levi said in an aggrieved voice, "I'm not asking Aidan Flynn, QB1 for the Toronto Thunder, right now. I'm in your *bed*. You can talk to me. Really talk to me."

He was. Levi was in his bed because Aidan had invited him there. Would he have done it if he knew Mo was coming back?

Probably yes, because Mo coming back changed the way their offense played on the field, but not really anything else—and God knew, Aidan would have still wanted Levi.

Maybe acting on it would have taken longer, if Mo was around all the time. Maybe Aidan would've spent more time trying to get out of his own fucking way. But there was no way it wouldn't have ended up exactly the same, in the end.

Levi in Aidan's bed.

"The thing that keeps getting me is that nothing's really changing," Aidan said quietly.

"He's going to be around."

"Yeah. On the field, sure. Hanging out with us at Vault or whatever bar we find, sure. But nothing else."

Aidan supposed he should be sad about that. Mad, even. Resigned, *surely*. But instead, he just sounded matter-of-fact. Like it was just a reality, and he'd accepted it.

"So you're not like . . ." Levi trailed off. It was unlike Levi to not confront things bluntly; it was one of the things Aidan liked most about him. They had that in common. He'd always know where Levi stood, because he'd never bother to hide it.

"I'm not what?" Aidan could guess, but there was a perverse part of him that wanted Levi to say it out loud.

"Sad or whatever."

"No," Aidan said. He could say definitively, no, he was not sad.

Confused. Freaked out. Unsure. All of those things, *yes*.

What would Mo have to say about this thing with Levi? Was he even going to tell him about this thing with Levi? He'd not told a lot of other teammates. Just Dawson. Wes knew something, too, but not who it was.

"Not sad. That's uh . . .good," Levi said.

Normally, *before*, Mo would have been one of the first people he'd have told. Landry and Riley, too, but the unique circumstances had made telling either of them impossible.

"Yeah," Aidan said. He wanted to tell Levi things had changed. That he felt different—so fucking different—than he'd felt in July when they'd first talked about this. But chances were Levi would want to know how he felt. Would want him to identify the emotions he was experiencing.

Of course, that was probably only if Levi *liked* that things had changed.

Maybe he wouldn't.

That *maybe* was fucking Aidan up even more.

How would Levi react if Aidan said, *well, actually, I might be sad, but it's not about Mo. I'm kind of fucked up about you.*

"You're normally so quiet, but you're freaking me out now," Levi said. He hesitated. That hesitation was fucking Aidan up even more; when did Levi hesitate? "Should I get Landry on the phone? Riley?"

"No. God, no." That was easy enough. They'd definitely want him to talk about his feelings.

He wanted to say, *I don't want Landry or Riley. I don't even really want Mo. I just want . . . you.*

But the words stuck in his throat. Maybe that was actually okay because Levi was already here, without Aidan even asking him to be.

He tried to relax into the mattress, into Levi's big warm body. Found it was actually easier than he thought it might be.

"I'm . . . I'm actually good right here," Aidan said.

"Awesome." Levi's uncertainty had morphed into his normal smug delight. Aidan found he could relax even more, hearing it in his voice.

"It's just gonna be really fucking weird tomorrow."

"Bad weird?"

Aidan hummed under his breath. "No. Having Mo around can never be bad weird. He's a solid guy. You'll see. Just . . . just *weird*. I keep thinking I wasn't used to him being gone, but I think I was. I had accepted it. And now I have to go through and un-accept it."

"You got used to not having him around, so yeah, that makes sense. It's been three years," Levi said.

"Doesn't really feel like three years, but yeah."

"Can I . . ." That hesitation was back in Levi's voice. "Can I ask why it took you so long to tell him?"

There was no real truthful answer that made Aidan look good. He *could* tell Levi he didn't want to talk about it. Levi would accept that, no question. But Aidan didn't want to lie, even if it wasn't exactly flattering.

"I was afraid," Aidan admitted.

"About liking guys?"

"God, that would be less embarrassing," Aidan said.

Levi's arm around him tightened further.

"More like, I was afraid that what would happen would happen. And guess what? It did," Aidan continued. "And maybe I was right to be afraid. It did suck. But I can't say it was all bad."

"Kind of seems like it was from this angle," Levi pointed out softly.

But then I wouldn't be here, with you.

"Good things came out of it, though," Aidan said firmly. He didn't say what the good things were, but he hoped Levi realized that he was the biggest. The best.

Levi's hand stroked his back, all the way up to his shoulder. "Glad to hear it, bro."

"I should probably deal with all that shit on my phone," Aidan said after a long, surprising peaceful moment. Surprisingly, because his phone was still going off.

"You could just turn it off."

He could. But if he did, then he wouldn't be Aidan Flynn, QB1 for the Toronto Thunder, and as much as he liked being the Aidan lying here with Levi, he was that Aidan too.

Couldn't stop being him.

"Yeah, and I will after."

He rolled over, catching a glimpse of Levi's smile as he did.

It was going to be fine. Everything was going to be fine.

Levi thought if he told himself he was fine enough times, that might make it true.

He was not freaking out. He was *not* freaking out.

Okay. He was freaking out a little. Or a lot.

He'd never imagined that Mo Jeffries might come back to Toronto. Sure, he probably hadn't fallen miraculously in love with Aidan, back, but the fact he was going to be here, in Aidan's face every single day, was giving Levi the kind of complex he'd never personally experienced before.

Because this was what jealousy felt like, wasn't it?

He stood in the middle of the field, getting some of his extra reps at left tackle with the second team offense, and tried very hard not to watch Aidan and Mo standing next to each other, chatting.

Levi had very pointedly not looked up Morris Jeffries when Aidan had told him about his unrequited feelings, but of course he knew of the guy. He was one of the best wide receivers in the NFL, hands down, even though he was in his late twenties. He'd lost a bit of speed, maybe, but he'd gotten smarter and craftier.

Any team would want him on their roster, and it didn't really surprise Levi that the Thunder had decided they needed him back.

Trevor and Lane were great tight ends, but they needed a dynamite receiver to round out the offense, and there was no better choice for that position than Mo.

He stood next to Aidan, dressed in his practice uniform even though nobody really expected him to participate in the walkthrough or play tomorrow. He was laughing at something Aidan said, dark hair glinting in the late afternoon sun, eyes crinkled with amusement.

Yeah.

Levi had always passingly thought he was good looking, which felt like a huge cosmic joke now.

"Hey, you good?"

Levi looked over towards Trevor. "Yeah, dude. I'm fine."

What was Trevor even doing out here? He didn't need extra reps. Had he come all the way out to the middle of the field to wonder if Levi was okay?

Shit.

"You're kind of glaring at our new wideout."

"No way," Levi said. Had he been glaring? God, he hoped not. And if he had been, he prayed Aidan hadn't noticed. He was trying to be chill about Mo showing up in Toronto and glaring at the guy who might be the death of all his secret hopes was not being very chill.

"Yeah way," Trevor retorted. He was being nice, in that particular Trevor way—pointed but with big brown kind eyes. It was the kind of thing that would put everyone else but his stepbrother, Lane, at ease.

"I . . ." Levi moistened his lips. Wishing that Zane and Ned would finish up with the backup center sometime in this century. He didn't want to have this conversation with Trevor, even though he liked the guy.

"You've got a huge-ass crush on Aidan and now you're worried Mo being back means you're going to stop being so buddy-buddy?"

Levi made a face. Considered denying it. "Possibly," he finally admitted.

"It's okay, dude, I think everyone's got a little bit of a crush on the guy. He's Aidan Flynn, you know?"

"Who's got a crush on Aidan?"

Oh great. Wes had wandered over now.

"Levi's sort of down bad, but I was just telling him it's not all that surprising," Trevor said, still sounding so kind. So sympathetic.

Levi made a face.

"Seriously?" Wes said. At least he looked surprised.

"Seriously," Trevor said, nodding eagerly. "He's been staring over at Aidan and Mo during the whole walkthrough."

"I couldn't have done it for the whole walkthrough," Levi protested, even though this was probably closer to the truth than he felt comfortable admitting to himself.

"If you say so," Trevor said, and even he sounded doubtful.

When it was obvious even Trevor thought you were full of shit, it was a problem.

"You think he likes you too?" Wes asked casually. A little too studied.

Levi didn't know what Wes thought he'd realized, but he wasn't going to play that game. "No idea," he said brusquely. "It's not . . .it's not anything."

Wes patted him on the shoulder. "My dude, it's okay if it's something."

"I can't be the only one who thought Aidan fighting so hard for Mo to get his contract with the Thunder meant something?" Trevor said. "So yeah, maybe it's okay if it's something."

The urge to confess the whole truth was on the tip of Levi's tongue. He couldn't tell anyone. That was the problem. His brothers were his best friends and he couldn't tell them, because of Landry's relationship with Riley. There'd been friends in Seattle, sure, but he wouldn't call any of those guys for advice or even to unload his frustrations.

They wouldn't get it.

They only knew the old Levi, who'd enjoyed a solely hookup lifestyle. They'd tell him to get under someone else and it would be fine. Or even worse, they'd suggest he still keep hooking up with Aidan, as long as Aidan was into it.

Aidan still seemed into it. They'd shared handjobs in the shower this morning and Aidan had seemed just as into it then as he had the night before, before the news about Mo had come out.

"Dude," Wes told Trevor, "how would that make it okay? That would mean Aidan wasn't into Levi, he was into Mo."

"I don't know, I was there when they saw each other for the first time, and it wasn't exactly a romantic reunion," Trevor said.

"Maybe they were hiding it?" Wes suggested.

Levi wanted them both to shut up before they accidentally stumbled on the right answer. "Guys," he chided. "It's fine. It's not . . .it's not something. It's not anything. Just let it go, okay?"

Wes didn't look convinced but Trevor was too nice to keep up the interrogation after Levi had told them to quit it.

At least then, Zane got their attention, deciding they were going to run another play.

He kept Levi in for another few plays, which was a great distraction, but then he sent him back to the sideline after that.

Turned out watching Aidan and Mo chatting it up like the last three years hadn't happened was bad enough from a few dozen feet away, but it was worse up close.

Levi resisted the urge to run up to Aidan, plant a flag on his back, and hiss at Mo like a cat, because Aidan was *his*.

Except Aidan was not his. Aidan didn't belong to anyone but himself.

Logically he knew that. The problem wasn't with logic, it was with everything else—all those stupid feelings that kept churning away in his heart.

"Hey, Banks," Aidan called out, "come over here and meet Mo."

God. Aidan hadn't called him *Banks* since this summer, since they'd kissed for the first time.

Still, what was he going to do? Argue? Tell Aidan *no*? That would make everything even weirder.

He could go over there and perform basic new teammate niceties, but he still dragged his feet doing it, stopping by and grabbing a bottle of Gatorade before heading over to where Aidan and Mo were still standing together.

"Finally," Aidan said, shooting Levi a fondly exasperated look. "Mo, this is Levi Banks, my new left tackle."

"Hey," Levi said, accepting Mo's outstretched hand. They shook briefly.

Mo was even better looking up close. Tan skin and dark eyes and hair. A jawline that looked like it had been chiseled from marble.

Levi wanted to hate him.

Wanted to hate the affectionate glance, full of a long familiarity, that Mo sent Aidan's way. "So this is the guy that meant I couldn't crash in your condo, huh?"

At least there was that. Levi supposed it could be worse. Mo could be moving in with Aidan. Aidan could be *asking* Levi to leave, so Mo could move in.

Of course, it wasn't like he was doing much sleeping in the guest room these days, but Levi had a feeling that Aidan wouldn't be admitting that—especially not to Mo.

"Yep," Aidan said, not sounding like he regretted that at all. "You got places you can stay, dude."

"Yeah, I'm just giving you shit," Mo said. "Makes me wish I hadn't sold the condo in your building though. I'm sure to buy it back is gonna cost me more."

It was petty but Levi hoped that it was so ridiculously expensive that Mo went someplace else. Levi didn't want him that close, and Aidan hardly needed that either.

Though Levi could see the potential in making Aidan scream so loud Mo finally got the memo that he belonged to someone else now.

"A lot more, probably," Levi said, not quite eliminating the hopeful note from his voice.

Aidan shot him a questioning look. Mo, on the other hand, didn't look all that surprised. Had Aidan told him? No. There was no way Aidan would've.

"So you're the youngest Banks, huh?" Mo asked. His gaze slid over Levi's body, not in an *I find you hot* way, but more in an *I can't quite believe you're the youngest* way. Levi got both of those a lot, but he wasn't surprised Mo had landed on the latter. He was straight. Or at least that was what he'd told Aidan.

And if a guy didn't go gay for Aidan Flynn, then he was pretty damn straight.

"Yep," Levi said.

"And the others, they're bigger than you?"

"Nah," Levi said, subtly flexing. Sure Aidan had said he loved Mo. But if it came down to it, he could totally take Mo in a fight. Maybe he was strong, rippling biceps evident under his practice jersey, but Levi was stronger.

"No way," Aidan added, chuckling. "Levi's just built different."

"Well, you're gonna keep this dude safe, so you're a friend in my book," Mo said, giving Levi a reassuring smile.

The problem with hating Mo on sight was that he wasn't particularly hateable.

He clearly cared about Aidan, and so did Levi. As much as he didn't like it, they had that in common.

"You're the worst," Aidan said fondly but Mo just grinned.

Levi had expected that some of Aidan's feelings might bleed out when he had to watch him and Mo interact one-on-one. But so far, they only seemed to him like old friends, reunited again.

It left Levi so confused. He'd been so positive that he could see beneath Aidan's mask, but now he wasn't so sure. Was there another, deeper one, underneath? Had he missed that? Levi didn't think he had.

"You looked good out there," Aidan said, turning to Levi. "Solid."

"Felt solid," Levi said.

Football was blessedly simple, compared to whatever the complicated shit was going on in his personal life.

"I'm not playing tomorrow." Aidan made a face. "Zane just told me."

"I'm sure I'm barely gonna play," Levi admitted.

"I told Zane to put me out there, but he just laughed," Mo said, commiserating.

Aidan elbowed him. "You don't even know the playbook yet."

"Yeah, I do. Run down the line and let you hit me." Mo grinned. "Just like old times."

"Yeah," Aidan agreed, "just like old times."

Chapter 16

IT WAS IN THE middle of the third quarter when Mo sidled over to where Aidan was standing. Zane had told him to not even bother dressing. Wes was going to play the whole first half and their-third string backup, Nelson Perez, was going to play the second half.

Aidan wouldn't be on the field except on the sidelines, and then only in an advisory capacity.

He'd argued that he and Mo should both get out there, at least for one series, to shake the rust off. But Zane had just shot him an incredulous look. "You've got rust?" he'd asked.

And okay, that was a little ridiculous. He didn't have any rust. Mo probably had even less, but then he'd actually played in the Rams' first preseason game.

"Are you gonna tell me what's up with you?" Mo asked as Perez bent down, taking the snap.

"Don't know what you're talking about," Aidan said.

"Yeah, dude, you know. You're . . . like lighter. It's good. I'm happy for you."

Part of Aidan—a much tinier part than had existed in early July—wanted to say, *yeah, you only knew me eating my heart out over you for so long, you don't even know what me being happy looks like.* But that wasn't Mo's fault. It had never been Mo's fault.

"I feel good," Aidan said.

Perez hit one of the backup tight ends for a twelve-yard gain, and Aidan listened in on his headset as Zane called in a running play.

Once Aidan's initial freakout had ended, once he'd actually had a moment to think about what Mo being here meant—and once he'd actually seen him again—he'd relaxed.

Could even say now that this was good. He'd get Mo on the field again, giving him more options in the passing game, and he'd get his friendship off the field. And this time, his brain and his heart wouldn't be confused about what he wanted or what he was getting. He'd know it was friendship and only friendship.

He was even considering telling him at some point, in the long-off faraway future, about what had happened with Levi. What was *happening* with Levi.

Mo was quiet for a moment. Then he spoke up again. "I actually thought you might not want me here."

Aidan didn't know what to say. At least he knew what he shouldn't say: that at the very beginning, during his initial freakout, he kinda hadn't.

Zane called another passing play, and Aidan focused on Perez, watching as the ball snapped. It was a good distraction; gave him another twenty seconds to figure out what the fuck he was supposed to say.

It didn't help. He still didn't have the words, but he'd try anyway, because Mo was a friend and he deserved some kind of answer.

"I—"

But Mo interrupted him before he could put together a coherent thought that wasn't a lie. "I know you asked for space. I wanted to give it to you, but when they told me I could come back—it was all I could think about. It was all I wanted. And when Toronto met the Rams' offer? I just wanted you to be happy about it. 'Cause *I* was happy. Feel like I've been trying to get back home for ages."

"You have," Aidan said.

"So yeah, maybe it was selfish," Mo said, shrugging. "You can tell me it was selfish."

"I promise you, it's okay," Aidan said, patting him on the shoulder. They'd hugged when Mo had first arrived, but he'd gone out of his way to avoid touching him. For his own peace of mind, but also because he wasn't stupid. Even if it was only sex to Levi, this had to be awkward for him, too.

But Levi was on the field and wouldn't be able to see this.

"Good." Mo looked relieved. "I just . . .I just want things to be the same again."

"Yeah, me too, bud," Aidan said and patted him again.

What he didn't say was that he already knew they wouldn't ever be the same again. Too many things had changed. He was no longer keeping his feelings secret. Mo knew about them. Then there was Levi. Mo didn't know about his feelings for *him*.

Because Aidan was pretty sure that was what this was. It felt different than it had with Mo. Maybe that was because Mo was such a different person than Levi. Maybe it was the fact he hadn't pined for ages before actually confessing them.

But Aidan couldn't deny anymore that he felt *something*.

The third quarter ended, and Levi came off the field, Zane subbing in one of the backup offensive linemen for the last few drives.

Aidan went to check in on him on the bench, not just because he should as the starting QB but because he *wanted* to.

"Good work out there," Aidan said as he approached.

Levi glanced up as he shot a stream of Gatorade in his mouth.

Aidan had spent way too many fucking years around sweaty guys, but he had to admit he'd never found it appealing. Not once, not until now.

Now, he wanted to lean in and lick the sweat off Levi's tanned neck.

"Thanks," Levi said.

Things between them had been a little shaky since Mo's return, but Aidan wasn't surprised. At least Levi hadn't left his bed. If he'd returned to the guest room, Aidan would've been actually concerned, but instead, it felt like more and more of Levi's possessions were finding their way into Aidan's bedroom.

First it had been the phone charger. Then an old Seattle sweatshirt, draped haphazardly over the bench at the end of the bed. And then his iPad, on the bedside table. His pillows, moving from the guest room to Aidan's room.

He'd say something, but to his own surprise, he found he liked it. Like Levi was wordlessly staking his claim.

"You were right," Aidan said. It was funny; he'd shied away from speaking his truths forever, but once the dam had broken, he couldn't seem to stop.

Levi grinned. "Oh, I'm sorry, what was that, bro?"

"You heard me." Aidan nudged him with his knee.

"Maybe I just wanna hear it some more," Levi teased.

Aidan leaned in. Instructed himself very firmly not to cross a line and get too close, no matter how much he wanted to. "I can arrange that," he said. "Tonight?"

"What's the play?" Levi asked, eyes gleaming.

"You. Me. In bed. Me, telling you how right you were about getting fucked."

Levi licked his lips. "I'm down."

"Had a feeling you might be," Aidan said, straightening. Trying not to sound smug and mostly failing. He'd never imagine telling Levi that he was right—about more than one thing—would be as hot as it was.

"Hell yeah," Levi said, falling just short of an actual fist pump. Like Aidan was everything he'd ever wanted.

"And," Aidan said with faux-seriousness, "you were right about play-ing left tackle, too."

Levi was going to kill him, but Aidan was pretty sure that if he did, he'd die a very happy man.

Even though he hadn't even played in the game, the reporters had wanted to talk to him. So there'd been *that* delay, and then Aidan had needed to do his good leader-slash-QB1 act, talking to every guy, even the guys who definitely weren't going to make the fifty-three-man roster.

Levi couldn't be surprised, but every time their eyes met across the locker room, he could practically *feel* Levi's eagerness and his hunger, rolling off him in waves.

Aidan finished talking to Nathan, the backup center, who'd blocked for Wes and Perez today, trying to ignore the way Levi's foot was tapping on the ground, just a few lockers over. Levi wasn't even bothering to *not* look impatient. Anyone who noticed no doubt thought that the reason was because Aidan was giving him a ride home, but the truth was, Levi was probably impatient for a whole different kind of ride.

Just the thought made Aidan go hot and cold all over.

He was absolutely gonna give Levi shit about this later.

Maybe make him beg a little more about it. Now *that* was a thought. But before Aidan could spend any more time on it, he realized he'd moved on to the next set of guys.

Wes and Nelson Perez.

"Great game, guys. Solid team win," Aidan said, holding his hand out. Perez gave him a bro hug, which was exactly the right move, since they weren't any more than semi-friendly teammates, but Wes ignored his outstretched hand and pulled him into a real hug.

It made Aidan want to smile, but he scowled instead.

Couldn't let Wes figure out that he liked him. Because if he did, he'd never leave him alone.

"You're doing the rounds," Wes said, as Perez finished getting dressed.

"Yeah," Aidan said. Didn't say, *you should be too,* but only because Wes already knew. Aidan had seen him on the sideline, during the fourth quarter, working the o-line guys. Checking in with all the second-string skill players.

If Zane hadn't already told Aidan that Wes was going to get the official backup spot, then he'd guess that Wes' performance today—and not just on the field, but off it, too—had sealed that deal.

Perez would head to the practice squad, lying there in wait if anything happened to either of them.

Aidan felt a little bad about it, but it was also just the way the NFL worked, and if he cried about every unfair thing they endured, he'd never stop.

"Sucks that some of these guys aren't going to be here," Wes said quietly.

"It's that way every year," Aidan pointed out. Wes was still young and sentimental. Aidan had been forced to ruthlessly cut out much of his football romanticism. Sports was a business, as much as any other job.

"Levi waiting on you?" Wes asked, his voice dropping even further, glancing over to where Levi was still not pretending to do anything but look at Aidan.

Aidan nodded. It was on the tip of his tongue, the sudden desire to ask about Wes' ex. The one he was still hung up on. *How did you know he wasn't the one? Or that he was, and that's why you can't move on?*

But Wes had never even told Aidan the ex's name, and Aidan supposed that wasn't surprising, because he'd never done anything more than barely tolerate Wes' existence.

For legitimate reasons, sure, but he couldn't expect Wes to suddenly be his friend. Even if he was beginning to wonder if maybe he should be.

"Don't fuck that up," Wes said under his breath.

Aidan wasn't sure at first that he'd heard correctly. "What?"

Wes shrugged a shoulder in Levi's direction. "*That*," he said. "I'm not stupid. You've got something going on, and it's Levi. Don't fuck with him."

The last thing he'd expected was a shovel talk about Levi from *Wes.*

"What about if I want him to fuck with *me*?" Aidan said, before he could overthink it.

Wes' mouth opened and then snapped shut again.

"That's what I thought," Aidan said, unable to stop the smugness from leaking into his voice.

"Well," Wes said, sounding gratifyingly flustered, "*that's* a visual."

"Sure is." And Aidan was going to have that visual spread out across his bed tonight. *Naked*. Could anyone blame him for being smug when that was waiting for him at home? Staring at him like Levi could barely wait for it?

"Congrats?" Wes squeaked.

Aidan surprised himself by taking pity on the guy. Slid onto the bench next to him. "How did you know?" he asked.

"I'm heartbroken, not dead," Wes retorted without much heat.

"Dude, I don't mean how did you know you were into guys. I mean, how did you know you weren't ready to move on?"

Wes' eyebrows shot up. "Is that what you're doing with Levi? Moving on?"

"Sort of."

"You never met my ex," Wes said wistfully. "Marcus was . . .Marcus *is* . . .unbelievable. The most amazing guy I've ever met. Hot and funny and so fucking smart he makes me look like the Cro-Magnon man. I always knew I'd lucked out with him, that he'd even be willing to look my direction."

"Dude—you're in the NFL," Aidan said. And though his tastes were running to enormous, built offensive linemen these days, even he could acknowledge Wes wasn't exactly hard on the eyes.

"So?" Wes' voice was defensive now. Not mad, but *sharp*. "Marcus is the best thing that ever happened to me."

"And you fucked it up?" At least he'd *had* Marcus. Though Aidan could acknowledge that might make it worse. Knowing you'd loved and then lost . . .

Well, at least he'd never had a shred of real hope when it came to Mo. He'd always, in the back of his mind, known that score, and it wasn't in his favor.

"No, life fucked it up, and then I fucked it up worse," Wes said, resigned. "Anyway, the way I know I'm not ready—no matter how many times Ramsey tries to cajole me into moving on—is that he's still the only guy I can think about. Your visual? A fun way to pass a few seconds. Then I'm back on the Marcus shit. Like always."

There'd been a time when Aidan had thought he'd end up like this. Never feeling for anyone the way he'd felt for Mo. But that hadn't been true at all.

"That . . .that helps, actually." Aidan rose to his feet. This time it was him who pulled Wes into a real hug. "I'm sorry about it, though. Sucks."

"Yeah," Wes agreed. "You know how else I know I'm not ready? I actually *like* missing him, because it means I have an excuse to think about him, still. To have him in my head."

"Shit, man," Aidan said. Suddenly feeling horrible for his backup. He hadn't realized Wes was this bad off.

Wes shrugged. Like he hadn't expected to hear any different. "Don't tell me I'm pathetic; I get that enough from Ramsey."

"I won't, then," Aidan said.

The sadness didn't really fade from Wes' eyes, but it took a backseat to his smile when he said, "Enjoy your visual, then, tonight."

"Oh, I'm gonna," Aidan said.

By the time he made it over to Levi, the guy was already on his feet.

"How's it going?" Aidan asked casually as they walked out of the locker room. Like this was every trip home they'd had since Levi had shown up in Toronto.

Levi shot him a look. "Seriously, bro?" he asked, aggrieved. "You can't act like—I'm going out of my fucking mind here."

"Oh?" Aidan had never pretended he didn't have an ego, and it was being stroked, nicely, by all of Levi's eager anticipation.

Did that make him a bad person?

Maybe only if he rubbed it in.

Levi shoved an elbow into Aidan's side and laughed. "God, you're such a dick. You kept looking, too."

"I can't stop," Aidan admitted. Even with Mo hanging out in the locker room, the man his eyes had returned to, over and over again, was Levi.

Sure he'd passingly imagined asking Mo to fuck him. But he'd never been possessed by the thought of it, not the way he was with Levi, like they were already together on his bed, Levi pulling pleasure he'd never experienced before out of his body.

"Good," Levi said, and it was apparently his turn to be smug.

"Thank God the stadium's closer than the practice facility," Aidan muttered as they reached his car.

Levi shot him a knowing glance as he climbed into the passenger seat. "Eager much?"

"Hell yeah," Aidan said. He'd wanted it two nights ago, before Mo had shown up, and he'd spent the last two days not being able to dislodge the thought of it from his brain.

Maybe if he'd played today, if he'd actually had the distraction of football, he could have done it. But he hadn't.

"You've never before?" Levi asked as Aidan pulled out of the players' garage.

"You *know* I haven't ever before," Aidan reminded him.

"Well, obviously, but that? You can absolutely stick a finger or two up your ass," Levi said. "Some girls are even into that."

Aidan's fingers tightened on the steering wheel. "I don't know if you've noticed in the month since you got here," he said, "but traffic here in Toronto fucking blows. So like, let's not try to distract me so much I crash us before you ever get inside me."

Levi shot him a hot look, and a second later, his hand was on Aidan's thigh, squeezing hard, and Aidan yelped.

"Seriously!" he said.

"I asked you a question," Levi said, all perfect innocence. "It was only a question."

"It wasn't *only* a question."

How could it be, when Aidan's cock was already throbbing in his slacks, desperate for Levi to slide his hand up further?

"I'm still waiting for an answer," Levi said, squeezing again.

Aidan realized he was literally holding his breath and let it out. "No," he said. "Never. Not with anyone. Not even just myself."

"But you want it." Levi said it like a phrase, not a question, and Aidan gave him credit for that, at least. He hadn't asked the damning version either. *How do you even know you want it?*

He wanted it.

Couldn't explain it. But there was no question.

"Yeah," Aidan said.

"If you don't like it, it's alright. I like it plenty," Levi said, stroking his thigh now. Aidan was fully prepared to admit to his obsession with Levi's thighs, but lately, it seemed that fixation went both ways.

"I know," Aidan said, between clenched teeth, trying not to think of just how much Levi liked it. He was going to crash this car and destroy both their careers and the only explanation he was going to be able to give was that Levi was a master in sexual torment.

It was the longest ten-minute drive of Aidan's life, and he'd never hated the Toronto traffic more than he did tonight.

Finally, he pulled into his tower's garage, Aidan pulling both their bags out of the backseat, Levi grinning at him.

"Eager much?" he asked as they walked to the elevator. Levi's hand ghosted across the small of his back. Not touching, but close enough Aidan could feel the heat of his touch through his clothes.

"Wanted this two nights ago," Aidan admitted. "Been thinking about it longer than that."

Levi groaned in the back of his throat. "You're kind of killing me, here."

"*Me* killing *you*?" Aidan questioned. They walked into the elevator. He knew there was a security feed—one of the reasons he'd moved into this building was how secure it was—and that was all that stopped him from leaning over and kissing Levi.

Just not telling him how much he wanted him, but showing him.

Levi fumbled with his keycard, pressing it against the sensor, and hit the button for their floor.

"You're so hot," Levi said, glancing over and licking his lips as the floors flashed past on the display.

Aidan knew that was objectively true; enough people had told him that over the course of his adult life, but he'd never *felt* it, so viscerally, as he did right now. Like his skin might melt right off his body just from the heat of the looks Levi kept sending from under his dark eyelashes.

The elevator doors dinged open, and once they were in the foyer, Levi pressed Aidan's body against the door as he shoved his keycard against the reader—the last step before they were finally alone.

Aidan half expected when the door finally opened, both of them stumbling into the privacy of the condo, Levi might press him into the nearest wall. But Levi didn't. He did shove their bags off Aidan's shoulder, though, and take him by the hand, practically dragging him to the bedroom.

"Come on," Levi panted breathlessly, even though he hadn't done anything more strenuous than ride in an elevator and he'd played a quarter and a half of football earlier today without looking particularly winded.

Aidan sank down to the edge of the bed and yanked Levi in, their mouth sliding together into a fierce kiss.

Levi leaned harder into him, one hand on his shoulder and one on the side of his head, knocking his hat off, pushing him further onto the bed.

"Clothes off," he said, barely breaking the kiss as he yanked Aidan's polo off. "God, you looked so douchey in this, and I wanted to take it off with my *teeth* the whole fucking game."

Incredulous laughter bubbled up from inside Aidan. He didn't get it, but then he didn't need to. He could only be grateful that whatever it was about him and his boring-ass clothes, they did it for Levi. Hopefully they would *keep* doing it for Levi.

Levi kissed him again, tongue slipping between his lips as he managed to undo his belt and the fastenings of his khakis.

"And these—" Levi broke off. "Jesus, do you know what your ass looks like in these?"

Aidan couldn't help his giggle. "Obviously not."

"Shit, bro, it's so good." Levi slid a hand underneath it, squeezing him through his briefs. "Need you bad. Been dreaming about it."

It wasn't like they hadn't had plenty of sex. They had—basically every night found them pulling their clothes off during a makeout session that ranged from sweet and gentle to hot and frantic.

Even though they weren't exactly denying themselves, it didn't matter. It was like the fire between them just kept getting stoked hotter, and this time Aidan had been the one to light the match.

"Fuck," Levi groaned as his mouth slid down, mouthing at the stubble along Aidan's jawline, then lower, to his neck, and then lower still, teeth grazing at his collarbone.

Aidan felt lightheaded and could only hold on—grabbing at Levi's broad shoulders, warm and solid under the cotton of his T-shirt. He needed skin too. Wrenching his mouth away for a second, he pulled the shirt off and dug his fingernails in.

Didn't care if they left marks. They'd fade by their next practice day or, if they didn't, maybe Levi would wear them with pride.

"Gotta get you ready. I'm gonna just explode if I don't." When Levi pulled back, his pupils had swallowed nearly all the honey brown of his eyes and his expression was full of desperation.

Levi shucked his sweatpants on the way to the bedside table to grab the bottle of lube. Aidan watched him go, enjoying the flex of his ass and his thighs as he pulled his own briefs off. He couldn't help the question that tumbled out of him.

"Why? You've done this before, yeah?"

"Sure," Levi said, returning to the space between Aidan's legs. "But I've never done it to *you.*"

Aidan wanted to ask more, wanted to interrogate Levi on exactly why that was. What was it about him that made Levi unhinged like this? And was it maybe the same thing that kept catching Aidan by surprise, that feeling lingering at the base of his stomach?

But before he could get his shit together to do it, Levi was pressing two wet fingers between his legs, not pushing them in but caressing with just enough pressure Aidan was already wild for him to do it.

He'd wanted it for so long. Couldn't say that the guy he'd pictured doing this to him had always been Levi, but since July—since that first kiss—the guy in his fantasies had always, *always* worn Levi's face.

Desire wore his pride down to practically nothing, and it felt way too easy to just beg. "Please, *please*," he murmured.

"I got you," Levi said. His other hand stroked Aidan's thigh sweetly, almost possessively. Maybe Aidan was imagining that, a fever dream brought about by the white-hot desire surging through his blood, but he *liked* thinking it.

Liked being wanted this much.

The first inch of his finger that slipped into Aidan's body made him swear. Forcing himself to relax, he felt more of it slide inside.

"That's it," Levi crooned. "You got this, baby."

It felt the same as Aidan might've expected it to, but wildly different too. He felt another pressing against the first, suddenly full in a way that made it hard to even catch his breath. But that fullness slowly melted into pleasure. Easy, languid, everything in him loosening. Then Levi did something new, crooked his fingers, and Aidan was gasping with the sudden spiky thrill of it.

"God, yeah, that's it." Levi was still murmuring to him, talking him through it. Sweet words, sure, but sexy words too, about how good Aidan looked like this, and how much better he was going to look on his cock.

Aidan couldn't quite get a breath now, desire flaring and catching fire inside him, and he hadn't been *sure* he would like this, no matter how much he wanted it, but now there was no question.

Another finger nudged up against his hole and Aidan groaned.

"You can take it," Levi coaxed. "One more and then you can have more."

"Want it," Aidan panted.

His cock was untouched, the tip bouncing against the planes of his stomach, leaving trails of wetness, and Aidan wanted nothing more than to reach down. Close his hand around it, let himself be taken by the force of his orgasm.

But he bit down hard on his self-control and kept his hands where they were—one curled around Levi's shoulder and the other clenching in the bedspread like only its existence was keeping him grounded.

"Yeah, that's it," Levi said, voice rough now. "God, I want you."

"Feeling's . . .uh . . ." Aidan gasped as Levi's fingers went deeper, harder. "Feeling's mutual."

"Good." Levi sounded so smug, and it shouldn't have been a turn-on, but at this point, it felt like everything about Levi was a turn-on.

Just looking at him in the morning, with bed head from the pillow and Aidan's fingers, shirtless and drinking coffee in Aidan's kitchen, made him want to drop to his knees.

That couldn't be normal; Aidan didn't feel even remotely normal about it. But then maybe this wasn't normal. If it wasn't, Aidan didn't even *want* normal anymore.

Aidan gasped when Levi pulled his fingers out. "We should use a condom," Levi said.

That seemed like the smart thing to do.

But Aidan shook his head insistently. "You said it. We've both been tested," he insisted. "Come on."

"Are you—"

Aidan kicked him with his foot. "I swear to God if you ask me if I'm sure, *I'm sure*. Come on, Banks, fuck me already."

Levi squeezed his eyes shut and then he was pushing Aidan further up on the bed. Tucking a knee tight against his chest. "It's uh . . .not as easy like this, the first time," Levi admitted softly, gazing down at Aidan, "but I want to see your face." He paused. "It's such a good face."

"Yeah," Aidan said, because anything more was beyond him at this point. He'd used up the remainder of his coherency on the condom argument. Now he just wanted to get fucked.

Despite how thorough Levi had been with his fingers, it was a stretch when Levi slid into him for the first time.

"Fuck," Aidan groaned, head falling back against the mattress. He wanted to keep looking at Levi, at the particularly warm look in his eyes, but it was almost too much.

"Just breathe." Levi's voice wobbled.

Aidan got it. When he'd first slid into Levi's tightness, he'd just about died and gone to heaven. Not thrusting away immediately had been a serious test of his self-control.

But he'd hung on, just like Levi was doing now.

Levi pulled back a little and thrust again, grinding deeper, and Aidan gasped.

"Yeah, yeah, that's it." Levi crowded in closer, the whole of his big body surrounding Aidan.

He'd never imagined he might like that, but he *loved* it.

"Kiss me," he begged, with his last little bit of brainpower as Levi began to thrust quicker. "Fuck, you gotta kiss me."

"I got you," Levi said, and he *did*.

Levi's kiss was intense and hot, lots of tongue pushing into Aidan's mouth, kind of the way Levi's body was currently sliding into Aidan's like it was meant to be there.

Was it any wonder that Aidan felt like he was being possessed from the inside out? Like after this experience he might never be the same again, not after he'd finally, *finally* gotten this?

"God, you feel so fucking good," Levi rasped out against Aidan's mouth, barely kissing as much as them just breathing into each other's mouth in a way that shouldn't have been sexy but was unbearably hot anyway.

"I'm . . ." Aidan groaned again. His cock kept rubbing up against Levi's stomach, against the hot muscled plane of it, and it was sending him closer and closer to the edge. He didn't want to come and let this end, but it was beginning to seem like a question of *if* not *when*.

Levi's cock was lighting him up inside, and every time he thrust, the hair of his happy trail pushed against him in exactly the right way.

"Yeah, baby," Levi murmured and kissed him harder.

He'd apparently been erring on the gentle side of the spectrum, because then he really put his strength into it, and Aidan lost it three thrusts later, tilting his hips up, cock catching just the right way against Levi's stomach, and he was *gone*. Coming harder than he'd ever in his entire life.

If this was sex, truly he got it now.

Why people would go to war for this. Would betray friends. Would fly across the country for a hookup.

Because when it was good, it was extraordinary.

Levi shuddered over him, mouthing at his neck, and finally his hips stuttered to a slow insistent grind as he worked them both through the remainders of their orgasms.

"Shit," Levi groaned. "So good."

That felt like an understatement and Aidan suddenly, stupidly, needed to know if he was downplaying how good it had been for him.

He was new to this. Maybe just getting your dick wet wasn't the be-all and end-all.

"Just good? 'Cause I'm thinking like . . .worldview changing," Aidan asked softly. He could hear the thread of worry in his own voice and hoped that Levi wouldn't.

Levi lifted his head, eyes meeting Aidan's.

Maybe he shouldn't have worried. They were blown wide, and as Aidan looked at him, it felt he saw whole universes in Levi's gaze.

"Uh, yeah? Same," Levi said. He pulled out, a careful and tender hand on Aidan's hip. Flopped over next to Aidan like he wasn't worried about the state of the bedding. Like his mind had been so blown he couldn't be bothered to even think about such an ordinary concern.

"But you've done this a lot." Why was Aidan bringing that up? He ignored the surge of jealousy he felt, because it was stupid. But he was thinking it, wasn't he? Surely he—a gay-sex newbie—couldn't measure up to all of Levi's legendary hookups.

But Levi nuzzled closer, lips against Aidan's shoulder. He didn't seem particularly perturbed by Aidan's questioning. "Yeah, so? It's not about the act, it's about the person."

For Aidan, it was definitely about the person.

Aidan nodded. "Yeah, um. Couldn't imagine doing this with anyone else." *Even Mo*, he didn't say, but he hoped Levi got what he wasn't saying.

"Good," Levi said.

CHAPTER 17

WHEN THE LAST SEASON had ended, Levi had always known it was a possibility that he'd leave Seattle. That they wouldn't want to pay him the kind of money he deserved, and that he'd move on by necessity.

But of all the places he thought he'd end up, Toronto had not even been close to the top of the list.

Now he was hearing the pounding drums of the Thunders' infamous lead-in song, fake lightning and thunder crashing through the stadium as the PA got the crowd pumped up for the team running onto the field.

Aidan looked over at him, eyes clear and determined through his visor. He leaned in, knocking their helmets together.

"You got this," Aidan told him.

Levi patted him on the ass. God bless the tight white pants the Thunder wore for their at-home uniforms and also the football culture that allowed him to do that, no questions asked. Nobody even blinked twice.

"So do you," Levi said.

Aidan grinned as the AC/DC song built to its crescendo. "Fuck yeah, we do," he said, raising his arms. "Let's go play some football, boys," he yelled, and following their captain, their quarterback, they ran onto the field, the sounds of a faux thunderstorm echoing around them, lightning blazing bright on the dark blue video screens circling the stadium.

"Fuck yeah," Lane yelled as their bodies crashed together in the middle of the field. "Let's cream some Cardinal ass!"

"You got a problem with Arizona, man?" Trevor wondered, hitting their group with high fives all around.

"Yeah, I'm gonna dust their shit," Lane boasted. "You feel me, little bro?"

Trevor grinned, and even though they were in Toronto and not Seattle, nothing was fundamentally different.

Everyone got hyped up, their competitive spirit sharpening all their edges.

"Come on, guys," Aidan said, gathering the offense together on the sideline after the big intro. He looked every inch the calm, collected, Super Bowl–winning quarterback he was, so much more like this than in practice or even during the preseason games.

But now?

Levi would do anything for him, push his body to its limit and past, just to make sure his crisp white uniform with its midnight blue and silver accents stayed pristine.

"You ready?" Griff asked him as Levi circled up near the rest of the offensive line. Acker was on his other side, still not looking *happy,* but at least less like he wanted to kick Levi's ass.

"Never been readier," Levi said. He was glad he'd managed to convince Zane to put him in for more preseason snaps, because now he wasn't lying. He *was* ready.

"Yeah, you got this," Griff said.

In the huddle, Mo leaned in and tapped his helmet against Aidan's. For a second, they didn't move, just stood that way, and Levi was pretty sure they were saying something to each other.

There were so many years of history there, and Levi didn't want to be jealous of those. Mo had helped Aidan get his two rings. He was hopefully going to help them all get another one. Get Levi his first.

He had to remind himself, for the millionth time, that it was *him* in Aidan's bed, not Mo. That all week, he and Aidan had been waking up together and falling asleep together. Even making out in the kitchen together.

It had been a really good week, but every single time Levi saw Mo, saw them look at each other with all that shared history, he experienced a jolt he couldn't quite tamp down completely.

He kept hoping that with time he could. That in a week or a month or by the end of the season, he'd like Mo and appreciate his long friendship with Aidan with no strings and no jolts to be found.

"Let's show them what we've got," Aidan said, meeting every player's eyes in the huddle. Levi swore his gaze snagged on Levi a second longer than anyone else, but he couldn't be sure, no matter how much he wanted to be.

Aidan called out the play then—a crossing route pass—and then Levi *knew,* no question in his mind, Aidan met his eyes again. Levi nodded, his acknowledgment of what Aidan was asking for. He knew what they needed. He knew the kind of protection Aidan had to have, and he was going to do everything in his power to deliver.

Preseason was one thing, but playing in a regular game was always different. More real, like every movement you made mattered. And it wasn't only him that felt that way—*everyone* on the field felt the same.

What it really meant was that even though Levi thought he had a good handle on what *real* defensive pressure felt like, coming at him in a rush, it was still tougher than he'd anticipated to plant his feet and work the guy back, one step at a time.

Levi did it, barely managing to turn the linebacker away from Aidan's pocket at the last moment, shoving him to the ground in enough time to watch as Aidan let the ball fly, soaring over their heads.

And Mo missed it by an inch.

Had the pass been too high or had Mo misjudged it? Hard to say.

Aidan muttered a sharp *fuck* behind him.

Mo had been mostly open, and that wasn't something that happened all the time—considering how often he was double- and sometimes triple-teamed by the defense's backfield. But none of that mattered because that was a pass Aidan wasn't going to get back.

"Shake it off," Aidan ordered when they huddled back up. Turned to Levi after he'd called Jaden's number for a running play. "You good?"

Levi had done *his* job, so he wasn't sure why Aidan was checking in. Shouldn't he be saying that to Mo, who was still half glowering on the opposite side of the huddle?

He gave Aidan a sharp nod.

It wasn't the greatest drive Levi had ever been a part of, or the smoothest either—which made sense, they'd barely played together in the preseason, and then there was the new arrival of Morris, who was still getting up to speed on the playbook—but they pushed deep-ish into the opposing team's territory, and when Trevor came up a yard short on a third and five, Coach sent Dawson out to kick a field goal.

Before the last season, that would've been a no-brainer. Even fifty-yarders had consistently been in Dawson Hall's wheelhouse. He didn't *ever* miss but it was rare enough that he'd been considered one of the best kickers in the NFL.

No longer.

He had something to prove, after a disastrous final season. A chip on his shoulder that Levi could see a mile away.

Levi thought that if you *didn't* know, didn't know Dawson, like he'd begun to, maybe he wouldn't have noticed.

But there was an undeniable tenseness to his shoulders, even under his pads, as he jogged out with the rest of the kicking unit, including his new holder, the rookie punter, Cam.

"Hey," Aidan said, coming up to where Levi was standing to the side. He always stood for kicks. Extra points and field goals both. He'd join Griff and Acker and the rest of his line on the bench in a minute, but only after Dawson was done.

"Good drive," Levi said.

Aidan made a face. "Felt like we were behind from the moment I missed Mo on the opening pass."

"You guys are still getting your chemistry back," Levi said.

Dawson lined up, Cam kneeling less than a dozen yards in front of him.

"Should be easier," Aidan said. He wasn't complaining, exactly, but Levi could hear the confusion in his tone. Like he'd expected it to be easier, even though it had been three years since he and Mo had played together.

"A lot of things should be easier," Levi pointed out dryly.

"You handled the pass rush well," Aidan said. "Was a little shaky on that first pass."

"Yeah."

Aidan didn't say that was maybe why the ball had floated a little high—had he rushed the throw because he hadn't been entirely sure the pocket wouldn't collapse onto him?

Maybe.

But this wasn't time to overthink what had just happened. They had to move forward, *look* forward.

"You've still got this," Levi said, giving his back a little pat. His hand drifted closer, towards his solid-gold peach of an ass, and Aidan shot him a look, then grinned.

"Not washed up yet."

Dawson sent a picture-perfect kick right between the uprights and half embraced Cam, half pushed him away, like he was embarrassed he'd need reassurance after what was a very routine field goal.

"Not just you either," Levi said, glancing over at Dawson.

"Nope. He's got this." Aidan sounded more confident about Dawson than he did about himself, which was not something Levi remembered.

Aidan had always been so sure of himself. Almost bordering on cocky.

He was as good as he thought he was, plus Levi had a competence kink a mile wide, so that had never bothered him.

The opposite, in fact.

He didn't like Aidan taking the blame for anything.

"Gonna give you that extra second," Levi promised.

Aidan glanced over. "I didn't—"

"Didn't have to," Levi said and then turned and headed to the bench to rest for the Thunders' next drive.

Aidan didn't like being tied midway through the fourth quarter.

Probably *nobody* liked it, unless they were used to not winning and then even the thought of being close enough to taste it might be gratifying.

But Aidan was actually used to *winning*, and he wanted to win this game. Mo's first back with the Thunder and the first of their new season.

Set the tone and all that jazz. Plus, the Cardinals were a fairly easy opponent, not picked to make the playoffs, and even though the Thunder were still shaking a bit of the offseason rust off, Aidan didn't want to play down to their level.

"Get me the ball," Mo said to him as they jogged out onto the field for their next drive. It was one of the first things Mo had said to him since that missed catch in the first quarter.

Aidan did not roll his eyes. "Sure," he said. "I'll just snap my fingers. Make it happen."

They'd been double- and even once triple-teaming Mo all game. He was a pro and there'd been windows. He'd caught two vital passes for first downs in prior drives. But Aidan knew what he wanted.

What the Thunder *needed*.

A nice long drive to suck up the rest of the time in the game. A drive that ended in a game-winning touchdown.

The kind of thing that had been his and Mo's bread and butter in their heyday.

"Hey, you're Aidan Flynn. Isn't that how it works?" Mo asked.

It was funny how Aidan loved and kind of hated the guy in equal measures. "No pressure or anything," he huffed.

Zane called in the play. Slant to Trevor, with optional curl pattern to Lane. One of those double tight end patterns they'd been working on during camp and preseason.

"You fucking love the pressure," Mo said, shooting him the kind of smile that had always lit Aidan up inside like a pinball machine. The smile was the same, but his reaction wasn't. Instead of a white-hot heat, it was more like a friendly comfortable warmth.

This isn't the time, Flynn. It's go time.

Aidan focused. Called out the play. Checked in with Levi—who'd been solid as fuck the whole game. The Cardinals had only sacked him once, when even Aidan could admit he'd held on to the ball about three seconds too long, waiting for Mo to try to evade the corner and the safety who were blanketing him.

Even then it hadn't come from Levi's side, but Acker's.

The ref blew the whistle and the ball shot out of Griff's hands, landing in Aidan's.

He dropped back. One step, then two. Trevor shot the gap perfectly between the safety and his coverage. Whoever decided to only put a linebacker on Trevor was going to get their ass reamed in meetings this week.

Aidan pulled back and threw the ball. Trevor caught it mid-stride, and went for another five yards, a total of a seventeen-yard gain. Perfect play. Perfect execution.

Zane called for two run plays after that, trying to eat up time on the clock. Jaden got a decent chunk of yards on the first carry, and even more on the second.

Aidan had a feeling after they were able to run the ball fairly well that he wouldn't be throwing much the rest of the drive.

He did take a shot down the field to Mo on a second down, but the corner batted the pass away at the last moment.

Still, they marched down the field, running more plays for Jaden and then a few more of Zane's double tight end formations. Trevor caught another pass, and then Lane. And finally, Mo got another one to set them up at the six-yard line with less than two minutes remaining.

The Cardinals had been using their timeouts to try to save time, but it was clear if they could get in the end zone, it would all be a moot point.

With that much time on the clock though, Aidan didn't want to send Dawson out to make a short field goal. It would break the tie, but it would leave the Cardinals with a chance, if they could go down the field and score a touchdown.

He wanted the Thunder to get in the end zone, and he knew who he wanted to catch the pass.

Just like old times.

Zane must have known what he wanted, because he called for a little misdirection—one of the new plays they'd come up with in the last week, since Mo had been traded—but they'd not had a lot of time to practice it.

It was all in the timing, the play starting like the double tight end formation the Thunder had been relying on all game, but then at the last moment, Mo releasing and heading to the corner of the end zone.

The hope was that whoever was defending Mo would lose track of him, thinking he wasn't getting the ball.

Aidan took a deep breath and then let it out slowly. To make this work, everyone had to do their jobs flawlessly—especially him. It would be a tight window to thread the ball in. He trusted Mo, but if Mo was even the tiniest bit off, it could be an interception, not the touchdown they needed.

"Let's do this," he said, clapping his hands.

He met Mo's eyes across the huddle. Mo nodded at him. He was as ready. They could do this. They'd done this so many times before.

Levi nudged him. "I'll get you the time," he said.

Aidan hadn't even worried about that, but it was true; he'd need the time for the play to develop. If he got pressured, he wouldn't be able to wait for Mo to release to the end zone.

"I know," Aidan said.

Levi smiled. "Let's get a W, then, bro."

They lined up. Griff snapped the ball.

One.

Two.

Lane and Trevor shot out, running their misdirection pattern. Aidan did a pump fake, trying to sell it.

Three.

Mo released from where he'd been blocking, which left the line to contend with one extra defender and one less lineman.

Four.

He sprinted to the corner.

Aidan saw Acker getting backed up, knew he only had a second more to make this work.

Sidestepped, trying to buy another precious half a second.

Five.

Aidan threw the ball, just before Mo got set, but he knew Mo could adjust. *Would* adjust. Had to believe he would, like he had so many times before.

They'd always had each other's backs.

Today was no exception.

Mo snatched the ball out of the air, came down with a quick toe-tap on the right side of the line.

The side judge threw his hands up and so did Aidan, as he raced in to celebrate.

Mo was an inch taller than him and a little broader and it felt natural, felt like déjà vu when Mo caught him mid-jump, mid-laugh, and raised him up towards the sky.

Aidan couldn't help it, he looked down at Mo's ecstatic expression and it was like the last three years hadn't happened.

All the pain, all the sadness. Every moment he'd missed him.

Every time he'd railed at fate for separating them. For Mo not returning his feelings.

Maybe it was written in the stars, or even in fucking fate that Mo would never love him like he'd loved Mo, but they *could* have this again.

"Thought I wasn't even going to breathe, watching them try to drive for that TD," Cam joked as Aidan leaned on the bar next to him.

He'd suggested two days before the game that they all head to Vault for what would either be a celebration of their first win or a consolation drink for their first loss.

"The defense was solid. They had our backs," Aidan said, and Cameron nodded excitedly.

"They sure did," Cam said. "But I was *still* freaking out."

"Aw, you're such a rook," Dawson teased as he lifted a glass of whiskey to his lips.

Cam made an outraged noise and elbowed him. "I played in college, you know."

"Oh, honey, we know." Dawson slung an arm around him. "You're cute."

He still thought maybe he should talk to Dawson. Dawson was such a solid guy—had been in college, and from everything Aidan had seen, nothing had changed now—but even solid guys went through it and could take advantage of someone without realizing it.

And that hero worship in Cam's eyes was *very* sweet.

But now he didn't want to talk to Dawson. Didn't want to warn him off. Just wanted to celebrate with his team.

Speaking of his team, it felt like he'd barely gotten a chance to celebrate the big win with Levi. Mo and Griff and Trevor and Lane had all been surrounding him. Jaden too. But it was like he was always on the opposite side of whatever group Levi was in. Then he'd had to do the press scrum after the game, and then it turned out that on their way to Vault, Levi had caught a ride with Griff instead.

Aidan sipped his drink and looked around the room, hoping that he'd see Levi. But he didn't. There was Nate, chatting with Jaden and one of their starting corners. Ramsey was here, in a corner with Wes, their heads tipped together.

Maybe that was something—no matter how much Wes protested that it wasn't.

So many guys here, but he couldn't find *his* guy.

Aidan ignored the voice that screamed at him that Levi wasn't his guy, no matter how much he wanted him to be, because he hadn't said something.

He knew he should, even though he was half terrified that Levi would tell him it was only sex. He'd done everything he could this week to show Levi that it wasn't just sex for him, and Levi hadn't exactly protested.

They'd even grabbed pizza again from Moretti's, mid-week, and it had felt even more date-like than the last time. And that wasn't even counting the long, slow blowjob he'd given Levi when they'd gotten back to Aidan's condo.

"Hey."

Aidan looked over but it wasn't Levi there. It was Mo, glass of red wine in his hand and an only slightly dimmer version of that celebratory smile on his face.

"Hey," Aidan said, tapping him on the shoulder. "Great game, man."

"So happy to be home," Mo said. "Feels like old times, catching your darts."

"Yeah," Aidan agreed.

"Missed it," Mo said, all earnestness. Too earnest. Something in the back of Aidan's brain pinged, but he ignored it, because he was just being stupid.

"Yeah, me too," Aidan said, even though he'd deliberately gone out of his way to not say anything about how he'd missed talking to Mo during their enforced silent period.

He hadn't wanted to touch on personal feelings.

"I forgot how good it was. How good it felt," Mo rhapsodized. He hadn't always been the most expressive guy, but maybe the last three years had taught him that if he felt it, he should say it.

Aidan could say *he'd* learned that. Of course if he had, then why was he still being hesitant about bringing it up with Levi?

One reason, and it was standing in front of him, grinning at Aidan like nothing had changed.

"Three years is a long time," Aidan said noncommittally. He wasn't sure he wanted to venture down memory lane with Mo, if only because he *still* wanted to find his guy.

Mo nodded. Slid closer, until their elbows were nearly brushing. "Actually," he said, tongue flicking out and wetting his bottom lip in a way that would've used to fuel Aidan's fantasies for *weeks*, "I wanted to talk to you. About something private."

Aidan really didn't want to rehash what they'd talked about last June. It had been ugly enough then, and there was nothing more to say about it. Aidan had felt one way and Mo had felt another.

Being back on the same team together didn't change that.

But how could Aidan say no? He felt caught between his long friendship with Mo, a friendship that meant he'd give Mo whatever he needed, no questions asked, and being QB1 and a captain, who should always be willing to hear a teammate out.

"Sure," Aidan said and, inclining his head towards the library, guided him and Mo that direction.

He had no idea what Mo wanted to talk about—though he had some idea—but he was still surprised when they stopped in front of a set of bookshelves, lined with leather-bound, gold-embossed volumes, and Mo said, "I've been thinking."

"A dangerous hobby," Aidan tried to joke.

"I mean it," Mo said, still so earnest. Where had all this earnestness come from? Aidan didn't quite recognize it, and it was making him uneasy.

"Okay," Aidan said. "What have you been thinking about?"

Mo took a deep breath. Set his wine down, which made Aidan even more anxious. "You know what we talked about in June."

Like Aidan was going to fucking forget. "Yes."

"I know I blew you off—"

Aidan wasn't going to let that slide. Had Mo turned him down? Yes. But he'd done it nicely. Thoughtfully. There'd been no blowing off of anyone.

"No, you didn't," Aidan said. "I told you how I felt and you told me you didn't feel the same. End of story."

Mo's dark eyes seemed to be pleading with him to understand what he was trying to say without him actually fucking saying it. "You surprised me. Fucking floored me, to be honest."

"I got that." That hadn't felt great either, but it hadn't been too shocking, considering that Aidan had spent years trying to keep his feelings under wraps.

"I didn't know what to say. I hadn't thought about it. I still don't know if I . . ." Mo hesitated. "I don't know if I do like guys, but God, being back here with you, playing together again, catching your passes again, I just . . .it makes me wonder."

Aidan told himself to be sympathetic, but his voice came out flat. "Makes you wonder what?"

He should be thrilled that they were having this conversation but all he felt was vaguely nauseous and like he should absolutely be finding Levi sometime in this century.

"Makes me wonder if I was too quick to dismiss it. Maybe we should . . .I don't know." Mo's smile was guileless. He had no fucking idea what was going on now. He only thought Aidan had been in love with him in June and now, in September, that Aidan was still in love with him.

"You're trying to say that you want to what . . .*date* me?"

"I don't know?" Mo was still trying to say it, which Aidan got. He had struggled with what to say for three years. It had only been three months for Mo.

"Yeah you do," Aidan said.

Mo blew out an unsteady breath. "I'm not saying I feel the same. But maybe I could. I think I was too quick to dismiss it before."

It was not a grand declaration of love. It was not Morris falling to his knees saying he'd made a massive mistake. It was too wishy-washy to be considered any of those things. Way too many "maybes" and "mights."

Three months ago, Aidan would've jumped on it anyway.

Now he just hung back, uncertain what he should say.

"We're just . . .we're good together, Aidan," Mo said.

Aidan had always believed that, but now he wasn't sure that extended to all the ways he'd once hoped for. But it would be *crazy* to tell Mo no. The Aidan of three months ago was screaming at him to take Mo up on whatever he was offering. But the Aidan of three months ago didn't know what it was like to have Levi.

"Yeah, we are. On the field."

Mo shot him a look. "Seriously?"

"I don't know what you want me to say. I told you I was in love with you and then you said it wasn't going to happen. That was almost four months ago."

"Yeah. But then I got traded here, and I'd been thinking, and now . . .it was like we got a second chance." Mo wasn't begging exactly, but there was a part of Aidan—much quieter now, but not completely silent—that wanted to believe he sort of was.

"I don't know," Aidan finally said.

He should tell Mo about Levi, but he didn't know if he could.

Regardless of anyone currently in his bed or worming their way into his heart, Aidan *was* sure he didn't entirely like the idea of *let's see how it goes.*

That sounded like a recipe for *Aidan getting his heart broken a second time.* And the first time hadn't exactly been a picnic.

Mo was staring at him like he hadn't believed how this conversation was going. That was fair; Aidan couldn't really believe how this conversation was going.

"You don't *know*?" Mo questioned.

Aidan huffed out a breath. "You know how you didn't know what to tell me three months ago? I don't know what to fucking say to you now, Mo. This is . . .it's a lot. I wasn't expecting it."

"I know." Mo had the nerve to look understanding.

Part of Aidan—the heartbroken part from three months ago—wanted to say *yes*, if only because if he said yes, maybe it would erase the way he'd felt. But the other part was screaming at him that if he agreed, it would mean that the next time he saw Levi, it wouldn't be to celebrate his first win as a Thunder player, but to tell him that he'd need to move back to the guest room.

Aidan could not imagine doing that.

He also couldn't imagine looking Mo in the eye and telling him that *no*, he wasn't interested after everything that had happened.

What would that say about his supposedly strong feelings?

Aidan didn't know.

He just plain fucking *didn't know.*

Maybe that was all he could say right now.

"I really don't know," Aidan said again. "Obviously you want an answer but I can't. Give me some time."

Aidan wasn't sure what time was going to buy him—hopefully some kind of clarity—but there wasn't anything else to say.

"That's only fair," Mo said wryly. "Considering what I said to you three months ago."

Aidan nodded. He finished his drink. Wished he already had another one even though he rarely had more than one during the season. But this? This called for it.

"I'm gonna—" He gestured towards the doorway which led to the bar.

"Alright," Mo said. Patted him on the back. Maybe if Aidan had given him even slightly more encouragement, his fingers might've lingered. But the touch was brief, and Aidan couldn't even say he was disappointed.

When he emerged into the main room, there was Levi, hanging out at the bar with Griff, Lane, and Trevor.

"Hey," he said, catching Levi's elbow. Unlike Mo, *his* touch lingered. Aidan couldn't help it, even though he was touching Levi in front of three of their teammates.

"There you are." Levi grinned. "Wondered where you went to."

Like Aidan hadn't been looking for Levi for fucking ever before Mo had dragged him into their private conversation.

"Been looking for you," Aidan said. He didn't know how to tell Levi what Mo had just said to him—and he obviously couldn't say it in front of any of these guys.

"Yeah?" Levi wiggled his eyebrows.

It should've been stupid. Not hot.

But it was hot.

"Have another drink," Levi said. "Then we're going."

"Oh, we are?" Aidan raised an eyebrow.

"Got a better celebration in mind," Levi said.

There was no question in Aidan's mind that he wanted it. Wanted Levi. Because didn't he always?

It was on the tip of his tongue to say *yes, your victory party sounds like the best fucking idea ever*. One hundred and ten percent, ten out of ten, all gold stars.

But then he thought about what Mo had said. What Mo had just suggested. And even though he wanted it, *craved* it nearly, he didn't know what kind of person that made him to take advantage of Levi's desire while not being totally honest about what was going through his head right now.

"Um," he said.

Levi looked surprised. Not disappointed, at least. But surprised.

"Hey, bro, it's all good. You played a hard game today. We'll table it for later." Levi smiled at him, as bright as ever, and his touch on Aidan's shoulder lingered.

Maybe it *would* be fine. Aidan let out the breath he'd been holding.

He had another drink. Laughed with his teammates. Lifted his glass in so many toasts he lost count.

Even joined in the chorus of boos when Cam said something careless about where they'd be in February.

"Can't jinx us, rook," Dawson teased him, slinging an arm around the punter's shoulders.

Cam had blushed, Dawson ruffling his hair with his other hand. "You're good, rook."

When Aidan had finally finished his drink, quietly consulting with the bartender to cover everyone's tabs, he met Levi's gaze and Levi nodded.

But Levi was quiet in the cab as they headed back to the condo.

Aidan knew he should say something—he didn't think he could tell him what had happened with Mo, because that would mean having to parse out what it *meant*, and Aidan had yet to figure that out—but he could make small talk.

Normally, conversation flowed between them so easily.

Maybe Aidan had brought on Levi's silence by not being enthusiastic about sex. Or maybe he was just tired from the game, and Aidan was being neurotic, imagining the worst-case scenario.

"You good?" Aidan said, nudging him with his leg. He couldn't kiss him, even though he wanted to, because they were in the back of a cab, and the driver had definitely recognized them, congratulating them on a great game when they'd first climbed in.

"Yeah, 'course," Levi said, their eyes meeting in the dark.

The cab stopped in front of their building and they climbed out, Aidan nodding along and giving the guy an autograph on top of a really healthy tip.

"It was a good day," Aidan said when they were in the elevator, floors flashing past. "Would've liked it if it didn't come down to the last few plays, but I'll take it."

Levi shot him a wry smile. "Overachiever," he joked gently.

Between the fond tone and the teasing, Aidan was fairly certain everything between them *was* okay, but then they walked into the condo and instead of Levi heading with Aidan into the bedroom they'd been sharing for weeks now, Levi went straight into the guest room without a word.

What the fuck. Aidan didn't want that. Aidan *hated* that.

Aidan hesitated in the hallway, eyeing the open doorway. Listening to the noises of Levi undeniably getting ready for bed.

Maybe Levi wanted his space, but fuck that noise. Maybe it was unfair, but Aidan didn't want to give it to him.

They hadn't talked about it, but Aidan liked having Levi in his bed for more reasons than just sex. It *was* more than just sex. Aidan believed that, and he wanted Levi to believe it too.

He made the decision in a second and didn't let himself overthink it.

Approaching the guest room, he leaned against the doorframe, trying to appear casual about it. Like internally he wasn't strongly considering grabbing Levi's arm and dragging him to his bed like a caveman with a particularly tasty morsel he didn't want to share.

"What's up?" Aidan asked, watching as Levi unbuttoned the shirt he'd worn to Vault, tossing it into the empty laundry hamper. Empty because he'd been using the one in Aidan's room.

The one he should still be using, the voice in Aidan's brain screamed.

Levi glanced over at him. "Going to bed," he said. He didn't sound short, but there was an edginess to his tone that Aidan also hated.

He'd fucked this up. *Don't fuck this up,* he could imagine Riley yelling at him right now.

I'm fucking trying, he yelled right back.

Try harder. These days it felt like Riley always got the last word, and Aidan loved him so much, he couldn't even be angry about it.

"In here?" Aidan questioned as carefully as he was able. Because damnit, Riley, he *was* trying.

A flush climbed up Levi's cheeks. "I wasn't sure, I didn't want to overstep and you didn't seem interested earlier . . ."

"Was a long day." That much *was* true. "Doesn't mean I don't want you in my space. Doesn't mean I want you to come back in here. But if that's what *you* want . . ." Aidan trailed off. Hoping desperately it *wasn't* what Levi wanted.

"I don't," Levi said.

Aidan hadn't even realized his shoulders were tense until they were relaxing, sloping downwards again.

"Well then," Aidan said.

Levi smiled, goofy this time, but it felt like they were both in on the joke. *We're both being stupid, bro,* he could imagine Levi saying, but Levi didn't have to, because it was so obvious.

Levi hadn't even gotten far in getting ready for bed without Aidan, but it still felt so right to have him back in the bathroom next to Aidan, brushing his teeth and getting water everywhere, splashing up on the mirror in a way that Aidan tried to pretend didn't bother him.

It turned out though that the most important thing was that it was *happening* at all. Aidan couldn't even imagine if Levi had ended up dotting the guest room bathroom mirror.

They crawled into bed, and for a second, Levi seemed like he was going to keep to his side in a way he rarely did, then he turned over, sliding a hand over Aidan's hip.

"You know if you still want to talk about it—the Mo stuff—you can," Levi said quietly, his expression hard to see in the dark.

"I know." Aidan hesitated. He wanted to say more, but what could he say? He'd just freaked out internally because Levi had tried to give him space he didn't want. "When there's something I need to say, I'll say it."

Levi was quiet for a long moment. "Alright," he said.

This too, Aidan realized, was about trust.

Trust that when Aidan had something to say, he'd say it. But it didn't just go one way. Aidan was going to have to trust that when he figured out what the fuck he was doing, when he *did* find the words, Levi would be willing to listen to them.

Levi leaned in and pressed a quick kiss to Aidan's cheek. "It's all good. Go to sleep," he murmured.

And to Aidan's surprise, he closed his eyes and actually did.

CHAPTER 18

Levi was not jealous.

He was *not* jealous.

But two nights ago, he'd watched Mo lead Aidan to the library at Vault, clearly intending for the two of them to have a private conversation, and ever since, Aidan had been . . . *off*.

Quieter than usual. Intense. And the most damning piece of evidence of all: Levi might still be in Aidan's bed, but other than some kissing and a hug that *Levi* had initiated, there'd been zero orgasms.

Aidan hadn't touched him since whatever he and Mo had discussed.

It was freaking Levi out.

The last time he'd checked, Mo *hadn't* returned Aidan's feelings for him, so Levi shouldn't have been worrying—but he couldn't help it.

He liked Aidan *so* much. Maybe even loved him. Probably *did* love him, if he was being honest with himself, and if this horrible crawling feeling in the base of his stomach was to be believed. But he'd thought he had *time* to deal with it. To slowly, carefully, relentlessly seduce not just Aidan's body, but his heart, too.

Then Mo had shown up, and at first that hadn't really seemed like a big problem.

It felt like a big problem now.

A problem Levi didn't know how to solve. A problem he couldn't even ask Aidan about, because Aidan seemed entirely predisposed to *not* talking about it.

Even practice today, the typical Tuesday-after-a-game grind, hadn't distracted him sufficiently to keep him from worrying about it.

"You're still glowering."

Levi looked over at Trevor. "Yeah. So?"

"Are we going to kick Mo Jeffries' ass? Is this what this is about?"

Levi rolled his eyes. Trevor had never kicked someone's ass a day in his life. He was on the painfully straight and narrow path and committed to sticking to it, probably because Lane was so devoted to the opposite.

"Are you even sure you know what that means?" Levi asked. He'd much rather discuss how Trevor was a beast on the football field but ridiculously mild-mannered off of it.

"Come on, dude, I *know*. 'Course I'm not sure I'd be able to take him alone. But if you joined in . . ."

"Wouldn't it be the opposite? Wouldn't it be *me* taking Mo and you joining in?"

Trevor shot Levi an embarrassed look. "I don't know if I could do that."

"Yeah, don't go around admitting that," Levi said.

"Don't worry, man, I wouldn't. Lane wouldn't ever let me forget it."

"No shit."

Trevor nudged him with his elbow. "So are you gonna tell me why we're even discussing kicking Mo Jeffries' ass? What did he do to you? Did he steal your man? Or did he steal him *back*? Does that even count, if Mo had him first—"

Levi cut Trevor's ramblings off. They were too close to the thoughts trapped in his own head and it wasn't doing him any favors to hear them repeated out loud.

"No," Levi said. "Things are just . . .complicated."

"That's usually code for you can't admit what you really want."

Levi normally liked Trevor a lot. He was entertaining, both with and without his stepbrother, Lane. They weren't called the demon twins for nothing. But right now, Trevor was working his last nerve. "I can admit it," he ground out.

"Okay, code for you can't admit it to more than just yourself."

"Not helpful, Trev," Levi retorted.

"Actually," Trevor said blithely, apparently unaware of how frustrated Levi was getting—how frustrated Levi already was, "it's super helpful. I'm trying to encourage you to talk about your feelings, and to do it with the one person who might be able to fix it."

"Unless Morris Jeffries falls back into a hole, there's no fixing it." And Levi really, really hated that.

Maybe this wasn't why he'd stuck to hookups before, but now he was beginning to see why that had felt so easy and casual. Because hookups, by definition, *were*. This whole thing was messy and complicated and made Levi want to bash his head against a wall.

Also made him want to drag Aidan to the locker room, so he'd stop smiling over at Mo that way. Made him want to be the one who drop-kicked Mo back to where he'd come from.

"You should just talk to him," Trevor tried again.

But Levi was beyond words now, and just growled, chasing Trevor off once and for all.

Levi knew he should feel at least a little bad about that, but he didn't. He was too messed up in the head. Jealous and hating how nasty it felt.

Because, obviously if it was as easy as just *talking* to Aidan, he'd have already done it.

But every time he got even the beginning of the conversation out of his mouth, tongue thick and body buzzing with nerves, Aidan shut down.

He'd tried twice now. Once, the morning after the game, when Levi was sucking down an enormous cold brew and Aidan was teasing him about his caffeine addiction, and that had seemed like a good time to bring it up, since the mood was already lighthearted. But then it had suddenly gotten quiet and tense, the moment Levi had brought up the game-winning touchdown.

He hadn't even *said* anything else, but it hadn't mattered. Aidan had clammed up and that was the end of that.

Then later last night, while they'd been playing *Mario Kart*, he'd slid his hand way up on Aidan's thigh and he'd frozen.

Not gotten pissed, in that cute way of his, about Levi cheating.

Nope, just gone totally still, like he didn't want Levi's hand only a few inches from his dick, even though it *clearly* disagreed with Aidan's assessment of the situation.

Levi had tried to play it off, moving his hand lower, to Aidan's knee, squeezing there. Had still gone to bed with Aidan later, but neither of them had tried to initiate anything, and Levi had lain there for hours, sleepless, as he tried to imagine all the reasons why their situation had suddenly changed.

Zane blew his whistle and they gathered up for the last set of plays at the end of practice.

"Let's go," he clapped. "I wanna see all our two tight end formations. Nate and I chatted about the Condors' defense yesterday and he thinks they're not as prepared for those, so we're gonna be leaning on them heavily this week."

They had the Condors this week, and since Riley had become their quarterback three years ago, the Thunder had yet to win against them.

Levi knew, from before, that this bothered Aidan.

Sure, he wanted his brother to succeed, but Aidan still had his own competitive drive. Still wanted to win.

Levi wanted to do it for him. To prove that even though Riley was great, Aidan was *also* great. The OG Great, so to speak.

In the huddle, prepping for the first play, Aidan put a casual hand on Levi's shoulder, leaning in as he walked him through the coverage.

"You're gonna need to pull to the left, more," Aidan said, and Levi nodded.

Levi was focusing—he was a pro, by now, and knew how important all this preparation was for the upcoming game—but he couldn't help the stray thoughts that kept sprinkling into his consciousness. *I wonder if Aidan ever leans in like this and wants to kiss me, too? 'Cause I'm burning with it. Miss it. Sure not getting my dick wet sucks, but not kissing is worse.*

Something crossed over Aidan's face then, before he pulled back. A flash of desire, suddenly reined in. At least that was what Levi hoped.

But if that was true, why wasn't Aidan *letting* himself?

They ran the first play, Levi blocking against the second string defense, pulling to the left, the way Aidan had thought he should.

"All these double tight end formations," Mo complained when they huddled up again, after.

Lane shot Mo an amused look. "Feeling a little left out, bro?"

Mo shrugged. "Like a little action in between blocking."

"It's 'cause you're shit at it," Aidan said. He sounded fond, but Mo still grimaced.

"I'm better than I used to be."

"Yeah, and you used to be utter shit at it," Aidan only said.

Levi did not do a fist pump of delight. But he *thought* about doing a fist pump of delight. Did that make him a bigger person? He didn't know.

On the third play they worked on, Trevor curled the wrong direction, nearly colliding with Lane, and Lane exploded, yelling and gesturing at his stepbrother.

"Fucking get your playbook memorized," Lane exclaimed. He didn't shove Trevor, but his hands were up like they were itching to.

Mo slid between them before anyone else could get down field in enough time to do it.

"Yo," Mo said, "everyone chill, okay? It was only a mistake."

"Yeah, he should know this shit," Lane huffed.

"Like you do any studying," Trevor retorted, sounding really deeply pissed.

Levi had a feeling it was more because of Lane calling him out in front of the entire team than it was embarrassment over not running the pattern right.

"Hey, you two, calm it down," Aidan called out and clapped his hands. Forever the eldest brother and peacemaker. "Let's run it again."

Trevor shot Lane one last dirty look, and they all lined up again.

This time Trevor curled the right direction, and Aidan hit him mid-stride.

They only ran about twenty more minutes of plays, Zane clearly pleased with what he was seeing. After he dismissed them, Levi dawdled by the entrance to the locker room, waiting for Aidan. Hoping to catch him by himself and suggest they grab some dinner, just the two of them.

He'd told himself this morning that he was going to stop trying to get Aidan to open up to him. If Aidan didn't want to tell him what was going through his head, that was on Aidan.

But it *wasn't* only on Aidan. Maybe Aidan didn't realize, but Levi was going through it too, as a result.

Maybe if he kept trying, Aidan would see he was trustworthy enough to confess to.

But when he did catch Aidan, Aidan spoke first. "Hey," he said, "can you get a ride home with Griff tonight? I wanna go over some more film with Nate and the rest of the defense for the Condors game. Nobody knows Riley's moves like I do."

It wasn't very surprising, and it wasn't anything that Aidan wouldn't have normally done. But Levi still wanted to make a face.

Instead, he reined in his disappointment and didn't. Just smiled, easy, like it was no big deal, and said, "Sure thing, bro."

"Great," Aidan said, nodding. "I don't know how late I'll be."

AKA *don't bother waiting up for me.*

It was harder to swallow that, and there was a part of Levi that strongly considered, when he got back to the condo, heading into the guest room.

But he didn't, his feet taking him into the room he'd been sharing with Aidan instead, like his feet knew what he wanted and they weren't giving it up all that easily.

"You're probably going to be disappointed," Levi told his feet. But it was probably a good message to *all* of him, because his whole body was still suffused with hope.

Like against all odds, when Aidan got home, he was going to reach for Levi again.

Aidan was tired when he got in the car for his drive home. Almost considered *not* doing what he'd been debating all day, but he also knew this situation was not as elastic as he wanted it to be.

At some point it was going to snap and someone was going to get hurt.

He was more afraid that the person who did was going to be Levi, more than he even cared if that person was him.

There was a strong voice inside of him that kept insisting if *that* was true, then a whole lot of other things—emotions and feelings that Aidan wasn't quite ready to face yet—had to be true, as well.

But he wasn't sure, and no way could he say anything until he was sure.

Talking to Riley wasn't a guarantee he *would* be sure, after, but he'd never found clarity like he'd found when talking things over with his little brother.

Sighing deeply, he plugged his phone in and dialed.

It was late enough Riley should be on his way home or actually home, and like clockwork, Riley answered on the third ring, his voice echoing like he was in the kitchen of the townhouse he shared with Landry.

"Hey," Riley said, "what's up? Everything okay?"

Over the last three years, they'd discovered that it was better for their relationship if they didn't talk the week before a matchup. Aidan knew that, and he'd called anyway.

"I didn't call about football," Aidan said.

Riley huffed out a little laugh. "You want to talk about Mo, finally?"

"Um. Yeah. Sort of." Aidan groaned under his breath. "I don't know how to start, even. But first . . ." He didn't want to ask if Landry was there, listening in. If he was, he'd probably have said something already, but the last thing he wanted was for Landry to think he didn't want to talk to him.

"First?"

"Landry's not there?"

Riley was quiet for a long moment. So long Aidan thought that maybe he was and now Riley was worried that something serious was going on.

"He's upstairs," Riley said. "Why?"

"I . . .I need to tell you something, but it's . . .it's awkward."

"Please don't tell me you discovered you were wrong this whole time and you were actually in love with Landry," Riley joked.

"No," Aidan scoffed.

"Well, you're freaking me out, Aidan. You gotta tell me what's wrong."

"It's not Landry. It's . . ." Aidan huffed out again. Annoyed that he couldn't quite spit this out. Riley wouldn't judge—*much*, anyway—and he would keep this secret, probably, as long as Aidan swore a blood oath that he'd eventually tell Landry himself.

"Bro," Riley warned.

"I'll start at the beginning. You know back in July, when you and Landry and Levi came to Michigan?"

"Yes," Riley said cautiously. Aidan heard him open and close a door, and he had a feeling Riley had just gone out onto the screened-in patio they'd added to the back deck last year.

Good. He'd finally taken Aidan's concerns about Landry overhearing seriously.

"You know I was bummed about Mo. I'd finally told him how I felt, and it didn't go well."

"We were there. We saw how upset you were."

"You weren't the only one who noticed. Levi noticed too. We . . .well—"

"Oh my God," Riley interrupted. "Do not tell me Levi hit on you."

Aidan was not going to go into all the pact details because every time he told someone, it sounded stupider and stupider. "I guess we could call it that. And I hit on him back."

Riley sucked in a hard breath. "And then he went to Toronto. And you're *living* with him. Aidan, don't tell me you're fucking with Landry's little brother while you're in love with someone else."

"Am I in love with someone else though?" That was the real heart of the issue. The most important question.

"I don't know, are you?" Riley's snark could be relentless. Aidan tried to remember a time when he'd admired that about him.

"I wasn't even thinking about it, we were just having a good time. And it was a really good time. I like him, and you know I don't like many people."

"I know," Riley said dryly.

"Anyway, it was good—"

"Please don't tell me any details," Riley interrupted again.

"It was probably heading towards more than a hookup, honestly, I could feel it going there, though I was understandably . . .nervous, about that."

"Of course you were," Riley soothed. He'd known Riley would see it, the same as Aidan felt it. "You'd just had your heart broken."

"Exactly," Aidan said.

"But then Mo got traded back."

"Right. I thought it wouldn't change anything, at first, and it *didn't*, because Mo hadn't felt the same back in June, and so why would anything be different?"

"He did not." Riley didn't sound so soothing now. Now he just sounded really fucking pissed. "Mo did *not*."

Aidan winced. "I mean, I get where he's coming from. Sometimes you don't know how you feel about someone until they're not there anymore, and I hadn't talked to Mo since June. He was giving me space."

"Please tell me he didn't pull that whole *oh, but fate made sure I was traded back to Toronto and now we're reunited and that means I should love you*."

Aidan couldn't tell Riley that, because that *was* the sort of thing Mo had said.

"I guess it comes down to, I'm torn. I *like* Levi. Three months ago, I was in love with Mo. But whenever I think about telling Levi it's over, I feel fucking sick to my stomach."

"Huh." Riley paused. "Tell me what it's like with you two—not the details, *please*—but like, how is it? What are you two like together? I can sort of picture it, but I don't have a firm grasp on it, not yet. You two have been around each other, sure, but other than July, I'm trying to remember the last time you two actually hung out."

"God, he's so great. Funny and chill and doesn't take my shit. Teases me, but not in the way that would've pissed me off before. I don't know . . .it's like he helps me relax. Pulls me out of my own head. Keeps me from overthinking everything, and it doesn't even seem like it's hard for him. He just *does* it." Aidan hesitated. "I like seeing him in the morning. I like how he's in my bed at night. I don't want him to leave."

Riley hummed under his breath.

"But for so long, Mo even considering returning my feelings . . .that was everything I wanted. It feels crazy to turn him down without even trying. Like, what did I feel if I don't want him now?"

"Bro, I've got a really simple answer for you," Riley said.

This was exactly why he'd called Riley. Riley would see through his bullshit and boil it down for him.

"What?"

Riley laughed under his breath. "You can see it, I know you can. I can hear it in your voice. There's no way you don't feel it."

"What *is* it, Ri?" Aidan demanded.

"You said you like Levi, but, bro, I gotta tell you, you don't sound like you just *like* him. You love him. Levi's who you love."

"I—" Aidan didn't know what he was going to say, because Riley was right, he shouldn't even be surprised by it, but before he could figure it out, Riley interrupted him.

"I don't know what you felt for Mo. Maybe you loved him too. But you're *in* love with Levi." Riley chuckled darkly. "God help us all. Landry is gonna lose his shit."

That was definitely a serious consideration. "In a good or a bad way?"

Riley just laughed. "I wish I could tell you. But I think it's gonna be good. *Eventually.*"

"God," Aidan groaned.

"But *only* if you tell him. Like right away. Don't make me keep this secret from him."

"I don't want to, but that means . . .I can't tell Landry I love his brother before I tell Levi."

"Yeah, you *definitely* have to tell Levi. Does he—"

"If you're gonna ask if he feels the same, *don't*. You think I know? You think I'd be this torn up if I knew how he felt? I mean, the Mo shit complicates things, sure, but you know Levi. He's only ever hooked up. He doesn't do relationships."

"And it would make shit really fucking awkward if he just wanted to fuck you."

"God, Ri. *Please*," Aidan nearly begged.

But Riley just laughed. "I think you're gonna be okay. Seriously."

"How do you *know* that?" Aidan questioned. He was around Levi all the time, and he didn't possess even a fraction of Riley's confidence.

"Just a feeling."

"A fucking feeling," Aidan said flatly.

"You need to talk to him," Riley chided. "Tell him everything."

"But—"

"And if it's awful, I'm gonna be there next weekend. Landry's gonna be there." Riley's voice had gone soft. "We're gonna be there to pick you up. And kick Levi's ass too, while we're around. Convince him he's wrong."

"Ri," Aidan warned.

"I mean it," Riley said firmly. "He feels like that for you. I can't believe I didn't see it before, but I do now. He switched to *left tackle* for you, bro."

"That's football," Aidan dismissed. Which . . .had he *ever* dismissed football? Jesus, he was *fucked*.

"It's really not, though," Riley argued. "Levi doesn't put his neck out like that. Landry's been whining about it for years. Worrying about his kid brother. But then when he switched, and he was the one who wanted to make the switch? It's practically all Landry and Logan have been talking about for *weeks*. And he did it because of you. He wants to protect you."

Riley didn't have to add the natural conclusion to that sentence. *Because he cares about you, bro. Because he's in love with you, and there'd be nothing worse than watching you get beat up every week.*

"That doesn't mean he loves me," Aidan said, but he could hear the hesitation in his voice. The yearning that he felt for it to be true.

"You won't know unless you ask. And it's gotta be you, because you know he's not going to say anything. Not when he thinks you're still in love with Mo."

That was fair. Levi wouldn't. He was a good guy, the *best* guy; if he thought Aidan's heart belonged to Mo, he wouldn't interfere. Wouldn't push.

"God, how *can* I?" Aidan asked, the question torn from the heart of him. It terrified him, standing in front of the guy and putting everything on the line for a second time.

"It's scary as shit. No question. But you know what, bro?" Riley asked. But before Aidan could answer, Riley kept going. "You're Aidan fucking Flynn. You've got two rings. You're probably gonna win another one, despite my best efforts trying to beat you. You're one of the best, if not *the* best quarterback in the NFL. Nobody can stop you when you want something. Not even *you*."

Aidan sucked in a long breath and then let it out, feeling suddenly perilously close to . . .well, *tears*. He didn't know what he'd ever done to deserve Riley's faith and loyalty in him—God knew he'd actually done a lot of things that proved the opposite—but he wasn't ever going to turn them down.

"You got this," Riley said quietly.

Aidan cleared his throat. He was nearly to his building. Levi would be waiting for him upstairs. He might not be able to do it tonight, but maybe in the next few days? He'd need to work up the nerve. Find the right scenario. Moretti's wasn't the right date-night vibe, not for a love confession, but there were lots of places he could take Levi. Even during a week that was full of game preparation, like this week. He'd *make* the time, damnit.

Riley was right. He was Aidan fucking Flynn, and he was going to get his man.

"Thanks, bro," Aidan said. "God, I mean it. I know I was shitty to you—"

"No," Riley said firmly. "I mean, yeah, you were definitely overprotective, and you overstepped one time or ten—"

"Or a hundred," Aidan corrected.

Riley laughed. "Or a hundred. But you listened, when I told you how I felt about it. And you haven't, not a single moment since. Been scrupulous about it. Maybe even *too* scrupulous, if I'm being honest. So don't say you were shitty. You made it possible for me to have this life, this career, even my guy. 'Cause you were right about so many things. It's tough to be a quarterback in the NFL. I'm only tough enough because you made sure I was."

"Did my best," Aidan said, throat clenching tight.

"Did *the* best," Riley said quietly. "Keep me posted, okay?"

"Okay," Aidan said.

"And you'll tell Landry, right?"

Aidan choked out a laugh. "You promise he's not gonna hit me in the face?"

"Did *you* hit him in the face when we got together?"

"Thought about it—but no. I was happy for you. Knew you deserved someone good. Someone like him."

"Exactly." Riley sounded smug now. "You think he's gonna feel any different?"

Aidan really hoped not.

"There you go," Riley said after Aidan was quiet. "Now I gotta go. He's gonna get suspicious, and you *will* be the one telling him. Not me, okay?"

"Okay," Aidan promised.

Aidan parked the car after he'd hung up with Riley. Grabbed his bag and headed up in the elevator to his condo.

He told himself firmly during the ride that he was not going to see Levi and immediately be tempted to confess.

He was going to take his time. Formulate his approach. Time it right. The way he approached game prep, or when he was on the field and he took that extra half second to make sure the play unfolded exactly the way it needed to.

But then he walked into the condo and there Levi was on the couch, shirt off and the shortest shorts known to man clinging to his thighs. *Neon pink* fucking shorts.

Levi grinned at him. "Hey, bro," he said.

Riley had just called him bro like half a dozen times and it had never done anything to his insides, but Levi did it, and Aidan wanted to drop to his knees and press his mouth to all that inner thigh that was currently showing.

But he couldn't. He *couldn't*. Not until he told Levi everything. Not until he told Levi what he really wanted.

"Thought you'd . . .uh . . .be in bed." *In my bed.*

"That's where you want me, huh?" Levi teased. He patted the couch next to him. *Right* next to him. "Come here, babe."

Babe not during sex was new. It made Aidan hot under the collar.

He hadn't thought it would be so difficult to resist a seduction. But then resisting Levi's seduction was another thing entirely.

"Um," Aidan hesitated.

Levi shifted on the couch, and the neon pink fabric of his shorts crawled up his thighs, revealing another inch of skin.

"Fuck," Aidan muttered under his breath. He was moving to the couch before he even registered that he'd given in.

"That's better," Levi said smugly, like he knew just how much he was leading Aidan around by the dick.

Damnit, that shouldn't have been hot. But it was getting Aidan there, for sure.

"Let's play," Levi said, reaching out for the controllers. He handed one to Aidan, and when he settled back onto the couch, his arm was around the back of the couch, his fingertips brushing the edge of Aidan's shoulder. It wasn't much of a touch, but it lit him on fire.

Aidan made the mistake of glancing down, and the stupid neon pink fabric of Levi's shorts was cupping his dick, clearly half hard and getting harder by the second. Just because Aidan was sitting pressed up against him.

Aidan was not proud. He scrambled back, Levi eyeing him steadily the whole time. Like he'd known exactly how he was seducing Aidan and also like Aidan panicking was hardly surprising.

"Dude," Levi said flatly. He tossed his controller onto the coffee table. "What the fuck is going on with you?"

Aidan licked his lips. "Are you trying to seduce me?"

"And doing a piss-poor job of it if you're running away from me," Levi retorted.

Aidan opened his mouth and then snapped it shut again. "I can't. I want to, but I *can't.*"

"Why the fuck not? You want me, I can tell. The shorts never fail."

"The shorts are . . ." Aidan glanced down at them again and felt his heart rate pick up. "We're gonna revisit the shorts, for sure."

"Why not visit them *now*?" Levi asked.

"I can't," Aidan repeated. "I can't, not until you know about Mo."

It was crazy how fast Levi's expression morphed from amused seduction to something intensely feral.

"What about Mo?" he demanded.

God, this was not the way he'd wanted to do this. In a ratty T-shirt and a pair of shorts that had seen better days, in his living room, *Mario Kart* music playing in the background.

Levi wearing neon pink shorts. *Just* neon pink shorts.

It was either the most awful atmosphere for romance or the most perfect moment for *them.* Maybe it didn't matter. Maybe that was really what Riley had been trying to say. That the extra half second didn't matter, in this, and maybe he only needed to just make the throw.

"The other night, Mo told me that he might've been wrong."

"Wrong?" Levi asked flatly.

"About me. About his feelings."

"And what, he loves you too, now?"

"Um well, maybe?" Aidan was vaguely aware he was not handling this well. The growing thundercloud on Levi's face told the whole story.

Levi stood up suddenly. "I can't listen to this," he said, sounding awful.

A second later he was striding towards the door, like he was going to leave *now*, only wearing that tiny pair of shorts. Aidan scrambled to follow him.

"Where are you going?" Aidan asked. Three quarters of his brain was panicking, because he *hadn't* done a good job expressing his feelings—shocking, really—though one quarter was cheering because why else would Levi be pissed if he didn't care?

If he didn't care, he'd just leave Aidan to Mo.

"I told you," Levi ground out, "I can't listen to you telling me you want Mo. That who you really love is him. I know you do. You told me. And I was too stupid to listen."

Aidan grabbed his arm right before he opened the front door. "You *are* being stupid," he said.

Levi made a face and tried to shake him free, but Aidan wouldn't let go.

Riley had told him he was *Aidan Flynn*, and he *was*. He wasn't going to let his stupid guy go, no matter how ridiculous he was being.

"Just let me go," he begged.

"I'm trying to fucking tell you that you don't *have* to," Aidan ground out. "If you would wait for a single second, I'd tell you that I know if I gave it a go with Mo, it would only be out of obligation, because I loved him before. He's not who I want *now*."

Levi froze.

"You stupid man," Aidan said, and it was nothing like how he'd envisioned it, no roses or candlelight or sweet words, "*you're* who I want."

"What?" Levi asked, jaw dropped.

"I love *you*," Aidan said. He was, no question, the tallest guy in the world. He'd gotten the words out, and once he'd said them, he realized just how true they were.

"I love you," he repeated, because now that he *knew*, it was like he couldn't stop saying it, especially when Levi was gazing at him like he'd just gone seventeen and zero in the regular season, and the Lombardi trophy was practically in his hands already.

"I'm stupid? You're the stupidest. I love you so fucking much," Levi said and kissed him.

Levi didn't think anyone would blame him for lifting his mouth every five seconds, even though he had *Aidan Flynn* underneath him, squirming like he was dying for it, despite *just* having sex, to say, *again*, "I love you."

They'd stumbled to the bedroom—to *their* bedroom, Levi was already calling it in his head, his heart full of joy—and Aidan had barely managed to wrench his pink shorts off, before they'd fallen into each other.

It hadn't been particularly pretty or memorable. Except that yes, Levi decided, it *had* been. The first orgasm he'd ever had while being in love and being loved in return.

Who cared if it was the most basic handjob, if Aidan had been looking at him like *that* during it? Like he was everything Aidan wanted, the look in his dark blue eyes making Levi breathless with joy.

Aidan grinned. "You gonna keep saying it?"

"You gonna stop me?"

Even though Aidan tucked his head into the crook of Levi's neck, he could feel how big Aidan's smile still was. "Might try."

"Nah, you won't," Levi said smugly. "You like it."

Aidan hummed under his breath, agreeing without words.

Levi's hand stroked his back, wondering as he did how Aidan's skin could be so soft when he showered so often in the crappy practice facilities.

"I'm gonna have to tell Mo about this," Aidan murmured into the silence.

Levi, who'd spent the last forty-eight hours eating his heart out with jealousy over the guy and what he'd believed *he* had that Levi never, ever would, suddenly felt horribly bad for the guy.

"Shit, yeah," Levi mumbled. There was more he wanted to ask—more he probably should know about that whole situation—but he was afraid to puncture the blissful bubble with Mo-related questions.

"Not right away, but at some point," Aidan clarified.

"What did you tell him?" Levi gave up; he couldn't help it. *Did you tell him about me?*

"Just that I was surprised. Shocked, really. I thought about telling him about you, but I didn't. Didn't know if I should." Aidan made a self-deprecating noise. He'd probably handled it better and with more grace than lots of other people would've, but no big surprise, he was being hard on himself.

"And then," Aidan continued, still with that thread of guilt in his voice, "I was weird to you, after."

"Bro, it was a weird situation," Levi reassured him. "I wasn't . . ." Okay, he kind of *had* been, but that wasn't Aidan's fault. "I was jealous, sure, yeah, because I was crazy about you, and I thought you were crazy about *him*."

"Not anymore." Aidan hesitated. "You believe that, right? I don't want—I don't want you to be worrying about him all the time—"

"Stop it," Levi interrupted, before Aidan could spiral into more overthinking.

"But—"

"I'm *serious*," Levi retorted. "We're good. I believe you. This . . ." He stroked Aidan's back pointedly this time, so he knew exactly what Levi was talking about. "It's so damn good, I wouldn't doubt it. Couldn't."

"Okay." Aidan let out a breath. "*Okay.*"

"Yeah, fucking breathe, bro."

The smile was back on Aidan's face, which Levi was having trouble not being smug about again. "What happened to not calling me bro in bed?"

"What happened is that I figured out how hot it makes you."

Aidan rolled his eyes. "It does not."

"Yeah, it fucking does," Levi gloated. How was he supposed to *not*? When Aidan wanted—*loved*—him, and looked like that about it?

"We're also going to have to tell them," Aidan said changing the subject but not bothering to clarify who *them* were. He didn't have to, because it was obvious who he was referring to. Their collective brothers.

Levi froze and Aidan lifted his head. He nearly pulled him right back down, but Aidan was staring at him in that way that meant they should probably talk about this.

"I told Riley," Aidan added.

"How did that go?"

"Riley told me to get my head out of my ass." Aidan sounded delighted by this, and wasn't that a fucking trip? "But he also told me that I had to tell Landry. Not that I didn't want to."

"Right," Levi agreed.

It wasn't like Levi was particularly worried that his brothers or Lyla would lose their shit. Landry loved Aidan. Logan mostly tolerated him, but he only wanted Levi to be happy, and if Aidan made him happy, that was all he'd care about.

Lyla would make a face and tell him that if Aidan was really who he wanted, then he shouldn't let him go.

Well, that wasn't going to be a problem. Levi was holding on tight, and nobody—not Mo, not his brothers, not *anyone*—was ever going to make him let go.

"I'm not *worried*," Aidan said. "Just . . .are they gonna freak out?"

Levi chuckled, amused at how alike they really were, under all their external trappings. "Probably. You wanna do it on Sunday?"

"We should," Aidan said hesitantly. "Before or after?"

"After. You're already gonna be a fucking mess before the game," Levi said.

Aidan squawked and elbowed Levi gently in the side. "I am *not*. I'm gonna be chill and prepared and ready to go win a game. *Finally.*"

"Right. So freaking out underneath all that chill-ness."

Aidan groaned.

"I *know* you, bro."

Aidan settled back on Levi, chin on his chest, blue eyes full of that look that Levi knew was love, now.

"Yeah, you do," Aidan said, and Levi knew, no matter what happened on Sunday—before or during or after the game—they were going to be fine.

More than fine.

CHAPTER 19

LEVI HAD BEEN THINKING about this all week. He'd been thinking about it for longer than that, to be honest, but ever since he and Aidan had become *them*, he hadn't been able to stop.

"Hey," he said, approaching where Aidan was sitting on the bench in front of his locker.

Aidan raised a questioning eyebrow. "What's up?" he asked.

Last night they'd FaceTimed Logan. He wouldn't be at the game, because he'd be in Chicago, the Piranhas playing the Bears. He'd looked surprised when it was both Levi and Aidan crammed together on their screen.

Levi could swear that Logan hadn't actually been all that surprised when he'd learned that the guy he'd been pining over had been Aidan Flynn. "Huh," was all he'd said. "You tell Landry yet?"

"Not yet," Aidan had said. Levi had added that their plan was to tell both Landry and Lyla tomorrow—after the game. "Good fucking luck with that," Logan had teased.

Levi told himself he wasn't nervous to ask. If Aidan said no, he'd say no. But he really, really wanted him to say yes.

"Griff says you typically are the guy who addresses the room before games," Levi said. He had last week, but Levi hadn't been sure if that was a weekly ritual, or a first-game-of-the-season kind of thing.

"Yeah," Aidan said, nodding. "Typically."

"I wanna do it, today."

Aidan looked skeptical. "But—"

"I know, it's the Condors and it's your brother," Levi continued in a rush. "But . . .just let me, okay?"

Aidan shot him a knowing little grin, the corner of his lips tilting up irresistibly. "How do you know I haven't spent the whole offseason composing a killer motivational speech perfect for the first time we play Riley and Landry and the Condors?"

"I don't," Levi said. "But let me do this, okay?" *For you*, he didn't say, but he hoped Aidan heard it anyway.

"Alright," Aidan said.

"Seriously?"

"You want me to change my mind?" Aidan teased. "Besides, I'm very curious what you've come up with."

Levi couldn't say his speech was brilliant or anything—but it was going to come straight from his heart, which they'd already established belonged entirely to Aidan.

"Okay. Awesome."

Aidan was still smiling, his *Levi* smile. The one that filled Levi's stomach with warmth, until it felt like he was drowning in love.

"Have a good game, alright?" Aidan said, reaching out and wrapping a hand around Levi's wrist, squeezing.

"You're gonna kill it," Levi said, because he already believed it was true.

"Hope you've got more than that up your sleeve," Aidan joked.

He did.

A few minutes later Coach Robertson walked in, and he gave his sweet and very short motivational speech. "Get out there and execute," he challenged, meeting each and every guy's gaze as his eyes swept over the locker room. "I know what you're capable of. You know what you're capable of. Deliver it." He paused, and the room exploded in yells and cheers. Coach, Levi had been learning, didn't have to say much for what he did say to be effective. "Flynn, you've got anything?" he added, when the noise finally died down a bit.

Aidan tilted his head at Levi, who stood. He wasn't usually the kind of guy who spoke out. At least he'd never been in Seattle. He knew both his brothers could be—when the occasion called for it—but to Levi's thinking, he hadn't felt the need. Not until now.

"I might be new here," Levi said, looking around the room. "But I'm not new to this rivalry, not really. You know my brother's going to be lining up against our defense. You know Aidan's brother will be too. I keep hearing this bullshit chatter that Riley's the new Flynn. That he's the better Flynn. But I don't have to have spent tons of time here to know what Aidan brings to this team. How he has every single one of your backs. How hard he works for you—so he can give his best on Sundays. You know what it's time for? For *you* to have *his* back. To give him back some of that dedication. Let's show the world who our QB is, okay?"

Levi couldn't look at Aidan while he was talking. If he did, he was afraid he'd fucking chicken out. Not go where he *knew* he wanted to go.

But now he glanced over at him, among the catcalls after Levi had sat, and Aidan's cheekbones were flushed pink.

He looked embarrassed and totally fucking pleased.

Good.

Levi raised his chin as they stared at each other, daring Aidan to argue with anything he'd just said, but Aidan only finally smiled back.

That's right, baby, I got your back. Forever.

That had never felt like more than the truth than when the game finally started.

The Condors had a tough defensive line—aggressive and strong, but also surprisingly fast, and Levi was glad he'd gotten his feet under him during the last game, because he felt like he was fighting every single play.

It wasn't just the linebacker corps that was making their jobs tough, though. Beckett West and Micah Rose were in the backfield, shadowing Mo and even Lane and Trevor. Making it hard for them to get open.

Every time Aidan dropped back, he was holding the ball a second longer than he normally did, trying to wait out the coverage, hoping someone might break away so he could hit them.

Two times on the first two offensive drives Aidan had ended up scrambling, trying to avoid a sack and not quite getting there both times.

"We've got to get something going," Lane complained on the sideline after the second drive went nowhere.

At least the Condors were also struggling with getting their offense down the field—they'd only scored three points.

"We're gonna find a way," Aidan said, picking up a tablet, flicking through the last drive. He glanced over at Levi. "Can't keep expecting you guys to keep the pocket clean that long."

Levi wanted to tell him that they could, but he wasn't naive enough to think he could keep that promise. He had his hands full, and so did Acker, on the other side.

On the last play of the last drive, Griff had been straight up driven back, practically into Aidan.

"Put Trevor on the line," Lane suggested.

Trevor was an inch taller than his brother and slightly bigger, but despite that, Lane was a better blocker than his younger stepbrother.

"Zane says no," Aidan relayed, listening to their offensive coordinator's instructions in the headset. "We're going to try some more running plays. Try to find a rhythm on the next drive.

It sort of worked.

They made it to the thirty-five-yard line and ultimately stalled out.

Dawson came out and tied the game, kicking the ball right between the uprights, like he'd never had a reason to miss last year.

Aidan should've been happy about that, but Levi could see the remnants of frustration on his face.

The Thunder and the Condors traded punts back and forth, but late in the second quarter, the Condors found the rhythm that the Thunder seemingly couldn't and pushed deep into the red zone.

And on fourth down, instead of going with the safe move of kicking the field goal, Riley took the snap and, after pump faking to the right, ended up dodging through traffic to run the ball in himself for a touchdown.

In the locker room, Aidan leaned in and said to Levi, "I fucking want to win this game. I'm tired of losing."

He didn't have to say why. Once had been fine. Twice had sucked. Three times was pretty terrible.

Four would be catastrophic, and Aidan was going to do whatever it took to change the narrative.

Zane had come down from the upper booth and he and Aidan huddled around with Mo, Lane, Trevor, and the rest of the offensive line, working on some more plays that might give them a drive or two.

The defense held the Condors to a punt on their opening drive, and then it was Aidan's turn.

Levi looked at him across the huddle and knew whatever Aidan was determined to do, Levi would be right there with him.

But it wasn't just him. Aidan was pulling them all together through sheer strength of will, ten years of leadership in the NFL showing in this moment.

"Let's get it done," Aidan said earnestly after he'd called out the play.

He didn't need to say that everyone was going to need to go above and beyond to make it happen.

They all knew.

A team as good as the Condors? When you wanted to be that good or *better*? They were going to have to bring the dedication.

Aidan clapped, breaking up the huddle, and Levi took his position on the edge, his focus narrowing to only the player in front of him. The guy was a good rusher, pushing Levi's skills and athleticism every single down, not letting him take a single breather. He fought hard, but Levi was going to fight harder.

He dug down deep, deep into the well of motivation, and after Griff snapped the ball, pulled out a great block, feet moving fast, his bulk pushing the guy forward instead of letting him move both of them backwards, right into Aidan's space.

Behind him, he heard Aidan call out, and a second later, Mo was crossing over the middle of the zone and he had the football. He pulled a fancy cut, almost reminiscent of his old speed, and Levi knew it wasn't only him who wanted to pull this win out for Aidan. Mo wanted it too.

They went down the field like that. Not every play gained the yards they needed—and they had to get third downs twice, but they made it to the red zone, and on second down and goal, four yards away, they ran one of Zane's two tight end formations and Lane snagged the ball, fooling the defense by not blocking on the line like he had been most of the drive, but rolling out just past the goal line.

Aidan was pumped up on the sideline after that, and even though there were a few touch and go moments—Riley scrambled and broke into a thirty-five-yard run at one point that had thunderclouds descending across Aidan's face—the Thunder marched down the field three more times, and by the end of the fourth quarter, the scoreboard read Thunder 27, Condors 13.

Levi was nearby when the last seconds ticked down and he was the first person Aidan turned to, the widest smile on his face that Levi could remember seeing. No—that was not quite true. Levi when he'd kissed him after telling him he loved him, *that* had been the best smile he'd ever seen on Aidan's face. But this was a close second.

Riley and Landry met them in the middle of the field, cameras everywhere documenting every moment of the game that Levi had heard called the Brothers Bowl. "Great game, bro," Riley said, hugging Aidan.

"Thought we were in trouble there for a moment," Levi said to Landry, who just rolled his eyes in delight. He'd almost snagged a high pass that Riley had let float just a little too far, and if he had, the end score might've been a little closer.

"Wasn't our game today," Landry said, shrugging.

"It was your turn," Riley said, always generous and gracious. "But next time?"

Aidan laughed. "All bets are off. I get it."

Riley nodded in delight.

"Know you've got a flight to catch, but after media, come find me—find us," Aidan said to him, letting his hand linger on Riley's shoulder for a second. "Got something we need to talk about."

Riley nodded, and the knowing gleam in his blue eyes as they slid over Levi made it clear he knew exactly what it was about.

It was a mass of their families in the hallway outside the Thunder locker room.

Riley was there, of course, and his best friend, Paige, who'd just moved to Atlanta. But it was the entire Banks clan, minus Logan, that threatened to exceed the space required.

Landry and Lyla were chatting with Levi, and the Banks parents were there, too, Larry and Linda, watching over three of their four children with an affectionate gleam in their eye.

At one point, so long ago Aidan couldn't even remember exactly when it was, he'd hoped that maybe his parents might come around and end up at their games, just like this.

But that had never happened—first, they'd been preoccupied with their own petty dramas, and then after, because Aidan had forbidden them from showing up. He'd known they'd only be doing it because suddenly their two sons had done something worth paying attention to.

That ship, Aidan had decided—a decision that Riley had echoed, later, when Aidan had told him what he'd said to them—had long since sailed. There was no putting it back in the harbor.

"I said it before, but I'll say it again," Riley said, approaching Aidan and pulling him into a hug, "great game, bro."

"That run?" Aidan shook his head in disbelief. "I wish I could run like that."

Three years ago, it would've just about killed him to admit that Riley had skills he didn't. That he could be better than Aidan was, even theoretically. Not because he hated Riley and didn't want him to succeed, but because of what that would mean for *him*.

"You used to," Riley said, giving Aidan a teasing nudge. "I gotta do it now, while I still can."

Irrelevant. Washed up. Has-been. Aidan had thought them all. Riley's comment would have derailed him into a panic attack before. Aidan still fought the urge to ignore Wes because he represented a future that had always terrified Aidan. What was he going to do when he was done with football? Riley would have his own life—he already *did*, frankly—and Aidan would be alone.

He looked over Lyla's head and met Levi's gaze.

Realized, with a hard, joyful jolt that he wouldn't be anymore. Maybe, if he played his cards right and didn't fuck up by pushing Levi away, he'd have *Levi* and whatever life they could build. *Together.*

"I better see you doing it every week, then," Aidan said, grinning.

Riley stuck his tongue out at him. "What's up?"

Aidan looked over at Riley. "You know."

Riley grinned. "Oh boy, fireworks time. Hey, Landry," he called out. "Get your fine ass over here."

Landry came, Levi, Lyla, and Paige trailing after him.

"What is it, baby?" Landry asked.

"Aidan and Levi have something to tell us."

Aidan met Levi's eyes. He looked happy. Thrilled, in fact. Warmth practically spilling out of his brown eyes.

"Well, don't make me do it alone," he told him.

Levi only smiled harder. "Like I was ever going to leave you on an island, bro."

Aidan barely had a moment to brace himself before Levi was pushing in his space, cupping his cheeks with hot palms and pulling him into a not entirely PG-rated kiss.

He couldn't help it; he stiffened a little. Levi's parents and his brother and sister were *right* there. But then he couldn't help it. Levi kissing him made it so easy to kiss him back.

His hand went up to Levi's shoulder, tugging him in closer. It was amazing how the rest of the world faded around him when they got their hands on each other. Like nobody else even mattered.

They kissed for probably a fraction longer of time than anyone needed to get the picture, but Aidan decided he didn't care.

How many times had Riley and Landry fucked around in the kitchen of his Michigan house? He didn't want to know, but the number was *not* zero. They could take a little PDA.

Aidan broke the kiss and the rest of the world came back into sharp focus.

The first thing he saw was Landry's face. His jaw was dropped and he looked like someone had just socked him right in the face.

Not angry, necessarily, but stunned.

"Guess you *didn't* tell him, Ri," Aidan said.

Riley smacked him on the back. "Ass," he said fondly. "Of course I didn't. I wanted to see this, front and center. And honestly? Zero notes. Fantastic execution. Wouldn't change a goddamn thing."

"Riley," Landry said dazedly, "did you just see that? Or did I just hallucinate it?"

"Nope, it's happening, baby. Our brothers are following in our footsteps. Enthusiastically, I might add."

Aidan looked over at Lyla. He knew her the least. If he hadn't known how Landry would react, he really wasn't sure about her. She just raised a questioning blond eyebrow. "How long has this been going on?" she wanted to know.

"Awhile," Levi said vaguely.

Aidan realized that they hadn't talked about what they'd say their origin story was, but probably being ambiguous was better than the details. If he never needed to explain to another person that he and Levi had made a sex pact because he'd been in love with someone else, he'd be totally fine with that.

Especially if the someone else consisted of anyone from Levi's family.

"It sort of started this summer," Aidan added.

Lyla looked surprised. "Oh," she said, comprehension dawning then. "When Landry and Riley dragged Levi to your house."

Aidan nodded. "So really, it's their fault."

"You mean, it was our good deed of the fucking year," Riley said impudently. "You're welcome, bro."

"We're happy for you two," Linda Banks said, tugging him in for a quick hug. Larry held out his hand and Aidan shook it firmly. "Can't say we saw it coming, only because Levi hasn't seemed particularly interested in finding the right guy, only the next guy."

"Dad!" Levi exclaimed.

Aidan settled an arm around Levi's waist. PDA would probably never come naturally to him—you'd catch him over his dead body fucking in someone else's kitchen—but it felt right touching Levi like this. Looking up at him and feeling the warmth of his love spill out of his eyes.

Landry scrubbed a hand over his face. "I'm . . .I can't believe this is happening."

"Told you, Aidan," Riley said, a mischievous expression on his face. "You blew his mind."

"How, what, *why*," Landry whined.

Levi laughed. "You really want to hear about it?"

"No, *no*," Landry retorted.

Lyla turned to Paige. "I think my brother's brain is broken. If that's all that comes out of this, I'm good."

Paige laughed. "When Riley told me, I thought he was kidding. Are you guys gonna have one of those 'seven brides for seven brothers' weddings?"

Aidan froze, deer in the headlights. *Wedding*? They'd *just* gotten together.

"Hell no," Riley said easily. "You think I'm sharing the spotlight with this guy more than I have to?"

Aidan relaxed a fraction.

"Besides," Levi added with a devilish grin, "I'm enjoying fucking around in sin way too much."

"God," Landry groaned, putting a hand in front of his face.

Riley elbowed Levi in the side. "Your parents are *right* there, dude."

"And they've heard so much worse," Levi said smugly.

"So I guess you're not going to move out, then," Landry said. "I couldn't figure out why you didn't want to find your own place immediately."

"Yeah, he was having conniptions about it," Riley teased. "On the phone to Logan every other day about it. Never occurred to him—pretty stupidly, I might add—that might be because Levi didn't want to leave."

"I thought he was just . . . I don't know . . . being lazy about it!" Landry exclaimed.

"Bro," Levi said flatly.

"Yeah, be nice to my boyfriend," Aidan said, and realized with another jolt that it was the first time he'd said it out loud and that he and Levi hadn't really talked about specific verbiage.

But Levi beamed like he totally approved of Aidan's word choice. "Yeah, be nice, Landry."

"Why am I not surprised that you two are going to be totally smug about how happy you are, all the time?" Lyla wondered, not sounding particularly upset about that.

"I'm not surprised," Paige echoed.

Levi broke away from Aidan to argue with his sister, good-naturedly. Something about how both of them deserved to be smug about finding each other.

It was cute and Aidan was totally endeared, but his best friend was still staring at him like he'd just seen a ghost.

"Hey," Aidan said in a low voice to Landry. "Are you sure you're okay with this?"

"I'm not *not* okay with it," Landry said. He let out a heavy sigh. "I'm just . . .I don't know, *shocked*. Last I heard, in July, you were in love with Mo and he didn't feel the same. And now suddenly you're with Levi?"

"It's . . .well, it's complicated."

"Why am I not surprised that you ended up with the messiest relationship of all of us?" Landry said knowingly.

"That's not true," Aidan argued. He wasn't *messy*. Him falling in love with Levi wasn't messy either; it was like an inevitable slide into the most natural-feeling emotion he'd experienced in possibly his whole life.

But how to express that to Landry?

"I didn't know what we were doing, not at first," Aidan said simply, because honesty usually was the best policy, "but I just knew I kept wanting more of him. I'd never felt like more myself than when I was with him. It felt . . .*right*. Even when Mo came back, nothing changed."

Maybe someday he'd tell Landry how Mo's confession had spurred the realization he was in love with Levi, but for right now, this was good, and it was true.

Landry stared at him for a moment. "And you really love him."

"I really, really do."

Landry hesitated for one more second before he tugged him into a long, tight hug. "I believe you," he said, "because Levi's one of the most lovable people I know. Makes sense you'd see it, too."

"Yeah," was all Aidan could say, his throat suddenly tight. He hadn't worried that Landry would react badly. He wasn't that much of a hypocrite. But he *had* worried that Landry would have doubts and concerns he couldn't answer. That he wouldn't believe that Aidan's feelings were as serious, as *lasting*, as Aidan knew they were.

But he shouldn't have worried; Landry had always seen right through to the core of him, better than just about anyone else.

"If Levi was going to settle down, of course he'd pick you," Landry said, after he'd pulled back.

"Hey, I heard that," Levi squawked, and the whole group, even including Larry and Linda burst into laughter.

"It's 'cause we love you," Landry said, reaching out to ruffle his little brother's hair.

"Yeah," Aidan said, "we really do."

CHAPTER 20

IT FELT LIKE THE most perfect morning Aidan could remember.

Waking up in his bed, no alarm, nowhere they *had* to be except tonight at the Vault victory party, wrapped up in a pair of arms belonging to someone who loved him, who he loved back.

He'd never gotten this before, not ever, and now Aidan didn't know if he'd ever be able to live without it again.

"Don't go anywhere, okay?" Aidan mumbled into the pillow, half hoping Levi would hear, and half hoping he wouldn't.

"Like, *right now*, or forever?" Levi asked sleepily.

Aidan tried not to freak out that he'd heard. "Both?"

Levi nuzzled his shoulder. "Not going anywhere," he promised sleepily.

And something inside Aidan finally let go—an edginess he'd never thought he'd dismiss completely. An anxiety he felt like he'd carried around forever. Maybe since his parents' divorce. He wasn't naive enough to think it was gone for good. He'd need it, sometimes, and he knew he'd find it then. But for right now? He relaxed into Levi's touch and let it soothe him.

Even the thought that, tonight, he knew he needed to talk to Mo—to let him down easy—didn't spike his nerves. Sure, he wasn't looking forward to it, mostly because he didn't know exactly what he was going to say, and he never liked going into a situation feeling clueless. But Aidan decided he and Mo had been friends for long enough, he should be able to feel him out.

Like he could read his mind, Levi murmured, "Are you stressing about it?"

"About?" But of course, Levi could only be talking about Mo. He'd told Levi last night, before they'd fallen asleep, that it was his intention to pull him aside tonight, to tell him that he'd fallen in love with Levi.

Levi hadn't looked particularly fazed by it, but he *had* asked, "Do you think it's gonna 'cause any problems in the locker room?"

Aidan didn't think so. But then he didn't really think Mo loved him. Not the way he loved Levi anyway. Maybe not even the way Aidan had loved Mo.

"It's gonna be awkward, maybe," Aidan had admitted. "But Mo's a pro, and we were friends before any of this. I think we can find our way back to that again."

He was still hoping that this morning, and he had a feeling he'd be thinking about it all day, in the back of his mind.

"Not really *stressing*," Aidan said, because he wasn't. Not like Levi meant.

"Good."

Aidan turned over, tipping his forehead against Levi's. How had he not realized how deeply in love with him he was? Even weeks ago, seeing the pillow creases on his cheeks had filled him with a buoyant thrill, and now? Aidan thought he might float right to the ceiling. The only thing keeping him down was Levi's arm, heavy and warm against his bare side.

"I think you gotta just be honest," Levi said quietly. "That's what I would've wanted you to be with me, if it hadn't gone my way."

"Levi, it was always going to go your way," Aidan said gently, because it was true.

"But—"

"No," Aidan interrupted. "It was always going to be you. Maybe Mo helped me see that I liked guys, that what I really wanted was something

I wasn't getting with every other hookup I'd had, but the moment you wanted to know why I was so bummed? The moment you flirted with me? It was inevitable. *You* were inevitable. I slid right into you, no questions, no hesitation, no wondering how it would've been if things were different. Because they weren't ever going to be. Mo's my friend. But you're the guy I'm crazy about."

Levi's smile was slow and wondrous. "And people say you're pragmatic."

"Never when it comes to you," Aidan admitted.

But Aidan wished, a little bit, that he was more pragmatic when it came to love when he pulled Mo aside in Vault, hours later.

He repeated his own words back to him in his head. *Mo's a pro. We were friends before any of this. I think we can find our way back to that again.*

"You look like you're about to puke," Mo said frankly as Aidan leaned against the side of the bar. He had deliberately *not* brought them into the library. It wasn't going to take a long time to have this conversation, and they weren't going to need privacy for it, not the way Mo had hoped they'd need it the first time.

That was not a lie. Aidan felt a little nauseous. He took a big swallow of the whiskey the bartender had poured him a few minutes ago.

"You didn't ask if there was someone else, before," Aidan said, because that was easier than admitting how much he didn't like this. Not being honest. Not being in love with Levi. But letting Mo down, the way he'd been let down.

It wouldn't ever feel *good*. Even if Aidan was semi-convinced Mo wasn't in love with him. Not really the way he wanted to be in love.

"No," Mo admitted. "Is there?"

"Yes," Aidan said.

Mo looked surprised but also resigned. "I guess I knew you weren't going to be into it, when you looked so shocked, but not happy about it."

"You shocked me, for sure," Aidan said.

Mo's dark eyes slid away from his. "I wouldn't even hate you, if you were doing this because I did it to you."

"Morris," Aidan chided. "Come on. You know me. I don't do that shit."

"I didn't know you were into guys, either," Mo argued, but his voice was still flat, matter-of-fact. "I didn't know until you told me you loved me. And now I find out it's not just me, but there's someone else, even. You gonna tell me who it is? I can tell you want to."

One of the benefits—and drawbacks—of being friends for so long. Aidan had told himself before this conversation started that would make it easier, but he hadn't realized it would make it harder, too.

"Yeah, I do, but not if you're going to be stupid about it," Aidan said bluntly.

He started a laugh out of Mo. "I guess if I don't feel like I want to kill him, like I'm actually happy you're happy, does that mean I didn't love you after all?"

"I was pretty sure you didn't." It didn't really feel better being proven right.

"But this other guy does?" Mo asked.

Aidan nodded. "A lot. Like I love him."

"I just thought . . ." Mo shrugged. "Fate pulled me back here, and I'd missed you so fucking much, and the thought of being with you, you know, *like that*, didn't really disgust me. I could've wanted it."

"That just means you're not straight, you idiot," Aidan teased carefully, "and that we're friends."

Mo looked like he was considering that. "Yeah, I guess that makes sense." He paused for a second. "You can tell Banks to stand down. I'm not gonna freak out on you or burst into tears or tear you into tiny little pieces."

"How did you know—" Aidan stopped abruptly, and then laughed. "I guess it probably wasn't very hard to figure out."

"Not really," Mo said. "I meant it though. I'm happy for you, really happy."

"Me too." Aidan tried to not be as smug as he felt, being *this* happy, but it was hard. He wasn't sure he'd quite pulled it off. Especially not when Mo made a face.

"No big surprise you're gonna be insufferable. He gonna be the same way?"

"I don't know. I'm kind of a catch?" Aidan joked.

He'd been told that so many times, by so many people, but he'd never really believed it was true. Not until now. In the back of his mind, Riley telling him, *I told you so.*

"Oh geez, you *are*," Mo said, and he was chuckling now. He took a long drink of the red wine in his glass. "God, I'm almost regretting saying anything to you now."

"*Almost*," Aidan repeated wryly.

"Well, it's good to know, you know? I bet you felt that way too."

"Yeah," Aidan agreed. "It was. It was what really allowed me to move on and fall in love again. So thanks?"

Mo rolled his eyes. "You *are* the worst. Why do I love you again?"

"Those darts I keep throwing you," Aidan said.

Mo burst into laughter, and yanked him into an unexpected hug, and Aidan knew, without a doubt in his mind, that it *would* be okay.

They'd be okay.

And for the first time, he allowed himself to be really, really happy not just about Levi, not just about their 2-0 record so far, but that for the first time in three years, he had his good friend back.

Levi kept telling himself that Aidan had this handled, but even though he knew it with like ninety-nine point nine percent certainty, it still felt good to hear Mo, and then Aidan, laugh, and even better to watch as Mo tugged his boyfriend into a very bro-y hug.

Nothing like Levi wanted to hug him.

Though if he was being honest, hugging him was the least of what he wanted to do to him.

Over Aidan's head, Mo's eyes met Levi's, and he gave a small nod.

It was up to interpretation, but Levi was pretty sure he was saying, *hey, I get it. It's okay. We're okay.*

That was a relief.

Levi didn't want to end up with someone in the locker room who hated him—someone who made it impossible for him and Aidan to exist in a normal couple kind of way.

Aidan was never going to be a big PDA person. Maybe here, at non-official events, but Levi already knew what he'd be like once he went to work.

But he didn't want to keep his distance, because neither of them wanted to rub their loved-up-ness into Mo's face.

Levi tried not to look over as Mo and Aidan hugged again—this one lingered a hair longer, but it was very much a *goodbye* sort of hug.

He was right, because a second later, Aidan walked over.

"It go okay?"

Aidan shot him a knowing look. "You know how it went. You were looking at us the whole time."

Levi wasn't going to apologize for being worried. For caring. Or for wanting to make sure he wasn't about to get his ass kicked in the middle of this fancy bar.

"Was watching both of our backs," Levi said.

Aidan's face softened from amusement to that look that Levi was beginning to realize was the *I love you so fucking much.* Never thought he'd see something like that on Aidan's face, but the more he saw it, the more he knew it belonged there.

"It was fine, honestly. He's fine. Probably shouldn't make out in front of him for a few months."

Levi moved closer, tucking a hand around Aidan's waist. "What about *not* in front of him?" he murmured under his breath.

"Hmmm, I like the sound of that. We didn't get our proper victory celebration last game," Aidan said. "You ever seen the library in here?"

"The library?"

"Come on," Aidan said, tugging him with intent. "I can guarantee there'll be nobody in there tonight."

"No big readers on the team?" Levi asked as he let himself be tugged.

"Trust me, nobody's gonna be in there," Aidan said.

"We could always wait until we get home," Levi suggested. He'd just been thinking that Aidan wouldn't be a fan of PDA, but here he was suggesting they go to a room of this very public bar—even though it had been rented out for just the Thunder, tonight—and kiss.

"Hell no," Aidan said. "I can't bug out early."

He led Levi into a room lined with bookshelves. Interspersed every dozen or so feet were little alcoves with dark blue velvet seats and long curtains held back with antique brass holders.

"I didn't know *you* were a big reader," Levi teased as Aidan gently pushed him down onto one of the bench seats, hovering above him.

"Are we alone? I'm a big fan of that," Aidan said, leaning in and kissing him. Tenderly at first, but it didn't take long for the kiss to turn hotter, fiercer. Levi nibbled at his bottom lip and wrapped his legs around Aidan's calves, pulling him in more insistently.

"God," Levi murmured into Aidan's mouth. "I want you."

"You had me this morning." They'd had a long leisurely fuck that had demolished Levi in the best possible way. But the truth was he couldn't get enough; didn't think he'd *ever* get enough.

"And?"

Aidan chuckled. "Point taken." He tugged on the curtain, dislodging it from its holder and darkness enveloped them.

It wasn't difficult to know what Aidan had in mind. The bench seat wasn't huge but it was big enough—barely—for both of them together. He lifted himself on it and Aidan crawled over him, kissing him intently. Fingertips trailed down Levi's chest, warm through the fabric of his shirt, lingering at the fly of his jeans, teasing fleeting touches that drove him crazy, until Levi was swallowing his moans. Hoping his kisses with Aidan might muffle them enough.

"You want it?" Aidan murmured.

"With you? Always," Levi said.

Aidan ducked his head, like he was going to hide his pleased face, but Levi reached out, pulling his chin up so he could see.

Levi's cock throbbed in his jeans and finally Aidan touched it, his eyes never leaving Levi's.

Aidan bent down, unzipping his jeans, and Levi squeezed his eyes shut as Aidan's mouth enveloped him, hot and tight and perfect.

They hadn't done this that much yet. It still felt new and filled him with incredulous disbelief every time. But Levi was beginning to wonder if that would be true when they were doing this ten years from now. Would it always feel like this?

Levi hoped so.

"Yeah, baby, suck me," Levi whispered to him. Aidan gave a half groan around him and his mouth slipped lower, Levi's cock moving deeper into his mouth, nudging against his throat.

As much as he'd want to drag out this pleasure, he was also aware of where they were. Nobody was going to kick Aidan Flynn out of this bar, but Levi also didn't want to have that conversation either.

He let himself sink into the pleasure of Aidan sucking him, so hot and wet, his mind drifting as his hands tangled in Aidan's hair.

"Can't believe you. So fucking lucky," Levi said. "Love you so much."

Aidan groaned around his dick again, and that was rapidly getting him to the edge. Between Aidan's mouth and the sheer insane hotness of the situation, he was going to lose it.

His fingers tightened in Aidan's hair and he came down his throat, Aidan swallowing around him.

"Fuck," Levi moaned out unsteadily.

Aidan huffed as his dick slipped from his lips. "I'm so fucking—"

Levi could see now that he'd been touching himself, grinding a palm against his hard cock, and Levi pulled his shirt up the same moment as Aidan pulled himself from his pants.

A second later come striped up his torso as Aidan shuddered above him. Levi didn't think he'd ever seen anything so beautiful in his whole freaking life.

"Shit," Aidan said, falling back on his heels. "*Shit*."

"It's okay, baby, we got this," Levi cooed and swiped his finger through the mess before sucking it into his mouth.

"Holy fuck," Aidan said, looking like he'd be ready to go again, if he hadn't *just* come. "Shit, that's hot."

"Yeah?"

Levi picked up another thick stripe of come and held it out this time, and Aidan didn't waste a second, sliding it into his mouth so he could clean it off.

A minute later, Levi was mostly clean-ish, and they were both panting.

"We need to, I don't know, start traveling with wet wipes or something," Aidan said.

"Who knew you had an exhibition kink?" Levi asked airily. "Or a come kink?"

"Nobody til you. Nobody after you, either," Aidan promised, blue eyes warm and intent on Levi's face.

"Good," Levi said. Couldn't help the smug edge to his tone. He didn't want Aidan to be with anyone else, either.

Aidan was perfect for him, and he hoped he could be perfect for Aidan, too.

They kissed for another long moment, Aidan's lips plush and wet against his.

"We'd better rejoin the party," Aidan said reluctantly. He tugged Levi's shirt down but didn't make any other moves.

"I can't believe I was just thinking you weren't a fan of PDA," Levi said. "And then you freaking lure me into the library to fuck."

Aidan grinned. "Expect the unexpected, baby."

He finally pulled the curtain back and they both froze, because they were no longer alone.

Ramsey was leaning against the doorway, a knowing look on his face.

"Hey," he said casually. "Flynn. Banks."

"Hey," Levi croaked out. God, what had he heard? What was he going to say?

"I can explain," Aidan said as they slid off the bench seat. Aidan didn't let go of him, though, like Levi had expected he might.

But Ramsey just laughed. "Sure," he said, sounding amused.

"Or not," Levi added.

"No worries," Ramsey said lightly. "I actually *don't* want to know."

Aidan nodded jerkily but took Levi's hand as he led them out of the library, towards the main bar.

He ordered them both green apple Manhattans, which the bartender recommended, but before they could even take their first sip, they were joined by a whole group of teammates.

Dawson and Cam. Nate. Trevor and Lane. Coming up the rear was Wes, looking like he knew exactly what was going on.

For a second Levi worried that Ramsey *had* said something, but then he probably didn't need to. They weren't exactly being subtle.

"You two have fun?" Dawson joked.

"Don't make them uncomfortable," Cam whispered to him under his breath. "Aidan's not—"

"Aidan's fine," Aidan said bluntly. He laced his fingers back with Levi's, prominently displayed on the bar top. "Anyone got an issue with this?"

"Nope," Dawson said with a smirk. "Just glad you finally got your head out of your ass."

"Anyone else?" Aidan's gaze scanned the group of their friends and teammates, like he was waiting for someone else to protest.

That was the moment Levi realized that Mo, too, had approached the knot of people grouped at the bar.

Even he shook his head, and the corner of his mouth was quirked up, like he actually found this whole thing funny.

Levi relaxed, and felt Aidan do the same thing, next to him.

"We're actually pretty dang happy for you," Nate said, clapping him on the back. "Banks is gonna keep you on your toes."

"I sure hope so," Aidan said, squeezing Levi's hand.

"Would be my genuine pleasure, bro," Levi teased. He lifted their hands and brushed his lips across Aidan's wrist, blushing a little at how Dawson and Lane catcalled them.

Aidan's eyes were soft when they met his, and Levi didn't think he'd ever been happier.

EPILOGUE

Next July

"You know," Levi said casually, as Aidan tossed a log on the fire, "it's been a year. Exactly a year."

Aidan glanced back at the chair Levi was sprawled in. The chair that until a minute ago they'd been sharing.

"Guess it has," Aidan said. He brushed off his hands on his jeans and stood, wandering back to where Levi was sitting.

Levi grinned up at him, clearly very delighted with himself. "I think that means we can finally have sex now."

Aidan opened his mouth and nearly said something like, "Yeah, yes, let's go do that right now." But before he could, the back door opened and a whole group of people spilled out onto the patio.

Too many brothers. *So many brothers.*

Landry and Riley, of course. Logan and Dylan.

But it wasn't *just* brothers. Even Lyla had come along this time, and she'd brought, to everyone's shock but most especially Riley's, Paige.

"Hey," Lyla had said, "if you're allowed to couple up with each other, so are we."

Riley had only stared at them in shock and had finally tugged his best friend into a long, tight hug. "You should've told me!" he'd said to her, and Paige had only shrugged with a bright smile on her face. "This is me telling you," she'd said. "We hung out at the game last fall and, well . . .one thing led to another."

All these siblings meant it was a very full house. Such a different vibe from last year, when Aidan hadn't wanted to talk to or even *see* anyone. He'd sulked when Riley had shown up with Landry and Levi.

But now he was surrounded by people he loved, that loved him right back.

None of them was as important as Levi, though.

Maybe they'd been together less than a year, but already Levi was the most important person in his life, and they'd become inseparable.

"Oooooh," Logan teased as the group of them spread out among the chairs surrounding the firepit. "Someone was thinking about breaking the PDA rule."

Aidan had been forced, after the second day here, to enforce a no-PDA-in-public-spaces rule. Not for him and Levi—but for everyone else.

"It's my house," Aidan just retorted and sank back into the chair Levi was sitting in. Levi's arms went around him and pulled him in close until he was practically sitting on his lap.

Riley raised an eyebrow. "Seriously, bro?"

"Seriously," Aidan said.

"Did you realize they were gonna be like this?" Lyla asked Landry.

"So smug, like they were the first ones to discover how great falling in love is?" Landry retorted fondly. "No. But I guess I shouldn't be very surprised."

"You shouldn't be," Riley said affectionately. "A Flynn's gonna Flynn, even if he's a Flynn in love."

Landry pressed his lips to Riley's cheek in a lingering kiss. "Especially when it's a Flynn falling for a Banks."

Lyla and Paige had pulled out the makings for s'mores, so they spent the next hour or so toasting marshmallows. Levi got chocolate smeared all over his face and Aidan felt duty bound to lick it off and didn't even feel bad, because Logan had Dylan's sticky fingers in his mouth twice already.

"This is perfect," Levi said with a happy sigh as he relaxed back in the chair, his legs bracketed around Aidan's thighs. Aidan was leaning against his chest, feeling the contentment spread through him, the steady pulse of Levi's heartbeat aligning with his own.

"We should do this every summer," Riley agreed.

"Kind of ballsy, don't you think," Logan asked, "volunteering your brother's house?"

"What do *you* think, Levi?" Riley asked again, smirking.

Levi just laughed. Maybe Aidan should've felt some kind of way about everyone assuming that his house was basically Levi's house, but it *was* and it was impossible to even be upset about it because he liked it so much.

Levi turned to him. "Bro, what's your take on this?"

"I'm down," Aidan said.

Levi didn't look surprised because he probably *wasn't* surprised.

He liked—no, he *loved*—having Levi in his space. Even when he stole all the blankets in a cold Toronto winter. Even when he was driving Aidan crazy by prancing around in electric yellow short shorts. Even when he invited half the team over for a *Mario Kart* tournament on a Monday afternoon that was supposed to be a day off because, "Aidan, you need to loosen up some."

Levi was usually right, which had sort of chapped Aidan's ass at the very beginning, and now he just found both reassuring and comforting.

He *did* usually need to relax, and often Levi could take him out of his own head with sex, or with teasing, but sometimes there was nothing like the distraction of having twenty football players eating him out of house and home, slumped all over his couch and his barstools, arguing about whether someone cheated.

Levi always knew what he needed, and Aidan sometimes wondered how he'd made it through a whole football season without him before.

He had. Many times. And yet, when he thought of how plain fucking *great* he felt now, versus then, he wondered how he'd ever managed it.

"You guys are adorable," Lyla said quietly.

Landry groaned. "Don't give them any more ammunition! They already know how hot and built and cute they are."

Aidan glanced back at his boyfriend and wasn't surprised to see a tender look on his face. "Hey, babe," he said, "did you hear that? We're hot and built *and* cute!"

Levi looked delighted. Delighted and in love. Aidan's two favorite looks.

"Yep," he said, "it's true. Now y'all get out of here. I am gonna be a lot cuter in a second and you don't need to be witnessing it."

"The magic words," Logan said, jumping up and tugging Dylan with him. "Come on, babe, we've got plenty to keep us busy."

"Us too," Paige said, wrapping an arm around Lyla's waist.

Riley and Landry were the last up. Landry had already turned to go in the door, but Riley lingered.

"Bro," he said, "he's good for you."

Aidan smiled. "Yeah," he agreed.

Levi's arm tightened around him. "He's good for me, too."

"Yeah, but Aidan? He was sort of messed up before," Riley said.

Aidan knew it. In the back of his mind, he'd known it and pretended like he didn't, because that was easier than thinking of how he'd felt, back then. Before the sunshine of Levi had come streaming into his life, turning everything technicolor and bright.

"Not anymore," Levi said, pressing his mouth against Aidan's neck.

"Aaaand that's my cue," Riley teased, covering his eyes and making a face. "Go be cute, but don't do it in front of me."

"Big words for someone who literally fucked my big brother in your kitchen," Levi murmured against Aidan's neck as he turned in his arms so he could get his mouth on Levi.

"You're not going to get any arguments from me," Aidan said and kissed him.

Levi was the best possible reminder that even though sometimes things sucked and it felt like they were never going to get better, often right around the corner there was an unexpected miracle, just waiting for you to grab it.

To grab it, to hold it, and to never let it go.

Levi leaned back and took Aidan with him, tipping his head to look at the stars. "I meant it," he said, "it's pretty much perfect out here."

Aidan had been coming here forever. Pretty much every summer since he was a kid had been spent in Michigan. His parents had owned a house here. He'd gone to college here. He'd bought his own summer house with the money from his first NFL contract. But he'd never, not once, felt like that was true.

But it was now.

-

Preorder *Stealing His Thunder*, Dawson and Cameron's book, coming in early 2026.

-

Don't miss Aidan and Levi's bonus scene – where they finally get to attempt a Banks brothers tradition, the Date Box!

-

Want to read the other Banks brothers' books? Check out Riley and Landry's book, *The Star*, and Logan and Dylan's book, *Playing the Player*.

-

And yes, for those of you who are already screaming at me, Ramsey's book will be third in this series and *Hell or High Water* is available for preorder now.

INTERESTED IN READING MORE OF
BETH'S BOOKS?

CHECK OUT A FULL LIST OF TILES
BY SCANNING THE QR CODE
OR VISITING HER WEBSITE

WWW.BETHBOLDEN.COM/BOOKLIST

WANT TO FOLLOW BETH?

MAKE SURE YOU NEVER
MISS A RELEASE?

SCAN THE QR CODE BELOW
OR VISIT HER WEBSITE
FOR A SOCIAL MEDIA LIST,
NEWSLETTER SIGNUP,
AND SO MUCH MORE!

WWW.BETHBOLDEN.COM/ABOUT